About the Author

Chris Bailey-Green was born in Suffolk in 1973. He spent nineteen years in the police, both as a civilian member and as a police officer, before leaving to become a full-time writer. He has a degree in philosophy and lives in the heart of Norfolk with his wife and numerous pets, where he spends a lot of his time in reading and thinking about writing. *Living With It* is his fifth novel.

Living With It

Chris Bailey-Green

Living With It

Olympia Publishers
London

www.olympiapublishers.com
OLYMPIA PAPERBACK EDITION

A CIP catalogue record for this title is
available from the British Library.

ISBN: 978-1-80439-036-8

This is a work of fiction.
Names, characters, places and incidents originate from the writer's
imagination. Any resemblance to actual persons, living or dead, is
purely coincidental.

First Published in 2023

Olympia Publishers
Tallis House
2 Tallis Street
London
EC4Y 0AB

Printed in Great Britain

Dedication

As usual this book is for Debbi, as they all are. She is the inspiration behind all my words and the reason why I am a writer in the first place.

Now

Daniel's wife died two weeks before Christmas.

There is, arguably, never a good time to die, but to die so close to Christmas has got to be one of the worst times that you can die. Worst for the family and friends that you leave behind, that is. Daniel could easily imagine that Christmas would never be the same for him again. He would constantly be reminded of his wife while everyone else was hanging tinsel and putting up their trees and feeling in the festive spirit. All he would be able to think about was the loss that he had endured and the pain that came with it. That first Christmas was going to be the most difficult, but he didn't imagine that they would get easier as time went by.

It had been a long time coming. Claire had been diagnosed a year previously, another Christmas which had been endured under a cloud of worry and fear. She had been determined that she was going to 'beat it' though, and for a time it looked like she might be winning the struggle, but it ultimately got the better of her and in the last few months things had been going downhill. She had lost an incredible amount of weight. She joked that if she had known it was going to be this easy then she wouldn't have bothered with all of the diets that she had forced herself to go on over the years. It was a joke that Daniel didn't laugh at. He found that there was very little that could make him laugh from the moment of diagnosis.

When it became obvious to all that Claire was not going to

win her fight, she became determined that she would not end her days in either a hospital or a hospice. She was adamant that she wanted to die at home, among her books that had played such an important role in her life. It hadn't been easy, but Daniel had done his best to ensure that her last wish was one that would come true for her. The house soon started to resemble a hospital anyway with all the equipment that was required to make Claire's last few weeks as comfortable as they could be. She was around her books though and that was all that really mattered. She was as happy as she could be, when she knew that she was dying and knew that there were books that she would never read.

Daniel did his best to keep her spirits up, but there was no one that was able to keep his spirits up for him. Consequently, he performed an act with Claire, but when he was alone, he sank into dark moods. For a time, they tried to pretend that what was happening was not happening, but cancer demanded to be acknowledged, and there was nothing that they could do but to give in to it, like they had with everything else that it had demanded.

Claire spent her days getting her sustenance from soup, that Daniel would carefully bring to the boil for her, out of a can. Some of the time she was able to keep it down, but for the majority of the time it just came back up again. She didn't feel like anything else to eat and she wasn't able to keep anything else down when she tried.

Daniel did his best to make it a normal Christmas. He wasn't the one that normally put the decorations up, to be honest it was something that he felt that he could take or leave, but that last December, he had crawled into the loft and got the decorations down in their dusty, cobwebbed boxes and struggled down the ladder with them and made the effort to put them up throughout the house in just the way that Claire would have done. He wondered why he was doing it as Claire was certainly not well enough to get out of bed to come and see them. He supposed that he did it because he wanted life to be normal. He wanted it to be a pre-cancer world. He knew that was impossible, but he had to try. He had to try for his own sake more than Claire's. It seemed that they had been living with cancer for a long time now. It was almost an impossibility to imagine a time when the cancer had not been there.

It wasn't easy for Claire, he knew that. He knew that there was pain and that the morphine helped a little with that, but it wasn't easy for him to see the woman that he loved slowly waste away before his eyes. There were support groups out there, he was aware of them, but he didn't belong to any of them. He couldn't bear the thought of being in the same room as people that were going, or had gone through, what he was going through. He didn't want people telling him that when it was all over things would get better. He wasn't convinced that things would get any better. He was pretty sure that they would never be better again. He didn't need that kind of advice. What he felt he needed was to shut himself away and try to pretend that none of it was happening.

That wasn't the healthiest of options, but it was what he most felt like doing. It wasn't something that he could do though. He had no idea how he would handle the grieving process when the time came. He had had almost a year to accustom himself to the fact that he was going to lose his wife. It hadn't been an easy thing to become accustomed to. A year later he wasn't accustomed to it now. Nothing can really prepare you for that. No matter what people said.

It had been a year of operations, radiotherapy, chemotherapy and numerous hospital visits. They had thrown everything that they could at the cancer that was ravishing her body, until the doctors had finally thrown up their hands and admitted defeat.

'It is only a matter of time now,' the consultant had told them on that fateful visit.

Daniel found himself wondering if you ever got used to telling patients that? Did you ever get used to the fact that there was nothing that you could do? Did you remember the individual patients, or did they just slip from your mind when they had left the consultancy rooms? He was pleased that he was not a doctor so that he didn't have to find out for himself. He didn't imagine that it was an easy job.

Claire had found time to be sympathetic to the doctor when she had told them the news that it was all but over.

'Thank you,' she had said, 'I know you have done the best that you can.'

That was just like Claire. To care about other people before herself. Daniel had just sat there in shock and hadn't known what to say. He had run through in his mind that there must be other things that they could try. Perhaps some alternative medicines. Hell, he would even go to a witch doctor if he thought that it would do some good. He was prepared to do anything possible, but the doctor had made it clear to them that this was the end of the road.

There had then been that awkward silence when nobody had known what to say. They were just digesting the news. The doctor probably wanted to get them out of the room so that she could tell the next patient the good or bad news that they were to receive. Claire seemed to be taking it all in. To be fair she had told Daniel that from the moment of the diagnosis she had expected to die. She feared that it was the end a year ago. She told him that they had to be thankful for the extra time that they had received. Daniel didn't feel that it was quality time though. He felt that the frequent trips to the hospital and the gradual decline in her health had been a struggle for them both.

It was raining when they left the hospital. People were scurrying about, caught in the shower, desperate to get cover, but Daniel knew that there was no amount of running that they could do. He knew that there was no cover that they could take that would shield them from the storm that was coming. Everyone else seemed to be going about their lives as if nothing had happened. Didn't they realise that none of it mattered any longer? Didn't they know that the world had just been turned upside down?

They had discussed with the doctor the care that could be put in place to make the remaining time for her as comfortable as they could. She had reinforced the idea that she had wanted to be at home and the doctor had nodded her head as if this was a common request that was easy to arrange. Perhaps it was a common request. Who would really want to die in a cold, alien place after all?

Daniel and Claire made their way to the hospital car park, not feeling the rain that battered against their faces. Neither of them spoke. Perhaps there wasn't anything that there was left to say. Perhaps there wasn't anything that either of them could say. Later on, there would be words, but for the moment there was nothing. They redeemed their ticket, found their car, and made their way home.

'You know,' she told him, 'You're going to have to get used to the idea of being without me.'

'It's not something that I like to think about,' he had replied, looking up at her.

'I know it isn't, but not thinking about it is not going to prevent it from happening. I need to know that you are prepared for this. I need to know that you are going to be all right.'

'How can you worry about me?'

'Because it's what I do, I do worry about you. I always have done, and I always will do.'

'Do you want the truth?'

'Of course.'

'I can't imagine life without you.'

'I can't imagine life without you, but it's something that you're going to have to face when my time comes.'

'I don't know how I will be able to carry on.'

'You don't mean suicide?'

'I don't know what I mean.'

'I don't want you to have such dark thoughts.'

'How can my thoughts be anything other than dark?'

'For my sake, you have to carry on. You have to live your life the way that you are meant to. You must do that.'

'I'll try. It won't be easy.'

'I know it won't. I want you to promise me though that you won't resort to suicide. For my sake, but also for Toby's sake.'

'Okay.'

'Promise me.'

'I won't.'

'Promise.'

'I promise I won't kill myself when the time comes.'

They lapsed into silence, each lost to their own thoughts. There were many things that were going through Daniel's mind. Of course, he had considered suicide. It seemed the most natural and the most immediate reaction that he could give to the loss of Claire. He had loved her for the greater portion of his life and now he was going to lose her. There were no ifs or maybes. There were no miracles that would come along at the last minute. No *deus ex machina* that would solve everything for them.

This is what people went through. This was life. This was death. This is what couples, and single people went through all of the time. They weren't the only ones going through it now. Somewhere, not too far away, someone similar to him was having this same conversation with the person that they loved. That person who had been handed a death warrant as well. It was only a matter of time. That was what the doctor had said. Time. Nobody could put a figure on it. Days, weeks, probably not months. Certainly not years.

You never really truly know what you have until you are faced with losing it. That is what they say. Only Daniel was aware of what he had. He knew that he loved Claire. It wasn't just something that he said because it was what she said first, or because it was habit. He said it because he felt it. He said it because he believed it. He made a point of telling her it every day that they had been together. He had wanted her to know it and to feel the love that he had for her.

Knowing what he had didn't make it any easier to know that he was going to lose it. You always lived with the possibility of loss. That was what being with someone meant. There was always an end to every relationship. Whether it was a divorce or breakup, or it came to a natural end. Either way, it was always going to end. He had just always assumed that he was going to be the one that was going to die first.

Statistically, women lived longer than men. He had counted on this fact. Maybe it was heartless of him, because he knew that it meant that he would be leaving Claire with the heartache rather than having to experience it himself. He just believed that it was going to be him that went first. Sometime when they were in their seventies, or eighties. Not when they were forty-two. When there was still so much life left in them. Still so much that was left to be done.

It wasn't going to be easy. He was sure of that. There was no doubt about it. He was going to be hit very hard by what was coming, but there was no ducking from it. There was nowhere to hide where the cancer wouldn't find them out. That was the thing about cancer. It knew all the hiding places and could find you.

There were many nights, after the diagnosis, when he would lie in bed, both of them awake, but pretending to be asleep. He would wish that he could take the illness from Claire and take it on himself. Let it happen to him, rather than to her. He knew that it was an impossibility, but he wished with all his heart that he could take this thing from her and take away all the suffering that she would go through. It didn't matter what happened to him, so long as she was all right.

Some people might have found this strange, that he was wishing his life away, but they have probably never been in love the way that he and Claire were. When you were in love then you were prepared to do things like that. You didn't want to see the other person suffer.

It isn't easy preparing yourself for such a loss. It takes a great deal of courage to face the inevitable. Daniel wasn't sure that he had the level of courage that was required of him.

'You must find the strength,' Claire had told him, 'For both of us.'

'It won't be easy,' he had replied.

'I know, but that's what it's all about. The price for being together is that we'll have to face the loss that comes with not being together.'

'I can understand why some people don't like forming attachments.'

She put her head on one side. 'Is that what this is? An attachment?'

'That's not what I meant, and you know it.'

Around the time when the doctors had given up hope on her, Claire started to sleep in the spare room. A hospital bed was used to replace the bed that had been there. It was easier for her to sleep in the hospital bed than it had been in a normal bed. She had moved into the spare room because she had said that she slept so badly that it would have been a disruption for Daniel to sleep with her.

Daniel missed having her in the bed that they had shared as a married couple. The bed seemed to be too big without her. It was like she had already died, and he could feel her absence. He hated the idea of them sleeping apart but went along with her wishes as he normally always did.

If the purpose of sleeping separately had been to enable him to have a better night of sleep, it wasn't working. He slept badly, fitfully. Her absence keenly felt. The sign of things that were to come. When he did sleep, he had bad dreams that resulted in him waking up in a sweat, with his heart beating irregularly.

His dreams were always the same. He was in a boat, a rowing boat, or something like that. He was on a lake, which was still with hardly a ripple. Claire was waving to him from the shore, but he was unable to reach her. There were no oars in the boat and his attempts to paddle with his hands resulted in him going nowhere. Gradually he would become more desperate to reach her. His attempts frustrated. If anything, the boat was moving further away from her, and she remained a distant figure. Calling to him. Wanting his help and there was no way that he could reach her to give her the help that she clearly needed. In the dream he would become more desperate to get to her. Annoyed at his inability to help her. Frustrated by the distance that was between them, and then he would wake up. He would immediately feel for the empty space that was next to him and his heart would sink when he realised that she was not there and realised the reason why she was not there was because she had terminal cancer and was slowly dying in the spare room.

This happened night after night until it became something that he dreaded going to sleep for. This kept him awake as well, perhaps more than anything. He hated to be awake, and he hated to be asleep. There was no winning in the situation. It was hopeless.

He tried to disguise his levels of tiredness as much as he could from Claire. He didn't want her worrying about him when she had enough on her plate as it was. She didn't need the extra worry of realising that he was not coping all that well with what was happening in their lives. He was not entirely successful in his deception, and she could easily see through to the levels of tiredness that he was experiencing. She would see the black rims under his eyes and know that he had had a fretful night of sleep.

'We have to tell Toby the truth,' Claire had said shortly after the diagnosis. 'He isn't stupid, and he will soon realise that there are things that are going on that we can't explain away any other way than the truth.'

'It would have been nice to have kept it from him for as long as we could,' said Daniel, feeling awkward.

'We have no right to do that. He deserves to know the truth as much as we do. We have never hidden things from him. We have always treated him with a maturity beyond his years.'

'I'm not sure how he will handle it, that's all.'

18

'He will handle it in the manner that we all will handle it. I'm going to beat this, Danny, I'm going to be all right. There's no need for either of you to worry, but as I go through all of the therapy and the like, there's going to be changes that will be difficult to hide. We won't be able to hide that from him.'

'He's only fifteen.'

'Old enough to be able to handle the fact that his mother has cancer. Old enough to understand what's going on. He's a young adult now, not a little boy any longer.'

'He always seems like a little boy, as far as I'm concerned.'

'I know.' She moved in closer to him. 'But he's not a baby any longer. We can't treat him like one, if we did, he would just end up resenting us for it.'

'I suppose you're right.'

'I usually am you know,' she had smiled at him.

Back in those days there had still seemed to be so many possibilities. It had not seemed to be out of the question that the cancer was something that could be beaten. People beat cancer every day. It wasn't the automatic killer that it would have been a generation ago. There were better treatments now. Better understanding. Medical practices and knowledge had advanced a great deal in the last few decades.

There was hope. When Daniel's mother had died of cancer there had been no hope. It was a death sentence the moment that you got the diagnosis. Nowadays you had a better-than-even chance of beating it.

These were the things that he had said to himself to try and convince himself that all was not lost. He wasn't entirely sure that he had been successful in this attempt. It was true that there were people out there who beat cancer every day, but there were also those that died from cancer every day.

He had it in the back of his mind that nobody actually won against cancer. Yes, you could go into remission, and you could be cancer-free for a while, but it seemed to Daniel that it always returned. No matter how many years passed, it would always come back. It would always win in the end. Once you had it, it was just a matter of time. Could be days, weeks, months, years or even decades, but it would always win in the end. It was a bleak view, but that was what he believed. It was a persistent disease.

These were the thoughts that went through his mind when he had heard the diagnosis about Claire. He had that immediate sinking feeling as if his world was being sucked through the floor, which in many ways it was. He wasn't sure how much he heard about the rest of what the doctor was saying. He knew that the doctor and Claire were discussing treatments and various therapies. They hadn't given up on this and were preparing to fight, whereas Daniel was already looking to ring up the white flag and admit that all was lost.

He hated the fact that people personified cancer by saying that they were fighting it. You saw it in obituaries all the time. 'Lost the brave battle against cancer.' 'Lost the fight to cancer.' Battle, fight, it made it sound like you were fighting a person and he hated the idea of giving cancer that kind of personification. He wanted to think of it as what it was, an invading cellular destroyer, so intent on eating away at you that it didn't realise the logic of the fact that killing you would also kill it. But that was to personify it again, and it didn't deserve that.

The conversation with Toby had not gone all that well.

'Is mum going to die?' he had asked and had never seemed so much of a little boy as he did at that moment. Claire had said that he was a young adult, but he didn't seem to be like that. In

20

Daniel's mind he was looking like it was his first day at school once again and that he needed his parents to protect him.

Daniel's first reaction had been to deny that she was going to die. To tell him that of course she wasn't going to die. But they had agreed that they would be honest with Toby. That it was what he deserved.

'I don't know,' was the only honest answer that he could give. He didn't know. He had no idea. He hoped not, of course. He prayed not, but he was aware of the fact that you didn't always have your prayers answered. Sometimes you just had to go with it and hope for the best. It didn't help all that much that he didn't believe in God and so it was difficult to pray to something that you didn't believe in.

'I hope she doesn't die,' Toby had stated.

'So do I. So do I.'

Did Daniel know then that the chances were that she was going to die? He didn't know. It was possible. It had always been at the back of his mind and sometimes at the front of his mind. It was impossible to think otherwise from the moment that you heard the words that she had cancer. It was the automatic reflex to hearing the news. This was about as bad as it could get.

Each morning, Daniel would wake in his solitary bed and push the memories of the disturbing dream from his mind as he grounded himself in his surroundings. He would then slowly get out of bed and go to the en suite bathroom and splash some water on his face to try and bring himself around to the fact that he was going to have to face another day.

He would then wrap his dressing gown around him and shuffling into his slippers would feel decidedly middle-aged and would make his way into the kitchen. He would bring the kettle to the boil and while that was happening would set the coffee pot up ready to deliver some strong coffee to him, which was the way that he really liked to start the day. He would make tea for Claire which is what she liked to start the day with, although she wasn't drinking as much of it as she used to. Everything seemed to be something of an effort for her at the moment. He supposed that it was rather difficult when you were that ill to be able to do the things that you used to do.

When the tea was made, he would take it through to the spare bedroom and lightly tapping on the door would bring the tea in and place it on the bedside table. He would then open the curtains and let the winter light into the day. It had been snowing recently, but the weather forecasters said that there was little chance of a white Christmas. It always seemed to fall on either side of Christmas, but never on Christmas itself. He supposed that if he wanted a white Christmas then he would be better off moving to Scotland or somewhere like that, where the chances of snow on Christmas Day were an almost certainty. He didn't think that there was much chance of a move to Scotland, although he did picture himself in a log cabin somewhere in the middle of nowhere, perhaps on the shores of a loch, or in the deep mountain glades. Cut off from the rest of the world and not having to deal with the bustle and the demands that everyday life created. He couldn't ever see it happening though. There had been that time that they had gone to Scotland, and it hadn't been as romantic as he had pictured it. It had rained a lot and been very cold.

Once the curtains were drawn, he would come and sit on the edge of the bed and talk to Claire about how her night had been. He would see to anything that was needed and wanted by her. He would then help her to drink her tea and they would chat about the mundane, the ordinary, and avoid the topic that was the elephant in the room.

After a while of doing this, he would then go and make sure that Toby was getting up for school and return to the kitchen where he would make breakfast for him which usually consisted of a bowl of muesli (which was something that seemed far too healthy for Daniel's tastes). He hardly ever had any breakfast and if he did it was a slice of dry toast. He knew that breakfast was the meal that was supposed to set you up for the day, but he just was never hungry enough in the mornings to be able to stomach it.

He would drink his coffee and chat to Toby about how school was going and what subjects he had for that day and had he done all of his homework. Toby always did his homework though, so there was little chance that this would be answered in the negative.

With breakfast over, Daniel would see Toby off to school, who always walked. Some parents drove their children to school even though the distance was not all that far. Daniel liked to think that he was doing his bit for the environment by not driving Toby to school, but the truth of the matter was that Toby liked his independence and simply didn't want to arrive at the school gates with his dad. He would rather meet up with his friends and walk to school with them, probably chatting about the things that they had seen on television the night before, or whatever it was that fifteen-year-old boys talked about when they got together. Girls probably, thought Daniel as he placed the breakfast things in the dishwasher and cleared the table. He would probably then help himself to another cup of coffee.

He lived on coffee. He knew that it probably wasn't all that good for him, but he drank copious amounts of the stuff. He needed it to help him stay awake during the day and do the work that he needed to do. It was fortunate that he worked from home so he was able to look after Claire, otherwise they would have been forced to get an impersonal nurse in and Claire didn't like the idea of a stranger being about the place.

He would try and get on with his work while trying not to think too much about cancer and the devastating effect that it was having on their lives. He would periodically check in on Claire who spent most of the day sleeping now, partially because she was so tired, and partially because of the levels of medication that she was on. The morphine seemed to help with the pain at least. Daniel wondered if he could get any for himself so that he wouldn't feel any pain.

This was Daniel's morning routine. It was the same every morning. There was no change to the humdrum nature of what he did. One morning though, he took the cup of tea into Claire and upon opening the curtains on the frosty morning, realised that she had died in the night.

Dad thought it would be a good idea if I recorded some of my thoughts in a diary so that I could make some degree of sense of what was going on in my life. I don't think you can make any sense of all of this. From the time that they told me about the cancer I felt that the bottom had fallen out of my world. I can't imagine how it was that dad felt. I immediately thought that mum was going to die. Well, you do, don't you? Cancer is such a death sentence. I know that there are people that beat it and live on, but there are probably a majority of people who don't live on, who succumb to it and the pulling power that it has. I really can't explain how I felt when they told me the news. How do you react to that? You think your parents are going to be there forever. You never think that they are going to die. In the back of your mind, you know that they must do, that everyone is going to die at some point, but you somehow never think that it is going to happen to those that you love. I'm not sure that writing these words is something that is going to help with the matters. My parents have lived with words all of their lives, so they put a great deal of importance in them. Maybe they will help. I don't know. I'm not convinced.

Then

Daniel and Claire met when they went to university together. They were both reading English and found that they had a shared love of reading. This was not particularly unusual for those that were studying English, but it seemed to be a passion with them. Something that they did to live, as surely as they took breath. Daniel had first been interested in Claire when she aired her opinion of the novel *Frankenstein* by Mary Shelley.

'Most of our knowledge of this book has been tainted by Hollywood,' she had announced when asked to address the tutorial.

'Proceed,' said the tutor with his fingers laced together, looking at her over some half-moon glasses.

'Hollywood has bred an image that it's the creature that's the monster, when quite clearly it's Frankenstein himself who's the monster.'

'Continue,' replied the tutor who seemed to communicate most of the time with one word, gently prompting students and getting them to fulfil their ideas.

'The creature is a newborn, Frankenstein is his father. He abandons the child because of the abomination that he sees in it. He abandons his child, and the entire world is turned against the creature. He has no recourse but to submit to violence because everyone he encounters turns against him and shuns him. The real monster is Frankenstein for abandoning his child. He is the maker of his own fate and brings all of the violence onto his own head.'

The tutor nodded his head. It wasn't a particularly revolutionary point of view, and you got the impression that it was something that he heard every year that he introduced *Frankenstein* onto the syllabus. He was always glad that someone made the connection though, and in this particular year it was Claire that had got there first.

Daniel had sat across from her, and although he had also made the connection about the abandonment of a child and true abomination, he looked on Claire as if she were bringing a divine revelation for the first time. Looking back on it he had no doubt that this was the moment that he had fallen in love with her. They had not spoken two words together so far, but he knew that this was the woman who he wanted to spend the rest of his life with. It might have sounded creepy and an obsession if he had voiced this to anyone, especially to Claire, but he was determined that they would have to get to know each other better. He admired the way that she spoke, the sound of her voice, with no discernible accent. The way that the sun came through the window behind her and gave her an almost halo effect to her hair. Daniel had had girlfriends before, but they had never encapsulated him the way that Claire was doing now.

He was by nature something of a shy person, so it surprised him (more than anyone) when he asked her after the tutorial if she would like to go and get a coffee.

'Sure,' she had replied, smiling at him as though she already knew the depth of his soul and everything that he had been thinking.

'We can discuss *Frankenstein*,' he had continued, not knowing when it was best to keep his mouth shut and when to go with the flow.

'We can discuss anything,' she had returned with the smile

still on her face. Daniel felt that if he had died in that moment then there wasn't really anything that he could complain about.

They had gathered their books and materials together and had walked to the coffee shop on campus. Numerous students were crowded in the place, either in groups that laughed long and loud, or on their own, hunched over books or laptops. They found a table that was free and sat down and began to get to know each other better.

Daniel may have noticed Claire, but she had equally noticed him. Both of them had butterflies in their stomach as they talked about this and that. It was as if they both knew that this was the start of something bigger. As if this was so much more than just a coffee and a budding friendship. It was no hyperbole to state that, to a degree, they both felt that they were destined for this moment.

'Who's your favourite writer?' Daniel had asked when they had been talking for some time and he was not sure on what he should say next. He felt that literature was the best topic to stick to for the time being. It was safe. He would dearly have liked to ask her out and was scared that she might say no, scared that she might say yes. He didn't know how best to proceed, so literature was safe at the moment.

Claire sucked in her lip and thought for a moment. 'I suppose I'd have to say Shakespeare. It sounds like a cliché to say Shakespeare, as it's an answer that everyone gives, but I'm truly mesmerised by his work. He was an incredible talent. I love his words so much. What about you?'

Daniel sipped his coffee and thought about it.

'Don't say Shakespeare,' Claire laughed. 'That wouldn't be fair.'

He smiled back at her. 'I suppose I would have to go with

Thomas Hardy for something classic, and Albert Camus for something more modern.'

'Interesting choices. Why?'

'Camus just fascinates me and he's a great believer in drinking coffee, so that isn't such a bad thing.'

'And Hardy?'

'I love his themes of unrequited love.'

'Have you had experience of this?'

'I suppose so. Hasn't everyone? Isn't there always someone that you fall in love with that's unobtainable. Someone that will never be able to love you back, even if they wanted to.'

'I suppose.' She tilted her head on one side and looked at him with a penetrating gaze that made him feel that he was never going to be able to have any secrets from this woman. 'Don't you find that depressing though? As a theme?'

'I don't find Hardy that depressing. I find him less depressing than Dickens. Things often seem to work out well for Hardy. You can't always say that with Dickens.'

'Things don't work out well for everyone in Hardy. Maybe some characters work out well enough in the end, but there is still a fair amount of death and heartache for the rest of the characters.'

'Well, I don't suppose that I can argue with that.'

'I suppose I'd better go and write my essay on *Henry V,*' Claire said, beginning to gather her things together.

'Whether or not he is a war criminal?'

'That's the one.'

'Do you think he is?'

'I'm not sure.' She chewed her lip in a habit that Daniel would come to know and love over the years. 'You mean because he orders that the prisoners be executed?'

'Historically, Henry ordered that no prisoners be taken as he couldn't spare the men to guard them, so they were outnumbered at Agincourt.'

'But everyone disobeyed the order because they wanted the ransom money that would come with having noble prisoners.'

'Absolutely,' said Daniel, feeling for his coat. 'It's worth remembering that in the play he orders them to be killed after the French kill the boys in the luggage train.'

'So, it's an act of vengeance as well as a means of getting his men back into the fight. An act of necessity, in other words.'

'Possibly.'

'But then doesn't he fight an unjust war to begin with and that makes him a war criminal for invading France in the first place?'

'It's an argument.'

'I'm not sure that I know which way I'll come down on this one yet. I think I'll just have to start writing and see where my thoughts take me. That's the way that I take most of my essays anyway.'

'Perhaps we can do this again some time,' Daniel said, aware that his heart was in his mouth when he said it.

'We can do this anytime you like and as often as you like,' she had replied as they had got up to leave.

Friendship came before dating, as is often the best way. By the time that they moved out of student accommodation at the end of their first year and into private digs, they were an 'item' and they moved in together.

Early on, Daniel had confessed to Claire that he had aspirations to be a writer, which was the true reason why he was studying English. He firmly believed that in order to write books, it was first necessary to read books.

'Why don't you do a creative writing course?' she had asked him.

'I don't believe that writing is something that can be taught. I believe that it is something that can be learnt, but not something that can be taught.'

'You might have to explain that one to me.'

'Well, we can learn from books, both good books and bad books, on how we should write, but I don't think that someone sitting up front of a class of people and telling them how to write is the way that it goes. Writing is so subjective. Someone will read your work and make an opinion of it, and you may learn from that, but another person could read what you have written and get a completely different point of view, which is just as valid. Who is right? One person marking your writing and giving an opinion is dangerous.'

'You probably don't think that much of critics then?'

'I think it is easy to criticise, but more difficult to create. As someone famous once said "nobody put up a statue to a critic". What about you? What do you want to do?'

'I want to work in a publishing house. I love the idea of reading other people's work and finding that one gem among the rough that will go on to make someone's career.'

'Fame and fortune.'

'Is that why you write?'

'Not at all. I write because it is something that I have to do. It's something that I am *compelled* to do. I have little choice in the matter. The ideas pop into your head and you just have to get them out.'

'What's the worst question that you think you can be asked as a writer?'

He thought about this for a second. 'Where do you get your

ideas from? You never ask a plumber where they get their tools from. Ideas are just the tools of the writer. It's what you do.'

'It would be like asking you where you get your words from.'

'Exactly.'

'Perhaps I could publish your books.'

'What an amazing partnership we would make.'

'I think we make a pretty good partnership already.'

With that they kissed, and all thought of writing and the business of writing was lost for the moment.

When Daniel was not studying or writing essays he would be writing. His attempts did not produce greatness and they were often very clumsy, but he maintained that the best way to learn to write was to write, and he was learning from the mistakes that he was making.

Initially he didn't feel confident with sharing his work with anyone. He thought about sharing some of it with Claire but was ashamed that she might think badly of him. It took a lot of courage to allow someone else to read something that you were so close to. That you had sweated over and tried to turn into something meaningful. He didn't think that Claire would be disparaging, at least not intentionally, but he didn't want to run the risk that she would, somehow, be disappointed in what he had to offer. Despite numerous attempts that she made to allow her to read his work, he continued to write in secret and then slowly file away what he had written.

He completed one novel but knew that it was not very good and burnt it in the large Victorian fireplace of the house that they shared together with a number of other students. He watched the flames licking at the words and wondered if he would ever make it as a writer, or whether it was just a dream that he had no right to believe in. Something that he should probably have put away with childhood.

He never gave up though, and that was one of the things that he felt most keenly about. You had to have the talent to write in the first place, but almost anyone could do that if they really put the time and the effort into it. What you needed as well was the talent to persevere. You had to keep going despite whatever obstacles were put in your way. You had to keep working at that manuscript until you reached a level where you finally felt that you could let go. That was always the difficult thing. Knowing when to let go. Knowing when you could put your baby into the world and let other people treat it kindly or harshly. And then you had to have the talent for collecting rejection slips and not allowing it to get to you every time that a new one hit the doormat. Some offered good advice on what it was that they were looking for. They gave pointers on how they thought that you could improve your technique, but most didn't say a word, and left you not knowing if you were doing everything wrong, or if it was just wrong for the publishing house that you were aiming for.

He learnt that it probably wasn't the best thing to send manuscripts off to the really big publishing houses that had hugely famous authors attached, maybe even the odd Nobel laureate. They wouldn't be looking for something from a first-time author that nobody had ever heard of, not unless your work was something of genius. Which it invariably wasn't. He also learnt that many of the really big publishing houses just didn't have the time to read all the unsolicited manuscripts that came into them on a daily basis. There were only so many books that they could publish in a year, and they were more likely to go with the authors that were already established with them then to take on someone new and untested.

Most of all he learnt that it was about money. This was the side of writing that he really didn't enjoy. He loved the creativity. Coming up with plot and character, finding the right words for them to speak and to think. He loved the buzz that he got from a really good day of writing. What he hated was the business side of it that came next. This is where the next talent came in. The talent for doing the rounds of the publishers and then getting all of the things done that you had to do if a publisher agreed to publish you. Getting the numerous edits done, approving the proof reading, agreeing on the cover of the book, writing the blurb for the back of the book, writing the author biography, and signing all the legal side of things. The thought of book talks and signings filled him with dread. The way that he looked at it; for every time that he was sending unsolicited manuscripts out and doing all the necessary other things that were required of a jobbing author, he could be writing. He resented all the time that was taken away from doing what he loved, what he was really passionate about.

All of this business side of things was in the future for him though. He still had his degree to finish, which was his main priority. He was the first person in his family to go to university. It had never been something that had come up before with any of his other relations. He enjoyed his time and was determined to make the best of it that he could. He read. He didn't just read the set books that he was instructed to read for his course, but he took the advice of his old high school English teacher and read around the subject. If an essay or piece of literary criticism mentioned another author, then he would seek out that author and read what they had to say as well.

Claire read at the same time. Very often they were reading

the same things and so were able to discuss them with each other. They enjoyed their literature chats almost as much as they enjoyed sex. They indulged in both freely. Claire read because she wanted to know the answers. She had a thirst for knowledge, and she would read late into the night, often all night. She loved it when she found a writer who had been dead for a hundred years or so, had the same thoughts that she had. The same dreams and desires. She sought out the answers to life and wanted to know what the meaning of it all was. She also read because it was something that she enjoyed doing. She couldn't understand the people that didn't want to own and read books. How could there not be a place for books in your life? Books were as important in life as friends were. She couldn't see how she could live without either of them.

She had come from a family that had believed that books were important. She had grown up with her mother reading to her the stories of Enid Blyton and then she had progressed onto her own reading when the bedtime stories had stopped. She had never stopped her reading. Every day she would read, and she would always have a book on the go. The moment that she had finished one and set it aside she would reach for the next book. She vowed that if she ever had children then she would teach them to love books from an early age as well. She thanked her parents for giving her a love of books and felt sorry for those that had been raised without that love. It felt like they were somehow unloved, in some degree, by their parents because they were missing this essential part of their life. She had never understood it when she had gone to visit friends, as a child, and seen that there were no books in the house. Having no books in the house was like having no furniture. Better to have no furniture, but still have books.

And so it was that they settled into their relationship as they continued with their studies. Numerous books were read, although Daniel struggled with the poetry element of the course.

'I just can't see the point of poetry,' he said to Claire.

'I suppose it's an acquired taste.'

'I mean, I like the war poets and people like Edward Thomas, but I just don't get the majority of other poets.'

'I'm not a huge fan of poetry either, I much prefer to have a novel to get my teeth into. I have the same problem with short stories, I like longevity to be able to develop a plot and characters. To really be able to get into them. Short stories don't give you the chance to get to know anyone before it's over.'

'I know what you mean. I suppose I could try my hand at short stories though. They are, in many regards, more difficult to write than novels. You have to be so much more concise than you can be in a novel.'

'You mean you can ramble more in a novel?'

'I suppose that's one way of looking at it.'

'When are you going to let me read your writing?'

Daniel sighed. 'I don't know.'

'Don't you trust me?'

'It's not that I don't trust you. It's more that I don't trust myself. I've such self-doubt about my writing that I'm not sure it's worthy of anything.' Daniel stirred his coffee and watched the people going about their business outside of the coffee shop where they were making one coffee last for as long as possible.

'I'm sure that you're not *that* bad.'

'I'm really not sure at the moment. Perhaps my confidence will grow with time, but at the moment it's very fragile.'

'I suppose I can understand that.'

'I haven't shown my work to anyone. It's not you that I'm

being exclusive about.'

Daniel was not alone in this feeling. A lot of creative people live with self-doubt and a lack of confidence in what they are working on. There is a school of thought though that believes that this is a good thing. It's better to be full of self-doubt and worry about what you are creating, rather than the arrogance of believing that it is a masterpiece worthy of brilliance and recognition throughout the world. Daniel would go on to write numerous novels throughout his life, and there would be a time with each one of them that he would stop and wonder if it was any good, or if he was just wasting his time.

The important thing though was to ride the self-doubt. Come out the other side. Have the talent to persevere and keep at it no matter what. It was one of the biggest talents that you could have. Numerous times he would see something in print and wonder how it had got there. He was convinced that if he put his mind to it that he could do better and achieve more.

'The important thing about creative writing,' he said, 'is that there are no rules, no matter what anyone says. You just have to keep chipping away at that marble block until the statue appears that was hidden there all of the time. It's just a case of revealing it. The novel is there. It's just waiting to be written.'

'Do you think you will ever let me read anything?'

'Probably.'

'What about sending stuff off to publishers?'

'I did send one novel off to a few publishers and collected a few rejection slips, some of which were not all that polite, if you read between the lines of what they are saying.'

'And where is that novel now?'

'I burnt it.'

'Oh yes. I remember you saying. Seems a bit of a radical

thing to do though.'

'It was trash, and I knew that it was trash.'

'A lot of trash sells. Some of the bestselling novels are trash and are never going to win any prizes.'

'That may be, but this was *really* trash. No hope for it, but to consign it to the flames.'

'Seems a waste of effort.'

'I've done better since.'

'I look forward to reading it some time.'

'I'm sure you will at some stage.'

There was no rivalry between them as they studied. No attempt to get one up on the other. They shared ideas and books. Helped each other with their essays and worked together to get the best out of their studies that they could. After three years their studies were complete, and they both obtained their degrees.

'I'm toying with the idea of doing a Masters,' said Daniel. 'I just don't know if it will be a colossal waste of time and money.'

'I suppose that depends on what you want to get out of it.'

'It might be just delaying my inevitable entering of the real world and doing a real job.'

'There is that.'

'I just don't know if I have the patience for a Masters. I've been in the education system for a long time, and I don't know if I want to stay in it any longer.'

'Don't do it then. Go and do something else.'

'I'm not sure what though. All I've ever wanted to do is write. If I can't make a living from writing, then I don't think I will know what else to do.'

'It's very difficult to make a living from writing. Even published authors often have something else that they do on the side. Lecturing or teaching for example.'

'In which case a Masters would make some sense.'

'It would be a backup for you if you don't make a living from your writing.'

'I don't know if I could teach though. Imagine becoming so trapped in it that there is no time to write and to do what I want to do. Imagine a job that has no creativity. It would stifle me.'

'Plenty of people do it. Most novelists write their first, and several other books, while working in some other occupation.'

'I know. Doesn't make it any easier though. I'm worried that I might get trapped in a job that doesn't allow me to follow my dreams.'

'Why don't you take some time to follow your dreams then, and if after a year or two you haven't been able to achieve what you want to do, then you can get yourself a different job and keep working at it in the meantime.'

'It's an option, I suppose.'

'You have your whole life ahead of you. You don't have to achieve fame and fortune by the time you are twenty-three.'

'I suppose not.'

They lapsed into silence for the moment. Claire continued to read *The Tenant of Wildfell Hall*, and Daniel thought about his future and what it was that he wanted to achieve. It was very daunting looking at things from this point of view. He wished that he had the ability to know if things were going to work out. If he could look at the end of his life and know whether he was ever going to make it, he could know whether it was worth trying for or not. He voiced this opinion to Claire who looked up from her book.

'But if you don't try, you will end your life wondering what would have happened if you had tried. You have to try and if you don't succeed, at least you can say that you tried. Much better to do that than to not try and wonder what would have happened if you had.'

'I guess you're right.' He lapsed back into thought for a few minutes. 'I've reached a decision.'

'You have?'

'Yes.'

'What about?'

'I want you to read my manuscript.'

'Okay.'

It was no small thing for Daniel to offer his book to Claire to read. Never having had any kind of feedback he worried what she would make of it. She spent the next two days reading the manuscript with Daniel often by her side, constantly asking her where she was in the manuscript, what was happening. He didn't dare ask her what she thought of it. He was sure that he would find that out with time.

'It's good,' she said when she finally finished reading it. An activity that Daniel had felt had taken her an age.

'Is it?'

'Yes, it is. You should definitely try and get it published. I think that it will get published. Someone out there will want it. It's just a matter of finding the right person who wants it.'

'Easier said than done.'

'Yes, but nothing's achieved that's worth anything without a little hard work. If it was easy to do, then everyone would be doing it.'

'Everyone seems to think that they have a novel in them.'

'And most of them would never get published. Besides, I think you have more than one novel in you, if this is anything to go by.'

'What did you like about it?'

'I liked the structure. I liked the characters; I could really believe in them. A nice plot twist as well. I didn't see that coming.'

'Thank you.'

'I would read more by you.'

'You might be the only one that ever does.'

'I doubt that.'

And so began the period that Daniel hated. The period when he had to sell himself. He hated selling himself, which is why he never did all that good when it came to interviews. It took him away from what he really wanted to be doing – writing. He knew that if he wanted to make a career out of it though that he would have to get work out there and be seen. He would have to make a name for himself. He was sure that if he did find a publisher then sales would be slow, and it would take some time for him to take off. He knew this, but he still didn't like having to do it.

There were worse things that people had to do in life though and he realised that he was rather privileged in being able to do the things that he was doing, so despite complaining about it all of the time he realised that he couldn't complain about it all that much.

Claire started the round of job interviews at publishing houses and was finally offered a job working at a small, but respectable, publisher where she was tasked with reading the unsolicited manuscripts that came in and deciding whether or not it was worth exploring the new authors more closely. It was her dream job, and she was very happy about it. She went to work each day hoping that this was going to be the day when she would discover a new Ian McEwan or Kazuo Ishiguro. Invariably she wouldn't, but she knew that everyone had to start somewhere, and you never knew what was going to cross your desk from one day to the next. Most of the time she would reject the manuscripts. Sometimes because they were simply no good, and at other times because they were good, but just not the kind of thing that the publishing house was looking for at the moment, or because it was too similar to something else that they were working on.

Daniel and Claire kept things professional, and he understood that he was not going to submit his manuscript to her, to place her in a difficult position if it was inevitably rejected. He plied his trade elsewhere and it was with a degree of surprise one day that one of the publishers that he had sent his book to, replied. They liked the sample chapters that he had sent them and wanted to see the rest of the manuscript.

Two weeks later they offered him a publishing deal.

The story of how my parents got together is something that they have told me, like, a zillion times. I'm sure that each time that they tell me the story they have forgotten that they have already told me. I just smile and listen to the story once again. A love forged in the pages of literature. I rather like that as an idea. They certainly installed a love of books in me. It would be difficult not to love books, growing up, as I was, surrounded by them. I suppose I could have gone the other way and rebelled, but it just never seemed that it was an option. Some people think that books and reading is something that is dying out. I think that books will survive. Bicycles have survived the invention of the car. Books will survive a lot of things that are thrown at them.

Now

Daniel found that he didn't have the words. For a writer this was a pretty bad state to be in. He knew that there must be words, but he couldn't find them. What words are there when your wife has just died?

He knew that there was business that needed to be taken care of. He knew that he would have to get a doctor out to sign the death certificate. He knew that he would then have to get some undertakers to take her away (she had already chosen the firm that she wanted to operate for her). He knew that he would then have to go and register the death. There would be relatives and friends that would need to be informed. Perhaps it would be easier to put something on Facebook to let as many people know in an easy and simple way, although it seemed impersonal to him. He knew, most importantly of all, that he would have to tell Toby, who was, even now, in his own room oblivious to what had happened.

There would be time for all of this, but right now what he most wanted was to just be with her. To hold her one last time before all the bustle took over and he was never able to hold her again. He couldn't imagine not being able to hold her, to talk to her, to hear her laugh or discuss the books that they had been reading. All the things that he had so often taken for granted during the time that he had known her, that would never happen again. It was abysmal. He couldn't imagine how life would go on without her. It seemed impossible for life to go on.

Outside of the window people were going about their business as if the end of the world had not happened. Nobody was noticing. People were not howling in the streets. The sun had still come up that morning and would go down that night. People were hurrying along the streets doing their Christmas shopping and preparing to sit down with their wives, husbands, and families as if nothing had happened. Daniel couldn't understand why it was that things were going on this way. He couldn't imagine that the world should still be turning on its axis. Surely there was no point to any of it any longer?

Claire was so cold. He hadn't believed that she could be so cold. He knew that she would hate it. She always hated being cold and irrationally he pulled a blanket onto the bed and covered her up with it as if it would somehow be felt by her and would bring her back to life. Her eyes were closed so he was spared the horror of having to look into her dead stare. He was pleased about this. It suggested that she had died peacefully in her sleep. Had probably not even known what was happening. Probably the best way to go, he thought as he tucked around the blanket.

He thought of all the people that were out there at this moment, wasting love. Cheating on their spouse, not enjoying the love that they had while it lasted and taking their love for granted. He wanted to shake these people up and explain to them that love was not eternal, as the greeting cards suggested. There was an end to it, at least in a physical sense, and you had to be prepared for that day by making the most of it that you could while it was there.

After a while he got off the bed and thought about Toby. He would be getting ready for school. Expecting his breakfast. There would be no school today. Daniel didn't think that you could go to school when your mother had just died. Some people thought

44

that after a death you should just carry on as normal. But Daniel knew that there would never be such a thing as normal ever again.

Toby had already showered when Daniel entered his room, and he was changed into his school uniform. Daniel had no experience with telling someone that someone had died. He knew police officers did it all the time. He suspected they probably had training in how to do it. He wasn't sure that he was up to the task. As it happened, he didn't need to worry about this. Apparently, the look on his face and the fact that he had unexpectedly come into Toby's room was enough.

'Mum's died, hasn't she?'

Daniel thought about what he was going to say and how he was going to say it. He should have been better prepared for this moment. He had known that it was coming for some time now.

'Yes,' he said, feeling that this was an inadequate response, but not trusting himself to say anything else.

Toby sat down on his bed and Daniel felt that he looked like a deflating balloon. He looked exactly how Daniel felt. Daniel sat down on the bed next to him and put his arm around him. Suddenly, Toby was not a big, tough fifteen-year-old any longer, but was a small child that needed comfort and reassurance. Comfort Daniel could give, but he wasn't sure that he could offer any reassurance. He would have liked it if someone had been able to provide it to him.

'Can I see her?'

This was an unexpected request, but in many regards, Daniel should have been aware of the fact that it was likely to come up. Toby had never seen a dead body before, and Daniel wasn't sure about how you handled such a thing. He had been too young when his grandparent had died. His parents had not kept the idea of death from him but didn't think that it was appropriate for him to see the dead body. Many people managed to go through their entire lives without seeing someone dead. Why would you particularly want to see a dead body, anyway? But Toby wanted to see his Mum. He wanted to say goodbye to her and pay his respects and Daniel didn't think that this was something that he had any right to deny.

'Yes,' he lamely replied, but neither of them made a move off the bed. They sat in silence. Toby being grown up enough to feel that he shouldn't cry in front of Daniel, and Daniel being unable to feel that he could cry in front of his son as he needed to hold it together for the pair of them. It was just them now. Them to face the world and they would forever feel the absence that was Claire. It would forever be there, like a big void that would not be spoken about, but that they would always be aware of.

They managed not to cry in front of each other, because of some macho bullshit that they somehow felt the need to keep to, despite the fact that this was the twenty-first century, and there really wasn't time for all that stuff any longer. They managed to keep it together until they went in to see Claire, and then Toby broke down and began to cry at the sight of his mother. With Toby crying there was nothing to hold things back for Daniel and he began to cry too. It was just the two of them alone in the house, before the bustle would start and so there was no need to put up fences and pretend any longer.

And then came the time that Daniel could not delay any longer. He called the GP and arranged for the doctor to come out and see Claire. He seemed a little disgruntled at the fact that he would have to come out to see a dead person when there were live patients that required his attention, but he came nevertheless because Daniel was insistent that he needed to come out and make sure that she was actually dead and had not just fallen into a deep coma or something of that kind.

Daniel knew that she wasn't in a deep coma. He knew that she was dead. He may not have seen that many dead bodies in his life, but he knew that it was pretty obvious when someone was alive and when someone was dead.

'There's no need for the police to get involved,' the doctor said.

'Why would the police need to get involved?' asked Daniel with a confused expression on his face.

'When someone dies suddenly, the police have to be called to act as agents of the coroner,' sniffed the doctor. 'In this case it was clear that Claire was going to die, and it was only a matter of time. Her death was expected, so as I say, no need for the police to get involved with this. You are free to arrange an undertaker of your choice.'

'Thank you,' said Daniel feeling bemused by the entire thing. Toby had taken himself back to his room but had not bothered to change out of his school uniform. Daniel could vaguely hear some distant music coming from his room and imagined that he was immersing himself in it to distract his feelings following Claire's death. Everyone had their own way of dealing with things.

The doctor left and Daniel went into the kitchen to get a mug of coffee and make the phone call to arrange the undertakers. He spoke to a charmingly polite and adequately commiserate receptionist who informed him that the undertakers would be with him within the hour.

Daniel drank his coffee and tried not to think about Claire lying in the spare room, all alone. He wanted to go and sit with her, but he also didn't want to go. He wanted to be with her, but he didn't want to remember her like that if he could help it. He knew this was irrational as he would have many memories of Claire and it was unlikely that the image of her dead would be a prominent memory among them.

True to their word the undertakers arrived within the hour. They were two sombre men (in dress and demeanour) that arrived on the doorstep. They were quietly spoken and respectful with their hands clasped in front of them as if they were standing at the side of the grave already. Daniel supposed that you had to have a certain kind of character to want to go into this business. He wondered what they did to let off steam after a day of being softly spoken and restrained. Probably abused their wives or drank heavily.

They went with Daniel into the spare room and looked at Claire as if they were sizing up a motor car that they were thinking of buying.

'Was the passing expected?' asked one of the men who appeared to be the senior.

Passing. So, the euphemisms had started. People seemed reluctant to use words that actually expressed the way things were, so they made up other words to somehow soften the blow of death.

'Yes, it was,' replied Daniel.

'Then there is no need for the police to be involved,' the man said. Everyone seemed obsessed with the police. Didn't they have enough to do without visiting everyone who had died? Surely there was crime that needed to be solved and things like that.

They looked at the bed and the angle of its position and where the door was located and then returned to their van. Daniel was quite surprised that they had turned up in a van that discreetly had 'Private Ambulance' written on the side in small letters. He had expected them to arrive in a hearse. They opened the back and pulled out a trolley, the kind of which was seen in hospitals throughout the world and what Daniel believed the Americans called a 'gurney'. He wasn't aware of anyone in Britain referring to them as this though.

They went into the bedroom with the trolley and placed a white plastic sheet on the bed which they proceeded to roll under Claire. When it was under her they covered her up with it and lifted her onto the trolley. All of the time they worked in silence or with whispers, with the practised hands of people that had done this thing countless times before and knew exactly what they were doing. When she was on the trolley, they pulled a black, velvet covering over her and then placed straps around her that they buckled in like seatbelts, as if they were afraid that she might decide to get up and leave at any moment.

They then wheeled her out to the van and pushed her into the back through the open rear doors. As one of them closed the van doors, quietly, the other turned to Daniel and gave him their business card and a leaflet on bereavement and what he could expect to happen next. Quietly nodding at him they then got into the van and drove away. Daniel stood for some time with the literature in his hands, watching where the van had disappeared to. Unable to move. Unable to go about his day now that Claire had left the house for the last time.

Eventually, he turned around and returned to the house placing the leaflet and business card on the kitchen table as he passed by. He walked up the corridor to Toby's room and quietly knocked on the door. Toby answered and he went in to find Toby lying on the bed with Mozart's *Requiem* playing at a decent volume from his iPod. His eyes were red and inflamed.

'She's gone,' said Daniel.

Toby nodded his head with nothing to say to this.

'Do you want something to eat?' asked Daniel, aware that Toby had not had any breakfast.

'Not hungry.'

'No, me neither. Okay, I had better get on with some things then. Call me if you need anything.'

'Okay.'

Daniel closed the door and returned to the spare room which seemed so empty now and yet was still filled with her presence as if she had only nipped out to the toilet and would be back at any moment. He looked at the crumpled sheets and decided that he had better start putting stuff into the washing machine. He gathered up the various items that would need washing and thought that he would have to contact the hospital about bringing back all of the equipment that they had lent him during the final weeks of Claire's illness. So many things to do.

He placed the laundry in the washing machine and started it off on its cycle. He then went into his study and sighed deeply as he sat in his leather chair in front of his desk. His computer blinked at him in front of him as if daring him to start work. He looked at the open word document that he had been working on last night. The cursor flashed on and off at him as if waiting for the words that would flow from his fingers. He knew that there would be no words that would come today.

He picked up his mobile phone and getting contact numbers, used the landline to start ringing around to all the places and people that would need to know about Claire's death. He rang the school and explained why Toby was not at school today. They were sympathetic and told him to take all the time that he needed. He didn't need to ring the hospital and speak to the oncologist as the doctor said that was something that he would do. He looked at the death certificate in his hands, the words making little sense to him.

He then started the rounds of family and friends, all of them expressing their condolences and their sympathy, offering to come around, asking what it was that they could do to help. He assured them all that there was nothing to be done, and yes, he would let them know about the funeral arrangements just as soon as he had sorted them all out.

Daniel felt immensely strained by it all. He felt tired, but he knew that he would not be able to sleep. Word was getting around that Claire had died and in between making calls, the phone was ringing all the time. So many people to speak to. So many people that had been a part of Claire's life that now wanted to be a part of her death. It was exhausting work.

Neither of them felt very much like eating, but that night, Daniel cooked himself and Toby spaghetti bolognaise, and they ate in silence. Toby had still not changed out of his school uniform and his eyes were still red. Daniel wished that he could find the words of comfort for him. He wished that he could tell him that it was going to be all right, that his mother had gone to a better place. He wasn't sure that any of that was true. All he could really think to say was that at least her suffering was at an end. That she wasn't in pain any longer. He took little comfort from these words himself.

'I want to go back to school tomorrow.'

'Are you sure?' asked Daniel looking up from his food that he had been moving around the plate, without really eating any of it.

'Yeah.'

'You don't have to, you know.'

'I know, but it's exam year and I can't really afford to miss all that much time.'

Toby was a conscientious student who studied and worked hard. In many ways Daniel was amazed that he was the son of the pair of them who had taken a more relaxed attitude towards studying.

'You're a grade A student, a little time off is not going to cause you any problems.'

'I know, but if I stay at home, all I do is lay there and think. I would rather have something to concentrate on. Something to take my mind off of things, you know?'

Daniel knew exactly what he felt like. 'Okay, you can go back to school if you think you are ready for it. It won't be long before you break up for the holiday though.' It seemed strange to refer to it as a holiday when neither of them felt remotely like being in the holiday spirit.

'Thanks, Dad. I will have to have some time off for the funeral, won't I? I would rather get back to work in the meantime.'

Daniel always found it amusing that he referred to school as work. It hadn't ever felt like work when he was at school. More like one long party with some bad memories thrown in when he was made to do things that he didn't want to do.

'Okay.'

Come bedtime and Daniel dreaded the idea of sleep. It wasn't that the bed was going to be too empty. He was used to sleeping alone now, but he knew that the space next to him would never be filled again. He supposed that this was something that he had known for some time. It had been weeks since they had shared a bed together, but there had always been the possibility that they would share a bed once again.

It wasn't this that was worrying him so much. It was more

to do with the fact that he didn't want to surrender to his sub-conscious. He didn't want to think about what dreams might come were he to go to sleep. He was sure that he was likely to be plagued and would have a troubled and turbulent night. He didn't want to have to think but being awake was causing him to think as well. He was in a pretty hopeless situation.

Toby took himself off to bed straight after dinner and Daniel imagined that he wouldn't be getting much sleep either. Claire had not been noisy in the last weeks of her life, but the house felt so quiet now that it was eerie. He could hear the ticking of the clock that he had normally taken for granted and wouldn't hear during the course of a normal day. He thought about putting some music on or watching some television, but he didn't feel like either of those things. He picked up the book that he had been reading, and then put it down again. He didn't feel like that either. He was re-reading *The Trumpet Major* by Thomas Hardy. He was re-reading all of Hardy and Claire had been re-reading all of Dickens. He supposed that he could go to bed. Try and slip into oblivion, but he doubted that oblivion was something that was going to come tonight.

Eventually, at eleven o'clock, he decided to take himself off to bed and locked up the house for the night. He had a very disturbed and restless sleep.

The next day he woke up as usual and went into the kitchen and turned on the kettle. He started crying when he automatically reached for Claire's mug to make her the morning tea. He gently put the mug back on the shelf and tried to pull himself together. He was used to a routine that had now been disrupted and would never be the same again.

He tried not to think about the mug that would never be used

53

to make her tea ever again and concentrated on making himself a mug of coffee. He couldn't remember where the coffee was and spent a while looking for it, even though it had not been moved and was in the place that it always was. He felt that he was cracking up, falling apart. Of course, the coffee hadn't moved. It was always there. He set about setting the breakfast things out for Toby and making himself some toast as he felt that he ought to eat something. He was going to have to visit the registrar today and register Claire's death. It wasn't something that he was particularly looking forward to. He didn't know why. He didn't think it would be that hard, but somehow registering her death made it more formal. Made it more real. It was almost possible to deny that it had happened up until the point when it became legal. He would also have to visit the undertakers as well and prepare the funeral arrangements. There was much to do. He imagined that one day, Toby would be doing all of this for him.

Toby came and ate his breakfast, as he had every morning. They were both acting out a ritual as if nothing had happened. Toby was quiet though. Very quiet. Daniel wondered if he was going to be all right. If he was going to pull through this without falling into a depression, or doing drugs, or something. Daniel dismissed the thought from his mind. Toby was more sensible and mature than he had ever been at his age. He had his head screwed on right.

With Toby off to school, Daniel made his way to the registrar to get the legal side of things out of the way.

'I'm very sorry for your loss,' said the registrar with a kindly look on her face. Daniel was getting used to people saying this to him, or offering him sympathy or empathy, when they heard the news that his wife had died. He wondered if the registrar got tired of saying it to people. She must have to say it to everyone that walked through the door.

When he had entered the building, he noticed that there were separate rooms. One for registering marriages and births. The happy room. And one for registering deaths. The sad room. He wondered if the registrars took it in turns to work the sad room for that day. Otherwise, it was bound to get depressing all of the time. They probably hated working the sad room, unless they were sadists. He didn't suppose that they were.

'Thank you,' replied Daniel, not yet used to how you were supposed to respond to someone who was offering their condolences. He wondered why strangers offered them in the first place. It wasn't as if they had known Claire. They never would now. Yet they felt the need to say how sorry they were that someone that they had never met had died. He supposed it was some kind of human empathy.

Fortunately, the registrar moved quickly onto dealing with the death and they were able to conduct their business. Daniel felt that then came a social awkwardness. The business was concluded, and the registrar was more than happy for Daniel to leave so that she could get on with the next case, but she was also aware of the fact that because of the nature of why he was there, she was unable to rush him out of the door. She had to let him dictate the pace of the interview. Fortunately, Daniel was all too keen to get out of the stuffy office and get on with the next appointment that he had to go to.

This was to the undertaker. He entered the building with a feeling of dread, knowing that somewhere within the walls of this building, Claire was lying, probably in a fridge somewhere. It felt strange. It felt unnatural. He supposed in many ways it was unnatural. There was nothing natural about being shoved in a fridge when you died. With Claire's feeling of the cold, he knew that she would hate it. He felt like he needed to break her out of there and take her some place warm, but he knew that, biologically, that would be a very unwise thing to do.

The funeral parlour was a strange place. There was a blank tombstone in the window and some artificial flowers. Inside everything was quiet and the staff spoke in whispers as if the grief was coming off the walls. In many regards, it was. Daniel sat quietly and waited to see the funeral director. Even the receptionist's telephone was set to a quieter ringtone, as if out of respect for the dead and the grieving. Daniel felt uncomfortable.

Eventually he was shown into an office with the director.

'My condolences for your loss,' the man said. A slight man, in his fifties, was Daniel's estimate. A look of vague malnourishment about him as if he deliberately starved himself to give him a cadaverous appearance that fitted well with the trade that he had chosen for himself.

'Thank you,' replied Daniel, shaking the man's hand, which was limp and moist, rather like shaking a dead fish. He fought the urge to wipe his hand on his trousers as he sat down.

'What kind of funeral plan were you looking at?'

'Claire was adamant that she wanted the cheapest funeral possible.' This had been something that they had discussed in the last weeks of her life. She hadn't wanted him spending a lot of money to bury her. She couldn't see the point of an ostentatious display of grief and mourning.

'Our basic funeral service includes all of the things that you would expect. As you know, your wife is here at the Chapel of Rest and you, or anyone else in the family, or friends, are free to visit her at mutually convenient times, should you wish to do so.'

Daniel had thought about this and wasn't sure that he wanted to see her in such a place. He and Toby had already seen her when she had died at home. He wasn't sure that there would be anything to be gained by seeing her again. He couldn't speak for anyone else that wanted to see her. He hoped that there was some kind of vetting procedure in place, so that members of the public couldn't just walk off the street and view a corpse whenever they felt like it, like some kind of Victorian tourist attraction.

'The cost also includes the use of a hearse and staff to help conduct the funeral. We will transport your wife directly to the place where the burial or cremation is taking place. Have you decided on which you are having?'

'Burial.'

'That's fine. The price also includes a standard coffin which is suitable for burial. Will you be having flowers?'

'We thought donation to a cancer charity might be more appropriate.'

'Those donations can be handled and coordinated through this office, should you wish it, so that people know where to go with their donations.'

'Okay.'

For the next twenty minutes, the director went through the plan and everything that it would entail.

'Do you have any questions?'

'No. No, I don't think so. Thank you for your time.' Daniel stood up, keen to get out of the office. It was all becoming a bit too much for him. He still had to arrange the funeral service, but that was something that could be done another day. Claire had decided to go for a humanist service, that was not overtly religious. She had never held much of a religious belief in life and didn't care much to hold one on death. She thought that this would be hypocritical. The minister, or whatever you called them, was due to come and see Daniel at his home the following day.

That night was another restless night of sleep. Daniel had thought over all the things that he had done with Claire. Their holidays abroad and in the country. The times that they had laughed together and the times that they had cried. He thought of it all. He was of the opinion that they were soulmates. That was why they had been so close for the time that they had known each other. Ever since they had gone for coffee at the university. Their paths were destined to be together. It was hard losing that soulmate. Hard to have nobody in your life when they had been there near enough all of your life. There was a gaping hole in his life, and he couldn't ever imagine that it was going to be filled. He didn't know that he wanted it to be filled. He didn't want to hook up with anyone else. He didn't want to marry again, or all of that. He wanted to have that hole in his life to remind him of the fact that Claire had been there, and now she was gone.

He lie in bed and listened to the rain beating against the windows. It was a certainty that it wasn't going to be a white Christmas again this year, but then he couldn't ever remember snow at Christmas. It was just something that seemed to happen in the films and on greetings cards. Already the Christmas cards downstairs had started to be replaced by condolences cards. It couldn't have felt less like Christmas. He supposed that he ought to make an effort for the sake of Toby, but he really didn't feel like it and he imagined that Toby wasn't really up to it either. They would both have to deal with their grief in their own ways, he imagined. He didn't think that it was going to be something that would be easy for either of them.

I was expecting the death, we all were, but nothing quite softens the blow when it comes. I knew the moment that dad walked into my room that mum had died. It was written all over his face. It was hard for me, but it must have been doubly hard for him. I suppose though that if he wanted to, he could always marry again and get another wife, whereas I only had one mum and she was gone forever. Nobody would ever be able to replace her for me. I wouldn't want anyone to. You can't replace your mother, not really. You can get a stepmother but she never actually gave birth to you. Dad seemed surprised when I said that I wanted to go back to school, but I needed something to focus my mind on. I didn't relish the idea of sitting in my room listening to morbid music and going all Hamlet on everyone. Getting back to school would raise some belief of normality as if everything was okay and none of this had actually happened. I wish that it hadn't happened. You can try and hide in a fantasy, or one of dad's books, but it doesn't prevent reality from getting in the way. Fuck cancer.

Then

When they finished studying for their degrees, Claire and Daniel moved out of the student rented accommodation that they had been living in for the last two years and rented a small house of their own. They had decided that they would stay together in the city that they had been studying for the last three years. They enjoyed the city, which was vibrant with a number of good bookshops, both those in a chain and those that were independent. Bookshops were important to the both of them and they wanted to be somewhere where they could get a ready supply of books. The intention was to fill their house with books. Knowledge would breathe from the bookshelves. They were happy together.

Most of their university friends went their separate ways. Some went on to study at different universities elsewhere, others moved back to wherever home was, but a few of them stayed where they had studied like Claire and Daniel. They stayed in touch with most of these friends. Most of them were also Literature graduates, although there were a few that had studied other subjects.

The house that they lived in was modest but was the best that they could afford. Claire was working in the publishing house and Daniel was still going through the negotiations of publishing his first novel. He didn't expect that there would be overnight success. He hoped that he would earn enough to be able to live off his writing, and that was good enough for him. He didn't expect to be earning millions of pounds like Stephen King, but then he wrote very different books to King, so didn't expect to earn that kind of money, or that kind of popularity. Most writers didn't. The success stories were limited. It depended on what it was that you wanted to get out of writing. If you were going into it in order to gain fame and fortune, then you were probably choosing the wrong job. If you went into it, like Daniel did, because you were passionate about writing and wanted to do it all day, every day, then the chances were that you would be far happier than those that thought that they were going to get a number one bestseller and a Nobel Prize straight out of the door.

Miller's Revenge was Daniel's first novel. It sounded like an action thriller, but it was really about relationships and how people acted towards each other. The publisher had liked it, which was always a good start. Daniel was excited when he signed his first publishing deal, he hoped that it would be the first of many, but he was taking one step at a time and not taking anything for granted. He was even more excited when the contract came back signed by the publishing house. There was no turning back now.

He didn't expect to make a big splash with his first novel, but if he could build up a following then he might sell other copies of future works, and there would be a market out there for him. He had the support of Claire, which is something that was very important. Not only did she provide the financial support by paying the rent, buying the groceries, and paying all the other bills, but she believed in him. That was probably the most important thing of all. She believed that he would be a success. She had believed that he would be published, and she believed that he would continue to be published, and she believed that one day he would make it to the point where her faith in him was justified.

Her mother thought that she was doing all the work and that Daniel was slouching around the house all day, eating crisps, and watching daytime television. She didn't see the hours that he spent bent over his laptop, furiously tapping away at the keyboard, or the long walks that he took when he was looking for an inspiration or was mulling an idea over in his head. She didn't see any of this, and there was clearly a part of her that didn't approve of Daniel. She probably didn't think that any man was good enough for her daughter, so it wasn't anything against Daniel.

Daniel was concerned about opinion of him though. He had to be. Otherwise, he wouldn't have been a writer. You didn't spend hours writing a novel and then not care what people thought of it. You had to have a degree of care about the opinion that people had of you. Bad opinion would mean that you sold less books, so you hoped for the best opinion that you could get.

'Your mother doesn't like me,' he told Claire.

'My mother doesn't like anyone, don't take it personally.'

'Kind of hard not to take it personally when she is directing it at me. Every time she comes to visit it is like icicles are dripping off of every word that she says to me.'

'I thought she hardly spoke to you.'

'Well, she doesn't, but when she does it's like icicles are dripping off every word.'

'It's just the way that she is. I really wouldn't worry about it.'

'That's easy for you to say. She's your mother. Was she like this with every boyfriend you ever had?'

'Most of them,' said Claire, nodding her head.

'No wonder it took you so long to take me home to meet

your parents.'

'What matters is what I think of you, not what she thinks about you, and I love you. That's all you need to think about.'

'I don't think she would like me even if I had a million-pound bestseller and we lived in a mansion.'

'I don't want to live in a mansion.'

'But you wouldn't mind the million pounds.'

'Well, it's a start.'

'I obviously need to write more.'

'Keep at it, Word-boy.'

They established a routine. Claire would go off to work and Daniel would sit down at the laptop and do whatever it was that he felt like doing for that day. Some writers believed that you should write every day and that you should set yourself a word limit, a thousand words for instance, and make sure that you did that amount of writing. Daniel didn't believe in that. He just believed in writing. Some days the words wouldn't come. Other days he would write a thousand words and on others he would write five thousand. He just believed in getting up each morning and going to the computer to try and make the words come. If they did, then all well and good. If they didn't come, then he would go for a walk or do some housework. Something to take his mind away from the writing for a little while, until he felt able to go back and face the blank, white page once again, with the taunting, flashing cursor that was always waiting to be moved across the page.

Money was tight, so they could afford few luxuries. One of the things that they tried to get the most of was books, but most of their book collection had been picked up cheaply in secondhand shops, so although it looked expensive it had actually been achieved on a budget. Most other things they did without.

Claire was heavily into classical music as her music of choice, and rather than spend a lot of money on CDs, decided that she would get most of her fix by listening to the radio. She was particularly into Chopin and Bach as her favourites. She would listen to classical music all day if she could get away with it.

Daniel started work on his second book. The publishers had said that they would be interested in anything else that he had to offer, and he felt that he needed to publish at least one book a year to keep things ticking over. He didn't have any novels in storage and so would have to start from scratch. The way he saw it he could spend six months working on a new book and the following six months on the business side of getting it published and promoted and so on. Once he had completed this he could start all over again.

Of course, it didn't always work like that. He couldn't have six months away from writing while he concentrated on the business side of things. Very often an idea would pop into his head and demand to be written and there was nothing that he could do about it, but to go along with it and the demands that it was making on him. He wasn't too bothered by this. It was the way that he worked. The ideas demanded attention and you had to obey them.

Miller's Revenge was not a bestseller, but it was well received, with some good reviews on Amazon and in some of the local newspapers. Daniel was hopeful that it was going to be the start of something new in his life.

'I'm so proud of you, Baby,' Claire said to him as they went out to dinner to celebrate his publication. They rarely went out for dinner, so this was something of a special extravagance. Something that they couldn't really afford, but that they were determined to do.

'Thanks,' he replied as they clicked glasses together. 'I hope that it pays its way, and I can begin to shoulder some of the household expenses.'

'Oh, you needn't worry about that.'

'One day I'll be earning enough for you to quit work and become a lady of leisure.'

'I'm not sure I would care all that much for that. I love my work, and I value my independence enough. Just earn enough to make you happy and for it not to matter whether you have to slave over a new book or not.'

'Well, I think we are a way off of that yet.'

'Just remember that everyone had to start somewhere. Every author had to start with a first step. Nobody was born successful.'

'And most of it has come with a lot of hard work, and a lot of false starts.'

'Exactly. You're doing fine, remember that. As I said, I'm proud of you.'

'I couldn't have done it without you.'

'I'm sure you could've.'

'I'm not so sure. You have been my rock. You're the one that has truly believed in me.'

'You would have got there. Look at you, one year out from university and you're publishing your first book. Most people have to wait, years, even decades, before they reach a stage like that.'

'Joseph Heller spent about seven years writing *Catch-22* after his day job, before he was able to finish it and get it published.'

'Exactly. You're lucky in that your day job has been your writing from the outset. You haven't had to toil over something that you've hated. Neither of us have.'

'That's true.'

'And I'm sure that this is just the start of a blazing career with you. I'm sure that you will eventually make it big. You will eventually write something that will really capture the imagination of the public.'

'That's the thing, isn't it? Being in the right place, with the right book, at the right time. It's almost more important than writing a decent book in the first place.'

Daniel's second book, *Lost Days*, was taken up by the publishing firm as well and sold even better than his first one had. He concentrated largely on writing about relationships and how people interacted with each other in different circumstances.

'It's what life is all about,' he told Claire.

'I suppose you're right. Don't get bored writing about similar things all the time though, and don't get caught in the trap of having to write the same stuff because it's what your audience expects from you.'

'I think I would like a bit of variety. I might jump from genre to genre. I'm sure it will really annoy the publishers. Get a hit in a certain formula and they are looking for you to repeat it time and time again.'

'That's because it's all about making them money.'

'Well, it's about making me money as well, I suppose.'

'It's more about the process of writing for you though, isn't it? You write because it's something that you want to do. Not because of the fact that you want the money.'

With the publication of his second novel, people were starting to take notice of him. He had received a national review and was not just known as a local author who was somebody of minor interest. His third book, *Out There*, was successful enough to make it into the top thirty chart of book sales. True it was nearer thirty than it was number one, but it was still something of a bestseller as far as he was concerned. He felt that he had arrived and was justified in his dream in wanting to be a writer. He was pretty sure that it was not enough for Claire's mother though. With the success of the book, he asked Claire if she would marry him.

It was something that he asked on Valentine's Day, because, as corny as it might sound, it felt like the right day to ask her. She immediately said yes. They hadn't talked of marriage before, but it was somehow assumed that it would be something that they would do one day. They had been together for six years now, they were twenty-three years old. Some said that they were too young to get married, but they had felt happy with each other. They had been living together, outside of university, for three years, and everything seemed to be going the way that they wanted it to go. They rarely argued and never seriously fell out over anything.

Claire's mother had been sceptical and had made it clear that she thought that it would never last.

'I think you're being very stupid,' she had told Claire, despite the fact that Daniel was standing there as well. 'If you marry this man, you will have nothing but a lifetime of regret. Now, Yvonne's son is a lawyer, a proper career. I could hook you up on a date.'

'I don't want a date, Mother. I'm going to marry Daniel.'

'You have never done what is right for you,' she had snorted. 'You went to the wrong university. If you had gone to the university that I had picked out for you then you would never have met this, this scribbler, and you would probably be able to settle down with a nice man who had proper prospects.'

'I'm more than happy with my prospects,' replied Daniel.

'That's because you have low expectations,' she shot at him

with barely a glance in his direction. 'I urge you, Claire, to be sensible about this.'

'I *am* being sensible about this. This is the way that I want things to be. It's my life and if I ruin it, as you seem to think that I will, then that is something that is up to me.'

'Your mother really doesn't like me,' Daniel had commented as they left the house.

'She doesn't much like me either. I'm sure that my father only died of his heart attack so that he might get some peace from her. I can't imagine what his life must have been like with her disapproval and nagging all of the time.'

'Are you sure you want to get married?'

'Yes, of course I am. Why, aren't you?'

'I've never been surer of anything in my entire life.'

'Well, that's sorted then, isn't it? We can forget about my mother and get on with our life. With any luck she will spend so much time sulking that she won't want to be a part of things.'

The engagement lasted two years while they saved up enough money to get married. They married when they were twenty-five years old. The same month of the marriage, Daniel's fourth book, *Dystopia*, came out and made it into the top ten. They moved out of their rented house and put the mortgage down on a house of their own. They continued to be happy despite the predictions of Claire's mother. She continued to haunt them like a bad dream but had as little to do with their life as she could. She was just *there*. Like a bad smell.

Claire had risen in the publishing house and was now more senior. Working with authors in getting their books published and helping to guide them to publication. She continued to enjoy the work and it didn't hurt that she was married to an author that many considered to be the up-and-coming thing. *Dystopia* also won some awards for Daniel, that he was particularly pleased about. He felt that he had arrived. Recognition was the justification that he had chosen the right career and it had not all been in vain.

With the success of *Dystopia* there was also interest in his back catalogue and he started to make sufficient money from writing to feel in his own head that he was finally doing a job. A proper job. Okay, he might not have been a doctor or a lawyer (like Claire's mother had hoped for her) but he was a successful man that was making money from his hobby that had now become a career.

His fifth book *Fog on the Distant Hills* went straight in at number one and stayed there for a couple of weeks. When he was not writing he was doing the tour of bookshops, reading from his books, being interviewed, and signing books to anyone that wanted to buy them. He remained a book lover and was always more interested in browsing the books in the bookshops than actually giving the talk that he was there to do. He would often convince the staff to allow him to buy some of the books that were on display while he was there. His hand began to ache from the amount of signing that he was doing. He would have a fear of spelling someone's name wrong and upsetting them when signing their book, so was always meticulous in his signing for them. Bizarrely there were even people that wanted to have their photograph taken with him. He felt like he was some famous actor, instead of a jobbing author who was trying his best to get his work out there.

From time to time, he would also be asked to write an opinion piece for one of the national newspapers. He didn't like doing this, as this was a bit personal. He could hide behind his words in his novels by saying that these were the thoughts and words of his characters and not necessarily the way that he thought. Writing opinion pieces made him put himself out there and be aligned with his own thoughts and words. It felt strangely vulnerable, and he was not a fan of doing it. It paid well though and he remembered the time when he was struggling and living off of beans on toast, and he was aware of the fact that things could easily go back to that way, so he tried to make his money where he could. When you have had little money, you are always mindful of the fact that you could go back to that way again if you are not careful.

'I've got something to tell you,' said Claire, with a hint of seriousness about her.

Daniel looked up from his keyboard. 'What is it?'

'Promise you won't be angry.'

'I can't promise that until I know what it is that you have to say. You might have to tell me that you have just murdered someone, at which point it would be difficult not to be at least slightly angry, unless it was your mother of course.'

'Be serious.'

'I *am* being serious.'

'It's important.'

'So, tell me about it. What's bothering you?'

'I have something urgent to tell you and I'm not sure how you will react to hearing it.'

'What is it? Just tell me.'

'I'm pregnant.'

Daniel stared at her as if he had not heard her correctly. There was a silence between them for a moment.

'You're pregnant?'

'Yes. You're disappointed, aren't you?'

'No, not at all. Not disappointed, just a little in shock. Wow. Pregnant? You mean I'm going to be a father?'

'That's generally a result of it, yes.'

'Wow.'

'You're not disappointed?'

'Of course not. This is wonderful news. I can't believe it.' He got up from his desk and gave her a hug.

'It's unexpected, isn't it?' she asked when they broke the embrace.

'Unexpected, but wonderful.'

'You really think so?'

'Of course, I do. It's fantastic news.'

'I was worried that you might be a bit put out by it all.'

'Why would I be put out by it all?'

'I don't know. I just wasn't sure. We hadn't planned it so I thought you might be a bit worried by it all and made to think that you have been forced into the situation.'

'I haven't been forced into anything. We both are adults. We both know what we are getting into with these things. It's only to be expected.'

'I have no idea what my mother will make of it,' Claire said with a frown.

'Well, she will never be happy no matter what we do. You could give birth to the second coming and she still wouldn't be happy about it.'

'I doubt it will be the second coming.'

'That's good news. Terrible to have your job picked out for you from birth with no choice of doing what you wanted to do.'

The news that they were going to have a baby was something that was unexpected. They had not planned for it, and it had taken them both by surprise. It was, nevertheless, still something that was welcomed by them as they thought of the fact that they were now going to go from being a couple to being a family. Neither of them had given all that much thought into becoming parents. They realised that they had a lot to learn, but they also knew that they were hardly unique in situations such as this. Most first-time parents went into it without really knowing what they were doing. Most people went through life like that. There was no guidebook that told you how you are meant to act on things. You had to make it up as you went along. It was the only way to do things.

Toby was born when they were twenty-seven. They felt it was about the right age to start a family, if there was ever a right time for this kind of thing. The labour had been difficult though and it had not been an easy birth. Claire had to have a Caesarean and was told by the doctors that it might be too dangerous for her to have children again. They became resigned to the fact that Toby was going to be an only child. It wasn't the way that they had planned it, but they could at least give him the unconditional love that he deserved.

The publication of Daniel's next novel *Time for Dreams* was a sufficient success for them to move into a bigger house that would be better for them as a family. Despite it being a bigger house, they had sufficient money to be able to afford a lower mortgage and were paying out less each month. Daniel felt that he was finally pulling his own weight in the marriage and had achieved something in his own right. There were talks about a movie deal based on one of his books as well, which was exciting as well as reassuring with the money that it would bring in. Daniel had been asked if he would consider writing the screenplay.

'I can't do that,' he told Claire.

'Why not?'

'I'm a novelist. I only know how to write novels. I couldn't do a screenplay.'

'You're a writer. You can turn your hand to anything that you want to. All you have to do is put your mind to it.'

'It's a completely different art form. I wouldn't feel comfortable doing it.'

'Then don't do it. The novels are bringing in enough money now. It isn't as if you need to do the screenplay. The only reason for doing it is to maintain control over your project and to prove to yourself that you are capable of working in another genre.'

'I'm not sure that I have anything to prove to myself. I would much rather just carry on writing novels. Screenplays require a completely different type of writing. You have to say things much more concisely than you do in a novel. Besides which, writing a screenplay and then getting involved in the film industry with all the rewrites and the like would be very time consuming and would take me away from the novels.'

'Nobody is going to force you to do it.'

'Plus of course, if I did write it, I would only get hacks messing around with it and changing it. Then I would have to be on set all the time ready to make rewrites and answer any silly questions that the actors might have.'

'I thought you might enjoy something of the showbiz lifestyle. You might get to meet some actors that you like.'

'I think I would rather have root canal surgery. I can't imagine anything ghastlier.'

'You have to think yourself lucky.'

'How so?'

'Ten years ago, you couldn't have imagined being in a

position where you had to agonise over whether or not you would write the screenplay to one of your books. There are worse things in the world to worry about.'

'I suppose you're right.'

'You know I'm right.'

'We have come rather far, haven't we?' said Daniel as he relaxed into an armchair.

'Yes, we have.'

'Are you happy in your life, Claire?'

'Of course, I am. Why do you ask?'

'You wouldn't have been happier marrying a lawyer or a doctor, like your mother wanted you to?'

'Not in the slightest. Why would you think so?'

'Just asking.'

'Well, you can set your mind to rest on that front. We have a great life together and I'm very happy and content. Are you?'

'Of course, I am.'

'Well, there's nothing to worry about then, is there?'

With the birth of Toby, they settled into a routine. Claire went back to work as soon as she had recovered from the surgery and had time off to spend with Toby. Daniel would split his day between looking after Toby and doing his writing. The movie deal went ahead without him writing the screenplay, and when it was released, it was received rather well but didn't set the world on fire. Daniel shunned the gala premiere as he didn't really fancy going to that kind of thing, and instead went to see the film with everyone else, like a normal member of the public, rather than someone that had a vested interest in the film.

He wasn't particularly impressed with the film at all. He thought that they had messed his book about and changed some

74

key elements of it. He supposed that he might have been able to prevent this from happening if he had been writing the screenplay, but he didn't fool himself for long. He was sure that if he had been reluctant to make the changes that they wanted, then they would have just got someone else in to make the changes for them. He was well aware of the legend that the writer was the lowest form of employment in the movie industry. He didn't understand this though. As he watched the credits roll endlessly at the end of the film, it occurred to him that none of these people would have been working, if he had not written the book in the first place. True, they might have found work on some other film, but all these people in the credits were employed because *he* had written a book. It didn't make sense, therefore, why writers should get such a bum deal in Hollywood. People overlooked them, he supposed. They were invisible, in many regards. Without them though the actors wouldn't know what to say. All those people – a thousand or more – that were employed all because he had sat, alone, at a keyboard and written something in isolation. It seemed very strange.

He did not regret that he had declined to write the screenplay though. He was happy with novels and that was where he wanted to remain. He always worried that he would run out of ideas, but every time that he took a little break from the keyboard, something else would suggest itself and he would be compelled to write once again. Sometimes he started writing one novel, sure of the direction that it was going in, only to have it morph in front of his eyes and become something completely different. In many regards he didn't feel like he had all that much control over his writing. It was like the words were there and he was just the instrument that allowed them to get down onto the page, other than that he had no say in what happened. It felt strange at times when this happened, but it also felt exhilarating. It was like a good guitarist who was so well crafted that they could run their hands all over their machine without their brain really realising what it was that they were playing. Daniel felt the same thing when his fingers flew all over the keyboard in a frenzy that it felt difficult to keep up with and words appeared on the Siberian white screen in front of him.

Everything was going well with Claire and Daniel. They had, what they thought of as a perfect life. They were content and happy in their love for each other. It was probably a good thing, therefore, that they had no idea of the disaster and tragic moments that awaited them.

Dad had written several novels before I was born, but it was some years before I got to read any of them. I think they were too mature for me and I had to be of the right age to read them and really appreciate them. I am impressed that both my parents had such a clear-cut idea of what it was that they wanted to do with their lives. I have no real idea of where I am going and what I am doing with my life. I know that I am only fifteen and perhaps I don't need to know at fifteen what it is that I am meant to be doing, but I have friends who are pretty clear on what they are doing with their lives. It's all mapped out. In some cases, this is because they have a calling and they know what they are doing. In most cases, though, it is their parents who are deciding what it is that they are going to be doing with their lives. I am pretty glad that my parents are not like that. They have always left me alone to make up my own choices, to make my own mistakes and follow my own path. It might mean I waste a bit of time going down dead ends, but at the end of the day, it's my time to waste.

Now

The death of Claire meant that it didn't feel remotely like Christmas at all. The songs were still playing in the shops and the carols were sung on the street corners, and all the things that you would expect from a Dickensian Christmas that had somehow worked its way into the culture. Daniel imagined that Dickens would have been very pleased at the effect that he had had on Christmas. It was the same as Queen Charlotte introducing the alien idea of having trees inside the house at Christmas, and the invention of the very first Christmas card. In brief, Christmas, as we know it today, was almost entirely an invention of the Victorians. A long-lasting legacy that they would undoubtedly have been proud of, had they of known of it.

Daniel tried to keep things as Christmas-like as possible for the sake of Toby (if no one else) but he secretly thought that Toby was as bothered about it as he was. With the loss of a wife and a mother, there didn't seem to be all that much point in celebrating. Relatives and friends had all invited them around to spend Christmas with them, but they were offers that were politely declined. Daniel did not imagine that he was very good company at the moment, and did not want to inflict that onto anyone else. Why spoil someone else's Christmas, just because yours had been ruined?

He informed the hospital that they could come and get their things back and they assured him that someone would see to it, possibly sometime in the New Year. They would be in touch, they said. They didn't seem all that bothered about getting their equipment back which irked Daniel as he imagined that there would be someone else that was waiting for it and would make good use of it, and it certainly wasn't something that he particularly wanted cluttering up the place any longer and reminding him of the illness that Claire had been unsuccessful in combating. The cancer that had finally beat her.

Daniel had a fear that the funeral would take place on Christmas Eve and therefore make the festive season something that was even more of a strain on him and Toby. As it happened, things did not happen all that fast and the funeral had been arranged for the twenty-ninth. That gave Daniel rather a long period of time to think about what was coming up. He wondered if he should speak at the funeral, or whether this would be something that would be too personal. Too difficult to manage to do. It would require him to pull himself together in such a way that he didn't think that he would be capable of doing. It was one thing to be able to hold himself together for the sake of Toby, but quite another to have to hold himself together in front of all the family and friends that would be there.

Toby was the reason why he got out of bed in the morning. If it hadn't been for Toby, then he would, very possibly, stay in bed for the whole day. Other than Toby there was no reason to get out of bed. Nothing really mattered any longer. He couldn't work. Didn't feel the inclination to type meaningless words onto paper any longer. What did it really matter? Nothing really mattered any longer. He had lost the one guiding light that he had in his life. The one reason that he had to go to bed at night, and to get up in the morning. Without that, without Claire, there just didn't seem to be any point in any of it any longer.

He had promised Claire that he would not end his own life.

He stuck to that promise. Promises were important. He had never knowingly broken a promise in his life. He had never lied to Claire. He had no intention of starting now. He promised that he would not kill himself, but he knew that there were other ways that he could die.

Each night, when he went to bed, as he lay down, he felt a tightness in his chest, and a pain in his left arm. He thought that he might be having a heart attack. He welcomed it. He knew that it would be difficult for Toby, and he felt some guilt over this, but he thought that it might be something for the best. Claire had been a part of his life for longer than she hadn't been there. It seemed only fitting that now that she was gone, he should follow her to wherever it was that she was now.

Sometimes he would also get stabbing headaches. He thought that maybe this meant that he had a brain tumour. Maybe he was destined to die that way. Again, he did nothing about it. He knew that there was nothing that he could do. He felt, in some ways, as if it was something that he had to suffer for the pain that Claire had gone through.

Ultimately nothing came of the headaches, or the chest pain. He knew that it was just tension and stress. He knew that nothing would be gained from these things. They were unlikely to kill him. He would just have to shoulder the pain that came with grief and carry on. It's what Claire would have wanted him to do. There was no doubt about that. He thought about going to see a doctor, but what would that achieve? Doctors had done nothing for Claire and there had actually been something wrong with her, whereas there wasn't really anything wrong with him. Nothing that time wouldn't cure.

But, was that true? Would he actually feel better in time or would the hollowness always be there? He suspected that there would always be that void where Claire had been. It might get easier with time, but he couldn't imagine that it would ever go away. He wasn't entirely sure that he wanted it to go away either. If it went away that would mean that he had, to some extent, forgotten about Claire, and he didn't want to forget about Claire. He wanted to remember her every day. He didn't want a day to go by without thinking of something that he meant to tell her. A joke that he heard that he thought that she might like. A story idea that he could run past her. Feeling sad because she wasn't there to read the first draft of the latest manuscript. She was always his first reader and she always gave honest opinions on what she thought of his work. He could rely on her. He had always been able to.

And now she was gone. There were so many things that he missed that he knew would never come again. He would never feel her snuggling into him when they slept. Holding hands as they fell asleep at night. The kisses at odd moments when there was nothing that had actually happened to warrant a kiss, other than the fact that they loved each other. All these years of marriage and they loved each other just as much as if they were giddy teenagers once again.

'How are you holding up?' asked Jordan when he came around to see him. Daniel made no reply, just shrugged his shoulders as if there were no words that could adequately explain how he was holding up under the circumstances. 'Tough call at Christmas time.'

'Tough call at any time of the year if you ask me.'

'Of course, I didn't mean to suggest anything else. You know, it's just extra tough at Christmas. You know what I mean …'

'I guess so.'

'How's Toby?'

'I think he's okay. He doesn't really want to talk about it all that much. I can understand his point of view, if I am honest.'

'Would you prefer not to talk about it?'

'One thing that I have discovered is that, regardless of how I feel, other people seem to have the need to talk about it.'

'We don't have to talk about it if you don't want to.'

'No, I really don't mind. Sorry, I'm being harsh. I'm not really myself at the moment.'

'I don't think that anyone expects you to be.'

'Oh, I'm sure some people expect there to be something of the stiff upper lip going on.'

'She was your wife. It's understandable.'

'She still is.'

'What?'

'My wife. Just because she's dead doesn't mean that she has stopped being my wife.'

'I understand.'

'Do you?'

'Probably not,' admitted Jordan sipping on his coffee. 'If anything happened to Natalie, I would be beside myself. I wouldn't know what to do. I doubt that I could function on any particular level that would seem even vaguely human.'

'I don't know how I'm doing it. I just put one foot in front of the other and hope for the best.'

They lapsed into silence for a moment. Sometimes this was the best thing. Guests came around and wanted to talk. The more considerate ones were just prepared to sit there. To have a companionable silence and to talk if the grieved felt the need to talk, otherwise to sit in silence. These people were few and far between. Most people don't like a silence and prefer to want to fill it with something, anything. Daniel had numerous offers of people asking if he wanted a cup of tea. He knew that this was less an interest people had in taking care of him, and was more to do with the fact that they wanted to do something. They had to keep busy. They probably looked at him and thought 'My God, that could be me.' They felt lucky for what they had in their life and dreaded the moment that might come when they felt the same way as he did. It was only human nature.

Christmas was upon them. Daniel tried his best to make it seem like a normal Christmas, but both he and Toby knew that it wasn't. He was sure that Toby appreciated the effort, but it was something that they both found difficult to get through. Opening presents on Christmas morning was a subdued affair. Daniel had removed the presents that were for Claire from under the tree and had placed them away in a cupboard somewhere. He knew that he would have to deal with them at some point, but he wasn't ready to deal with them at the moment. It was all too much to have to face at the present time.

Once the presents were unwrapped, Toby returned to his bedroom with his gifts. Daniel went into the kitchen to prepare lunch. The turkey had been in the oven since he had got up and he set about peeling the potatoes and preparing the vegetables. It took an enormous amount of effort. He wasn't sure why it was that he was bothering. Why was he trying to pretend like this was a normal Christmas? Why didn't they just have a sandwich or something and treat it like it was just a normal day? A normal day? Would there ever be such a thing again? It all seemed so ludicrous. It was difficult to deal with. The grief was overwhelming at times. The emotion would roll in from nowhere and Daniel would feel like collapsing on the floor and crying his eyes out.

He felt that he probably needed some help. He knew that if he went to see a doctor, he would be diagnosed with depression and placed on anti-depressants. He wasn't sure that it would achieve anything by doing this. He didn't want to fall into the trap of having to take medication in order to get through the day. He thought that once he started on tablets then he would be hooked for the rest of his life. Maybe he would even become a zombie under their influence. He wouldn't be able to work. He didn't feel like working at the moment. There was little that occupied his day, other than thoughts of Claire all of the time. He remembered all the things that they had been up to. He remembered the day that they met with startling clarity. He remembered things that he had forgotten. He felt that he remembered every little thing that they had done together.

Lunch was as subdued as the present opening had been. Daniel didn't know what to say to Toby. He didn't know what words to say to comfort him when he didn't know the words to comfort himself. If he had known how to comfort Toby, then he would have taken his own medicine and comforted himself. He felt that there was probably a gulf that was opening up between them. Maybe with time the distance would become worse and they would end up never talking to each other. He didn't know. He felt so helpless that he didn't know what to do. As a writer, not being able to find the right words was frustrating. He felt incompetent.

Toby had hardly come out of his room since Claire's death. Daniel knew that it was reasonably normal to expect a teenager to want to spend more time in their room than anywhere else in the house, but it felt as if the distance was growing. Toby would be in one part of the house, and Daniel would be in the rest of the house. Separated by their grief. He knew that he ought to make more of an effort with his son, but he could hardly move. Everything he did was a supreme effort and was difficult. He wished that he could just stay in his room like Toby, and deal with his grief that way. He found himself envying the fact that Toby didn't have the responsibility that he did, and could afford to spend his time in his room all of the time. He wondered if it would get any easier, like people said that it would. He couldn't see how it was possible for the moment.

He sat in his study for a few hours and stared at the flashing cursor that was taunting him to write. He knew that he should probably return to work. There was plenty of work to do. There was the writing of the new book that he had been working on and there was editing to be done on another. His publisher would be waiting for both books. Well, they would have to wait. There was no motivation in him to do any of it for the moment. Maybe he had lost the ability to ever do it again. Perhaps Claire was his muse and without her he was doomed to never write another word again.

He wasn't sure that he believed this. He didn't lack a muse, so much as he lacked motivation. He had had moments like this in the past, when everything had seemed to be such an effort that he had not felt like writing. There had been the odd moment (not too many of them) when writing had felt more like a chore than something that he enjoyed doing. The problem that he had now was that he had always written his books with the intention of his sole reader being Claire. He had written them all for her. The fact that other people liked to read them as well was a bonus, but each word that he had written he had written for one reader only. Now that she was gone, what was the point? She had always been the first one to read what he had written. He had valued her opinion before he had made edits and got it ready to send off to the publisher. Now he had lost that forever.

True, he still had several finished manuscripts that he had stored over the years. He had been more productive than his publishing permitted. He had written two novels a year and published only one. He had enough stored novels to still publish one a year without having to write another word. It would tide him over if he continued to lack the motivation to write. He just wasn't sure what he would do with his days if he wasn't writing.

Toby only really came out of his room for meals, and he wasn't always that keen to come out of the room for them. It wasn't unusual teenage activity, but it was unusual for Toby. Daniel respected his privacy though and allowed him the space that he obviously felt that he needed. Daniel had no idea what it was that he was doing in his room, he allowed him to get on with it though, without any intrusion from him.

Daniel spent most of his time listlessly going from room to room. Not doing much, waiting for the time when he could justifiably go back to bed and sleep once again. He didn't like sleeping as it brought dreams of Claire with it, but he didn't like being awake either as this gave him thoughts of Claire all of the time with the added disadvantage of not being able to slip into oblivion. He was sure that sleeping tablets would probably give him oblivion, but he didn't want to fall into the habit of taking medication in order to get to sleep. It was difficult to get off to sleep though. He had always suffered from some form of onset insomnia, but it was worse after the death of Claire than it had ever been before. He would, more often than not, cry himself to sleep. He believed that having a good cry was a therapeutic way of dealing with the grieving process. It just wasn't very British to do it in front of others.

So many things were worse after the death of Claire than they had ever been before. For the sake of something to do he took all the Christmas decorations down on Boxing Day. He knew that it was a bit early, but he couldn't face seeing them around any longer. As he packed them away into the loft, he could well imagine that they would never see the light of day again. He could live without them and he doubted that Toby was all that bothered. He didn't imagine that he would be celebrating Christmas at any time in the future with any particular vehemence.

When he came out of his room, Toby made no mention of the fact that the decorations had been taken down. Daniel wondered if he even noticed that they were gone. Probably not. The way things had been lately, he probably hadn't even noticed that they had gone up in the first place. Daniel hoped that Toby was going to be okay and that he wasn't going to fall into drug abuse or something like that, as a means of dealing with his pain. He knew that it was very unlikely, but you read stories about people where this had happened. It had probably been easier for him while he had still been able to go to school, but now that the holidays were upon them, he was as listless and claustrophobic in the house as Daniel was.

The days between Christmas and New Year were flat, uneventful, the way that they normally were anyway. Daniel tried to edit his book, but found that he was reading the same paragraph over and over again, with none of it sinking in or making any sense. He eventually decided that editing while in this frame of mind was probably not something that was for the best. New words were simply not coming at all. Maybe he was trying too hard. Staring at the flashing cursor until it was seared into his brain. He would go to sleep at night and see that flashing cursor, blinking in an Antarctic waste of white. Daring him to find the words to be able to continue his journey.

The days after Christmas and before the funeral were slow. Daniel had the option to go and see Claire in the Chapel of Rest, but decided against the idea. He had no wish to remember her dead. He wanted to remember her vibrant and full of life. He didn't want to remember her cold and empty. The minister, or whatever he was, came around to see him and spoke to him at length about Claire. He wanted to know everything that he could about her and discussed with Daniel what kind of music he would like for the service. Daniel had not given this much thought, but knew that Claire had written down some thoughts on what she wanted for her funeral service. In the end they decided on an excerpt from Elgar's *Enigma Variations* to enter the chapel with, *The Show Must Go On* by Queen to play in the middle of the service and the theme to *Schindler's List* by John Williams to play on the way out. These were some of the recordings that Claire had mentioned in her final days, although she had never concreted the plan and Daniel found that there were a number of other things that he could have chosen that would have been equally as fitting.

Planning the service gave him something to concentrate on and it enabled his mind to focus. He found it easy to talk to the minister about Claire and the things that they had gotten up to together. They talked of Toby and the love that she had for him. They talked about the way that they had met at university and Claire's passion for literature. Daniel decided that rather than deliver a eulogy about Claire he would read one of her favourite Shakespeare sonnets instead. He felt that he had all bases covered. Music that she had liked and her favourite writer being read at the service. All in all, he felt that she would have been happy had she been able to witness the service.

Daniel struggled with his belief in the afterlife. Neither of them were particularly religious. They had inherited some religious beliefs from their parents, but had quickly grown away from them. Claire's mother was mortified when she discovered that her daughter was not going to have a Christian service and burial. Daniel stuck to his guns though and refused to allow any of Claire's wishes to be changed.

When you weren't particularly religious or spiritual it was difficult to imagine what it was like after you died. Was that it? Did you just fall into a black pit like you did when you were under general anaesthetic? Was there simply nothing and you were unaware of it? Or was there a consciousness beyond the existence of the body? They were questions that he didn't have the answers to and he was not about to undergo a religious conversion in order to believe something. He had always believed that this life was the only one that you got and when it was over it was over, that was it, but now that Claire was dead, he found himself hoping that there was something else. He didn't like to think of her as slipping into nothing. He liked to think that somewhere she still existed in some manner or other. He just didn't like to think of her as no longer being.

His mind told him that it was probably all over and she was gone from all manner of life and there was no consciousness that continued, but his heart found him hoping that there was a continuation. For her sake he wanted her to still exist somewhere, but it was also for his sake, as that meant that he might see her again one day. His brain told him that it was a forlorn hope, but he couldn't help but dream that he had been wrong all of his life. It had never really mattered all that much until this moment.

He thought that he ought to do some work. He didn't

particularly feel like writing, but he had been brought up with what they called the Protestant Work Ethic. He was not particularly religious himself, but his parents had instilled in him the belief that work was linked to goodness and that you had to work in order to get things done. Those that did not work were lazy or incompetent in some manner. That was what he had been brought up to believe and so he felt that he had to work. He was lucky that he had a job that meant that he did not have to work every day. He was also lucky that this job had brought a degree of financial security with it that meant that he didn't have the pressure of working. He could work if he chose to do so, but he didn't have to work. He could take a day off if he felt like it and just do some reading. He could go to the cinema instead of sitting in front of the computer screen. In other words, he could afford the luxury of doing what he wanted to, and taking all the distractions that he could from actually doing any work. He still had to work because he was motivated to do so and because he felt guilty if he didn't work.

It was this guilt that made him work the most. Sometimes he would be inspired to write and would hammer away at the keys at a furious rate. At other times he would sit in front of the computer and the words just wouldn't come. He remained sitting there though because he felt that it was something that he had to do. He knew that he was fortunate. Fortunate to be doing a job that he enjoyed when there were millions out there that were stuck in jobs that they hated. Jobs that were pointless. Jobs that were there for the sake of jobs and had no meaning behind them, no point to them. He was lucky to be doing the job that he did, but he was also lucky that he had been successful enough to be able to take it easy.

Despite his financial security, Claire had insisted in

continuing to work at the publishing house. There were a couple of reasons for this. Firstly, it was because it enabled her to have a certain amount of independence, with her own wage coming into the household. Secondly, it was a job that she still really enjoyed doing. She enjoyed starting new writers off on their careers. Of course, there had been the conversation with her bosses of trying to poach Daniel to the publishing house, but he was well established elsewhere and content with the publisher that he had. Also, Claire felt it was important to have a little professional distance between them. She knew that her bosses would have loved to have been able to publish Daniel's work. It would have made them a great deal of money and very contented. You couldn't have everything that you wanted in life.

Daniel thought about the fast-approaching funeral and how he would deal with it. He had to keep himself together, for the sake of Toby, if no one else. Claire's mother would be there and would be dripping blame and accusation. Daniel was convinced that she blamed him for Claire getting cancer. In her own way she was certain that if she had never married Daniel then this would never have happened. There was no logic to this, of course. She just liked to blame Daniel for everything that was wrong in the world, particularly if it impacted on her daughter.

He was not looking forward to the funeral, did anyone really look forward to a funeral? It would be his last chance to have a physical connection to Claire. He wasn't looking forward to saying goodbye to her, although he knew that in reality, she would stay with him for the rest of his life. He was quite pleased about this. He wanted to feel her presence with him every day. He wanted to feel that she was there. He needed to feel that she was there. He couldn't go on with life without her being there. It was as essential to him as breathing was. There was no other path open to him.

He had chosen the suit that he would wear to the funeral. Claire had wanted it to be a celebration of her life, rather than a mourning of the fact that she was dead. To that end she had stipulated that bright colours were to be worn. Daniel had opted for a dark suit with a bright tie. He didn't really feel that he could go fully bright. Toby had opted for the same. Daniel felt that even this small concession would be enough to bring recrimination from Claire's mother who would probably be in full mourning, like a ship in full sail.

Daniel wasn't sleeping all that well and had dark circles under his eyes. He looked haggard, which was what he was. He also wasn't eating all that much, although he always tried to make sure that the meals were cooked for Toby. He just didn't fancy eating them himself. Most of the time he just moved the food about on his plate and then ended up scraping it all off into the bin. He was aware that all of this meant that he was falling into a depression. He didn't want to go to the doctor and get prescribed anti-depressants. He was against the idea; besides he didn't think that they really worked. He had no idea what he was going to do. He supposed that he would just keep sinking into the depression until such a time as he was able to see the other side of it and things would reach some degree of normality once again. Although he had serious doubts that things would ever return to normal. Too much had happened, and there was too much that was haunting him for that.

I spent much of my time in my room. I wasn't just being unsociable. I suspected that dad would really want some privacy at this time. I didn't want him to feel that he had to make an effort

91

for me. He was going through enough as it was. We both were. My room was my sanctuary though. It was somewhere that I could really be myself. Everything tangible that I loved was in that room. I liked to be surrounded by stuff that was important to me. Plus I was having a hard time of it all at the moment. I had known that mum was going to die. It just doesn't prepare you for when it happens. You think of it as something that is abstract and not really going to happen, even though you know it is. I would breakdown rather a lot and struggle with my growing depression. That's another reason I stuck to my room. I didn't want dad to see that. I needed to be strong for him. He didn't need me falling apart on him and being another problem that he had to deal with. I saw on Boxing Day that he had taken down the Christmas decorations. I didn't comment on this. I didn't want to get into a conversation that he probably didn't want to have. I understood why he had taken them down. I would probably have done the same thing. The coming days were going to be hard. I wasn't sure how we were going to handle it, although dad seemed to be holding up okay. Better than me.

Then

Although Claire couldn't have any more children, they were all happy in the little family unit that they had created. Eventually Claire returned to work, and Daniel did most of the looking after Toby, seeing as how he was able to work from home. It was an arrangement that suited them well. When Daniel was away on a book signing tour or was in meetings with his publisher and the like then they got a babysitter in who was able to look after Toby while they went about their business. One of the babysitters that they always tried to avoid though was Claire's mother, which in many ways Daniel felt would be like getting Adolf Hitler to look after your child.

Eventually Toby grew up and started school. Time seemed to be moving so fast. It had only seemed like yesterday that he had been born, and now he was going to school. They arranged for him to go to a good school in the hopes that he would prove to be academically gifted. While she was pregnant, Claire had insisted that Daniel play Mozart to him through her stomach as she had read that this helped children in their intellect. Daniel didn't know if this were true or not, but it was something that he was happy to go along with if it was something that Claire wanted.

'I sometimes wish that I could go back to his age,' Daniel told Claire, 'but be able to retain all the knowledge that I have now.'

'That would certainly give you an advantage over the other

students that you would be at school with. Don't you think it would be rather boring though?'

'How so?'

'Well, if you have all the knowledge and the mental capacity that you have now, but trapped in a five-year-old body, don't you think that it would get rather boring when all the other kids are learning the alphabet and you want to slink off and read Thomas Hardy?'

'I suppose that it might raise some suspicion if a five-year-old was reading Hardy.'

'They would either brand you as a genius and make life difficult for you, or put you in an insane asylum.'

'Perhaps you would have to keep this knowledge secret to yourself so that they don't discover you.'

'In which case it would be rather boring in hiding your knowledge while learning how to write and to read. How many times do you think you could cope with reading about the cat sitting on the mat before it actually did drive you insane?'

'Since you put it like that, it doesn't seem to be all that attractive a proposal.'

'I'm just saying. Maybe you need to think these things through a little bit before you wish for them.'

'Well, it's probably a good job that it isn't something that is likely to happen then.'

'I'm sure that you could find a novel in there somewhere with that kind of idea.'

'Probably.' Daniel didn't sound all that sure about that.

Daniel had fallen into the problem of success. He was not the first person to have done this, and he wouldn't be the last. The problem was that his last novel had been a number one bestseller. This had been a great achievement and he had been very happy with this. It made it clear that he had arrived as an author. He was popular. Now there were those that would deride him because of the fact that he was a popular author. They believed that in order to be a great writer, you had to live in obscurity and be virtually starving. Only then could you create great art. By being a bestselling author, you were considered to have sold out. People would look down their noses at you. There was no possible way that a bestselling author would win the Nobel Prize for Literature.

This kind of snobbery was not just linked to the book writing business. It was true throughout all art. Whatever line you were in – painting, music, theatre, writing, singing, whatever you cared to think of. The moment you became successful there were always those that were prepared to point the finger at you and accuse you of having sold out. They liked for you to be obscure, as if they were the only person who had discovered you. That exclusivity could not exist if you were number one.

It made no sense to Daniel. He didn't think that he had sold out, and nor did he think that he was creating great art. He was just doing what he wanted to do and if it was successful then all well and good, if it wasn't then it didn't matter. He didn't write with an audience in mind, other than Claire. He didn't try to write a bestseller; he didn't think that you could write a bestseller. It all depended on what caught the imagination of the public at the time. What they might enjoy one year, they might hate the following year. Your audience could be rather fickle. It was difficult to know what to do with them.

The pressure and the problem that Daniel had though was the fact that he had been a bestselling author. He had been number one. The pressure was now on to make his next novel a bestselling novel as well. Having done it once you were expected to do it again. Unless you had a fan base the like of Stephen King, you could not guarantee that your next novel was going to sell enough copies to make it a number one bestseller.

His first real success had been the novel that they had made the film out of. This had sold reasonably well in its own right, but had sold even more copies when the novel was re-released with the photographs from the film on the cover. It was a well-known fact that there were those that would see a film and then go and buy the book of the film. It was good business to be able to get your novel made into a film or a TV series. It gave you a second bite at the apple.

There was always much talk about the fact that the reading public was diminishing. There was little actual factual evidence for this. The book had been surviving the death knell for generations now. It had survived the advent of the cinema, TV, video and DVD. It had even survived the Kindle. Although Kindle sales were very popular, there were still those that could not resist the idea of actually holding a book in their hands. To feel the pages between their fingers. Bookshops still made sales, particularly the big chains.

Lots of people came to see Daniel when he was on his book signing tours. Nobody ever asked him to sign their Kindle. It was always books that people were buying and were happy for him to sign. He tried to make each dedication unique, but found that this was something that was virtually impossible to do, and ended up just writing the same thing over and over again, which was rather repetitive and boring. He also made sure that he used a different signature to the one that he signed his cheques with, not that he wrote all that many cheques these days. He might have been being a little paranoid about that, but it didn't hurt.

Daniel knew that there were some authors that absolutely hated to meet the public. They hated the idea of having to go out, to shakes hands with the great unwashed (as they called them) and sign their name numerous times to people that they had never met before, but for some reason wanted their name scrawled on bits of paper. Daniel had never subscribed to this point of view. He was of the opinion that the book-buying public were the ones that had put you where you were. You owed it to them to give them something back. If they wanted to meet you and for you to sign books for them, then that was part of the deal. Every time you signed a book, that was another sale that you had made. It was all about business, but it was also about giving something back to the people that helped you to live the way that you did. After all you were living in *that* house because people had bought your book. You were driving *that* car because someone had gone to see the film of your book. That's why Daniel couldn't understand people, like actors, who were in the public eye, but refused to give anything back to the public that paid their hard-earned money to go and see their films.

Daniel found book tours tiring, but he knew that it was all part of the package. It wasn't his favourite activity, but he knew that it was something that had to be done if he wanted to sell books and put food on the table for his family. It was really as simple as that. There was no argument about it. He did what he had to do. A lot of writers wanted to develop the idea of being reclusive. This meant that they didn't have to go on promotional tours, but also created an air of mystery about them, which they somehow thought would mean that they could sell more books. It was all a bit of a mystery to Daniel. As technology developed, he became aware of the fact that he would need to have a social media footprint. Social media was the up-and-coming thing, and if he wanted to be in touch with his fan base then it was important that he got in contact with them in that way.

He was something of a technophobe. He didn't understand technology all that well. He used it on a daily base, but when it went wrong or broke down, he was at a complete loss to know how to deal with it. He would then go wistful about the days of a typewriter, or even a fountain pen. He somehow thought that those days were simpler and didn't have the problems that the technical age held. He was pretty sure that they were making things more difficult for ourselves. We had become reliant on technology though. It had become an essential, rather than a luxury. It was also considerably easier to do edits on a computer than a hard copy would have been.

'I've been offered an honorary doctorate,' said Daniel when he was leafing through his mail one morning.

'That's nice,' replied Claire as she sipped on her tea and looked through the weekend papers.

'Not sure I ever saw the point of them though.'

'Snobbery. It's as simple as that.'

'You mean people collect them like cars, or something?'

'Something like that.'

'It always seemed to be a bit of an insult to me that you would be given a doctorate for not really doing all that much more than what is, after all, your job anyway, whereas the real students have to slave away for years to gain their degree and at great expense as well.'

'I can see where you might think that is a bit unfair. It's a bit like getting an OBE or something like that I suppose.'

'At least you can put an OBE after your name, or I could call myself Sir Daniel. Turns out with an honorary doctorate that you can't even call yourself Doctor.'

'Seems to be rather a pointless exercise then.'

'I think I will politely decline and allow the others to take up the snobbery. It's not for me. I would rather gain a doctorate the old-fashioned way. Problem is that I don't think that I have the patience for it any longer. All that studying, when I could be reading, or writing, or just chilling out and doing nothing, while pretending to work.'

'Is that what you do?'

'What?'

'Chill out and pretend that you are working?'

'It's pretty fair to say that there is a great deal of procrastination that goes on in the writing process. Sometimes you will spend hours checking social media, looking out the window, doing anything rather than face that blank page and actually do anything that even comes close to resembling work.'

'So, that's what you do when I'm out of the house all day?'

'Well, not all the time. These books don't write themselves, you know? But I will confess that there is a fair amount of thumb twiddling and sitting waiting for the words to come.'

'They always seem to come.'

'They do eventually. Sometimes, they just need a little coaxing to be able to come out. Otherwise, they might stay hidden.'

'So, you're not going to accept the doctorate?' Claire asked, looking up from the literary section of the newspaper.

'I don't think so. I think I'd feel very guilty about accepting it. It's a very nice offer, but not really my thing.'

'I bet you would accept a knighthood quick enough.'

'Well, that's an entirely different thing. Besides, if I did then you would become a Lady as well as me being a Sir.'

'I hadn't thought of that.'

'Is it an idea that appeals?'

'Not too sure how I feel about it. It's all academic anyway.

Do you really think that you are likely to be offered a knighthood?'

'Not unless I give a large sum of money away to charity, I wouldn't have thought.'

'Well charity begins at home.'

'So they tell me.'

'You better believe it.'

'We do our bit. I was struck by the amount of homeless people that there are about nowadays when I went into town recently.'

'I believe they are termed rough sleepers now.'

'Is that so? I didn't know that,' said Daniel thoughtfully. 'It seems wrong to be accepting a knighthood when there are so many people that are sleeping on the streets.'

'You haven't actually been offered a knighthood though, have you?'

'Not as such. I was just saying.'

'You can't save the world all on your own.'

'No, but I can do what I can to make what I see a little better. Donate a little money here and there. Help someone out. It all goes a little way to making a difference.'

'I suppose so.'

'I hope so.'

'You're an idealist.'

'It's my job, Claire.'

'That's one way of looking at it.'

'I create ideas. I create words from my fingers.'

'That just sounds weird.'

'It's true though. I tap away at a keyboard, and words come out of the ends of my fingers.'

'You have a very strange way of looking at things.'

'I guess that's because of the fact that I'm a writer.'

'Or you're a writer because you look at things in a strange way.'

'Either, or.'

'Would you like some more toast?'

'Don't see why not.'

Daniel and Claire had a happy marriage. They were now financially secure. Daniel was selling enough books and Claire was bringing in a respectable income from the publishing house. The frugal days of their early marriage were now behind them and they were very happy together. The introduction of Toby to the family made them complete. It's true that they would have liked to have had more children, but as this was not a possibility, they accepted their lot and were happy with it. There really wasn't all that much else that they could ask for.

They considered themselves lucky. Most of their university friends that had got together had long since split up, and a couple that had got married had ended in divorce. There is an argument that fulfilling an attachment when you are so young is something that will end in disaster as you grow and change into different people. Claire and Daniel were lucky that this didn't apply to them. As they grew and became older their love for each other grew and they became more comfortable in their surroundings and in the life that they had created for each other. It helped that they had so much in common, but where they differed, this only helped to cement their relationship further.

'I've been reading a biography of Dickens,' announced Claire one day. Outside of novels, she most enjoyed reading biographies about famous writers. She had already read biographies on Jane Austen, Thomas Hardy, Albert Camus,

Agatha Christie and Thackery, and had enjoyed most of them.

'How's it going?' asked Daniel looking up from his coffee as they sat in the evening and relaxed after a hard day at work.

'I haven't got all that far into it, but what surprises me the most is that he was able to achieve so much with such a poor level of education.'

'I suppose that was his genius.'

'He must have been. It's like the people who don't think that Shakespeare wrote the plays because he never went to university.'

'Snobbery.'

'I read a review by one man that said Shakespeare couldn't have written the plays because he had never been a soldier and he wrote about life as a soldier so well.'

'He had never been a king either, but he wrote very well about what it meant to be a monarch.'

'Exactly. These people just don't seem to understand what it means to be a writer. How you can take the experiences of others and turn them into something to write about.'

'It annoys me that there are people that don't like to give the credit to Shakespeare for what he achieved.'

'You might just as well say that Dickens couldn't possibly have written his novels because he never went to grammar school or university.'

'In a couple of hundred years they may well say that. It's snobbery to suppose that you can only be a great writer if you have been to university.'

'Some people,' continued Claire, 'are only happy if they are able to promote some scandal or take a contrary view to public opinion so that they can get the attention that they think they deserve.'

'So, you don't buy that someone else wrote Shakespeare's work either?'

'Not in the least. No more than I suspect that someone else wrote the books of Dickens and did it to keep their own identity secret.'

'You never know, you could start a conspiracy theory about Dickens. Make yourself famous.'

'I'm sure that is why people do it.'

'Well at least it keeps the debate alive, I suppose. There isn't much else going for the argument.'

'I feel so tired,' declared Claire with a yawn.

'Perhaps you have been reading too much.'

'That's never stopped us before.'

'Why don't you have an early night then?'

'It seems a waste to go to bed so early. Makes me feel like I have entered into old age and am no longer able to make it through a day without going to bed early, in some cases while it is still light outside.'

'If you are tired, you are tired. There isn't all that much that you can do about it. Sometimes it happens. It isn't as if you are going to bed early every night, is it?'

'I suppose not.'

'Why don't you have some hot milk or something to help you sleep?'

'The way that I feel at the moment, I don't think that I will need to have anything to help me sleep. That should be the easy part. I ache so much as well.'

'Busy day?'

'No more than normal. Perhaps it is just a sign of advancing age.'

'We are not that old.'

'Not so old that we ache in our bones at the end of the day and want to go to bed early? It's how I feel at the moment.'

'Everyone is entitled to one off day. Just don't make a habit of it.'

'I'll try not to. I think I will take myself off to bed though, if you don't mind?'

'Of course I don't mind. I might do some more writing and will see you in a bit.'

'I'm sure that I will be fast asleep by the time that you come in.'

Daniel went back to his study to work on his latest book. When he wasn't writing, he was editing what had already been written. He wrote at a faster rate than he published, and so he found that he always had a number of unpublished manuscripts that were stacking up in a filing cabinet, ready to be used when the moment seemed right. He saved them for any occasion when he might get writer's block. He didn't really believe that there was such a thing as writer's block, but he didn't like to tempt fate. If he ever dried up for months at a time, then at least he would have a stack of unpublished work that he could produce, which would make it look like he was still working with no problems at all.

The problem was that the longer the work remained unpublished, the more he tinkered with it, the more editing that he did, and the more it would morph and change from the original idea that he had set out with. There comes a time when you have to draw the line and say that enough is enough. Enough editing and re-editing. You have done the best shot that you can with the tools that you have and it is now time to release it into the world and let other people see what they think of it. That is always the hardest thing to do. For so long this has been part of your life. It has become like a child for you, and now you have to let the reins go and let it find its own way in the world. It isn't easy to do that. Particularly when you then hear other people making critical remarks about something that you have sweated over. You have put a lot of yourself into the novel, so it is easy to take it personally when someone snubs it out of hand.

Most parents would not respond all that well if you were critical of their child in front of them. The chances are that they would be upset and angry, and that was exactly the way that you could feel in the creative field when someone was critical of what you had created. There were those that could distance themselves from that kind of thing and not be affected by the remarks that were made, good or bad. Daniel pretended to not be all that interested in reviews, but secretly always hoped that they were good.

He had been described as a 'popular author' as if this was some unnatural smell. He didn't see the problem with being popular. True, the snobs looked down on you and you were never likely to win the Nobel, but you were making money and there were plenty of authors out there that were not making the money, so he didn't really see it as something to sneer at.

There would always be those that didn't think that you were making great art unless you were living in a garret somewhere in Paris, and slowly starving to death, while all the time bemoaning those that had sold out to the establishment. Daniel didn't think that there was anything that he particularly needed to worry about over the fact that you could buy his books in a supermarket. If someone decided to pick up one of his books when they had gone in to get a tin of baked beans then who was he to argue with that? Seemed perfectly reasonable as far as he was concerned.

Jordan would frequently pop around to see them. Jordan was

someone that they had met at university and had stayed in the area when so many others had gone their different ways.

'How's the novel going?' he asked Daniel when he was over for dinner one night.

'Which one?' replied Daniel.

'It's like that is it?'

'I always have more than one project on the go at any given time.'

'Daniel likes his work,' said Claire.

'It's a good life if you can get it,' replied Jordan. 'There are so many people that are unhappy in their jobs.'

'Probably the vast majority of people,' replied Claire. 'We are lucky to both be doing something that we love and are passionate about.'

'I wish I felt the same.' Jordan had left with his degree and had ended up working in an office as part of Human Resources. He had no idea how he had ended up in that particular career. Nothing that he had studied had particularly led him that way. He also found that he was daily surrounded by people that were incompetent, with only the slimmest of grasps on employment law and were consequently frequently making decisions that verged on being just illegal. He would try to point this out to his managers, but would be largely overruled to the point where he didn't feel that there was any point in highlighting their errors any longer. He just kept his head down, tried to do as little work as he could and accepted his wage packet at the end of each month. 'I wonder how I ended up in such a dead-end job.'

'Change it,' said Claire. It was something that had been advised a number of times by one or the other of them.

'It's all very well saying that, but I can't afford to lose the money. I have got settled down in there now. If I were to go and do something else then I would have to start again at the bottom of the ladder and wouldn't be able to afford the lifestyle that I have made for myself.'

'It's no good if you are not happy though, Jordan,' said Daniel as he tucked into his spaghetti.

'Well, there is more to life than work.'

'It's not much good though if you have to drink yourself into a stupor on a Friday and Saturday night to dull the pain of the week though,' said Claire.

'It's like you can read my life,' replied Jordan.

'Is it really all that much fun though?' asked Daniel. 'I mean you do go out to nightclubs and things. We stopped all that when Toby came along.'

'Plus, we think that the music is largely shit now.'

'It's not that great,' admitted Jordan. 'There are a lot of knobheads out at the weekend. A lot of police about as well. I don't envy them that job. Standing on a street corner waiting for a fight to break out. What kind of life is that? Makes me feel better about my job.'

'Why do you do it then?' asked Claire. 'Go out I mean.'

'Because I'm single and I'm looking for true love. A bit like you two have.'

'Do you really think that you will find it in a crushed nightclub with some drunk woman though?' asked Daniel.

'Probably not, but I might find someone that wants to have a bit of temporary fun if nothing else.'

'We need to find you a woman,' said Claire with confidence.

'Well, good luck with that. I am hoping for a nice rich woman that doesn't mind sharing her wealth with me and doesn't put too many demands on me.'

'Not much that you want then?' chuckled Claire.

'No, not all that much. I don't think that there is all that much chance of me finding it though. You're right, I am unlikely to find "the one" in a nightclub, but I've got to look somewhere.'

'Have you considered online dating?' asked Daniel.

'Oh God no, that's so sad a thing to do. It smacks of desperation. It's like you can't find anyone on your own so need help with it.'

'Not at all,' said Claire. 'It's a very popular way of finding people these days. People are living very busy lives and there is little time for actual dating. Online dating just makes it so much easier to hook up with someone. Saves a lot of the hassle.'

'Well, I'm not sold on the idea.'

'You should give it some thought. You never know what might happen and what sort of person you might find.'

'Serial killer, probably.'

'Don't be so negative, or you will never achieve anything and never meet anyone.'

'You might be right, Claire. I don't know. I sometimes think that a relationship is too much hassle. I've kind of got used to life on my own at the moment. Not sure how I would respond to someone else moving in and putting their things all over the place.'

'It's all part of life.'

'So they tell me.'

There seems to be something about the fact that happily married couples will want to get their unattached friends into a relationship as well. There doesn't seem to be any logical reason for this, other than perhaps the fact that they feel that they have to spread the love around and share it with other people that are not as fortunate as they are.

Claire and Daniel were happy in their life. They were aware

of the fact that they had had it reasonably easy. Yes, there had been financial difficulties to start with, but they had found each other early enough in their lives and had then settled down quickly. There were those that would say that it would have been better for them if they had been able to experience a few other partners first, before they settled down, but that wasn't how they viewed their life. They had both been fortunate enough to get jobs that they had always wanted and that they enjoyed, and they were blessed with Toby when he came along. In many regards Daniel felt that it had all been too easy for them.

It was why he was less than surprised when fortune decided that it was time to give them both a kick in the teeth.

I'm a naturally shy person. I find it very difficult to meet girls. I find it very difficult to talk to girls that I do meet. I wish I had more confidence, but I'm convinced that they don't like me. Maybe it's because in a small part I don't like myself. I don't know. It would be nice to have a girlfriend though. For most people of my age that also means that it would be nice to have sex. Of course it would. I would be lying if I didn't admit to that. I've hung out with a few girls in the past that I suppose could loosely be termed as girlfriends. I'm not sure if they would agree with the term. The most that has ever happened though is some pretty intense snogging. That's cool though as I discovered that I really like to kiss. I think I'm not that bad at it and with a little more practice I might actually become pretty good at it. It's getting the practice though. That's the difficult thing. I'm not the kind of person that would force myself on people. You can't make people want to kiss you. You can't make people love you. That's why mum and dad are so lucky. They truly found their soulmates and at a reasonably early age as well. After all they were not that much older than me when they got together. I have no idea if I'm going to go to university or not. I know my parents would like me to go, but I have no idea what it is that I would like to study. I'm pretty academic and good at a number of subjects. I could study English like they did. Perhaps I should do something different though, carve out my own path away from what they did. Make a name for myself in a different direction. Some people would say that I have plenty of time to decide what to do, but I don't think that is the case. Pretty soon I will be going to college and then from there I will be potentially off to university, so I will have to make up my mind before too long. I wish I knew what it was that I wanted to do with my life. I envy my parents for knowing from an early age what it is that they wanted to do. I just don't think that I'm like that.

Now

It hadn't snowed. It never did snow at Christmas. It was too much to ask for. If you believed all the American films, or the Victorian picture cards, then there was nothing but snow at Christmas. Maybe that was true of some places, but it wasn't true of where Daniel was. It never had been. It had snowed in November at times and it had snowed in January, but it always seemed to bypass December as much as it could. It was almost like it was a conspiracy to ensure that people lost their bets on it being a white Christmas. This particular year, Daniel couldn't have cared less whether it snowed or not. There could have been a stunning meteor shower for all he knew and he would have been entirely oblivious to it.

What it did do was rain. A lot. It rained all of the time. Making the sky battleship grey and miserable. A dismal, unappetising, festive time of the year. Nothing to write home about, you might say. It was cold as well. Oh yes, it was cold. That was something that Daniel would always remember about the day that he buried Claire. Just how cold it was, and how tragic it was to be laying her in the colder earth. It seemed unnatural to leave her there as well. To be walking away from her as she remained in the last place that she would ever be.

The morning of the funeral, Daniel shaved for the first time since she had died. It just hadn't seemed to be a priority up until that point. He supposed that he ought to try and look like he was coping okay with everything for the people that would come and see him at the funeral. He wondered how many people were coming because they actually wanted to pay their respects to Claire. How many others were there because they wanted to see or be seen? Some people actually enjoyed funerals. He wondered what was wrong with these people. There was clearly some deep trauma from their childhood that had remained unaddressed.

Having shaved and showered he put on his suit and the red tie that he was wearing in deference to Claire's wish that the funeral not be too morbid and had bright colours. She wanted it to be a celebration of her life rather than a cause for deep sorrow, but he really couldn't feel any other way about it. He was burying his wife. The person that he had known since they had been book loving teenagers together. They had spent all of their adult lives together, and now that was over. It had ended. Not suddenly, but after a long, drawn-out struggle. Where was the dignity in all of that? Where was the celebration to be had? He didn't feel like celebrating. He felt like crawling into a hole and remaining there for the rest of his life.

He supposed that the fact that it had been a drawn-out affair at least gave them the opportunity to say goodbye. If she had been killed in a car crash or had dropped dead of a heart attack, or something, then they wouldn't have had that opportunity to say goodbye to each other and say everything that needed to be said. It hadn't been a particularly dignified end for her though, and the pain had been something that even the morphine had been unable to mask. Perhaps it would have been better for her if it had been over quickly, without the pain and the lack of dignity.

He surveyed himself in the full-length bedroom mirror and decided that he was probably presentable to the world. He also decided that if he wasn't presentable then the world could go screw itself. It was asking too much of him. Much more than he was able to give at any rate. He went to check on Toby who was already dressed and wearing a red tie like his dad.

'Ready?' Daniel asked him in almost a whisper.

'Is it time?'

'Almost.'

'Okay.'

Daniel went back out into the kitchen and considered making himself a coffee to try and keep his caffeine levels at a sufficiently high level that he would be able to function throughout the day. He also considered the possibility of opening one of the bottles of wine from the wine rack and making a good start on it. He thought that would be a splendid way to be able to face the funeral. Turn up drunk. That would give Claire's mother something to really moan about. She had already informed Daniel that she would not be wearing anything colourful at the wedding despite what the wishes of her daughter might have been.

'I will be dressed entirely in black, as is fitting for these occasions. I am surprised at you for going along with such a ridiculous venture.'

Daniel refrained from telling her that he thought that the entire thing was a ridiculous venture and he would much rather that she hadn't died in the first place so that they wouldn't be having a debate now on etiquette.

'It was Claire's wish,' he feebly said.

'Well, clearly she wasn't in her right state of mind towards the end or she wouldn't have come up with something so insensitive. I think we would be best placed to ignore such a request and go with what is actually right.'

Daniel wondered who it was being insensitive to. He also marvelled about how Claire's mother had even managed to turn

Claire's funeral into being about her. He had snapped.

'Well, you wear whatever the hell you want. I'm going with what my wife requested of me and I am pretty sure that everyone else will do the same.'

He had then hung up the phone and opened a bottle of wine (which he had managed to entirely drink within the hour) and made him feel no better at all. Not even in the slightest. He had thought that mother-in-law jokes had been something of a cliché, until he had met his own who had lived up to every joke that Les Dawson had ever come out with.

Jordan arrived early for the funeral. He was always early for anything. He believed in arriving before the time that you were meant to meet. He hated the idea of arriving dead on time almost as much as he hated the idea of being late. Daniel doubted that Jordan had ever been late for anything in his life. They had agreed to meet up and as their closest friend, Daniel had allowed Jordan to travel in the family car to the funeral. A fact that would undoubtedly annoy his mother-in-law when she realised that she had been snubbed in this way. As far as she was concerned, she was the chief mourner. Daniel was just an unfortunate bystander that happened to get in the way of Claire's life.

'Are you ready?' asked Jordan, adjusting his tie, which was something that he rarely wore and was something that he felt very uncomfortable in. He had opted for a bright blue tie with a sport's jacket. He felt decidedly underdressed.

'Are you ever ready for something like this?' replied Daniel, spreading his arms out as if in supplication.

'No, I don't suppose that you are.'

'It's something that we have to do though, so I guess we just have to get on with it.'

'It amazes me where you're finding the strength from.'

'It beats me. I don't know where it's coming from, but somehow you find the strength to get out of bed every day and do the things that are required of you. I can't say that it's something that's likely to last though.'

'What do you mean?'

'I have the strength at the moment, largely because I've been carried along with the momentum of the thing. With Claire's death. There's always been something that needs to be done, relatives to phone, funeral to arrange, death to register and so on. Plenty of things to do and to keep my mind occupied.'

'You're worried that after the funeral you will have run out of things to do?'

'And then will collapse like a rather expressive jelly that nobody wanted to eat at a wedding.'

'Interesting imagery.'

'I'm still a writer, albeit one that has not written all that much lately.'

'Nah, well neither has Dickens. I wouldn't worry about it all that much.'

'I do worry about what will happen when I don't have something to occupy myself though.'

'You have Toby.'

'Toby has withdrawn into his own shell, and I can't say that I blame him. He's dealing with the death of his mother in his own way. I suppose I will have to deal with the death of my wife in my own way.'

'You could always return to work. I believe burying yourself in work is often the way with these things.'

'It isn't always the best way to deal with these things though, is it?'

'I suppose not.'

'The thing is, Jordan, I'm not convinced that I'll be able to work.'

'Why not?'

Daniel shrugged his shoulders. 'The words don't seem to want to flow any longer. It used to be that I could sit in front of the laptop and words would fly out of the end of my fingers at a furious rate, but they just don't seem to want to come any longer.'

'It's still too soon after Claire's death. You have to give it time. You will get it back again.'

'You sound very sure of that.'

'I am.'

'I'm not. What if it doesn't return? Claire was my muse. She was my inspiration. What if without her I'm unable to write a single word ever again?'

'I'm sure that you will be able to write again. You're worrying too much.'

'Do you think so?'

'Yes, of course.'

'Only it seems very real to me. It seems like a massive problem that I'm going to have to face at some point.'

'You've got stored up unpublished manuscripts though, haven't you?'

'Yes. I write twice as much as I publish.'

'Then why don't you ease yourself back in gently? Why not dig out one of the manuscripts and edit it and deal with it that way? Get yourself back into the actual new writing by means of the editing process.'

'Wise words. That has worked for me in the past when I have had a block.'

'I thought you didn't believe in writer's block?'

'I don't. It's just every now and then there's a blip and I can't seem to get the work done.'

'I think the death of your wife is more than a blip.'

'I didn't mean it in that way.'

'I know you didn't, but what I'm saying is that all the blips that you've had in the past don't amount to anything compared to what has happened to you now. You have to give it time. Build yourself back up slowly, but you will get there.'

'When did you become so wise?'

'I've always been wise, I'm just very good at hiding things.'

'I reckon you might be.'

'How is Toby holding up, by the way?'

Daniel sighed. 'It's difficult to tell. As I said, he has withdrawn into his own world at the moment. We haven't really talked about what has happened.'

'Do you think you should?'

'Yes, I suppose so. We will have to address it at some point in the future. For the moment I'm just trying to give him some space to come to terms with things on his own. Once the dust has settled slightly, I imagine that we will talk.'

'He will need you.'

'I know. I'm just not sure what it is that I am meant to say to him. How do I console him on something like this?'

'Share the common mourning that you have, him for his mother and you for your wife. It's a starting point. You don't have to have been in his boat to experience what he's going through just because your mother is still alive.'

'I never lost anyone so young. Even my grandparents didn't die until I was in my twenties.'

'You're lucky, mine died before I was a teenager.'

'Must make it difficult.'

'It means it's difficult to form a memory of them.'

'God, do you think Toby will forget his mum?'

'I doubt it. He is older than I was and he has a lot of good memories to look back on. He won't forget her.'

'He *is* old enough for it to really hurt.'

'Aren't we all? You will have to talk to him about it at some point though. You can't put it off forever, or it will drive a wedge between you and damage your relationship with him.'

'You might be right.'

'Are you sure you are okay? You look terrible. Are you sleeping?'

'Thanks. I feel terrible so it's only fair that I look terrible as well. I'm not really sleeping, no; or to be precise, when I am sleeping it's fretful and full of bad dreams and nightmares. I keep living over the events of her death, over and over again. I keep wondering if there is something different that I could have done to have made things better.'

'What could you possibly have done?'

'I don't know. Maybe there could have been something that would have made things easier for her.'

'You can't hold yourself responsible for cancer. Nobody can. It's an evil, vile disease.'

'I know it is.'

Jordan heard a noise and looked up. 'The cars are here. It's time.'

Daniel had been dreading this moment. Up until this point he had almost been able to deny that it was happening. He had been almost able to fool himself into believing that Claire was just staying with her mother, or something. Now when faced with the coffin in the car he was unable to deny any longer that she had died. He was able to fool himself no longer. The time had come.

They collected Toby and went out in the crisp December air and looked at the cars as they rolled up. The frost was still on the grass and the windows. Their breath was visible in the cold air. Daniel shrugged his coat and his scarf around himself a little tighter to try and ward off the cold.

He looked at the coffin and tried to imagine that Claire was inside. It didn't seem to be possible. It all seemed to be something of a nightmare. There was no denying that it was happening now. It was all very real and he would have to put up with it all.

They shuffled into the family car and prepared themselves for the funeral. The car was silent as they drove to the graveyard where the service would take place. Daniel couldn't take his eyes off of the hearse that was in front of them moving slowly down the road, as Claire left their home for the last time.

The air was biting cold after the warmth of the car when they arrived. The small party followed the coffin into the chapel, where Daniel noticed Claire's mother sitting prim and proper in the front row. If he was being disingenuous then he might have thought that she was actually enjoying herself and the attention that she was getting as the mother of the deceased. Perhaps that was unkind, but it was the first thought that entered into his head. In that moment he knew that he really did hate her. She seemed to be enjoying the death of her daughter rather too much for his liking. He wondered if the woman had any redeemable features and came to the conclusion that if she did, then he had not noticed any in the time that he had known her.

'I still think you should have had a religious ceremony,' she hissed at Daniel as he sat down. He bit his tongue and chose not to reply. This was not the place to have an argument, although she clearly wanted one. Perhaps that would come later. Perhaps after a few drinks he would let his guard down and tell her what he really thought of her. That would make for entertaining viewing. For now, he was not prepared to get into an argument that would take place over the corpse of his wife, no matter how much she wanted one.

The ceremony commenced with the songs that Claire had chosen for her funeral. Daniel could sense the annoyance from Claire's mother that there were not hymns instead of the music that had been chosen. He was in no doubt that she blamed him entirely for all of this. It would be to no avail to tell her that Claire had planned her own service. She would still have blamed him for influencing her. What they needed was a nice little Catholic service, she would have mused. Something where the congregation were informed that unless they believed in Jesus Christ then they were doomed to hell for all eternity. That was the kind of thing that would have made her happy. Daniel was certain that it was exactly the kind of thing that Claire would have hated. For one thing, he knew for a fact that Claire hadn't believed in Christ, so it would have been a hypocritical thing to have had happen to say the least.

The service eventually drew to a close and the congregation rose to follow the coffin to the graveside where she would be placed in the earth in her final resting place. Daniel found himself wondering how easy it had been for the gravediggers to dig the grave in the frozen earth, but then he imagined that they used mechanical diggers these days rather than shovels. That would make their work easier he thought. He had never really given it all that much attention before, but he imagined that was how it was done these days. He wondered where the mechanical digger was and then thought that they probably moved it from sight to ensure that it didn't upset the mourners.

When some handfuls of earth had been thrown onto the

coffin, people began to drift away. Some of them no doubt keen to get out of the cold and into the pub where the reception was being held. Daniel stood by the graveside looking down at the coffin, lost with his own thoughts.

'It was a beautiful ceremony,' said Jordan coming up to him.

'Why do people say that?'

'Say what?'

'That "it was a beautiful ceremony", nobody ever says that it was a shite ceremony, or that the service was crap. They always say that it was beautiful.'

'I suppose it is because at times like this, people just don't know what to say.'

'Then perhaps it would be better if they didn't say anything at all.'

'I'm sorry, have I annoyed you?'

Daniel sighed. 'No, I'm sorry. I'm just being contrary. So many things on my mind I suppose. I suppose it's also because of the fact that I have to face Claire's mother in a moment, and that is not something that I'm looking forward to.'

'Nobody has ever looked forward to facing Claire's mother. The woman is a dragon. Even Claire would've admitted that.'

'Yes, yes, I think she would've. I don't know Jordan, it's all so bloody pointless.'

'What is?'

'This is,' said Daniel indicating the coffin in the grave before them, 'it all seems such a waste. Why did she have to die? Why her and not someone else?'

'She never asked that question though, did she? She always accepted the cards that had been dealt to her without questioning.'

'Yes, she did. She was always so much better than I was. It

does seem such a bloody waste and a shame though. She might not have questioned why, but it isn't something that I can do. I have to know why this happened. Why couldn't they save her?'

'The disease was just too vigorous.'

'All the advancements that we have made in medical science, you would think that we would be able to come up with a cure for this bastard. Almost every disease and illness that is out there we are able to either develop a cure for, or are able to make medicines that prolong life and make things easier, but this fucker just won't submit.'

'They will sort it one of these days.'

'It's too late for Claire though, isn't it? Too late for her. I feel that it should be me down in that hole, not her.'

'You can't think like that.'

'But I do. A mother should be there for her child. He needs her.'

'He needs you as well.'

'He could have done without me if his mother had still been here. She would have handled things a lot better than I can. She would know what to say to Toby. I have no idea what to say to him.'

'It will come. It will just take time. You're both grieving.'

'I hope it comes. I hate being without the words for him.'

'It will happen. Just give it time.'

They lapsed into silence, both looking down at the coffin in the cold earth. After a while Jordan shivered. 'Shall we go and face the dragon?' he asked.

'I suppose so.'

They left the graveyard with a degree of reluctance. If the truth had been known, Daniel would have stayed there for a lot longer. Possibly forever if he could have gotten away with it. He hated the idea of leaving Claire behind. It all seemed too much to be asked to live with. He would have gladly lay down in the grave with her and stayed there until the earth was piled on top of them.

Daniel supposed that he had been prepared for the mental pain that would come with the grieving process of losing Claire. He had been aware of the fact that it would come, but there had been nothing that he could do to prepare himself for the wave that hit him when she was gone. What he had not been prepared for was the physical pain that came along with it. The aching and emptiness that was in his chest. The way that it felt like he was about to go into cardiac arrest. The aching of his limbs and the headaches, the damn headaches that felt like he was having his brain tumour and force its way out of his skull as if it couldn't handle the pain any longer. He had not been prepared for this. Jordan thought that he should go and see a doctor, but Daniel was still reluctant to do that.

He cried himself to sleep each night, the loss of Claire so painful that it hurt in every part of his body. If someone would have come along and offered to kill him then he thought that he would have gladly accepted if it meant that he was able to get away from the pain that was eating up his soul. They should teach about grief in schools. Learn young so you knew how to deal with this kind of thing. The truth was that there was no amount of preparation and learning that could prepare you for such a thing as this.

The reception back at a local hotel was everything that Daniel hated about this kind of thing. He was forced to listen to relatives and friends, all saying the same thing about Claire. How wonderful she was, as if this was something that was news to him. He spent as much time as he could in avoiding Claire's mother. She was sitting in a corner, surrounded by fawning old ladies, that were quick to treat her as the chief mourner. She was in her element. Daniel had no idea who any of them were. He supposed that it was the posse of people that she had invited so that she was always surrounded by sycophants.

He made his way to the food table and looked at the mess of sandwiches, that frankly looked like they had seen better days. He found this funny as he realised that he had seen better days himself. It was very probable that he was only half way through his life and that he would never see the good days again, not the way that they had been when Claire was alive. He thought about the fact that if he was only half-way through his life – that it would mean that he would ultimately spend more years with Claire gone than they had spent together. It was a sobering thought and not a nice one at that. He found himself wishing that he didn't have so long to wait until his own time came. He couldn't imagine living that long without her.

'You know you could write about it,' said Jordan as he came up to help himself to a soggy sandwich filled with egg mayonnaise, or something that looked very much like it.

'Write about what?'

'Claire. The loss. The grief.'

'I'm not sure that I could do that. I don't fancy any of this stuff,' he said surveying the buffet with a critical eye.

'That's because you're not eating enough. You'll waste away.'

'So be it.'

'Why couldn't you write about it? You're a writer after all. Surely it would be the best way to deal with all of this.'

'You might be right, but it doesn't seem to be the decent thing to do at the moment. It's a private matter. I don't think it's something that I could share with the public.'

'You don't have to share it with the public. I said you should write about it. I didn't say that you would have to publish it. You can publish it if you feel ready, when the time comes. Otherwise, you can just write it for yourself. Don't you always say that writing is a therapeutic process?'

'Yes, it is.'

'Well then, there you go.'

'I'm not convinced. It might be something that is a little too difficult for me at the moment.'

'Give it time and you might find that it is the best therapy that you can imagine.'

'I'm not sure that it will work in this instance.'

'Why not?'

Daniel sighed and suddenly felt very tired. 'Because it's too personal. The grief is too much, it's just all too much at the moment.'

'Give it time.'

'Maybe I don't want to give it time. I don't want to feel like this. I want this pain and misery to go away.'

'It will do with time. They say that time is a healer.'

'What a cliché that is.'

'Doesn't mean that it isn't true.'

'I'm not convinced that things will get any better with time. Not even if a million years were able to pass.'

'Well, in a million years we will all be forgotten. They probably won't even be reading your novels.'

'You're assuming that there will even be humans left. I'm sure we will have annihilated each other long before then.'

'You're probably right. Are you going to face the dragon?'

'I see absolutely no reason why I should. I've nothing to say to her and I'm pretty sure that she has nothing that she wants to say to me, that isn't an accusation or something like that.'

'She's a very bitter woman.'

'Always has been. Claire's death hasn't made her that way. I'm sure that she was born that way.'

'These sandwiches are truly awful.'

'I think I might go home.'

'What about Toby?'

'I think he's already gone. He said something about making his own way back.'

'He isn't handling this all that well, is he?'

'I don't think either of us are.'

'Want me to walk home with you?'

'Sure, why not.'

They made a few farewells to the people that really mattered and left them to enjoy their mourning with the level of happiness that they seemed to be enjoying. There was nothing like a good funeral to remind you that you were still alive and were able to carry on with your life.

Daniel and Jordan walked home the short distance from the pub to the house. Daniel and Claire had always liked the idea of having a pub that was so local to them that they were able to walk to it without that much fuss and bother. Saved one of them not being able to drink because they were driving. Claire had been particular about having the gathering after the funeral at the local pub so that Daniel could drink if he wanted to. As it happened, he had limited himself to one pint of ale. Not because he was moderating his drinking, but because of the fact that he just didn't have the taste for it at the moment. He could have crawled into a wine bottle if he had thought that it would help, but he wasn't convinced that it would help at all. All it would do would probably be to emphasise the situation and make him feel even worse, plus he would be feeling the same way that he felt now, with the added disadvantage of having a hangover as well.

The house was quiet when they arrived. Toby had returned to his room where he was doing whatever it was that he did in there to help him with the grief of his mother's death. Daniel and Jordan sat down in the kitchen and had a coffee together. They didn't say anything, but just sat in silence and each thought their own thoughts, without feeling the need to bother the other.

I've never been to a funeral before. You are supposed to start off by going to the funeral of your grandparents, not one of your parents. That seems to be the natural order of things. It should never have been the case that my first funeral was for my mother. I don't know how I am supposed to feel about this. I don't know how I'm expected to feel about anything any more. Perhaps all I will feel ever again will be pain. It seems to be all that I feel at the moment. A pain that goes on and on with no end in sight. I wish I could believe that the pain will end, but I have a feeling that it will be with me for the rest of my life. There's not much that I can do about that really. I suspect that the pain would have been there no matter when mum died. It has nothing to do with my young age. Pain is pain at any point in your life.

Then

Claire had been feeling more tired as time went on. She didn't seem to be able to recover from the fatigue that she was feeling. No matter how much she slept, it always seemed to be there with her.

'It's incredible annoying,' Claire told Daniel when they were discussing it one night.

'Perhaps you should go and see a doctor.'

'To be told that I am working too hard and I need to take a break? Perhaps that's what I need, perhaps we should go on holiday somewhere.'

'We've just come back from holiday.'

'Perhaps we need another one.'

'I really think you should consider going to see a doctor if it's something that's persistent.'

'Would you go to a doctor? Of course you wouldn't,' she stated before he had time to answer. Each of them was quick to say that the other needed to go and see a doctor over some ailment or the other, but each of them was slow to take their own advice.

'It might be something to do for the best.'

'I'm getting incredibly short of breath as well. I think I need to exercise more, but I feel too tired all of the time. Perhaps I'm just out of shape.'

'There's nothing wrong with your shape at all. You are perfectly fit. You shouldn't be feeling like this.'

'It's just one of those things, I suppose. A sign of advancing age.'

'You are barely in your forties. That's hardly old.'

'Well, sometimes it feels like it is. It's more to do with the number of miles that have been travelled rather than the age. Miles travelled both emotionally and physically.'

'I'm not sure that I'm following you on that one.'

'I'm just saying that a busy lifestyle can make you feel old, even when you're not old in years.'

'I suppose so.'

Daniel left it at that. He knew better than to push Claire into going to see a doctor. The more pressure he put on her about going to see a doctor, the more likely it was that she would push back and resist going. If she needed to go and see a doctor then it would have to be something that she came to of her own free will and in her own time. He was concerned about her, but that wasn't anything that was particularly new. He was always concerned about her. It was what being in love was all about.

So, things continued the way that they had done for all the years that they had been married. Daniel continued with his novels and Claire continued at the publishing house.

Toby came home from school one day with a copy of Daniel's novel *Dystopia* in his hands.

'Look what our teacher has us reading,' he said, proudly showing the book to Daniel as if it was a great prize.

'*Dystopia* is on the syllabus?' asked Daniel incredulously.

'I don't think it's on the official government syllabus. Our English teacher just likes to add things to the reading list that he thinks we should be reading. He recommended that I read Albert Camus.'

'I think you are probably a little young for Camus. He isn't the easiest of writers to get along with for some people.'

'But you like him.'

'Yes, I do. I think he was a great writer and a tragic loss when he was killed in the car crash.'

'He could've written so much more.'

'It's one of the great tragedies of literature. I think one of the other great tragedies is the fact that Thomas Hardy stopped writing novels after the critic's reaction to *Jude the Obscure*. If they had kept their mouths shut then we would have had another twenty years of Hardy novels to be able to read.'

'You like Hardy, don't you?'

'Probably my favourite author.'

'Mine is you.'

'Oh shucks, you're only saying that because you want more pocket money.'

Daniel found it strange that they were reading one of his novels at school. He didn't really think that his novels were suitable for that kind of thing. The teacher was obviously a fan, and knowing that Toby was his son was probably after an autographed copy of the novel, or more likely for Daniel to go into the school and give a talk on what it meant to be a writer. Daniel hated that sort of thing as he wasn't really sure what it meant to be a writer. If he didn't know, then how was he expected to tell others of it.

The world did look with a certain amount of disdain on writers. That was at least the way that Daniel felt that things went. Daniel had wanted to be a writer for as long as he could remember. When he was growing up, he would write short stories in an exercise book that were based around characters in his favourite television programmes. It was like he felt that there was something missing, not enough episodes, or something like that, so he felt the need to write more.

He had joined an amateur dramatics group in the hope that he might be able to meet girls and had fallen in love with theatre and for a brief spell as a teenager he had written a number of plays. None of which had actually been produced, but the enthusiasm was there. He had fallen out with the plan of being a playwright though. He didn't feel that there was enough money in it, although Tom Stoppard didn't seem to be doing all that badly, nor did Harold Pinter (not that he would have known who either of these two were when he was a teenager). He lived in a very insular world. It was possibly because of the fact that he lived in an insular world, that he naturally gravitated to the isolation that comes with being a writer.

He had moved on from writing plays to writing poetry. He had done this chiefly as a lovesick teenager, he was pretty sure that most of the poetry from this period (if it had survived) would be enough to turn the stomach of even the most fanatical of poetry fans. He was pretty pleased that most, if not all of it had been destroyed. He really didn't fancy the idea of some of that turning up and destroying his carefully constructed career as a novelist.

At the age of fifteen he had gone to see the careers advisor, which had been a compulsory thing that the school felt you needed to do in order to prepare yourself for the outside world.

'What do you want to be?' asked the advisor. He hadn't said it but Daniel could sense that the words 'when you grow up' were on the end of the sentence and had been left hanging in the air.

'I want to be a writer,' Daniel had replied with confidence.

The advisor sighed and palmed his face. Here was another kid that had come into his office and had unrealistic expectations on what he was going to be doing with his life. Why couldn't they come in with realistic expectations of what they wanted to do with their career? Why was he even doing this job in the first place? Was it really his responsibility to dash all these people's hopes and tell them that they were not going to be the next Picasso, or Wordsworth, Mozart or Monet?

'Well, I suppose they have got to come from somewhere,' he had replied and had then handed some leaflets to Daniel on Information Technology. He hoped that he would consider these as a more realistic career expectation.

That was the problem with the career's advisors. They were no bloody good. If you wanted to be a postman or a doctor, then they might actually be able to help you, but if you wanted to do something creative then you could forget it. They were out of their comfort zone and had no idea how to advise you. This man had no idea how you went about becoming a novelist. He didn't even read novels. He simply didn't have the time.

It would have helped if the advisor had taken the attitude that it didn't matter where you came from, but that it mattered where you were going. The problem was that he didn't have the imagination to see where he was going, let alone anyone else. That was the problem with school as far as Daniel was concerned. It left you dispirited. It was only there to churn you out with enough intelligence to be able to vote for the government, but not with enough intelligence to be able to question what they were doing. There was no room for creativity in the equation. Come out on the factory line and don't deviate from the plan.

Daniel was someone that deviated from the plan in a big way. He wasn't prepared to conform. He supposed that was what being a writer was all about. The need to conform was not something that your average writer did. He thought about all the Soviet writers that had gone to prison for what they had believed in. All those that had languished in the wastes of Siberia for writing things that were against what the state wanted you to believe.

Daniel had turned away from the plays and the poems and had decided that he would write a novel. He wrote a novel about neo-Nazis in Britain and how they wanted to get their hands on a list of prominent outspoken Jews that they wanted to persecute. It was called *The List Maker*. It was without exception completely awful and the kind of amateurish rubbish that you would expect from an adolescent. It contained immortal lines such as 'the gun spat venom'.

The good thing about it was that Daniel was able to recognise that it was complete rubbish and do something about it. He had burnt it. It had only been about sixty thousand words in length so was more of a novella than an actual novel. The important thing though was it was something that he was able to cut his teeth on. He had demonstrated that he was able to write something of a sustainable length. It might have been complete rubbish, but that was hardly the point.

Daniel was pragmatic enough to realise that there were bound to be moments when you fell when you were aiming for the stars. It was inevitable that this was the kind of thing that would happen. It gave him experience though and that was something that was so valuable it couldn't be ignored. He hadn't given up. It would have been easy to give up and go and work in a factory somewhere, or to do something else, but he had been persistent. This was something that he really wanted to do. If you want to do something enough then you will find a way to make it happen.

It wasn't that there was anything wrong with working in a factory. A great many people worked in factories and some of them might actually be happy. You have to follow the road that is laid out for you and working in a factory was not the road that was laid out for Daniel.

He had the good sense to ignore the careers advisor and the teachers that were dead in their jobs and were just going through the motions until it was time to retire. You can't let other people dictate your dreams to you. You have to follow your own path, and Daniel had followed his path and it had been a success. He was extremely grateful as he knew that there were those that were never as successful as he had been.

He was of the belief that with determination and hard work it was possible to achieve anything though. You just had to believe in yourself. If you didn't believe in yourself then nobody else would believe in you either. You could hardly expect them to do so if you were not committed yourself.

The careers advisor had been right about one thing, writers did have to come from somewhere. His unspoken criticism was that he didn't think that writers came from the place that Daniel had come from. He didn't believe that it was possible for someone like Daniel to become a writer, in other words. But they did have to come from somewhere, and why not from where Daniel was? It seemed perfectly natural as far as Daniel was concerned.

He had learnt the lesson that if you want to be a writer then the first thing that you need to do is read. When he went to university, he was able to read a great deal, not only the books that were on the reading list, but also the books that he could read, when he was reading around the subject. You might be tasked with reading *Hard Times* by Dickens, but it helped if you were able to read some of the other things that Dickens had written so that you got a perspective of his work. What had he written either side of the novel for instance? It might be viewed as a little excessive but he was able to advance his reading a great deal and he was able to learn a lot about the technicalities of being a writer.

This helped him when he came to write his first novel *Miller's Revenge*. He had decided that he wanted to concentrate on relationships rather than having a 'shoot them up' kind of novel. He had decided that he simply wasn't that kind of writer. It was probably a good thing that he had found his niche elsewhere. His first novel, an action thriller, if it could be termed as that, was something that he had written because he thought it was necessary to write a blockbuster. It probably came from watching too many Arnold Schwarzenegger films as a teenager.

With maturity he realised that you couldn't write a blockbuster and had to write what was inside that demanded to be written. That was when he came into his own as a writer. Now that he had settled on novels as the medium that he was happy with, he decided that he would not stray into anything else again. Yes, he could have written the screenplay for his novel that was turned into a film, but he really didn't feel that it was something that he would have been comfortable with.

'I get worn out just walking up the stairs,' Claire told him over dinner one night. It took Daniel a little time to ground himself back to the conversation. He had been thinking of the work that he had been doing during the day and had been engrossed in the world of his characters.

'You do?'

'Yeah. I'm really not fit at all.'

'I think you're fit.'

'Flatterer.'

'No, it's true I don't mean to flatter. There's hardly an ounce of fat on you. If anything, you have been losing weight rather than putting it on.'

'I could have been, I suppose.'

'I still think you need to see a doctor. It's possible that they might be able to do something to boost you. Maybe your calcium is unbalanced or something like that. That can make you tired.'

'How do you know?'

'I've been researching.'

'For a novel?'

'Yeah. I tell you, some of the things that we writers have to research are incredible. It's possible that if the police ever check my search engine, they will think that I'm some sort of sociopath.'

'Or serial killer.'

'Very probably. We do research some very strange things. Probably get the CIA knocking at the door at some point.'

'It's a good job that we don't live in America then.'

'Well that would be the FBI then.'

'Probably.'

'I think you should go and see a doctor.'

'I'll be fine.'

'I'm sure you will be, but I'm concerned about you and I think that you would be better off seeing a doctor. Put my mind at rest, if nothing else.'

Claire wasn't too sure about this. She was reluctant to have anything to do with doctors. She still remembered the birth of Toby and how difficult it had been. That was enough to put her off doctors and hospitals for life.

'I'm not convinced that there is anything wrong with me other than just getting older.'

'Then there will be no harm in going to a doctor to have that confirmed. If there is anything else wrong then they can sort it out and make you feel better.'

'Well, maybe.'

'Do it for me.'

Claire sighed. 'All right, I'll go and see a doctor.'

'Thank you.'

Daniel made the appointment to see the doctor. He was not convinced that it would ever happen if he was to leave it to Claire to organise. He went with her to make sure that she went through with the appointment. The doctor listened carefully as they outlined all of the problems that Claire was having, the shortness of breath and the feeling of tiredness all of the time. The doctor was sympathetic and assured Claire that there was probably nothing to worry about and it may well just be a symptom of working too hard and not getting enough rest. He did say, however, that he would like to organise a few tests to make sure that she was okay and there was nothing else that was sinister that was going on.

Claire didn't like the use of the word sinister. In truth, Daniel didn't care all that much for it either. He immediately assumed that there was something that was sinister that was going on. He was a natural worrier. Particularly when it came to Claire. There were blood tests that needed to be conducted. These were arranged quite quickly, with an urgency that worried Daniel. He was beginning to wonder if the doctor was telling them the entire truth or whether he was holding things back.

The blood tests came back and whatever the results were the doctor was cagey about it.

'I'm going to put in a referral to you for the hospital,' he said.

'The hospital?' asked Claire, 'what's the matter?'

'I'm not too sure, but I think they need to explore matters further and help you out. We need to rule out certain things and they will be in a better place to do that for you then we can in the local surgery.'

Daniel had his fears of what this might mean. 'What department?' he asked, dreading the answer and thinking that he probably already knew.

'Oncology,' the doctor looked a little uncomfortable with this.

'Cancer,' Claire said softly.

'At this stage it is a possibility. We have to do everything that we can to make sure that it isn't, and if it is, to ensure that the correct tests are carried out. Your x-ray showed some anomalies on your lungs that I think need checking out.'

'My lungs? But I've never been a smoker.'

'Unfortunately, if it is lung cancer, and it is only a possibility at this stage, so don't get worked up unnecessarily, but if it is, unfortunately you don't have to have been a smoker in order to get it.'

'Don't get worked up? How am I supposed to not get worked up? You've just told me that there is a possibility that I might have lung cancer.'

'Yes, and at the moment it is only a possibility and we need to do everything that we can to ensure that if it is lung cancer then it is treated properly and that will improve your recovery rate and chances of survival.'

'Jesus.'

'I know it is a lot to take in. I've got some literature for you to read through and the oncologist appointment will be arranged as soon as possible.'

Both Claire and Daniel were in a state of shock when they left the doctor's surgery. They had gone in expecting to be told that this was just a sign of middle age and that everyone felt the same way and she needed to knuckle down and get on with it, and now she was being told that there was a possibility that she might have cancer.

'I wish we had never gone to the doctor in the first place,' said Claire shooting an accusing look at Daniel.

'Surely it is better to know if you have cancer or not?'

'I'm not so sure about that. I think I would rather not know about it at all, thank you very much.'

'But if you have cancer, at least you can get treatment for it and start to get better. If we hadn't gone to the doctor then you would never have known, but things would probably have just got worse. At least this way there is hope of you getting better.'

'I'm not convinced of the positives at this particular point. All I can see is negatives.'

'You have to give it time. I will be with you each step of the way.'

'I know you will.'

'You won't have to face any of this alone.' He took her hand and they looked at each other, sharing a moment of their love, but also the fear that both of them had at the moment.

They lapsed into silence. Over the months that were to follow there would be a lot of silence. A lot of hand holding and a lot of crying. Anyone being told that they might have cancer inspires a level of fear in them that is hard to be equalled. Most people when they hear the word cancer, immediately think that they are going to die. Despite the fact that the survival rates are much higher these days than they were of the previous generation – that doesn't seem to matter. It is like being handed a death sentence. Knowing that you are going to die, and that the end is probably not going to be all that dignified.

The appointment with the specialist came through and they

went along for a chat and for further tests. Eventually after being put through more tests than Claire felt that she could cope with, they were back in the consultancy room once again.

'I'm afraid it's not good news,' said the consultant looking over her notes. Claire and Daniel held hands and took a deep breath. 'You have lung cancer.'

In some ways they were imagining that the news would be sugar coated, and were taken by surprise at the bluntness of the news. Daniel supposed that it was probably a good idea to be forthright, it saved any ambiguity and confusion that might arise from the news later.

'I've never touched a cigarette in my life,' said Claire.

'Unfortunately, not all lung cancers are caused by smoking. twenty percent of women that develop lung cancer have never smoked. It's a good thing that you are not a smoker though. If you were I would advise you to stop immediately. Lung cancer is the biggest cause of cancer in women. It causes more fatalities than breast cancer, uterine cancer or ovarian cancer combined.'

'Okay, so it's a big killer,' said Claire.

'Yes, it is, but it's not all bad news. There are things that can be done to improve your chances of survival.'

'So, what do we do?' asked Daniel.

'There are two basic treatment options. Local and systemic. Local treatments include surgery and radiation therapy. We will be looking at these options first. Local treatments are designed to remove cancer cells at their source. Systemic treatments include chemotherapy. Systemic treatments are designed to attack cancer cells anywhere in your body, not just the lungs. At the moment we will be concentrating on local treatments as there is no evidence, at this time, that the cancer has spread anywhere else in the body, other than the lungs.'

'Okay, so surgery first?' said Claire.

'Yes, we will attempt to remove the tumour that is in your lung with surgery. We will then put you on a course of radiotherapy to clean up the wound and any remaining cancer cells that are in the area. There is every chance that this will be a successful result for you.'

'I'm pleased to hear it.'

'We can keep working on this and monitor you to ensure that the cancer has not spread. If at any point it becomes clear that the cancer has spread to other parts of your body, then we will have to consider chemotherapy as the next available option.'

'Okay, so when do we start?'

'As soon as possible. Sometimes we issue a course of radiotherapy before we operate to reduce the size of the tumour to make it more manageable to remove. Looking at your test results, that doesn't seem to be an issue at the moment. I would say that we are clear to operate without radiotherapy first, and will put you through a course of radiotherapy after the operation to help clean things up a little.'

'Sounds like a plan,' said Claire.

'I know it's a lot to take in at the moment. If you have any questions, or if there is anything you want to know, then please don't hesitate to ask and we will see if we can answer them for you.'

'Thank you, Doctor,' replied Claire. All she wanted to do at the moment, was to get out of the consultancy rooms as soon as she could and into the open air. She felt that she was having trouble breathing in the room. It was so stifling, so hot and uncomfortable. She wondered how the doctor could stand being in there all day long.

They left the hospital in silence and walked to the car park.

They passed numerous people coming and going along the way, each of them with their own concerns, their own problems and their own health issues. Daniel wondered what these issues might be. He wondered if you could read it on the faces of the people as they passed him by. There were the obvious ones, the people who had a limb in a cast or similar. Most were impossible to guess at. From time to time, they passed a patient in a dressing gown that had escaped from the ward in order to get outside and have a much-needed cigarette. He felt like snatching the cigarette out of their mouths, crushing it under foot and condemning them for smoking when his wife had just been diagnosed with lung cancer. Somehow, he managed to restrain himself and satisfied his feelings with a glaring look at the individuals concerned.

'I thought this was a no smoking site,' he muttered to Claire.

'You're never going to stop people from smoking.'

'You would think that they would be a little more considerate, seeing how this is a hospital and all.'

'Are you going to become staunchly anti-smoking now?'

'I don't see why not. Disgusting habit.'

'It never bothered you before.'

'You never had cancer before.'

'But my cancer has got nothing to do with smoking.'

'Beside the point.'

'We have to work out what we are going to tell Toby.'

'Would it not be better to tell him the truth?'

'It does seem rather pointless in trying to keep this from him. He is going to find out sooner or later. I'm just concerned about how he will take it.'

'He's a sensible lad. He's got his head screwed on right. He will adapt to it. I don't think we need to worry about him. He will be concerned, but he will cope.'

'Do I need to worry about you?'

'How do you mean?' asked Daniel as he fumbled to pay the parking ticket.

'Do I need to worry about how you will take it?'

'I'm trying to keep optimistic about it all. You're going to beat this. I've no doubt of that.'

'I wish I had your optimism. I can't help but feel pessimistic about it.'

'You're bound to feel that way. Don't worry, everything is going to be okay.'

'I hope you're right.'

'Of course it is, you just wait and see.'

They told Toby when they got home and he seemed to take the news with good grace. He asked her bluntly if she was going to die, and Claire responded that she planned to stay around for a number of years yet and wasn't going anywhere. Toby seemed to take this assurance as something that was true and didn't question it any further.

While they waited for a date to come through for the operation, they tried their best to continue with their lives. Toby continued to go to school, and Claire and Daniel got on with their work. Daniel was working on a new novel *Tidal Wave* and was about forty thousand words into it. He continued to write and found that it offered him a distraction from worrying about Claire too much.

Claire wasn't feeling particularly ill, so was able to continue going to work, but had informed them that she would need time off for the operation and for the radiotherapy that would follow it. They were sympathetic and assured her that she could have all of the time that she needed.

As was expected, they both researched lung cancer online

and found that there were differences between men and women who had lung cancer. Men were more likely to develop a cough because of the placing of the tumour and would likely cough up blood as a result of this. Women were less likely to do so. This explained to Claire why it was that she was not coughing up blood, which was something that she associated with lung cancer and expected to happen to her. It seemed strange that there should be differences in this disease between men and women and she intended to ask the consultant if this were the case, or whether it was an internet fallacy.

I don't know how long mum had been sick before they finally told me that she was ill. I suppose they had to process it themselves first before they shared it with anyone, including me, but I felt left out of the loop. I wish I had known what they knew from the start. It would probably have given me more time to process things myself. I don't think you can come to terms with being told that someone you love is ill and might even be dying. I don't know how you deal with that. I don't know how I dealt with it. My first thought, when they told me, was that she was going to die. It's something that you associate with cancer. Surely, more people die from cancer than survive it. I don't know what the statistics are. I haven't looked them up and I have no particular inclination to look them up either. Mum assured me that she was going to be sticking around and was not going to die just yet. As it happened it was a promise that she couldn't keep. She shouldn't really have made that promise to me. You shouldn't promise people things that you have no control over.

Now

It was fast approaching New Year's Eve, and Daniel couldn't have cared less about the event. He had never been one that was all that fussed about New Year anyway. He would quite often prefer to go to bed with a good book, rather than to stay up to see the fireworks or watch any of the celebrations that were taking place. Frankly, he couldn't understand what all the fuss was about. So, a new year had started. So what? It didn't really change anything. Were people celebrating the fact that they had the next day off from work, so could get themselves as paralytic as possible before they were eventually forced to return to jobs that they hated, just so that they could pay the mortgage?

Another year could often be the start of a fresh slate. The chance to uphold those resolutions, that you would almost certainly break before the 3rd January. A chance to right the wrongs that you committed the previous year? He hardly thought so. It mattered even less to him this year as the turn over to a new year meant that he was facing the first year of his life without Claire being in it.

The prospect was not exactly one that seemed cause for celebration. In fact, he could think of no reason to welcome in the New Year at all. Toby had been asked out with some friends, but had politely declined, preferring instead to spend the evening in his own room, doing his own thing. This left Daniel at even more of a loose end than he would have been otherwise. Jordan had asked if Daniel wanted to see in the New Year with him and

Natalie, but he didn't feel like he was ready to spend time in company at the moment. The funeral had been bad enough. There was no reason to spend any other unnecessary agonies at the moment.

All in all, that meant that he was planning on spending a quiet New Year's Eve. He had no intention of seeing the New Year in. He planned to be in bed long before midnight chimed out the old and in the new. Claire had been someone that had enjoyed seeing the New Year in and would stay up to see the crossover. Daniel hated the idea for reasons that he had not been fully able to explain to himself, let alone anyone else.

He remembered once when they went to a party on New Year's Eve. It was possibly the worst party that he had ever been to. It was being hosted by one of Claire's bosses and the first thing that struck Daniel was that the man had invited people of influence rather than friends. As far as he could tell there were no friends that were present, and no family, it was all people that might be able to influence things in the publishing house or be able to do business with over the coming year.

It was the worst party that he had ever been to. As they didn't really know anyone (and nobody was particularly all that bothered about talking to them) they had spent most of their time in the room where the food was laid out, talking to each other and trying to pretend that there was not a party going on.

The problem was that as it was a New Year's Eve party nobody could justifiably leave before midnight. Daniel did think about picking up one of the forks and stabbing himself in the eye, so that they would have an excuse to leave the party to go to hospital. It seemed something of an extreme measure, but for a moment he had given it some serious thought.

As midnight approached, everyone had gathered around the

television set so that they could hear the chimes of Big Ben signalling in that it was a new year that had started. There was much congratulation and slapping on the backs. Five minutes later and people started to leave, seemingly as quickly as they could, so maybe it had been a pretty boring party for all those concerned anyway.

There were many things that Daniel found hard to cope with after the death of Claire. There were many things that he found hard to believe. Perhaps the strangest of all was the fact that the world continued to turn. That people continued to get on with their lives and time continued to tick by. The world had not ended, and yet it was as if Daniel's own world had ended. It was as if time had stopped ticking by and there was nothing left for him. He just found it bizarre that the rule for him did not apply to everybody and everything else.

Here they were at New Year's Eve, and it was a mystery how they had managed to get there. For him, life had stopped with the death of Claire. It was still two weeks before Christmas. It was as if he couldn't imagine how he had got from that time to this. And yet, here he was. He couldn't deny the proof of where he was and what he was doing.

He felt resentful that time had continued to tick by and the world had continued to turn. It wasn't fair. It should have all ended. He supposed that he should pull himself out of the pit that he was in and catch up with the rest of the world, that was resolutely moving on without him. He knew that this was something that he should do, but it was just something that he wasn't feeling all that inclined to do. It was all very well knowing what you were supposed to do, but it was no use at all if you didn't have the inclination to do it.

He couldn't summon up the motivation to work either. He knew that he had work to do. He knew that it was sitting there for him to do. There wasn't an urgency to work. It wasn't as if he needed the money. He had worked hard for years and was able to reap the rewards from it now. It didn't feel like much of a reward though, given the circumstances. He supposed he would have to consider himself lucky that he didn't have a 'normal' job, working in an office or something like that. He had no idea how he would have been able to drag himself in each day, put a smile on his face and pretend that, yes, everything was fine and there was no need to worry about him. At least as a writer he could hide himself away and keep distant from the world. Hell, being a recluse was pretty much what being a writer was all about.

He explained all of this to Jordan. Jordan was spending a lot of time at the house since the death of Claire. Daniel supposed that he was his best friend, although he had never really given it all that much thought.

'It's difficult to know how to respond to all of that,' Jordan said.

'I don't know what the answers are. I feel like Miss Havisham, in that time has stood still for me. It's rather difficult to suddenly find yourself within the pages of a Dickens novel. *Great Expectations*,' he said to Jordan's blank look.

'Ah, never read it.'

'You need to read more. It's perverse that you are a literature graduate who has hardly read anything. How could you possibly have graduated without reading *Great Expectations*?'

'It wasn't on the syllabus. As I remember it was *Hard Times*.'

'You didn't read that either I'm willing to bet. Just fluffed your way through it.'

'It's amazing what you can get out of *York Notes*.'

'Philistine. How can you be friends with a writer and have read so little?'

'I've read your books.'

'I suppose I should be grateful for that.'

'Plenty good enough, as far as I'm concerned.'

'I'm not going to win this argument.'

'I'll never be as well-read as you. You're a writer. It's your job to be well-read. It's my job to read for pleasure and I don't get all that much pleasure in reading books that were written so long ago. I don't have the attention span for them. Plus, Dickens writes such very long sentences. The man really didn't understand the use of a full stop.'

'Different times.'

'Well, that's as may be. I prefer my reading material to be a little easier on the eyes.'

'Each to their own, I suppose.'

'Indeed. The question is though not what we are going to do about my reading matter, but what we are going to do to help you move on with your life?'

'It seems a bit early in the day to be talking about moving on with my life. That makes it sound like we are talking about me getting married again.'

'I don't imagine, for one second, that you are thinking of getting married again. Even I wouldn't suggest such a thing. I wouldn't even suggest that you start dating again.'

'Good, because I have no interest whatsoever in dating again, or finding anyone to replace Claire. There isn't anyone that could replace Claire as far as I'm concerned. I will just have to face the prospect of being on my own for the rest of my life.'

'Sounds a bit grim,' said Jordan.

'Well, that's as may be. I will just have to live with it. I don't see it as a problem. Dating someone else would seem like a betrayal to Claire. Does that make sense?'

'It makes perfect sense. Nobody is going to expect you to date again. At least not yet. It's far too early to even be thinking of such a thing.'

'Too early or not, I don't see my position as ever changing in that regard. Even if it were to be ten years from now.'

'A lot can happen in ten years.'

'My love and devotion for Claire are not something that I see as changing at all.'

'No, I don't suppose that they will, but ask yourself this, would she want you to be alone for the rest of your life?'

'Why are we even talking about this? I have no intention of replacing Claire. My wife has just died for Christ's sake. It hasn't even been a month yet.'

'Okay, we are just talking. There's no need to get wound up about it. I was just talking about you moving on with your life.'

'Moving on with my life, doesn't mean that I have to find myself someone else to be with.'

'No, it doesn't, but nor can you stay frozen in time, watching as the world passes you by. You have to get on with your life. You have to get on with your work. You have to be there for Toby. You have to be a dad to him and help him through all of this and all of the other problems that he is going to have as he grows up.'

'Yeah, I know. It can't be any the easier for him.'

'No, it can't. He is probably in just as much pain as you are at the moment. You need to be there for each other. You are all the other has left now.'

'I know.'

'So, you need to pick yourself up and move on. For his sake if not your own.'

'Stop wallowing in self-pity, you mean?'

'I think you are allowed to indulge yourself in a modicum of self-pity. As you say, your wife has just died. You are allowed to grieve, but eventually you will have to pick yourself up from the floor and carry on. It's what Claire would have wanted you to do. She wouldn't have wanted you to stop your life on her account.'

'I suppose you're right.'

'Yes, I am. You know it.'

It helped to talk to someone else about the things that Daniel was going through, even if it did reinforce some of the things that he knew about already. Sometimes you just needed someone else to say it to you. Someone else who could reassure you that what you were doing was all right, and that you were going to get yourself out of the mess that you were in. You need someone that will tell you that it's going to be all right. That it's okay to feel the way that you do. It doesn't matter, nobody is going to think the worse of you for it.

Daniel was sitting in his study, trying to bring himself to work when the phone rang. If he had bothered to look at the caller ID then he possibly would have allowed it to go to answerphone. When he realised that it was Claire's mother he immediately regretted picking up. He didn't have the will to talk to her at the moment, or indeed at any moment if the truth were told.

'I think Toby should come and stay with me for a while,' she said without any preamble or greeting.

'Why?'

'I think he needs some maternal love at the moment.'

'Well, he isn't going to get that. His mother is dead.'

'But I'm the next best thing that he has to a mother, so I think he should come and stay with me.'

'I think he should stay with his father.'

'You will be fine without him.'

'It was him that I was thinking about.'

'I tell you; he needs a woman's love now more than anyone else.'

'And you think you can give him that do you?'

'Well, of course I do, why wouldn't I?'

'You never gave any love to Claire, what makes you think that you can give it to Toby?'

'What do you mean that I never gave it to Claire? I loved Claire a great deal and I feel her loss more keenly than anyone.'

'More than me?'

'You were only her husband. I was her mother.'

'Do you even hear what you are saying?'

'I knew her a lot longer than you did.'

'It isn't a competition.'

'I still think that Toby would be better off with me.'

'Toby is going back to school in a few days.'

'Well, you can easily keep him off school given the circumstances.'

'He doesn't want to be kept off school, and I don't want him to be kept off school either.'

'You are being unreasonable, Daniel.'

'*I'm* being unreasonable? You mean because I don't agree with you? Anyone that doesn't agree with you is being unreasonable?'

'I think you will find that I'm well within my rights to demand that Toby spend some time with me.'

'So you are demanding now, are you?'

'I had hoped that it wouldn't come to this.'

'I think you will find that as his father my rights outweigh your rights by quite a large margin, plus, of course, I'm taking into account the fact that Toby doesn't want to spend any time with you.'

'Have you asked him?'

'I don't need to ask him. I know my son.'

'I didn't think so. You will do me the courtesy of at least asking him.'

'No, I don't think I will. Goodbye.'

With that he hung up the phone and tried to control his anger at the woman. He ignored the phone when it rang again and allowed it to go to answerphone and deleted the message without listening to it first. He really couldn't be dealing with her at the moment. He had other things on his mind. He didn't think that he was being unreasonable in denying her the right to have Toby come and stay with her. He knew from previous conversations that Toby didn't really like his grandmother. He had nothing in common with her and she had hardly acted in a kindly way towards him. If the truth were known she had ignored him for most of his life. She seemed to resent the fact that Claire had become a mother, as if she were the only person in the world who could be allowed to be a mother. Obviously, she considered herself to be the greatest mother alive. If you judged these things by the lack of attention that she had spent on Claire, then she was possibly right.

Daniel couldn't be dealing with Claire's mother at the moment. She was in the position of being able to grab as much attention for herself as possible over Claire's death. He had no idea what the motivation was for her wanting Toby to come and stay with her. He was sure that there would be some ulterior motive for her in wanting it. It probably would give her an extra chance to show off to her friends and make them realise what a dutiful grandparent she was and how she was in such deep grieving for her daughter. He couldn't be handling all that crap at the moment.

'Your grandmother wants you to go and stay with her,' he told Toby.

Toby looked panicked. 'You're not sending me, are you?'

'Not if you don't want to go, and I suspected that you would not want to go so I told her no.'

'I don't want to go. I want to stay here with you and go back to school.'

'I thought that might be the case. I fear we may not have heard the last of it though. Your grandmother can be a forceful and determined woman when she has got something in her head.'

'Promise me you won't send me to her.'

'You're not going anywhere that you don't want to go, don't you worry about that.'

'Thanks. I can't think of anything worse than staying with her. I would rather have my eyes gouged out.'

'Thankfully that won't be necessary.'

January was a cold, unforgiving month. There was still no snow. It was rainy and dismal. The kind of weather that makes you depressed, even if you are not feeling depressed in the first instance. For someone like Daniel (who was definitely feeling depressed beforehand) it was even worse. He found it almost impossible to motivate himself and to continue with his day. Getting up in the morning was the hardest part of all. It would have been so much easier to stay secluded under the duvet and pretend that the outside world had gone away.

Having managed to get out of bed, the second hardest thing was to prevent himself from going back to it. When Toby had been packed off back to school, there really seemed to be no reason to stay up any longer. Daniel found himself disappearing off for a sleep mid-morning. He was sure that it wasn't doing him any good, but the more that he was asleep the better it felt for him. The more asleep he was the less of the day he had to face. The less of the day he had to face, then the less thinking he had to do, and all of that was a good thing as far as he was concerned.

He thought about what Jordan had said and how he should write about what had happened to him and Claire. He had to confess that it wasn't the first time that he had thought about it. He had thought about writing about it all during Claire's illness, but he didn't think that she would have taken too well to the idea that he was writing about her. He thought about writing about it all now, but wondered if it would just make for too depressing a reading. That was probably the way that it would turn out.

It was like Facebook. Really people only posted the good things that they were doing. They did this because maybe they wanted to show off about how good their life was. Be envious about how wonderful things are with me. Don't you feel jealous? Very rarely would anyone post anything negative about their life, because after all, who really wanted to read that shit? There were, of course, those that posted hints that there was something wrong in the hope that someone would become concerned and pick up on the hint and ask what was wrong. Daniel saw these people, but made a point of never asking them what was wrong. They were just attention seekers as far as he was concerned. He had no intention of fuelling their narcissistic tendencies.

Daniel hoped that February (when it finally came) would be a better month for his mental health. The problem was that there was a whole lot of January to get through before it was February. A whole lot of a depressing month. Perhaps as the year rolled on and spring finally appeared things would get better and he would feel more capable at facing the world. It was a lot to ask for.

In the meantime, he had fallen into the habit of his morning sleep and he convinced himself that it was doing him some good. He wasn't sure that it was, but he had convinced himself that it was something that he was going to do anyway. He was aware of the fact that it was a withdrawal tactic. By hiding away from the world, he was avoiding the possibility of having to face up to the ugly truth of the reality of what life was now. He knew all of this; he just didn't care.

He thought that maybe it was time to do some work, regardless of what he felt about it. The problem was he just didn't have the words. The words, which had flowed so naturally before, were just not coming to him. He supposed it could be a bit of writer's block, but he didn't really believe in that. He thought that was just an excuse for when you couldn't be bothered to write. In this instance though the words were elusive. They refused to come and he couldn't force them to come. It didn't work like that. No matter what he tried, the cursor and the arctic wasteland of the page just stared back at him. Taunting him. Teasing him with his inability to make anything appear on the page. He hated the flashing cursor more than anything else in the world. It was provocative and mocking of him. It seemed to be laughing with each flash. Daring him to make it dance across the screen, knowing full well that he didn't have the capability to do so. Not at the moment at any rate. It had never bothered him all that much in the past, but it bothered him now. It bothered him a great deal.

There was little that he could do about it though. Staring at the page would not make the words appear. Caressing the keyboard would not make his fingers dance across the page as they had once been wont to do. He was in a purgatory, waiting to find out if it was going to be a hell or not. He rather suspected that if such a place as hell existed, then he was already there. Hell was life without Claire. Being forced to continue breathing when she had stopped. Being forced to carry on when she was no longer there. Not able to offer her help, her support, or her love. It sounded like hell as far as he could see. He couldn't imagine anything else that could be worse. It must be hell because Claire's mother was in it.

She had plagued him with more phone calls, all of which he had chosen to ignore. He should have ignored her the first time that she rang, but he had not been paying attention. He didn't need to listen to the answerphone messages to know that she was still harping on about Toby spending some time with her. It didn't seem to matter to her that it was not something that Toby or Daniel wanted to happen. All that concerned her was what she wanted. She was that kind of person. The kind of person that only thought about herself and what she wanted, to the detriment of everyone else around her.

Daniel shouldn't have been surprised that there were people like her in the world. He had created enough of them, and people like them, in his novels. Indeed, although he would never admit it for fear of a lawsuit, he had even based one or two of his characters on Claire's mother. Whenever he needed a villain for a piece, he knew that he didn't have to look all that far from home to find one.

He was a writer, it's what writers do. They look around them at the world that is there and take, steal if you like, what they can use for characters and plot. Never piss off a writer. The chances were that you would end up in one of their books and it would not be a flattering portrait.

'Claire's mother wants to steal Toby,' Daniel told Jordan.

'Steal him?'

'Well, she wants him to go and live with her for a while.'

'How long?'

'Unspecified, but Toby has made it clear to me that five minutes would be too long to have to endure.'

'Why does she want him to go and stay with her?'

'She says it's so he can get some maternal love, but it's more likely that she wants to parade him in front of her old cronies and get some more sympathy.'

'How would she get sympathy for that?'

'She would probably claim that I had forced him on her because I was not able to cope as a father, or a human being, and so she was having to be a martyr to her dead daughter by looking after her offspring. Anything to really paint me as the bad guy and her as the saint of all that she sees.'

'What a vile woman. Is she really like that?'

'Yep, I'm afraid so. She is the kind of person that donates huge amounts of money to the Church, just so that she can be in with the priest and appear to be one of her favourites. She is the kind of person that goes to church to be seen, rather than because of any spiritual need.'

'I've never really thought about it like that.'

'She's really as bad as she sounds.'

'Sounds it.'

'So poor Toby is caught in the middle. Not wanting to go to her, but knowing that she is making a fuss about having him over there. It's really a very difficult situation for him to be in.'

'Can't be that difficult, surely? He doesn't want to go then he doesn't have to go.'

'That's the short of it. He's just concerned that she will make things difficult for me, or him, if we refuse.'

'What are you going to do?'

'Ignore her and hope that she just goes away, or dies or something. It should have been her to die, not Claire.'

'No parent should outlive their child.'

'That's what they say.'

'And I believe it's true. Are you growing a beard?'

'Not really. I just couldn't be bothered to shave. I used to shave for Claire and I can't really see the point of it any longer.'

'You have to keep up appearances. What about for the public when you go on your next book tour?'

'Plenty of writers have beards. I'm sure that they can cope with me having a beard for a while. Besides, the least thing I feel like doing at any rate is book tours. I really can't be doing with all that sort of thing. It would suit me if I never had to do another one again.'

'The public want to see you.'

'I can't imagine why. It should be enough for them to read the books without having to see the author as well. What do they gain by that?'

'There are some that would say that you owe it to the public who buy your books to let them see you once in a while.'

'I can't be doing with this entire business. I can't even write at the moment. Let alone think about all the business side of writing, which frankly gives me a headache just thinking about. I think it would be better if I could just write books in seclusion and never have anything to do with the business side of it.'

'I suppose you could do that if you wanted to,' said Jordan, although he didn't sound too sure of it.

'It's bad enough having to do my tax returns. I have given

159

little thought to doing them while Claire has been ill.'

'Well, you don't want to fall foul of the tax people. Not only will they sting you for a big bill, but you will end up in the papers as a tax evader.'

'They say that no publicity is bad publicity.'

'I think it would be enough to stop people from wanting to buy your books.'

'Well, that's their lookout.'

'I hate seeing you like this.'

'Like what?'

'So down. So depressed with everything. I know that your wife has just died and you arguably have a right to feel that way about things, but I hate seeing you like it. I feel that there is something that I should do about it.'

'There's nothing that you can do.'

'I know that, but I feel that there's more that I should or could be doing.'

'Honestly, there's nothing that you can do. I have to get through this on my own.'

Daniel was right. When he was in the position that he was, there was very little that anyone else could do about it. You just had to get on with it and hope that there was a way through to the other side. If not then you were trapped in it for the rest of your life.

I really didn't like the idea of going to spend time with my grandmother. I didn't like her all that much. She had never seemed to be all that interested in me. She even forgot my birthday more times than she remembered it. Maybe I picked up from my parents my dislike for her. I know that they didn't like her all that much. She was not an easy person to like. I was concerned about any problems that she might cause my dad. I wouldn't have put it past her to try some sort of lawsuit to get full-time custody of me. I couldn't think of anything worse. The problem was that I could see that dad was in a pretty bad way. He had taken the death of mum pretty hard and I could see that my grandmother would use that to her advantage to say that he was some kind of unfit father. He was far from it, he was just going through something of a rough patch, which was understandable (to everyone but my grandmother) given the circumstances. It was difficult losing my mother, but it must have been even more difficult to lose your wife. It made me wonder of the wisdom of being in a relationship. I'm sure dad would say though that the pain of being without mum was worth it for the time that he had spent with her. I don't think that he would have changed a thing if he could have. Life is about loss. Living is about death. They go hand in hand, there isn't much that you can do about it. I just hoped that he could hold it together enough that it didn't give my grandmother any justification for trying to take me away from him. He never said anything about it to me, he wouldn't, but I could tell that he thought it unfair that mum had died instead of my grandmother. He felt that it should have been the other way around. It's the natural order of things. Parents shouldn't bury their children, but, of course, they do so every day. It happens a lot more than people would like to admit.

Then

Claire's operation date came through quickly. She wasn't sure whether to be reassured by this, or worried that they were rushing her in because she was an urgent case that needed work. It was possible to view it that way. It wasn't as if she wasn't worried enough as it was.

'I really don't know how I'm going to cope with all of this,' she told Daniel as she lay in the pre-op area waiting to go in for surgery.

'You will do fine,' he replied, with perhaps more confidence than he felt. 'You will get through this and you will beat it. I have faith in you.'

'If anything happens to me then you know that I love you, don't you?'

'Hush, nothing is going to happen to you. You will be fine and yes, I know that you love me, and I love you as well. When you come out of this operation, I will be there waiting for you. It will all be over in a flash for you.'

'It's going to be a number of hours for you though.'

'I will cope. Waiting around is nothing compared to what you are having to go through. I wish that I could have the operation for you.'

'Just be there when I wake up.'

'I will be there. I promise.'

'Are you ready? Shall we do this?' said the surgeon as he came through the door in his blue scrubs.

'Better get it over and done with,' she said, putting a brave face on the situation.

'I love you, Baby,' Daniel told her as she was wheeled away from him, and he was forced to let go of her hand. If he could have then he would have gone into the operating theatre with her, but he knew that was something that was not possible. He also wasn't entirely sure that he wanted to see her cut open and lying on a table like that. It wasn't something that he particularly wanted in his memory.

The doctors told Daniel that if he wanted to, he could go home and they would call him the moment that Claire was out of surgery. Daniel declined the offer and decided that it would be better for him to wait at the hospital. They told him that it was likely to be a lengthy wait, but he told them not to worry as he had a book with him and would wait in the waiting area until it was time for him to see Claire again. They assured him that he could be there when she woke up. This wasn't normal practice, but they had paid to go private and so a little extra care was allowed in this case. It was also, Daniel had explained, the reason why the operation had been arranged so quickly. This hadn't stopped Claire worrying about it though. It was amazing what could happen when you paid for things yourself. It was the age-old maxim that money mattered and could get you anything that you wanted.

Claire had felt a little guilty about going private as there were probably people on the NHS that were desperate for operations, that were on long waiting lists and here was she jumping to the front of the queue. She felt that she didn't really have the right to do so. As far as Daniel was concerned if they had the money then they would pay for it, it was as simple as that. He was a lifelong supporter of the NHS and was proud of the institution, but when it came to his wife's health, then hypocrite or not he was only wanting the best for her. He didn't think that anyone else would have done any differently, if they had been in a position to do so. Most politicians wouldn't put their faith in the NHS. It wasn't because he felt it was failing at all, he just knew that he would get Claire seen quicker and more efficiently, if they went private. The politicians went private because of the fact that they didn't want to rub shoulders with the great unwashed. Being around sick people was so depressing, after all.

Claire had also pointed out that by going private there was less chance of a journalist getting hold of the fact that she was receiving treatment for cancer and making a news story out of it.

'You have to acknowledge that you are a public figure,' she had told Daniel when he had seemed incredulous about the entire thing.

'I'm an author. We don't inspire that level of passion. If I was an actor or a singer then maybe there would be interest out there, but nobody is going to be interested that the wife of a writer is in hospital. We just don't generate that level of interest.'

'Lots of people come and see you at book signings.'

'Yes, but I don't get recognised in the street, and people only ask me to sign my books, they don't ask for my autograph without the book.'

'Well, I think you're famous enough for it to raise an interest.'

'I can't say that I agree with you on that one.'

Daniel was right though; authors just didn't raise that sort of interest. They were not superstars. You had to be a serious bibliophile to want to treat them as such. Maybe in the days of Dickens they had been treated that way, but that was before Hollywood had come along and changed the entire thing.

Daniel tried to concentrate on his book, but found that his thoughts were more often drifting off to wondering how Claire was doing. The hospital was boring and his chair was uncomfortable, but he preferred to be there then at home worrying about her. At least this way he was on hand if he was needed for anything. The doctors didn't anticipate any complications, but you never knew with this kind of thing. They always made a point of telling you that every surgery had a risk involved. It didn't exactly fill you with confidence, but at least they were being honest.

Time ticked by. Daniel made odd attempts at trying to concentrate on his book, but eventually gave it up as an impossible task and spent his time flicking through his phone instead. There were times when you just needed to talk to someone. You scrolled through social media, hoping that there would be someone out there that you wanted to talk to and who wanted to talk to you as well, more to the point. It made you feel less isolated in the world. It was one of the reasons why Daniel often listened to the radio when he was working, just so that he would know that there was someone else out there in the world, and that he was not all alone, which is often the way that it felt most of the time.

Daniel became restless and started to pace up and down, like an expectant father in a maternity ward. He found himself wishing that he smoked so that he would have something to do, but it probably wasn't a good idea smoking when your wife was having surgery for lung cancer and there were so many oncologists knocking about the place. He just felt that he should be doing something with his time rather than this endless waiting that seemed to go on without end. The longer that it took, the more he began to worry that something had gone wrong. He wished that there was an observation room, as there seemed to be in so many medical dramas. At least that way he could watch to see how things were going and would have something to do with his time.

'Do you want a cup of tea?' asked one of the nurses as she passed him by. He supposed that this was another benefit of going private, they offered you tea, although the NHS might have done so, he wasn't sure.

'I'd love a cup of coffee, if that's possible.'

'Of course it is. Milk? Sugar?'

'Milk, no sugar, thanks.'

At least drinking coffee would give him something to do with his hands and his time. It wasn't ideal, but it was better than the nothing that he had been doing so far.

'Shouldn't be too much longer now,' the nurse said when she returned with his coffee. He couldn't help but notice that the coffee was in a china mug rather than the plastic ones that were normally so favoured by hospitals the world over. Maybe that was part of what he was paying for.

'Thank you.'

'We'll get you in to see her as soon as we can.'

'I appreciate that.'

Daniel hoped that it wouldn't be too much longer before he could get in to see Claire. He hated all this waiting about and not knowing what was going on. It was better to be at the hospital rather than having gone home though. He would have been climbing the walls by now and ringing the hospital every five minutes to get an update on the things that were going on. He would have been driving the hospital staff mad, as well as going pretty mad himself.

He picked up his book again, but just held it in his hands. He seemed to lack the energy to even open it, let alone to have the concentration required to actually read it. It was requiring too much of him. He wasn't up for reading at the moment. What if she had died on the table? What if they were just sorting out the details before coming to tell him?

'Would you like to come through now?' It was the same nurse that had brought him the coffee. He must have slipped into a day dream for a moment and was unaware of the passage of time. The coffee sat beside him, untouched and cold.

'Is she out of surgery?'

'Yes, she is.'

'How is she?'

'A little groggy. She will be fine though. Let me take you through to see her.'

'Thank you, yes.'

They walked through some double doors and into the recovery part of the hospital. Because this was a private operation Claire had her own room and didn't have to share with a lot of other people on the ward. Daniel was quite pleased about this. He was pretty sure that if he was in hospital he would prefer to be in a private room, rather than stuck on a ward of sick strangers, all of whom wanted to talk to you and tell you their life story. He couldn't think of anything that would be more depressing to him if he was laid up in a hospital.

He was led into the room where she was. It was exactly as you would picture any hospital room. Sterile and bare. There was little requirement for her to be on any machines and she just had oxygen being administered via her nose.

'Hey,' said Daniel as he walked over and took her hand.

'Hey you.'

'How are you feeling?'

167

'A little tired.'

'Are you in any pain?'

'A little, but it's not too bad. They have got me drugged up to the eyeballs with morphine. Something good to come out of this at least.'

'Well, don't you go getting used to it,' Daniel said as he brushed back her hair.

'I won't. Have you seen the doctor?'

'No. Why?'

'I was just wondering how things went.'

'I don't know, but I'm sure they went fine. You've nothing to worry about.'

'Aside from a course of radiotherapy to follow.'

'It will be a walk in the park compared to what you have just gone through.'

'I suppose so.'

'Do you want to sleep?'

'Yes. Will you come back later?'

'Of course I will. You just try and stop me.'

Claire was already back to sleep before he had finished talking. The nurse had not been exaggerating when she had said that she was groggy. It was only to be expected. Daniel bumped into the doctor as he was leaving.

'I was just coming to see you,' she said.

'How did it go?'

'I think we got it all. It was a successful operation as far as we can tell.'

'She will still have to have radiotherapy though?'

'Yes, we will need to eradicate any cancer cells that are in the surrounding tissue. Anything that might have been too small for us to cut out.'

'Will she be all right?'

'No reason why she shouldn't be. So far everything is going according to plan.'

'That's good news.'

Now that Daniel knew that she was safe, he left Claire behind to have a sleep and returned home. Toby arrived home from school and he told him that the operation had gone well.

'Can I see her?'

'Of course you can. We will both go back tonight after she has had a bit of a rest. She is very tired from the operation at the moment. In the meantime, I suppose I had better call your grandmother.'

'I've got some homework to do,' said Toby and made for his room.

Daniel was not looking forward to making the call to Claire's mother. She had approved of the fact that they had gone private for the medical care but felt that it really should have been someone in Harley Street that dealt with Claire, rather than a doctor who was moonlighting from the NHS. No matter what they did, she never approved of it, so it didn't really matter. It was such a drain having to talk to her though. It was something that he did his best to avoid at all costs.

There was a lot to be said by not surrounding yourself with people that hated all of the time. It was like a disease that could seep into open wounds and cause all sorts of manifestations. It was best avoided. It was problematic though, when it was a member of your family that was the problem and you couldn't really avoid them.

'Well, I don't know how I will be able to get down to visit,' she had said in response to Daniel telling her that the operation had gone well. Daniel expected that she was dropping a hint that she wanted Daniel to pick her up and put her up in his house for the duration of her stay. As far as Daniel was concerned, she could get the train down if she really wanted to come and could stay in a hotel. He couldn't think of anything worse than having her about the place while Claire was trying to recover from the operation. He also didn't think that it would help all that much for recuperation.

He chose to say nothing in response to this and she just sighed at the other end of the phone when she was proved right about the shortcomings of the man that her daughter had chosen to marry. She felt that she should be on hand. Daniel felt that if she was in another country, she would still be too near them.

The phone call with Jordan went better.

'She's all right though?' he asked.

'Seems to be,' said Daniel, 'for someone that has just had major surgery that is.'

'Bless her. Can't be easy.'

'No, no it can't. I can't imagine what she has gone through. I've never had any kind of operation. Not even to have my wisdom teeth out.'

'That's because you're not wise.'

'Thanks a lot.'

'It's my pleasure.'

Daniel and Toby returned to the hospital later that night. Claire was still a little groggy, but she had been able to eat a little dinner and was feeling better than when she first saw Daniel. Toby was a little shaken at seeing his mother in hospital. He was unused to hospitals, never having set foot in one since the time that he was born. It was a slightly alien experience for Daniel as well.

They stayed until Claire started to grow too tired again. The good thing about going private was that there was no real fuss over the visiting time regulations. You could pretty much go in whenever you liked. As long as you didn't get in the way of the medical staff doing their thing, then no one was going to complain about you. It was a liberating experience. Daniel was pretty sure that Claire appreciated the length and frequency of the visits as well. He didn't bother to inform her of the fact that he had spoken to her mother. He didn't want to cause her any further stress than she was already under, and he knew that mention of her mother was likely to cause her stress.

Claire was in the hospital for a week before she was deemed well enough to be able to go home. Despite her threats to do so, her mother never came to stay and didn't so much as even send a 'get well' card. In fact, Claire might not have even been in hospital as far as she was concerned. Daniel wondered why they had taken the time to tell her about the cancer. She wasn't interested in any real sense of the word. She paid lip service to it, but she wasn't as interested in it as she would be if it was something that was happening to her. She might have been able to get some degree of sympathy from the cronies that she surrounded herself with. Sympathy for the fact that her daughter had cancer, but wasn't she bearing up well with the news that her only daughter was ill. It sickened Daniel. He didn't talk to Claire about it though. One of the things that probably really irritated him about her was the fact that she consistently forgot Toby's birthday.

Daniel had no truck with the fact that she also forgot his birthday, and frequently forgot Claire's birthday as well, but Toby was a child and didn't understand the apparent snub that he was getting from his grandmother. Daniel had no doubt though that she consistently would remember her priest's birthday. She was that kind of woman. The kind that was all sweetness and light to strangers, and treated her nearest like complete shit. There wasn't much that you could say about it really.

Oh, but you weren't allowed to forget her birthday though. If you did then you would get a phone call from her, crying down the phone, complaining that her daughter didn't love her any longer. Daniel still remembered the phone call that Claire got from her on the first wedding anniversary after Claire's father had died.

'Have you forgotten something?' her mother had asked her without any preamble.

'I don't think so,' said Claire cautiously.

'It's my wedding anniversary today.'

'I know.'

'So you have deliberately snubbed it then?'

'Mum, Dad died.'

'Do you think I don't know that?'

'Well, you can't celebrate a wedding anniversary when one of you is dead. That's not how it works.'

'So, you think that just because your father has died that you can treat me with so little respect?'

'I really don't know what you're getting at here.'

'I am getting at the fact that you seem to have seen fit to ignore my wedding anniversary.'

'As I said, you can hardly celebrate it when one of you has not made it to the anniversary date. The best you can say is that it is another year that you would have been married, if the other one had lived.'

'I don't want to hear your excuses. This is just callous and hateful behaviour of yours. I'm surprised at you, Claire. Truly I am.'

'I'm consistently surprised at you, Mother.'

'And just what is that meant to mean?'

'Oh, nothing.' Claire didn't have the energy for the fight that was evidently something that her mother wanted so much. She had thought that she was in the right and she still felt that she was in the right. How could you celebrate a marriage when one of you was dead? That wasn't how wedding anniversaries worked surely? Not to the point where you got cards and presents from others. Maybe it was something that you could privately celebrate, but it wasn't a public event any longer.

Claire didn't think that she understood her mother. Daniel certainly didn't when she had explained the telephone conversation to him.

'The woman is off her rocker,' he had said with amazement.

'Well, that would be one explanation for it. Only it isn't dementia or anything like that. She has always been like this. Ever since I was a child. There is no explaining the woman at all.'

'Certainly no reasoning with her.'

'You're not wrong there.'

'She seems to think that this all makes sense in her head. I'm sure she thinks that she has genuinely been slighted by us.'

'More slighted by me. She hardly acknowledges that you exist.'

'A state that for most of the time I'm more than happy to be in. I know she is your mother, but Jesus.'

'I know what you mean.'

Daniel had wondered if Claire was pretending her frustration with her mother for his sake, but it seemed to be genuine enough to be real. Live with someone for long enough and you will know if they are lying or not, and Claire didn't seem to be lying about her mother. She seemed as bemused and as frustrated by her as he was. He was pleased that he didn't have to have all that much to do with her. The problem was that the little that he did have to do with her was more than enough.

He had got on well with Claire's father. It had been a mystery to him why he had married her in the first place. They couldn't have been more opposite each other if they had tried. Claire's mother was a snob, whereas Claire's father was a down-to-earth kind of guy that had no delusions of grandeur. He had worked as an electrician, but this had not been important enough for his wife and she had declared to all of her friends that he worked at the university in some undisclosed post that she didn't go into. He had made no effort to conform to her lies and had told the truth if he had been asked. If she was picked up on any of this, then she would just declare that he was confused. It was impossible that she couldn't be right. She made sure that everyone knew this.

In the meantime, she continued to boost her public profile by donating to the church and having the priest around for tea whenever it suited. She never practised her religion in any noticeable way. It was all for show, as was so many things with her. It would have been amusing if it had not have been so damn tragic at the same time.

Claire had no illusions as to what her mother was like. She was convinced that she had spent ages ignoring the warning signs of her father's impending heart attack. Whenever he had complained about any discomfort or pain, she had ignored him and shooed him away from her.

'He was always complaining about something,' she had told Claire when she had queried whether his heart attack had been entirely out of the blue.

'So, this might have been preventable then?'

'What are you implying?'

'I'm not implying anything. I'm just asking if there were any warning signs that were ignored. By either of you.'

'You would have to ask him that.'

'Well, that's a little difficult, seeing as how he is dead.'

'Well, then there you go. There is no use crying over spilt milk is there?'

'Crying over spilt milk? Is that really how you see the death of your husband?'

'Now, don't twist my words.'

'I'm not twisting your words. I'm just repeating what you were saying, and it sounded like that was how you viewed the death of your husband.'

'Well, it doesn't matter now, does it? If he suffered any pain and discomfort, he is out of his misery now.'

'In more ways than one.'

She looked at Claire with narrowed eyes. 'You have always been a most disobedient and unruly child. I really don't understand you at all.'

'I don't think I understand you either.'

With that, Claire's mother had gone off with her nose in the air and started to play her role as the grieving widow. It was a role that she was determined to play well. It was the kind of thing that she was really good at.

Claire was home from hospital, and she was glad to be there. It hadn't been so bad being in hospital, not as bad as she had thought that it might be, but it was nevertheless good to be home. It was always good to be home. If you were never pleased to be home, then there was something that was wrong with your life that needed to be addressed. It was fun to go away on holiday, but Claire was always glad to be back home, no matter how much of a good time she had while she was away.

If you were not happy to be home then there was something that needed to be changed in your life. Somehow you had got your priorities all wrong. It would take a hypochondriac to not be pleased to be home from a hospital though. Claire was still taking it easy and found moving to be something that was rather difficult. She knew that with time things would improve, and there was no sense in trying to run before you could walk. She had undergone major surgery and needed time to recover from it. She had brought her laptop with her to the hospital so that she could still do some work and answer some emails. Daniel had been against the idea, but Claire had said that she wanted to keep busy and was not prepared to give up work completely.

'It's only cancer, for Christ's sake,' she had jokingly said to him. Daniel had had trouble in seeing the joke. He didn't like it all that much when Claire joked about the cancer. He knew that it was her way of coping with it, but it was in bad taste and he didn't approve all that much. He supposed that if it helped her then there was little that he could do about it.

'I'm not looking forward to the radiotherapy,' she told Daniel.

'You've just had major surgery. It can't be all that bad for you. It's better than chemo at any rate.'

'Don't say that. I might have to end up having chemo at some point and those words will come back and bite you in the arse.'

'Everything is going to be fine.'

'You keep saying that, but I'm not always convinced that it will be fine.'

'The doctors are very pleased with the operation. They think that they have managed to get the majority of the cancer out. The radiotherapy is just a precaution against any tiny little cells that have been left.'

'Tiny little cells.'

'Yes.'

'That sounds ludicrous.'

'It's the truth though. You have to remember that. Thousands of people go through this each year.'

'And not all of them survive.'

'You can't think like that.'

'We have to consider the possibility that this is something that I might not survive. We've never really talked about that, but we are both thinking about it. It's something that we can't ignore.'

'You will be fine.'

'But I might not be, Daniel. You have to acknowledge that it's a possibility.'

Daniel looked sullen. 'All right, I acknowledge that it's a possibility, but it isn't one that I give much entertaining to.'

'Of course not. Neither of us want to admit that this is possibly it. This is as far as I go. But we have to consider it seriously, so that we can put things in place to ensure that things will be okay.'

'You mean with Toby?'

'I don't just mean with Toby. I worry about him, of course, but I also worry about you. How you will be if I'm not here to look after you any longer.'

'I'm sure that I will cope with it as best as I can. Do we really have to talk about this?'

'Yes. We've never mentioned it before, but I want to be buried. I don't want to be cremated. I don't think I could stand being reduced to a bunch of ashes. I would rather rest in the ground.'

'Jesus, Claire!'

'We have to talk about it. If we don't talk about it then you won't know what to do if the time comes. You won't know what I want. So I want to be buried, okay?'

'Okay.'

'No flowers at the funeral though. I always think that flowers are such a waste on a dead person. I would rather that the money that people waste on flowers was donated to a charity or something.'

'Okay, that's easy enough to do.'

'And I don't want an expensive funeral. Save your money. I would rather we did it on a budget.'

'We don't have to worry about the money, we can afford it.'

'But don't you see? I think it's all a waste of money. I would rather it all be cheap and nice rather than over the top and gaudy.'

'It's your funeral.'

'Yes, it is. And that is what I would like.'

'Okay.'

'I also don't want a religious service. A nice one where people speak that actually knew me would be ideal, but failing that, no priest. I know it will annoy my mother, but I don't really care what she thinks.'

'No priest.'

'That's right.'

'Anything else?'

'Probably, but I don't think that I can think of anything else at the moment. I'm too tired.'

'You know you're going to be okay, don't you?'

'So you keep telling me.'

'I will let you sleep. We can always talk again later.'

Daniel didn't really want to talk about it again, but he could understand that Claire had a desire to set these things right in her head. It didn't make for easy listening.

I hate hospitals. I've never spent any time in one, not since I was born at any rate, and I can hardly be blamed if I don't remember that at all. Who does? There is just something about hospitals. They are so clinical and impersonal. No matter where you are, the hospitals all seem to be the same. It's like they are all built to the same design and they all have the same chemical smell about them. Maybe it is used to mask the smell of death. A lot of people must die in hospital. I wonder what the ratio is to those that make it out the doors. You'd like to think that more people walk out of hospital than are wheeled out, but I'm really not sure. I hated seeing my mother in hospital. She seemed to be so weak, so vulnerable. So unlike herself. She was a strong woman and she had been reduced to this frail person lying in a bed with doctors and nurses buzzing around her, trying to make her comfortable. I think I made a resolution, then and there, that I would only go into hospital if it was absolutely necessary. If I could avoid going into the place then I would. It is probably from this point that I developed my dislike to all things medical. I can't even watch medical dramas. They just don't do it for me.

Now

There was a stigma attached to cancer. It really shouldn't have been like that in the twenty-first century, but that's how it was. People didn't like talking about it. They didn't like mentioning the "C word" if they could get away with it. It was like if they didn't mention it then there was some protection from it. People didn't like talking about it because they knew that there was too much of a possibility of them getting it themselves. It was a superstition that many people clung to, despite living in such enlightened times. You just didn't mention cancer and then you could hope that it wasn't there. That it wouldn't impact on you.

The truth was that almost everyone would either get cancer at some point in their lives, or they would know someone who had cancer. It was inevitable. It was such a promiscuous disease that it was prepared to spread itself wherever it could. It had no care for social status or age, gender or sexuality, race or religion. It didn't care who you were. You were all targets. That was the fear that so many people had. There was no protection from the disease. It didn't matter how much money you had. Money couldn't buy your way out of it. There was the Jewish saying that "if the rich could hire people to die for them, then the poor would make a good living."

People were prepared to use all sorts of euphemisms rather than saying the word. People had "a long illness" or were just ill or sick. Doctors wouldn't even use the word when they were diagnosing you or sending you for tests. They talked about tumours or growths. They talked about cells or words like that. They wouldn't directly come out and say that they were talking about cancer. Perhaps they felt that if they used the word then it would send their patients into a panic.

It was all too much for some people. They couldn't cope with it. They liked to fool themselves into believing that everything would be okay. You might be able to survive a tumour, but it wasn't so easy to survive cancer. A tumour was something that was less aggressive. You could have it cut out and that would be the end of the matter. Cancer was something that would aggressively take over your body and mean that there was no surgery that could be performed that would make you better. That's what people thought.

Now that Claire was dead, it didn't make it any easier to talk about it, if anything it made it worse. The simple fact was that people were afraid. They were afraid because they might get it, and they were afraid that someone like Claire, who had been young, fit and otherwise healthy, had died from the disease. If she died, what hope did everyone else have for the disease if they were to get it?

'What I really hate is the personification,' Daniel told Jordan. They had met up for coffee, which was something that was rare because Daniel had taken to not leaving the house if he could help it.

'How do you mean?'

'Well, all this talking about doing battles with cancer as if it is a person. It's incredibly insulting to talk like that.'

'How so?'

'To say that someone has won the fight or battle against cancer suggests that those, like Claire, who lose that battle are in some way losers.'

'I suppose they would argue that they are losers because they have lost their lives.'

'In a literal sense, that may be true, but it is incredibly insulting to suggest that someone who has struggled so much against the disease should be considered a loser, as if they hadn't put enough effort into the fight.'

'I see your point.'

'I just find it very insulting.'

'What words should we use instead of battle or fight then?'

'I don't know. Do we have to use any words to replace it at all? Just stop saying things like "lost her fight against cancer" and the like. Is it enough to just say that they have died without turning it into some mock battle against an adversary?'

'I suppose because that is the way that it is seen. Cancer is seen as invading the body, so it's only natural that people will use war analogies to talk about it. You invade then you are battled against.'

'I just don't like to think of Claire, or others like her, as losers. There was nothing of the loser about Claire.'

'No, there wasn't.'

Cancer was a self-destructive, suicidal disease. It grew and took over the body until the body could take no more and died, at which point the cancer would die as well. It killed the thing that it needed to live on. It was rather stupid in that regard. It was like many terminal diseases. Only it wasn't terminal for everyone.

Claire had never asked why it was that she had got cancer instead of someone else. She never asked why it was that she, who had never touched a cigarette in her life, had lung cancer while someone who smoked two packets a day was walking around fine. She never asked why it was that she was going to die so young when so many others lived to be so old. She never asked these questions.

Daniel did. Daniel was always asking why it was that Claire had been struck down with this horrible disease while there were so many hateful, spiteful and evil people that were allowed to wander around free, spreading their venom into the world. He was thinking primarily of politicians at this point. He didn't understand why his beautiful wife should be afflicted while everyone else was going about their business as if nothing important was happening.

Daniel's world had come crashing down. It had not been a quick, devastating revolution, but had been more of an evolution. It had started when Claire had first become sick, and then it had spread slowly as she had gone through the various treatments. It had taken a further blow when it had become obvious that the treatments were not going to work. It had become even worse when it had dawned on him that she was going to die. Then there had been the slow process while she had been dying. Slowly. Wasting away a bit at a time. Until there was nothing left. And it was when she died that the entire edifice had finally collapsed on top of him, and his world had finally crashed to the ground.

It was difficult to explain to someone who was not in a similar position. Yes, they could empathise with you, but could they ever really truly understand unless they had been through the same thing? Daniel thought not. To others he would probably seem to be self-indulgent in his grief. Yes, his wife had died, but nothing was to be gained by keeping on about it. He needed to move on. He still had his entire life ahead of him. He still had Toby to look after and care for. There was still much that was positive about his life. He had a wonderful son. A comfortable home. No debts. A steady income. He was a bestselling author.

Some people would kill to have been in his shoes. Okay, it was sad that he had lost his wife, but it was not the end of the world.

Daniel didn't really have anything to say to people who thought like this. He didn't have the energy required to put them on the right track and explain to them how he was feeling. Yes, he might seem to be overdoing the mourning process, but that was because they had never lost someone that they were so close to. It was easy to be superior when you had no common frame of reference. And yet, Daniel hoped that they never would understand. He wouldn't have wished his best enemy to be in the position that he was in right now.

The thing was that when you started a relationship you always knew that it was going to end one day. It might be that you fell out of love with each other and no longer wanted to be together. It might be that you realised that you were not meant to be together. It might have even just fizzled out. It might have done any of these things and a thousand more. Even if it didn't do that though, even if you were deeply in love and perfect together, there was going to come a day when one or the other of you was going to die. And then the relationship would come to an end. It was inevitable. There was no way that you could get around it.

Every relationship that you entered into would end in loss. Either because you were dumped for someone else or because the love of your life had died. There was always the possibility that you would be the person to die first, but then you would be the one that caused the other the pain and suffering of loss. There was always the possibility that you would both go at the same time, but although this would spare one of you the feeling of loss, it would still put an end to the relationship.

There were people that were fully aware of the fact that

relationships carried the possibility of so much pain, and so made a determined effort to avoid having a relationship at all. They preferred to go through life avoiding the relationship so that they didn't have to live with the pain and suffering that they had a fifty percent chance of happening to them. They would tell you that they were happy and content with this. But they had missed the point.

Yes, relationships would end in pain and suffering for one of you, but that was the condition that came with the happiness that relationships would bring. Daniel understood this. He knew that he had to shoulder the pain because of the years of happiness that he had shared with Claire. What he found difficult to get his head around was the fact that his life with Claire had been so short. He felt cheated. Why did she have to die so early? They still had a good forty or so years left in them and now she was gone. He could have handled the pain if he had been able to make it last for another forty years.

'I don't understand why she had to die so young,' Daniel told Jordan. 'Why couldn't she have died when we were both in our eighties?'

'You wouldn't have found it any easier then. If anything, you would probably have found it even worse after being together for so long.'

'Maybe, but we would have had our entire lives together. We would have lived to a decent age and there would have been less cause for complaint. I don't understand why she had to go so early.'

'I'll tell you something that a wise man once said to me. Maybe it will help,' said Jordan, shifting the coffee around the table. 'You have to think of life as being like an airport departure lounge.'

'Okay, sounds strange.'

'Bear with me. So, we all enter this departure lounge and we don't know anyone, but as we spend time there, we get talking with the other people that are there and we make friends and get closer to people. And then the flights are called. Now, some people have been waiting there a very long time before their flights are called, whereas others have arrived only recently and are called away straight away, but it doesn't matter because everyone is at the airport to catch a flight to go to a better place.'

Daniel was silent for a moment. 'And you believe that?'

'It's a way of looking at things and making sense of this life and the way that we live and die.'

'Do you really believe that we are going to a better place?'

'That's what the wise man said. We are all on our way to a better place. We are just waiting to get there.'

'I wish I could believe that.'

'Does it bring you comfort to believe that Claire has gone to a better place? That she still continues to exist in some way or another? Or would you prefer to believe that she's gone? That that's it, no more.'

'Naturally I would prefer to believe that things have continued with her. I can't imagine her not existing.'

'And that's why religion has such a strong appeal for so many people. It gives us hope that there is something else out there. That this is not the end of it all. That this is just the departure lounge and we will all eventually catch a flight to somewhere else.'

'I suppose you're right.'

'I'm not a religious man, myself, as you well know, but I would like to think that there is something else to this life – that this isn't the end for us.'

'What if it is though? What if this is all that there is? What if we have one shot at life and we are wasting it away with… coffee.'

'There's nothing wrong with coffee.'

'Stephen Sondheim said that the only things that were worth leaving behind you when you died were children and art.'

'You are lucky, therefore, that you are able to leave behind both.'

'I suppose so. At least in Toby, Claire is able to live on, even if she doesn't live on in any other way.'

'I don't believe that you think she has fallen into nothingness. I think you believe that she is still out there somehow.'

'Well, if she was then I wish she could find some way of telling me so.'

'You mean come back as a ghost or something?'

'I don't believe in ghosts.'

'There are plenty of sightings of ghosts by people. England is allegedly one of the most haunted countries on the planet. More sightings of ghosts here than anywhere else.'

'Wishful thinking. I think there are three explanations for ghosts.'

'Go on.'

'Firstly, it is wishful thinking by those that are in mourning. They want, like me, to believe that their loved ones are still out there somewhere. This grief means that they manifest this belief in seeing something that is no more than an hallucination.'

'Reasonable I suppose.'

'The second is that these sightings are just seen by people that are suffering from some kind of mental illness and believe that they are seeing things that are not there. These are the same people that believe that God is talking to them or that they are Napoleon or Jesus.'

'Okay.'

'The last explanation is a scientific theory that is of my own invention.'

'And what is that?'

'That what people are seeing are echoes of the past.'

'How so?'

'Imagine that instead of being linear, time is actually something that is like a ball of string, all crossing over each other and in a bundle.'

'Okay.'

'At some points the timelines cross. It's possible for there to be a worn area here and there, and what we see are echoes from another time. We see things from the past. Roman soldiers, monks, grey ladies. None of them aware that we are there as they are just enacting in their own time streams and are unaware of the fact that they are rubbing off into our time. That's why you see people walking through walls where there were once doorways. Why it is that you see people in old monasteries and old houses. You don't tend to see ghosts in modern houses.'

'It's a plausible explanation I suppose.'

'We could be rubbing off into some future time as we speak. We could be sitting here drinking our coffee, and in the future we are scaring the shit out of someone who sees two ghostly figures sitting at a table that is no longer there, in a coffee shop that has long since been turned into something else.'

'It's an interesting theory.'

'I'm a writer. I sometimes have too much time on my hands to think about things.'

'That much would appear to be true. Of course, the fourth

theory is that they are evidence of an afterlife.'

'There is that, I grant you.'

'You seem very resistant to the idea.'

'I just struggle with it all. Probably because the concept of an afterlife is so entwined with that of religion, and I have trouble following any religion. No matter what the religion, they all seem to be filled with hypocrisy and greed.'

'I can understand that point of view.'

'If you can separate the two then I might have more ease in believing that there is life after death.'

'I've read a lot about near-death experiences, and I don't believe that they have all that much to do with religion,' said Jordan.

'You've read a lot about near-death experiences?'

'Yes, I find it fascinating.'

'I've never really come across them all that much.'

'You should dig into them. They are quite fascinating and all paint a very similar picture of what it is like after you die.'

'But these people, by necessity, don't actually die. They come back. In theory, therefore, they have not actually died.'

'It rather depends on your definition of what it means to die.'

'I suppose if your heart stops beating,' said Daniel, sipping his coffee.

'Then that would be the definition that most people that have had near-death experiences have.'

'I'm a sceptic.'

'Of course you are. You're a writer. It's necessary to be like that in order to work.'

Daniel wanted to believe. He wanted to believe in an afterlife. He wanted to believe in aliens. He wanted to believe in the decency of mankind. He wanted to believe in Santa Claus.

Wanting to believe though, didn't make it happen. It didn't make it any more likely that it was true either.

It had been a month since Claire had died. Christmas was a distant memory that had been swallowed up by the coldness of January and it was a bitter January. The memory of Claire's death had not been swallowed up though. It still bit as sharply as the wind did. Daniel tried not to go out if he could help it. He would spend as much of his time indoors as he could. This was not an unusual activity for a writer. They were, by nature, secluded creatures that kept strange hours. He had always dealt with his publisher by email and if he really had to, by telephone, rather than actually having to go and see them. He now needed no further excuse to go out and see anyone. If he could help it he would arrange to see Jordan at his own house. Jordan did still try and get him to go out though, as if he was well aware of the fact that Daniel was trying to hide more deeply in his own home. Toby was old enough to be able to make his own way to school, so he didn't have to worry about that. As a matter of fact, Toby would have probably been horrified if his dad had tried to pick him up or drop him off from school. It just wasn't the done thing.

His seclusion led him to thinking about writing again. He knew that he didn't need to, but it was something that he had always done. He was fortunate enough to not have to do it for the money now, although when he told strangers that he was a writer, they still asked him what he actually did for a living. It was like it was impossible for someone to do something for a living that most other people just saw as a hobby.

He picked up his copy of *The Return of the Native* and leafed through the pages. He was still trying to work his way through Hardy. He was on the whole enjoying it. He found him to be a fascinating writer, even if he was rather obsessed with the concept of unrequited love (which was a major theme that ran through all of his novels).

He thought about having a read. He hadn't been able to concentrate on reading for some weeks now. Every time he tried to settle down and immerse himself within the pages of a book, he would find that his thoughts would stray elsewhere. He looked over to Claire's chair where the copy of *Barnaby Rudge* was still sat there where she had left off reading it, never to pick it up again. He supposed that he should think about putting it back on its place on the bookshelf, but that would somehow be giving in to the fact that Claire wasn't coming back, even though she clearly wasn't.

He had opened the wardrobe and looked at all her clothes that were in there. He supposed that he should really think about sorting them out and giving them to charity. There was no point in keeping hold of them now and some good should really come of it. The problem was the same as *Barnaby Rudge* though. Getting rid of the clothes would be like admitting to the reality of the situation that he was in. Could he really bring himself to get rid of all of Claire's things? Keeping hold of them wouldn't do any good, but he liked the reminders of her that were about the place. He liked the smell of her on her clothes. He liked the reminders around the house that she had lived there. He could almost fool himself into thinking that she had just gone out to work and would be back soon.

'You have to face up to the fact that she isn't coming back,' Jordan said when he came around one day and had seen the way that Daniel stared wistfully at *Barnaby Rudge* and her chair.

'I know that, of course I know that.'

'Only it doesn't seem to me that you do. It's been over a

month since she died and you are still holding onto things like a shrine.'

'It's too soon to think about getting rid of her stuff just yet.'

'Is it? When is it the right time to do it? You will never admit that there is a right time. You just have to grab the bull by the horns and get on with it.'

'I'm not sure that I'm ready to do that yet.'

'My point is that you will never be ready for it. You just have to do it. If it helps then I will happily help you with it.'

'Happily?'

'You know what I mean. I am happy to help, not that I'm happy we are getting rid of her stuff.'

'I appreciate the offer, but I don't think now is the time.'

'Well, the offer stands for when it is time to do it. When you feel it is right.'

Daniel spent a lot of time going to the graveyard. It was really the only time that he went out. He was able to order most of his groceries online and get them delivered because he couldn't face the hassle of going to the supermarket. He went to the graveyard and sat by Claire's grave almost every day. It was the one activity that he had.

He would sit there and talk to her. Tell her about the things that he had been doing, which wasn't really all that much. He would talk to her about the things that he was reading and the things that he was thinking about writing about, even though most of it was made up because he was not thinking about writing and was not reading all that much. He had always talked to her about these things, and it seemed only natural to continue to talk about them now.

He knew that it was illogical to go to the graveyard to talk to her. He knew that she wasn't there any longer. It was just her

192

earthly remains that were there. She was either completely gone or her spirit (or whatever you wanted to call it) was elsewhere. If he believed that her spirit was elsewhere then he knew that he could talk to her anywhere and she would be able to hear him. Possibly. He did talk to her anywhere. He talked to her all the time. He tried to do it when Toby was not around in case he thought that his dad was going insane with grief.

He came to the graveyard, not because of the fact that he thought it was the only place that he could talk to Claire, not because he thought that she was still there, but because of the fact that this was the last place that he had had any physical contact with her. She was there in the grave, or what was left of her was there. He didn't like to think about the decomposition that was going on, although he knew that it was. He knew that there would soon be nothing left of her but bones. He didn't like to think about it. He preferred to think of her lying there in some eternal, graceful and beautiful sleep, like Snow White. Only there was nothing that he could do to wake her from it.

He went there every day, no matter what the weather was like, he didn't feel the frost on his hands or the biting wind that whistled through the barren trees. He would come and he would spend a couple of hours there, sometimes more. He saw other funerals take place and got to know some of the regular mourners that appeared from time to time. He was a familiar figure in the graveyard.

He knew that he should be writing. He knew that he really should, but the motivation was just not there at the moment. He needed something to kick-start his imagination. Something that would get him back into the writing business and inspire him to hammer away at his keyboard for several hours a day. He didn't have that at the moment. He thought that maybe he should take up something of Jordan's suggestion and write about Claire. That felt a bit too personal. Maybe he could turn it into a novel about grief and loss. But then Jordan had said that he didn't need to publish it, he just had to write it. Something that would occupy his mind and get him away from the sadness that engulfed him all day long. He was still resistant of going to the doctor, no matter how much they assured him that anti-depressants really did work.

'I thought I might find you here.'

Daniel looked up and saw Jordan standing above him.

'You seem to be doing an impression of some Greek tragic hero, throwing yourself on the grave of the martyred,' said Jordan, sniffing away the cold.

'I'm always here.'

'I thought that might be the case. I called at the house, but got no reply. Where's Toby?'

'Football practice.'

'Well, at least one of you is going about a normal life.'

'What's that supposed to mean?'

'It means that you have had your life on hold for the last six weeks since Claire died.'

'As you say, it's only been six weeks. That isn't all that long really when you think about it.'

'Maybe not, but you can't allow it to get into a habit.'

'How long do you think you would mourn if Natalie died?'

'The rest of my life, but I wouldn't allow it to stop me from getting on with things.'

'You're clearly a better man than I am.'

'I don't know about that. I just don't want to see you consumed by this until there is nothing left.'

'Your concern is noted.'

'Thank you.'

'As it happens I have been thinking about how I move on from here.'

'Have you?'

'Yes, I have.'

'And what are your conclusions?'

'That maybe you're right. Maybe it's time to move on with things.'

'It doesn't look too much like you are moving on with things when you are sitting next to a grave all day long. In this weather you will get piles.'

'I come here because I want to talk to her, is that so strange?'

'Not strange at all, but you can talk to her anywhere.'

'Yes, I can, and I do. But this seems to be a good way of paying respects to her. I've been thinking about what sort of tombstone to get her.'

'I'm sure you will make it a good one.'

'I can't think for the minute what to write on it. How good is that? Me, a writer and I can't find the right words. Words are supposed to be my business.'

'They will come to you. They always do.'

'They always have done, but that doesn't mean that they always will. She was my muse, you know. What if having lost her I'm never able to find the right words again?'

'You will.'

'How can you be so sure?'

'Because I have faith in you. You will recover and you will get your talent back.'

'I've never really considered it all that much of a talent before.'

'I can't see why not. It's something that you are good at and something that you will be good at again. You just have to give it a try.'

'Maybe you are right. You are certainly right about one thing.'

'What's that?'

'It's time to sort out her things.'

My best friend is a guy called David. David's parents are divorced and he lives with his dad, like me, but he lives with his dad because his mum is an alcoholic and the court decided that she wasn't responsible enough to be able to look after him. David said that his situation was a lot like mine, but it really isn't. He can still see his mum whenever he wants to. She might be an alcoholic and she might forget about him a lot and not always want him around, but she is still there. They can still get together. I will never have that again. I will never be able to see my mum again. I don't know if I believe in an afterlife. Mum was a lapsed Catholic and dad is an atheistic Jew who is partial to the odd bacon sandwich. I was never really raised with any form of religion. I'm sure my grandmother would have liked to have had me raised as a good Catholic, but I frankly have a problem with organised religion. Dad goes to the graveyard a lot. He probably thinks that I don't notice, but I do. I'm not sure what he is hoping to achieve. I don't go there nearly as much. I can't see the point. There are only remains there. It's not mum. If there is anything left of mum, in the sense of something still continues, then it is not to be found at the graveyard. The problem is that I don't know where it is to be found.

Then

Claire's radiotherapy had started and seemed to be going well.

'You may notice,' said the doctor, 'that you lose your appetite and certain foods that you used to love you can't stomach any longer. It's just a side effect of the radiotherapy. You should settle down after a while.'

'How long?' she asked.

'Difficult to say,' he said, spreading his hands. 'Different effects for different people.'

'Will there be any other side effects?' asked Daniel.

'Yes,' the doctor replied. 'Not all people are effected with them though you understand.'

'I understand,' said Claire. 'What are they?'

'You may experience sore skin. If you do, there are various things that we recommend. Washing your skin with unperfumed soap is the first thing we suggest.'

'Okay.'

'We also recommend that you pat your skin dry, rather than rubbing it. You could also wear loose fitting clothes and avoid things like tight collars and shoulder straps. You may find that this helps.'

'Anything else?'

'You may find that you are very tired, in which case you should get plenty of rest. Avoid doing any activities that you don't feel up to. Perhaps get some mild exercise. Just don't push yourself too hard. Are you working?'

'Yes.'

'You may wish to ask your employer for some time off, or maybe let you work part time until your treatment is finished. It will be easier for you to deal with that way.'

'I've already thought about that, and they are fine with me going sick for the length of treatment and any time that I need off after it.'

'That's good.'

'Will I lose my hair, Doctor?'

'You might do, although that is more commonly felt with chemotherapy. Unlike chemo though, radiotherapy only causes hair loss in the area that is being treated. In your case, I don't believe that will present you with a problem.'

'No.'

'You may experience sickness though, particularly as the area that is being treated is so close to your stomach. We can provide you with anti-sickness tablets if this is the case. They should help you.'

'Sounds like there are a few side effects then,' said Daniel.

'Yes, there are. There are more. This leaflet will tell you the other side effects that are most likely. Naturally, if you have any questions, then don't hesitate to get back to me, or contact someone on the care team.'

'Thank you,' said Claire. 'Naturally the benefit of having the therapy outweighs the potential side effects.'

'Yes, it does, most certainly. Radiotherapy is considered the most effective cancer treatment after surgery, as in your case, but how well it works is something that is dependent on each individual person.'

Claire commenced the therapy. She found it mildly amusing that radiation was something that could cause cancer, and here she was being bombarded with radiation to kill the cancer that was within her. There was an irony there somewhere. She had done her research and knew that this was adjuvant radiotherapy. In other words, it was therapy that was being used after surgery to try and reduce the risk of the cancer coming back. She had been hoping that it might have been curative therapy that would cure her of the cancer completely. It might well do, but if that had been the case, then she wouldn't have needed to have the surgery. The worst kind of therapy was palliative, which was used to relieve the symptoms of cancer, when there was no actual cure for it. She didn't want to be going down that road, if she could at all help it.

There were three types of radiotherapy that were used. The first was that given by a machine, which was used to carefully aim beams of radiation at the cancer, or area where the cancer was. The second was where they implanted small bits of radioactive metal temporarily into your body near the cancer. She had not heard of this particular therapy before. The last was where you were given injections, capsules or a drink that was radioactive and was swallowed or injected into your blood. She was having the first treatment.

Claire had some very small ink tattoo dots on her skin so that they could be sure that they would always aim at the same area each time. It would be less effective if they kept changing the area each time that she had the therapy.

'I always wanted to get a tattoo,' Claire joked.

Daniel didn't really see the funny side of it and was rather amazed by the fact that she could continue to joke while all of this was going on. He supposed that if she was able to see the funny side of things, then he should really be able to see it as well, but this was his wife that we were talking about, and he couldn't face the possibility that this might not work, and he would lose her.

It was determined that she should have one treatment a day, five days a week, Monday to Friday, with the weekend to rest up, for the following four weeks. She knew that this was something that was going to be a great strain on her, and also a strain on Daniel. She knew that he wasn't really coping with this all that well. Yes, he kept it to himself, but she knew him well enough to be able to read the signs and knew that this was something that he was having a great amount of trouble with. She knew that he probably wished that it was something that he could take on himself, so that she didn't have to go through it. That wasn't possible, of course, this was the way that the cards had been dealt.

She lay down on the table and the machine was used to direct the radiation at her, while it was operated by people that were in another room, who watched her through the window.

'There's an intercom here,' said the nurse, 'should you need to talk to us, or should we need to talk to you.'

'Okay.'

'You need to keep as still as possible throughout the treatment. It will only take a few minutes and will be completely painless. You will be able to go home as soon as it is finished.'

'I thought that there might be some recovery time needed.'

'Not usually.'

The doctor had not sugar-coated it for her. He had made it clear that it was not a nice procedure to go through, and there were people who decided that the side effects outweighed the benefits of the therapy. Their quality of life had been so knocked by the treatment. These people often wanted to withdraw from the treatment.

'If this happens to you,' the doctor had said, 'then I advise you to contact us immediately so we can talk through all of this.'

'Don't worry,' she had replied. 'No matter how bad the side effects may be, I know that the alternative is probably far worse. I will just have to grin and bear it.'

'I think you are being very brave,' Daniel told her when they were two weeks into the therapy.

'What's the alternative?' she had replied. 'I'm half way through the therapy now. It won't be long until it's over.'

'Hopefully you will feel better when it is all finished.'

Claire had lost her appetite, as the doctor had predicted and was feeling very tired, but those were the only side effects that she had really noticed with the therapy at this mid-point. She knew that there was still time for other symptoms to present themselves though. She was just grinning and making the best of it. There really wasn't all that much of an alternative, not if you wanted a fair crack at getting rid of the cancer.

She could understand those that hated the therapy though. These were usually the people that had resigned themselves to the fact that the cancer was terminal, either because they had convinced themselves that this was the case, or because the doctors had told them that there was really no hope. She could understand why these people would not want to have a poorer quality of life for the rest of the time that was left to them. If there was no hope of a recovery, then you probably just wanted to spend the rest of your days as comfortable as possible. What was the point of having more days if you just felt shit about them? Sometimes, you just had to cut your losses.

Claire wasn't in that position. At least not at the moment, she told herself. Perhaps she would never be in that position. Perhaps the treatment would work and she would become cancer free. She didn't really know. It was early days as far as these things went.

She was lucky in the fact that it had been caught early. If it had been allowed to fester longer then who knows what might have happened.

'I'm really very proud of you, you know,' Daniel told Claire.

'Proud of me for getting cancer?'

'That's not what I meant, and you know it.'

'What did you mean?'

'Proud of you for putting up with all of this so bravely.'

'It's not like I have much of a choice. Not if I want to stay alive, at any rate.'

'You are doing marvellously well. I doubt that I could put up with things the way that you are.'

'You hate hospitals, that's why.'

'Well, everyone hates hospitals. I can't see that there is all that much to like about them.'

'I'm sure they appeal to some people.'

'Hypochondriacs, maybe.'

'Maybe. We have to think about what will happen if the radiotherapy doesn't work.'

'I suppose that will mean chemotherapy then,' said Daniel.

'My understanding is that chemo is used if the cancer has spread.'

'If the radiotherapy doesn't work then the cancer might spread. We have to put our faith in it and hope that it manages to zap the remaining cells that are there.'

'Zap?'

'Technical term.'

'Sounds it.'

It had been a long day and Daniel and Claire were sitting down in the living room discussing the first round of radiotherapy that

Claire had just undertaken. It was too early for her to really feel any of the side effects that she anticipated she would soon feel. It seemed only natural to her that she would feel them. It didn't seem possible that she would be able to go through four weeks of radiotherapy without feeling some kind of side effect.

'Only four weeks to go,' she said as she sipped on her tea.

'Less than four weeks now that you have started.'

'I look forward to when it is all over, and hopefully things will return to normal. If there will ever be such a thing as normal again.'

'I'm sure that there will be a normal again. Try not to worry too much about it.'

'How is the new book coming along?'

'It's on hold at the moment. The important thing is to get you sorted out first.'

'Well, don't leave it too long. You can't be a writer that doesn't write. It's not in your nature. You have to write. It's what you are born to do.'

'There will be time to sort all of that out later. Plenty of time to be had with writing once you are settled again.'

'I look forward to being settled. All of this is a terrible inconvenience.'

'Interesting way of describing having cancer.'

'Well it is. I can't work. I feel rough. I want to feel like I can get on with my life. That is the worst thing about cancer. It disrupts your life and takes things over in the same way that it takes over your body.'

'I can't imagine.'

'Hopefully you never will have to imagine. It's bad enough that one of us has got this without two of us going down with it.'

'You make it sound like you have got the flu. It's hardly

contagious.'

'Well, I don't know what words there are to describe this without sounding fatalistic. I don't want to give it the level of importance that it is trying to demand from me.'

Claire refused to give in to the illness. As treatment progressed, she began to feel some of the side effects. She felt the tingling of the skin and would often feel sick while the rays were bombarding her body, but this did not fortunately last for all that long afterwards. She became even more tired than she had been before and she lost most of her appetite. Food that had been appetising before she started treatment no longer held any appeal to her. She ate basic foods that were not extravagant in taste. She didn't feel that she had the energy to eat anything more exciting.

Throughout it all though she continued with grim determination. She knew that it was something that she had to get through. She had to get through it if she wanted to be well again. She felt as if the treatment was making her feel more ill than the disease had in the first place, but she knew that it was necessary. It was something that had to be endured. Four weeks seemed like a long time when you were having your body bombarded with radiation five days out of seven. She knew that in reality it wasn't all that long a time and she would be through it before she knew it. She just had to surrender to what the doctors had said that she had to do.

Some, no doubt well-meaning, but misguided friends told her that she should consider alternative medicine instead of what the doctors were telling her to do. They said that it wasn't natural to be zapped with radiation and she would be better off seeking more homeopathic medical assistance.

She was always polite to these people, but declined their advice. She had put her faith in doctors because she had to believe that they knew what they were doing. Taking some strange homeopathic medicine was likely to cause her more harm than good. She had to fight this in the approved manner. She couldn't run the risk that if she declined treatment and surrendered to some strange oil, or something, that the disease would be stopped. It was more likely that she would die if she turned away from accepted medical thought.

It was all very well her friends suggesting that she seek alternative medicine, but they were not the ones that had this disease. They were not the ones that were facing death if it was not treated correctly. She had to go with what she knew. It was the only way.

Claire was perhaps fortunate that her treatment was first thing in the morning on each day that she had it.

'It gets it out of the way,' she told Daniel.

She didn't particularly like the idea of having to wait around all day for the treatment to take place. She would have the treatment and they would return from the hospital to have a lay down and rest from the radiotherapy. Daniel would try and write while she was doing this. He was finding it rather difficult to concentrate on the writing though when he had so many other things on his mind. He was very concerned for Claire and everything that she was going through.

He tried to put on a brave face for her, but he was deeply worried about her and the situation that they were in. It was his greatest fear that she would die from this and leave him alone. He wasn't sure how he would be able to cope with that, were it to happen. It was something that he dreaded and something that kept him awake at night. He tried not to let the worry show though. He didn't want to worry her about how worried he was.

He was sure that she was in the same boat and was just as

worried, but was keeping how worried she was from him so that he wouldn't get worried. This is what being married was all about. Hiding your worry from your partner so that they wouldn't get worried themselves. It was rather futile really. They should have just owned up to each other about how worried they were. They might then have been able to find some common ground for dealing with the worry and getting through it.

Daniel tried to write. It wasn't easy. The words didn't want to come. It was no sense being a writer that couldn't write. He was too busy worrying all of the time to be able to bring the right levels of concentration to writing. Writing required a lot of effort and he just didn't have it in him at the moment. He told himself that he had time enough to worry about writing when all of this was over. When the radiotherapy had been successful and they were able to return to normality.

Before too long the radiotherapy sessions were drawing towards an end. It had been a hard month to get through, but they had finally got there.

'The good news,' the doctor said, 'is that the radiotherapy appears to have been successful in treating the surrounding area from where the cancer was cut out from you. There doesn't appear to be any cancer cells left.'

'And the bad news?' asked Claire.

The doctor looked up at her. 'No bad news. All good news. We seem to have nipped this in the bud before it has had the chance to spread and cause further damage.'

'Can you be certain of that?' asked Daniel.

'Well, to be honest there are no certainties in cases such as this. We have done the best that we can in getting rid of the cancer and it seems that it has worked. Now, cancer is a stubborn disease, and it is possible that it may flare up in the future and return. There isn't all that much that can be done about that at the moment other than to wait and see if there is a return, but we can be hopeful that there won't be one.'

It didn't sound as hopeful as Daniel would have liked it to have been. He wanted the news that the cancer had been destroyed and there was no chance that it was coming back. There was a school of thought though that once you had cancer, the chance of it returning was high. You were only in remission at the moment. There would come a time when there was a danger that it could return at any point. It was, as the doctor had suggested, a stubborn disease. It was used to everything that you could throw at it. Daniel wondered if there would come a time when it was ever beaten completely.

'There is a rumour,' said Jordan to Daniel, 'that they developed a cure for cancer years ago, but that they are making too much money from drugs to beat it to be able to issue it.'

'Sounds like a bit of a conspiracy theory to me,' replied Daniel. 'I am sure I heard the same thing about them developing a cure for the common cold, but the pharmaceutical companies were making too much money in cold remedies.'

'Could easily be true.'

'I'm not sure that it is. I think some people, you included, just like a good conspiracy theory.'

'Talking of which, did I ever tell you my thoughts on JFK?'

Daniel didn't really want to hear Jordan's thoughts on JFK. He had had enough of conspiracy theories. Maybe he could have written a novel about them if he had felt so inclined.

'All seems to be good news then,' Claire told him one evening when they were settling down in front of the fire to read their books.

'I think it's very positive. I think you've done remarkably well.'

'I should be able to return to work soon then.'

'There's no rush.'

'I know, but I would really like to get back to things. Try and get a sense of normality. We have been living with this thing long enough now and it is something that I really would like to put behind me and get on with life.'

'I can understand that.'

'So, I'll be returning to work as soon as I feel strong enough.'

'How's your appetite?'

'Still hasn't recovered fully.' This was true. Foods that had previously been a favourite of Claire's were now difficult to stomach. She found this to be really annoying.

'Give it time. I'm sure it will recover at some stage.'

'Well, they did warn that it was likely to take some time before such things returned to normal. Once I have my energy back though, I want to return to work.'

'I get that. Maybe you could start off part-time, or something, to begin with?'

'That isn't a bad idea. Would be a good way of easing myself back into things. What about you?'

'What about me?'

'Are you going to start writing again? I know that you haven't been writing while all this has been going on.'

'I suppose so. I just haven't had much of an inclination to do it recently.'

'You have to get back into it, just as I have to get back into my work. We have to get back to normal.'

'What's normal?'

'Normal is what was happening to us before this cancer

reared its head and made itself known to us. We can start to put that behind us now and get on with things.'

'I hope so.'

'I see no reason why not.'

'Toby has taken it all rather hard.'

'He is still young. It's all very confusing to him. He probably doesn't understand half of the things that have been going on. We should probably have spent more time answering any questions that he had and putting him in the picture.'

'I suppose we had other things on our mind.'

'Very neglectful of us as parents though,' she said.

'We will make more of an effort with him in the future. This was just something that was so unexpected. We weren't prepared to deal with this kind of thing. Not this early on in our lives.'

'I don't think we would have been any better prepared if it had happened twenty years from now.'

'No, probably not.'

That was the thing about cancer, you just weren't prepared for it. Statistically you know that there was a fair chance that you would either get cancer yourself, or someone close to you would get cancer, at some point in your life. The odds were in favour of it, but you just didn't think that it was something that was going to happen to you. Despite the statistics, you always thought that it was going to be something that was going to happen to someone else rather than to you. It was a survival instinct that made you think that it couldn't happen to you.

That's why people smoked. They knew the dangers that they were exposing themselves to, but they always thought that it was something that would happen to someone else. They talked about the fact that there were people out there who smoked two packets of cigarettes a day and still lived into their nineties. They talked about the concept of a cancer gene, and if you were going to get cancer then you were going to get cancer, regardless of whether you smoked or not. They justified it to themselves in any way that they could. Always prepared to say that it wouldn't be them that got cancer or heart disease as a result of their smoking habits, and each time they lit a cigarette they ran the gauntlet with this merciless disease.

Things returned to the normal that Claire and Daniel so much desired. Starting slowly at first, Claire returned to work and was soon back up to full hours and was working as she had been before she had heard the word 'cancer' uttered in the same breath as her name.

Daniel returned to his writing and was able to reasonably pick up from where he had left off and finish the book that he had been working on before all of this happened. Jordan thought that he should consider writing a book about the cancer experience, but Daniel thought that this was something that was just too personal for him to engage with. Some of his writing had been personal in the past, this was true, but he had always managed to maintain a distance and a wall between his private life and his professional life. He hoped that it would be something that he would be able to maintain.

And so life continued as if the cancer was something that hadn't happened, or as if it was something that had happened to someone else. They both got on with their lives and tried to put the entire affair behind them.

Claire was required to go to the hospital for regular check-ups. These were firstly weekly events and then they could be moved to monthly and then six monthly and finally yearly, assuming that everything was going to be okay on each of the checks that she went through. Once the final hurdle was complete then there would be no need to see her again. She would be cancer free.

That was the plan at least. As it turned out things were not going to be as simple as that.

'I'm afraid that the cancer is back,' said the doctor on one of the check-ups.

'Back?' Daniel asked as if it was the most difficult proposition that he had ever heard.

'Yes, I'm afraid so.'

'So, what do we do now?' asked Claire. 'More radiotherapy?'

'I'm afraid that radiotherapy won't do any good at this stage. The cancer had returned with a vengeance and has spread throughout the body. It was always a possibility that this would happen, you understand? The only thing that we can try at the moment is a dose of chemotherapy and hope that will do the trick.'

Neither Claire or Daniel liked the sound of that. They had discussed all the treatment options beforehand, and they knew that chemotherapy was very intrusive and was likely to make her feel rather sick, more so than the radiotherapy had done. Things had reached a point though, where it didn't seem that they had all that much of an option left open to them.

'I suppose there is nothing else that we can do?' asked Claire, hopefully.

'No, I'm afraid not.'

Daniel noticed that the doctor said that she was afraid rather a lot. He wondered what it was that she was afraid of. It wasn't as if she was the one that was having to undergo all of this treatment. Perhaps she was just afraid of telling people all this bad news all of the time. It couldn't have done her mental health all that good to be like that.

'When do we start?' asked Claire.

'I think it would be best to start as soon as possible,' replied the doctor.

'As bad as that?'

'I'm afraid so.'

And so it was that Claire began a course of chemotherapy. She had just reached a stage where she felt she was well enough to be able to return to work and now she was having to go off sick again. Her employers were sympathetic though and had told her that she should take all of the time that she needed. Daniel supposed that this was because they didn't want the bad publicity that might come with them applying pressure to someone that, after all, had cancer.

Cancer was still a word that people avoided using. It was like it was contagious. Admit that it existed and you might run the risk of catching it yourself. It was as if it was a cold or something like that. Something innocuous. Something that you could easily catch off of someone if they returned to the office too early. You could see the way that people withdrew from you when you told them that you had cancer. They were embarrassed and didn't know what to say about it all. They felt awkward and wished that they hadn't approached you in the first place.

It annoyed Daniel a great deal the way that people socially interacted with you when they found out that you had cancer. It was like they were behaving as if you were already dead, and yet somehow was still standing there in front of them, like some kind of zombie that had come to spread infection upon them. They expected you to keep out of the way and have nothing to do with them. Stay at home and keep your infection to yourself. Have the decency to do that at least.

Daniel took a break from the writing to care for Claire as much as he could. Someone needed to take her to the hospital each day and be there for her. Someone needed to care for her and make sure that she was going to be as comfortable as it was possible for her to be. They were under no illusions that things were going to be tough, but they were convinced that they would be able to get through it all if they were there for each other. It was the way that their entire marriage had worked and there didn't seem to be any reason why they should act any differently now.

They were convinced that if they stayed together and supported each other then they would be able to beat this cancer and get through to the other side.

I can't say when I really became aware of cancer. Of what it was and what it could do. Logic would state that I was aware of it before mum got sick, but I really can't remember. I think mum was pretty brave though. A lot of the things that she went through I was unaware of at the time. I only became aware of them from dad long after her death, when dad felt that it was something that he could really talk about at last. It took him a long time and I suppose I can understand the reasons why. I would hate to go through what mum went through although I realise that the odds are stacked against me. So many people will get cancer at some point in their lives. Some will survive it and some will not. Mum was just one of the unlucky ones.

Now

The first thing that went was your knowledge of current affairs. That's what Daniel thought. He had always been reasonably aware of what was going on in the world. He would check the BBC app on his phone on a regular basis, get important news updates and would usually have the BBC on in the background while he was working. He liked to know what was going on in the world. More than that, he thought it was important to know what was going on in the world.

Since Claire had died though he had no idea what was happening in the world. As far as he was concerned the world had ended, so what use did he have for what was happening outside of the walls of his house? He barely was concerned for what was happening inside the house.

He had no knowledge of what wars were taking place. Which politician was currently involved in some scandal, or if the American president had said or done something that could be classed as inappropriate. He had no idea what was happening. He didn't know if there had been a severe car crash on the M1 that had cost the lives of several people, or if there had been major flooding in Brazil, or an earthquake in Japan. He had no idea of any of this. He just wasn't interested any more. It was as if nothing mattered to him, because nothing did matter to him. Aside from Toby, of course.

He had to make the effort there. He had to be a father and they had to stick together, but it was difficult to do when it felt like you had lost a limb. He supposed that he was wallowing in self-pity. He didn't deny this, but it wasn't something that he was all that bothered about. He didn't care what other people thought about him. If they thought he was being self-indulgent with his grief. They could think what they liked, and they could really all go to hell anyway. He had no time for anyone else that might think that way. Let them think what they wanted to. It didn't matter to him in the slightest.

He thought some crazy thoughts during this time. He thought about taking up smoking. He had never been a smoker. Had never even tried cannabis when he was a student. He just didn't move in those kinds of circles. He thought if he took up smoking then maybe he could catch cancer and be with Claire. Wherever she was. Did you catch cancer? That made it sound like it was a cold. Surely, you had to contract it? He wasn't sure. He had never really thought of the terminology before. There had been no need for it. But surely, if he took up smoking it would take years before he would get cancer? It wasn't something that would happen that quickly. It wasn't like other drugs that could kill you on the first attempt.

But then who would look after Toby? If he was gone then it surely would be the disastrous thing that he would end up being looked after by his grandmother and that wouldn't be a good thing. No, not in the slightest. He couldn't do that to Toby. As much as he wanted to reunite himself with Claire he had to stay around for Toby's sake. At least for a few more years yet.

Jordan had told him that he should go back to writing. He thought that the process would give him focus. 'Take your mind off things.' Had been the actual words that he used. He couldn't imagine that it was likely that anything would take his mind off of the death of Claire. Least of all writing.

He wasn't sure that he would ever be able to write again. He wasn't being over dramatic. He actually felt that he had reached the end and the words would just not come any longer. They had been there for Claire and now that she was gone there were no more words left to say. There was nothing to say. Everything that could be said had been said.

Would it be such a disaster if he never sat down at the keyboard again? He didn't see it as a problem. He was earning enough in royalties for it not to matter if he never worked again and he still had a number of unpublished manuscripts that he could put out that would make it look to the world as if he was writing.

'I'm only taking a break,' he had told Jordan.

'Maybe this is not the best time to take a break. Maybe you need to work.'

'I'm not sure that I do. I've been working flat out for the best part of twenty years. I have achieved a huge body of work. More than a lot of writers do. It doesn't matter if I don't write for a few months, or even a couple of years.'

'But what will you do.'

'Read. Chill out. Do what I want to do. Maybe take some holidays.'

'Well, that's all well and good, but writing is something that has driven you for a great number of years. It will feel like it is a void in your soul.'

'The loss of Claire is like a void in my soul. Writing is just a job. It doesn't really matter.'

'You have never viewed it as a job though. You have always thought of it as a vocation.'

'Maybe.'

'That's what you've always told me, at any rate.'

'Well, maybe I was wrong.'

'I don't think that you were. I just think that you have lost your way. You will find it again.'

'I wish I had your faith.'

The truth of the matter was that Daniel couldn't write at the moment, and to say that he would spend his time reading instead was also something of a lie. He wasn't in the right frame of mind to be able to read. He just couldn't concentrate on the words. Words which had been so important to him for all of his adult life, had now left him and he was suffering from something of a double grieving process. Although he didn't feel all that inclined to read or write he knew that if he were to settle down to one or the other then he wouldn't be able to do it. He just knew that would be the case.

It wasn't even a case of determination. It wasn't as if that if he put his mind to it then he would be able to read or write. He didn't make the effort because he didn't want the disappointment that would inevitably come from failure to achieve either task. Why set yourself up for that sort of failure?

Life was full of enough disappointments without adding to them unnecessarily. At least that was the way that his thinking was going. There was a flawed logic to it. It didn't help all that much knowing that it was flawed.

He knew that he was in a rut and that he would have to do something about it. He knew it wasn't possible for things to continue for as long as they were, and were likely to go if left unchecked. How long were you allowed to be in a total period of mourning for though before it was deemed seemly to be seen as getting on with your life?

Queen Victoria had spent the rest of her life in mourning after the death of her husband, Albert. Was that overindulgence?

Or was that something that was acceptable? It seemed to be something that was overindulgent to Daniel. She had laid out his clothes every day on his bed as if he was about to come in and change. Something that he would never do again.

Daniel hadn't quite gone that far, but nor had he emptied the wardrobes and drawers of all of Claire's clothing. How soon was that permitted to be an acceptable thing to do? It seemed disingenuous to do it too early. As if you were keen to wipe away the physical presence of the person that had died. If you left it too long then maybe it seemed too morbid to be hanging on to a dead person's effects.

Daniel's head hurt. He had not previously considered any of this. There was so much of an aftermath that followed a death. So many things that you had to consider and action. Not just the funeral. That had been easy compared to some of the other things that he had to think about now. Too much to think about. Too much that needed to be done.

He was pleased that he was able to shield Toby from most of it, but then he knew that there was a fair possibility that one day Toby would be doing all of this for him. Working out what to keep and what to give to charity or throw away. Daniel knew that Claire would have liked most of her things, that Daniel had no need to keep, to go to charity. She was always in the business of helping others whenever she could. Even when she didn't have all that much herself.

When they had been struggling before Daniel had first been published, she would always give to those that were less fortunate than they were. She would give what change she could to those that were sleeping rough on the streets. She couldn't imagine what their lives were like. It must be hard. They would never be in a position to buy Daniel's books. They would have their own stories to tell though, if people were only prepared to listen.

Everyone had stories to tell. That was the thing. A few thought that they should be able to write these into novels. Daniel was really annoyed about the celebrities who thought that they could write novels. They were famous for something else but because they read books, they thought it was easy to write books as well. The chances are that they were all ghost written anyway.

The point was that everyone thought that they could write a book. Nobody thought that they had the talent to write a symphony as well as their day job. Nobody thought that they could paint something equal to the old masters. Nobody thought to do all that, but everyone thought that they could write a book. It was something that really pissed Daniel off. He had to work at his profession. It wasn't something that particularly came easily, although there were times when the words just flowed naturally. Then some celebrity would come along with a book that they probably hadn't read, let alone written and it went straight to number one. Purely because of who they were. Not because of how good they were as a writer.

Everyone thought they had a novel in them though and everyone thought that it would be easy to get it published. In fact, they thought it was their right to get it published. Because he was a published and established writer, Daniel often found that he had people passing their manuscripts on to him to read.

'Maybe you can pass it on to you agent?' they would ask him in hopeful tones.

This put him in a very difficult position. He didn't really have the time to read other people's manuscripts, which were invariably not as good as they thought they were anyway. Trouble is it was hard to say no to these people. Hard to turn them down.

Hard to tell them that they actually had no hope at all. It was difficult to puncture someone's dreams. Sometimes you served them best by just being honest with them. As hard as that might be.

It was difficult for Daniel because it wasn't really his job to do all this. He wasn't an agent or a talent spotter. He didn't really want the credit for spotting the next bestseller. He just wanted to write and he was having trouble enough doing that at the moment. Claire's illness and her eventual death had really knocked him and rocked him emotionally, as was to be expected really. He shouldn't find it all that difficult to realise why he wasn't able to work. He was sure that he would have problems with working if he were a bricklayer as well. It didn't matter what you did for a living when something like that happened. That's what he told himself, at any rate.

He wasn't sure that his temporary block would be temporary or if it was something that would become permanent. It was too early to really say. There was plenty that could happen in the future. There was plenty that couldn't happen as well.

The phone rang while Daniel was sitting in his office. He didn't pay much attention, but picked it up without looking at the caller ID. He soon wished that he had allowed it to go to answerphone.

'Daniel, it's Mrs Baldwin.'

Daniel sighed. Claire's mother never referred to herself by her first name, always it was 'Mrs Baldwin'. He made sure that he called her by her first name because he knew that it was a level of familiarity that annoyed her.

'Yes, Martha. What is it?'

'There is no need to take that tone with me.'

'What tone would that be?' Daniel knew exactly what tone

it was and he knew exactly the kind of tone that he would like to be taking with her. Right now, he thought the dialling tone would be a good one to take with her.

'That tone that suggests you are not pleased to hear from me.' He couldn't argue with her radar. She had excellent levels of perception. 'We really must talk about this Toby situation.'

'What Toby situation is that? I was not aware of the fact that there was a Toby situation.'

'The situation of you not letting him to come and stay with me.'

'As I've told you before, Martha, he doesn't want to come and stay with you. That's no reflection on you,' (this was not entirely true, Toby didn't like his grandmother at all) 'he just wants to be with his dad at the moment and I don't think we can blame him for that.'

'I feel you are poisoning him against me.'

'Nobody is poisoning anyone against anyone. You have a bed of your own making.'

'And what is that supposed to mean?'

'You never had all that much to do with Toby while Claire was alive, you never had all that much to do with Claire, if the truth be known. You can't expect him to come running to you now that his mother is dead.'

'Family is very important at this time and it's important for him to get to know his grandmother.'

'Excuse me, Martha, but you have had fifteen years for him to get to know you and you never showed much interest in it, so I don't think you can really expect it now.'

'Do I really have to get solicitors involved now?'

Daniel tried to contain his temper, which was not an easy thing to do these days. He was angry at the world for the loss of

Claire and now this silly old bat was threatening him with ridiculous things.

'Martha, if you really want to go and waste money on solicitors to get them to argue that you have more rights to your grandson, that you have seriously neglected over the years, than I do as his father, then by all means go ahead and waste your money. I doubt you would get a good solicitor to represent you at any rate.'

'You are being quite unreasonable.'

'No, you are being unreasonable. How dare you threaten me with solicitors over my own son when my wife has just died. Who the hell do you think you are?'

'She was my daughter, you know, that died.'

'You were no more of a mother to her than I was.'

'That's a terrible thing to say.'

'No, you just can't handle the truth so you have twisted the facts to fit what you think of as your own reality, which is entirely different to the reality of the rest of us.'

'That is libellous, I tell you, I shall have my solicitors onto you for that comment.'

'No, it isn't libellous.'

'I tell you that it is.'

'Libel is defamatory statements of the written word. I think you are thinking of slander which is spoken or oral. It still isn't slanderous though because it happens to be true.'

'You think you are so clever, don't you?'

'I don't think anything of the sort. I am what I am, and unfortunately you are what you are. Now if you don't mind this conversation is at an end.'

With that he put the phone down and saw that his hand was shaking. That woman really knew how to wind him up.

'Is everything okay, Dad?'

Daniel turned around in his chair and saw that Toby was standing in the door way. He had been unaware of the fact that he had raised his voice rather a lot during the course of the short telephone conversation.

'Yeah, everything is fine, Toby. Sorry if I got heated.'

'Was that grandmother?'

'Yes, it was.'

'She still wants me to go to her?'

'I'm afraid so.'

'You're not going to send me to her, are you?'

'No, not if you don't want to go.'

'I don't want to go. Most certainly not.'

'Then you won't have to go.'

'Promise?'

'I promise.'

Toby seemed satisfied with this and nodded his head.

'Do you want some dinner?'

'Not really hungry all that much.'

'You have to eat.'

'So do you and I eat more than you do.'

'Well, I am your dad, it's my job to look after you.'

'And now Mum has gone, it's my job to look after you as well.'

Daniel could feel himself welling up at this. He had never loved his son more than he had in that moment.

'Come on, let's get some ice cream.'

Ice cream was the answer to most things. It was the ultimate comfort food really. Daniel survived as a writer on coffee, but ice cream was a good back up when things were down. It was pretty much designed to cheer you up again and it served as something to eat when you were not feeling all that hungry. There was always room for ice cream.

Daniel's relationship with coffee was very similar. You poured coffee into his mouth and words came out of his fingers. Without coffee he was unable to operate. Claire had always said that this was an illusion, but if it was an illusion then it was something that Daniel was prepared to play up to.

Some writers developed alcoholism or snorted lines of cocaine to cope with the demands of the creative world. Daniel had never been all that interested in alcohol, and drugs were something that he didn't go anywhere near at all. He wouldn't have known where to get them for starters. Not that he wanted to know where to get them. No, Daniel's addiction was coffee. He thrived on it. He couldn't operate in the mornings until he had drunk his first cup of coffee.

Claire had tried to convince him that he didn't need caffeine to be able to function, but he had pointed out to her that she was exactly the same with her morning cup of tea. She had grumbled at this as she had realised that he was in fact right about it.

Aside from coffee, tea and ice cream, the other real staple in their lives were books. They loved their books. Their house was full of books that they had been collecting since their student days. They still had some of their university text books and the paperbacks that they had found in second hand shops when they had been starting out. They had steadily collected more over the years until there were now books in every room and on every subject that you could imagine.

Daniel, in particular, collected books on a range of subjects, because you never knew, as a writer, when they would come in handy for the purposes of research. He knew that there was the internet, but you couldn't beat having a book to turn to when it came to research. There was so much that you could find out on the internet, but a book was the reason why most people became writers in the first place.

There were books on just about every surface in the house. Books everywhere that you went and all over the place. There was no corner or shelf that had been installed that had not been taken over by books. Each of them always had at least one book that they were reading. They might be reading something new and, on the side, they would be re-reading a classic, perhaps something that they had studied when they were students and had not read since.

Art was long and life was short. There was two and a half thousand years' worth of literature to get through and it wouldn't read itself. They weren't limiting in what they read as well. They would read fiction and they would read fact. They would start back as far as Herodotus and Thucydides and work their way all the way up to what was in the charts now. There was no snobbery about it.

If they wanted plays, as well as Shakespeare there were modern classics from the likes of Noel Coward, Pinter and Stoppard, or they could turn their attention to Molière, or go further back to Aeschylus, Euripides and Sophocles.

When it came to novels the choices were endless. You could go back to the favourites of Dickens and Hardy, but there were the Brontë sisters, Mary Shelley, Trollope, Thackery and Forster to entertain those long winter nights and that was before you got onto more modern authors that were more numerous and just as good in their own ways.

There was plenty of literature out there and enough to keep you busy. Neither of them felt that you should be restricted in what you read but should read widely around your interests.

Every now and then dip your toe into something that was outside of your comfort zone and was not something that you were used to. You might find something that you were unaware of and that turned out to be really special. Claire had made excellent discoveries with the likes of Diderot and Voltaire that she had shared with Daniel.

Daniel felt very strongly that to be a good enough writer then you had to be a good enough reader. You had to read. He couldn't understand those that wanted to write a book, but never read one. If you couldn't read then you couldn't write either. It was as simple as that. It amazed him that there were people in the world that didn't like to read. He didn't understand these people at all, it was like saying that they didn't like to breathe. He was astounded that there were writers out there that didn't like to read. They were just missing out on the tools of their trade.

'It's like football,' said Jordan when Daniel had raised the topic with him.

'How so?' replied Daniel feeling a little confused.

'Well, you don't like football?'

'No.'

'Well, those that do like football, feel very passionate about it. They can't understand why it is that people, like you, don't care for it at all.'

'Because people get so worked up about it. It's only a game after all.'

'But to them it's not a game. It's more important than that. It's a way of life. They attach the same level of interest to it as you do to reading, or the theatre.'

'They are hardly equal terms.'

'But in their minds, they are.'

'Yes, but when the Royal Shakespeare Company have a

successful tour of Japan, they don't get paraded through the streets in an open top bus.'

'Maybe they should.'

'And people don't come out of seeing a production of *Titus Andronicus* and riot in the streets.'

'Given the nature of *Titus Andronicus* I'm rather surprised by that to be honest.'

'Well, that may be so, but it doesn't happen.'

'All that proves is that perhaps theatre goers are more sophisticated than football fans.'

'And less violent.'

'Maybe so, but the point that I was trying to make was that it's about the passion. They're passionate about football, you're passionate about theatre and reading.'

'I don't see the same thing in it at all.'

'No? Perhaps I'm not explaining myself very well.'

'No, I think you're explaining yourself well enough, I just don't see the two things as being comparable.'

'You're being a snob.'

'Perhaps I am.'

'You can surely see though why some people are passionate about one thing and other people are passionate about something else?'

'I can understand that, I just find it hard to believe that there are those out there that don't like reading, or to be more precise, are so anti reading as to be quite angry about it.'

'That's because for your entire life you have lived in a world centred around books. Everything has been to do with books. You have not had a life where books don't feature in it. With all that you find it hard to believe that there are others out there who have been raised in a bookless world.'

'Poor sods.'

'But they don't see themselves as poor. They don't know what they are missing out on, indeed they don't think that they're missing out on anything.'

'I still say they are poor sods.'

'They probably think of you as being sad that you have your head buried in a book all the time.'

'Well, that's their look out.'

Jordan sighed. 'I'm never going to make you see this, am I?'

'Probably not.'

It was difficult for Daniel to understand why there were those who didn't like books. Jordan was right. He had been brought up with books all his life. Ever since he was a baby. He didn't understand the football fanatics and a lot of them probably didn't understand him. Not all of them, of course. Being a football fan didn't mean that you hated to read. Plenty of football fans read books as well. It was perhaps not the best analogy that Jordan had come up with. It was the best that he felt he could do under the circumstances. He had tried to make Daniel see his point of view – which had not entirely been a successful mission.

Growing up with books for all of his life it was hardly surprising that Daniel had decided to become a writer. Some people grow up with a clear definition of what it is that they want to do as a career. For some this might be a less achievable goal, like being an astronaut. Others knew exactly what they wanted to be, a scientist or a politician, a baker or a teacher, dancer or actor. You name it.

Some chose their careers because it was a similar job to their parents. This was because people often naturally gravitated towards what they knew. Daniel could have followed suit and gone into the city, like his dad, or become a lecturer, like his mum, but he had not fancied either of these careers and had gravitated towards the only natural thing that he could think of. He read books. He liked books. The logical thing to do, therefore, was to write books. It made perfect sense to him.

His teachers, careers advisor and to an extent his parents had shrugged their shoulders, thrown their hands up in the air and acted as if he had chosen to be an astronaut. To become a writer had seemed as far-flung and as transient a career move as going to the moon would have been. It was just not the sort of thing that people did. Yes, it was true that people wrote books. It was known that people wrote books because there were bookshops that were full of books. It was understood that these had to come from somewhere, but no one had particularly encouraged the young Daniel to be one of the people that contributed to the stock of books sold.

He had been determined though. He was a very determined young man and he was determined that he was going to become a writer. The reason for this was not because of the fact that he felt any particular strong determination that this was the direction that he should be going in life, but rather because he couldn't think of anything else that he wanted to do. This lack of imagination for someone who wanted to be a writer was perhaps disturbing. It had never seemed to falter for him though, so perhaps it was something that he had grown into.

He had proven his teachers and, more importantly, his careers advisor wrong and much to the pleasant surprise of his parents had become a writer. His father had been concerned that there wasn't enough money in it, and he wouldn't be able to make a living from it. It is true that it had taken a few years before he was really able to make a living out of it, but there could be no argument that he was making a living out of it now.

He was so successful now that he didn't really need to worry about the break that he was taking from the writing. Either it would come back to him or it wouldn't and if it didn't then he had enough to keep him going for a few years with the unpublished manuscripts that were lounging around on his hard drive just waiting for the moment when he decided to email them off to his publisher.

No, he didn't really have any immediate concerns about his writing career. It would hold out for a good while and if it didn't then he could retire and think himself lucky that he had his health. No, he wasn't worried about that.

He was worried about other things instead.

Grief is a very strange animal. People handle it in different ways. My way of dealing with my mum's death was to throw myself back into life and make things as normal as I possibly could. In some ways to act as if it had never happened. Dad was having a far harder time of things than I was. His way of dealing with things was to withdraw in on himself and become very insular – even more so than he normally was. As a writer he was pretty insular to begin with. I don't think that this is a particularly healthy approach to life, or death. I personally think that he needed to interact with people more. I was also pretty convinced that he was not working. I felt that it would probably have helped him a great deal if he were to do some work. It might focus his mind and stop it from dwelling in a dark place that threatened to get darker.

230

Then

'I'm afraid that the chemotherapy is not working,' the doctor said as she sat in her chair with a sympathetic look on her face.

For a moment Daniel and Claire didn't say anything. They didn't feel that there was anything that they could say. Claire had gone through a bad time with the chemotherapy. She had lost her hair and had taken to wearing a headscarf for reasons of vanity, something that she felt she would never have stooped to before the chemotherapy, but now found that it was easier to cover her head rather than face the questions that people asked her about her loss of hair.

'Are you doing it for charity?' someone had actually asked her with an insensitivity that was truly amazing.

'No, I have cancer,' she had replied, looking the other woman directly in the eye. She hadn't known what to say to that and had quickly made her excuses and disappeared off somewhere else.

She developed bags under her eyes that no amount of make-up could cover up or hide. Frankly, she looked ill. There was no other way to describe it. She looked ill because she was ill. She had lost a lot of weight and her clothes didn't fit her any longer. She was loath to go out and buy newer clothes that fitted.

'If I buy new clothes then I will be admitting that this is more than a temporary thing and that this is how I am going to be now, that I'm never going to get back to normal again,' she had told Daniel. Daniel had seen her point, but the baggy clothes only went to highlight her condition even more. If that were at all possible.

'So, if the chemo is not working,' said Daniel, 'what does that mean that we do now?'

The doctor looked embarrassed for a little while and looked between the two of them. She flicked her hair back out of her eyes and sighed.

'I am afraid that it means that there is nothing more that we can do.'

'Nothing you can do?' he asked while Claire sat in silence absorbing it all and apparently taking the news better than Daniel was.

'No, there is nothing more that can be done. We have reached the end of the line as far as treatment goes.'

'So, what happens now?' Claire finally asked.

'It's only a matter of time.'

'Can you say how long?' asked Claire with a slight lump in her throat being the only sign of emotion that betrayed how she was thinking at the moment.

'I think you have to plan for weeks rather than months.'

'I see.'

'Weeks?' Daniel asked incredulously.

'I'm afraid so.'

'How is this possible? Things were going so well.'

'Sometimes it happens. Sometimes things take a down turn. Sometimes there is recovery from that and at other times there isn't.'

'I see,' Claire said again.

'We will make you as comfortable as possible. There will be a certain amount of pain and discomfort, but we will do what we can to ease that for you. You should be admitted to the hospital as soon as possible.'

'No,' Claire said sharply. 'No, I don't want to die in hospital. I want to die at home. I want to be among my books and the things that I love. I don't want to die in an anonymous room with lots of people that I don't know.'

'Okay,' said the doctor as if this was something that she had been expecting. 'We can make you as comfortable as possible. We can show you how to administer the drugs,' she told Daniel. 'And we can have a nurse visit at regular intervals.'

'If you think that is for the best.'

'I really do think that it is for the best.'

'We will be guided by you,' Claire said.

'I will make the arrangements.'

'Thank you, Doctor.'

They left the hospital and entered into the drizzle of the outside. They walked slowly to the car. Aware that a death sentence had just been handed out. You knew that this was always a possibility, but you never thought that it would actually happen. That it would come to that. There were ways that you could be saved and everything would be all right. Now, medical science had shrugged its shoulders and given up on you with the words that it was only a matter of time. *Only a matter of time.* Five innocent little words that didn't mean all that much on their own, but had been the death sentence upon Claire.

They were already sleeping in separate rooms by this stage as Claire had found it uncomfortable sleeping in bed with Daniel and disturbing his sleep when she was unable to get to sleep and tossed and turned. They went home and hugged each other in the kitchen and then Claire went to her room. She was exhausted and needed to lay down. She was also in need of a great think.

It is difficult being faced with your own mortality. We all

know that we must one day die. That our time upon this world is finite. Yet, most of us file this knowledge away at the back of our minds and try not to think about it. We don't like to think about it. It is something that we know will happen, but we try not to allow it to engage our thoughts all that much. We certainly don't want to know the day or the time that it will happen in advance. We prefer to think of the time of the future to be measured in years rather than weeks, or days. Even though we know it will be coming for us all at some point, it is hard to be told that your time is limited to only a tiny few grains that are left in the hourglass. When you reach a certain age most of us know that there are likely to be fewer days ahead than there are behind. To be told that this is so blatantly the case though is something that is hard to take in. Claire had a lot of thinking to do.

Daniel had a lot of thinking to do as well. He sat in his office chair and swivelled from side to side while he took in the news that his wife was going to die. He knew that the relationship would end one day. Of course he did. One or the other of them would die and that would be an end of things. He just thought that it might be something that happened in thirty or forty years. Not something that happened in a few weeks' time. That was far too early. He wasn't ready for that.

Were you ever ready for that sort of thing? Would it be any easier if it had happened forty years from now? Would they have been so close and so used to each other by that point that the wrench of separation would have been a harder burden to bear? Which was easier? Death after a long time together, or death after a shorter time together? The truth was that neither of them were particularly easy and it was impossible to say which was the better. There was no better. It was just a shit hand that you had been dealt. It would happen to us all at some stage though.

It was one of those things. If you wanted to be in a relationship then you would have to live with the pain of loss at some point. If you didn't want to deal with that pain then you could just live on your own, but then you might resent the fact that you spent your life on your own, unless you were someone that really preferred your own company. If you did then there was nothing wrong with this. You had to make your bed and you had to lie in it according to your own interests and beliefs. Nobody was really in a position to criticise you for the choices that you made when it came to your personal life. There would be plenty to criticise in your professional life, no matter what you did for a living. There was always someone that thought that they knew how to do your job better than you did.

Daniel had thought that by being a writer and self-employed he would avoid the criticism that came from having a boss that was always breathing down your neck. This didn't prevent him from having criticism though as he fell afoul of the critics that were paid to criticise other people's work. First of all, they accused him of not being good enough and then when he was successful, they accused him of selling out. There was no way to win really.

And now his wife was dying and it didn't really matter what the critics thought any longer. It was all an insignificant event of the past. They could think and say whatever they wanted. His wife was dying. The love of his life was going to die and there was nothing that he could do about it. It was the sense of powerlessness that got to him the most. He felt that there should be something that he could do to make things better. To make things right.

But there was nothing that could be done. He would just have to accept things for the way that they were, that they were out of his hands. It wasn't a feeling that he was particularly used to and it wasn't something that he liked.

A couple of hours later Claire woke up and walked slowly out of her room.

'Tea?' asked Daniel as he fidgeted in the kitchen.

'I'm not sure I can handle tea. Maybe just some water.' Daniel poured her a glass of water from the water cooler and placed it on the table for her where she had sat.

'Thanks.'

'Pleasure.'

'We should talk.'

'What is there to talk about?'

'Plenty, I'm dying, Daniel.'

'I'd rather not think about it.'

'I'm afraid you're going to have to think about it, Daniel. It's a reality. We can't avoid it now. We could pussyfoot around it earlier when there was a chance of recovery, but now that is has been made clear to us that's it only a matter of time then we have to come to terms with it.'

'How am I supposed to come to terms with that?'

'If you don't come to terms with it now, it will be more difficult for you to come to terms with it… after.'

'I don't think it will make any difference.'

'I don't want my last weeks on Earth to be spent with an elephant in the room.'

Daniel continued to polish some glasses which didn't really need polishing because they had already been through the dishwasher.

'It's not an easy thing for me to talk about,' he finally said.

'Do you think it's easy for me? I need to know that you will be all right with this.'

'How can I possibly be all right with this?'

'You know what I mean. I need to know that you will be there for Toby and not go to pieces. It's going to be difficult enough for him to lose one parent let alone two.'

'I will cope as best as I can. What other choice do I have?'

'Not much, I suppose. I suppose it will be easier for me.'

'Easier for you? How can you say that?'

'All I have to do is die and then there will either be nothing and I won't have to worry about it, or there will be an afterlife and I will move on with whatever that brings. I won't have to stay behind and deal with the grief and the mundane things of life any longer.'

'I don't know how you can talk about all of this so calmly.'

'What would you rather I did? Beat my breast? Go shout at God in a thunderstorm and blame him for bringing this on me? It's nobody's fault. I just can't believe that I'm going to die of lung cancer and I've never smoked a cigarette in my life.'

'I know that seems to be the great injustice in all of this.'

'If I had known that this was going to happen then I would have smoked. At least that way I would have nobody but myself to blame for what happened to me, plus I would get the enjoyment of smoking out of it.'

'I don't think smoking is very enjoyable.'

'No, perhaps not.'

'It just seems such a goddamn waste.'

'Of course it is. But I haven't had such a bad life. I have known love and that is more than a lot of other people get to experience. I have done a job that I have wanted to do. I married a man that I wanted to marry and I have had a wonderful son. I can't really complain about anything.'

'How about complaining that you are going too early?'

'But don't you see? I would rather lead the life that I have and go early than live twice as long and have none of those things. I've had a blessed time and there is really nothing to complain about.'

'I wish I could see it as philosophically as you clearly do.'

'Perhaps you will with time.'

'I can't ever imagine that.'

'That's the thing with life though. We are often asked to imagine the unimaginable at times. We get there. You will too. You will come to understand it all one day.'

They lapsed into silence for a moment. Daniel continued to polish and put away glasses in the overhead cupboard and Claire sat with her untouched water.

'Where's Toby?' Claire eventually asked.

'In his room doing his homework, I should imagine.'

'Have you told him?'

'No, I thought it was something that you should be there for.'

'That's a conversation that I'm not really looking forward to.'

'No, I don't imagine that it is.'

'It's going to be hard for him.'

'It's hard for all of us, Claire.'

'Yeah, I know.'

'But you're right. It's not a good age to lose your mum.'

'I don't suppose any age is really.'

'I don't know. If it was your mother... ' It was the first attempt at humour since they had heard the news and Claire smiled in response to it.

'My mother will never die.'

'Creaking doors hang the longest. That's what my

grandmother used to say.'

'I'm sure she was right.'

'I suppose you are going to have to tell your mother at some point what has happened.'

Claire snorted. 'Her only concern will be looking good for the funeral. She will pick an outfit out as soon as she hears. Talking of which, we should really talk about my funeral arrangements and what I want to happen.'

'Don't you think that is a little soon?'

'I don't think we have all that much time to be able to take the luxury of waiting.'

'I suppose you're right.'

'I don't want a religious ceremony.'

'That will upset your mother.'

'Yeah, well it isn't for my mother. If it was her funeral then she could arrange to have whatever she wants, but it isn't, it's my funeral and I'll have things the way that I want them to be.'

'Fair enough.'

'No hymns either. Some nice classical music with the odd bit of something modern thrown in.'

'Did you have anything in mind?'

'Not at the moment, I'll give it some thought and let you know what I think. I also don't want everyone in black. Some nice bright colours to celebrate my life rather than mourn my death would be nice, and no flowers either.'

'Sounds like you have given this some thought.'

'To be honest I always had it in the back of my mind from the moment I was diagnosed with cancer. You hear those words telling you that you have cancer and you immediately think that you are going to die. Turns out I was right. You start thinking about these things and planning for the worst, just in case.'

'I tried not to think about it.'

'I know you did, but hiding your head in the sand is no longer an option. You have to face up to the reality of the situation. We have to deal with this because it's going to happen.'

'I know. I will come to terms with it eventually.'

'Maybe you should get a dog.'

Daniel was momentarily confused. 'Why would I want to get a dog?'

'It will be company for you. Give you something to focus on.'

'Don't you think that Toby will be company for me enough?'

'Maybe, but he won't always be around and he could probably use something to focus on as well.'

'I'm not sure I could handle having a dog. I have never owned a dog in my life. I don't even know where you go to get a dog.'

'There are breeders all over the place. You could easily find one on the net and be able to pick one up.'

'I think a dog is a lot of responsibility.'

'Exactly. It will take your mind off of things.'

'I'm not sure that it is the best idea that you have ever had.'

'Well, it's just an idea.'

'One of your more unusual ideas.'

They decided that the best thing to do was to tell Toby together. They briefly considered the idea of keeping the latest news from him. To shield him from what was going to happen, but they had never been one to keep things from Toby in that way. They treated him like an adult and believed that he had just as much right to know about the dark things of life as well as the light things. It would do nothing to hide death from him. It was an inevitable part of life.

Telling him what was going to happen would give him the same amount of time to prepare for what was going to happen as they had. Otherwise, it would be a worse shock for him when his mother unexpectedly died. It seemed the best approach to the situation. There would be some who would prefer to keep such things from their children. To smother them in cotton wool and pretend that there wasn't evil in the world, but this didn't help the situation and only made it more difficult to face up to the matters when they happened.

He took the news well, or at least he took the news well in front of his parents. When they were not about and he was alone there was bound to be an amount of soul searching and questioning as to why this was happening. It was bound to happen. He could have expected his mother to live a lot longer than she was clearly going to. There was injustice in this. There is no sense in questioning it though, it is just the way that sometimes things go. That didn't stop Toby from questioning it though. It didn't stop any of them from questioning it. They quickly learnt though that questioning it was not going to help the situation. It was not going to change anything.

They knew that they only had a matter of weeks left now and they wanted to make the best of them that they could. The problem was that Claire was ill. She was not in the best of situations to enjoy the time that was left to her. She couldn't go anywhere or do anything. She spent most of her time in bed. For a great deal of time, she was in a lot of pain despite the supply of morphine that the hospital had supplied for her. Daniel had been given strict instructions from the doctor about how much morphine he was allowed to administer. The amount that Claire was given didn't seem to be enough to quell the pain. Any more would be dangerous. This seemed to Daniel to be a ludicrous situation that they should be worrying about Claire taking an overdose of morphine when she was going to die anyway. Still, he didn't want her to go before her time had come.

The doctor had told them that things would continue as they were for some time and then it would reach a stage where Claire would slip into a coma and it would be one that she wasn't going to wake up from. It would continue until she passed, reasonably peacefully, in her sleep and that would be an end of it. It was impossible to tell how much conscious time she had left to her. The chances are that the coma would creep up on them and would happen before they were really aware of any of it.

Claire wasn't able to read any longer and so Daniel sat by her bed and read to her whenever he could. He wasn't sure about how much she was taking in or whether she was just listening to the sound of his voice and was often lulled into a state of sleep by it. She took comfort in the sound of his voice. She had always loved him reading to her.

Daniel would have liked to have spent her last few weeks filling up her time with happy memories, but she wasn't up to anything energetic. She was pretty much bed bound now and couldn't even get up to go to the toilet. She found this to be acutely embarrassing and insisted as much as possible that the nurse who came in daily helped clean her rather than Daniel doing it. Despite the closeness of their marriage, she wanted to keep this from him. She didn't want his lasting memory to be one of cleaning up after her. Daniel had tried to protest, but she wasn't having any of it. He countered that he would do anything for her and she replied that there were limits to this expectation as far as she was concerned. He had, as always, given into her in the end.

'Do you think there is an afterlife?' she asked him when he was mid-sentence in reading her *The Mayor of Casterbridge*. He put the book to one side and looked at her.

'I would like to think so.'

'You never used to think so though, did you?'

'I was never sure.'

'Do you want to believe in one now because I'm dying?'

'I suppose I'd like to believe that this isn't it, that when you die you will continue to exist in some way. Still be out there somewhere. Looking out for me.'

'I will always look out for you if it is at all possible to do so. You can rest assured I will be there if there is any means in which it can be done.'

'I would like to think that you're still there. I'm sure I will still talk to you. Tell you about my day and the novel that I'm struggling to write.'

'I will be your muse if it is allowed.'

'If it is allowed?'

'Well, I don't know what the rules are going to be in the other place. I don't want to make promises with you that I can't keep.'

'You have always been my muse, Claire, you know that, don't you?'

'Yes, I suppose that I do.'

'You have always been the inspiration behind my books. Why do you think I dedicated them all to you?'

'I thought you were just grovelling.'

'Charming.'

'I'd like to believe that there is an afterlife. I'd like to think that there is a purpose to all of this. Maybe we get to go to a happier place and it's all explained to us. Get to be with our loved ones again.'

'Sounds like it could be a perfect place.'

'Do you think you will re-marry?'

'What?'

The question had come out of the blue and had taken him rather by surprise. Not the sort of question that he was expecting Claire to ask him.

'It's a simple enough question.'

'I very much doubt that I will re-marry.'

'Why not?'

'Because you're the only woman for me.'

'Don't be silly. The chances are that you will have a long time left to live and I would hate for you to be all alone for all of that time.'

'I would hate to be with anyone else. Nobody can replace you.'

'It's not a case of replacing me. It's a case of ensuring that you're happy and looked after.'

'I'm sure that I will be just fine if it's all the same to you.'

Claire fiddled with her blanket tassel as if she were nervous. 'It's not all the same with me. I want you to have a life.'

'I have a life. I had a life with you and it was glorious. I don't need another wife to make me happy. I will be just fine.'

'Promise me you will give it serious thought and if someone comes along that you like the look of you won't shun them because of some misplaced loyalty to me.'

'Okay, I promise that if I start to date again then I won't be misguided by my loyalty for you.'

'Thank you.'

'I doubt it's likely to happen though. I would always live with the fear that the person wanted to be with me because I'm a famous novelist rather than because of who I really am. At least when you fell in love with me you fell in love with a broke student rather than a well-off writer.'

'You think they will be after you because of the money?'

'Probably and because they will think there is something glamorous in book tours and launches, premieres and cocktail parties and all the things that I hate about the writing business.'

'You just have to find the right woman.'

'Hey, I found the right woman. I'm looking at her right now.'

'I won't be here much longer though.'

'I prefer not to think about that.'

'You have to think about that, Danny. You have to think about the fact that I'm not going to be around for long. You have to think about what happens next.'

'Next? There is no next.'

'I don't want you to grieve forever. I want you to get on with your life. I accept the fact that you're going to be upset, but you have to get on with things. You can't fall into a mire.'

'I can't believe you are so calm about all of this. I just want to scream and rage and shake my fists at the heavens.'

'And what good will that do? You have to be practical about all of this.'

'It makes me feel better.'

'Well, that's something I suppose.'

'I don't seem to be able to be as calm about these matters as you are.'

'I've had time to be philosophical about it.'

'You've had the same time as me and I haven't come to terms with it at all.'

'Maybe I'm just more philosophical about these things then you are.'

'You must be.'

'I just want you to be happy.'

'I've been happy for all the time that we have been together and I'm grateful for every day that we have spent in each other's company. I couldn't have asked for a better life. It may be too much to ask that I will be happy in the future though.'

'You might find some degree of happiness in some form or another.'

'The best that I can hope for is acceptance really.'

'Acceptance?'

'Coming to terms with what has happened. Learning to live with it. Learning to live with the grief and the hole that is in my heart.'

'Very poetic. You should be a writer.'

'I've thought about it. Don't like the hours though.'

'Maybe you should write about all of this.'

'That's what Jordan told me.'

'Maybe he's right. Let some good come of the situation.'

'I'm a bit too close to it at the moment. Maybe in the future.'

'I just want you to be happy.'

'Don't worry about me.'

'And promise me you will keep writing. Don't give up just because I'm not there to read your first drafts.'

'I've got to pay the bills someway.'

'Do it because you love it. Not because it pays the bills.'

'I suppose I'm lucky that my hobby is also my job.'

'Yes, but I have often thought that you need a hobby to replace the writing.'

'Well, there is always reading. I suppose that is my hobby.'

'You certainly do enough of it.'

'We both do.'

'Well, I used to. Not so much any more. I'm so tired.'

'Do you want me to leave you to sleep?'

'In a minute, there's something I want to ask you first.'

Daniel came closer and took her hand in his. 'Anything.'

'As the doctor said, this is going to get worse before the oblivion of the end comes. I'm going to go through a lot of pain before I reach the stage when I can't feel it any longer.'

'Yes, I'm sorry. I wish I could take the pain off of you. Take it onto myself.'

'I know you do, but that isn't possible, is it?'

'No.'

'But there is something that you can do for me all the same.'

'What?'

'I want to die on my terms. I want to go when I'm ready to go. I don't want all the pain and then to slip into a coma without being able to say goodbye properly.'

'What are you asking me then?'

'I'm asking if you would be prepared to kill me.'

Being told that your mother is going to die is a bit of a shock. It's a very strange feeling. I mean, you know, at the back of your mind, that your parents are going to die someday. You know that we all are. Including yourself, although that is perhaps more difficult to believe in as you feel that you are immortal and you can't imagine that the world will continue without you in it. If I was honest with myself then I always knew that mum would die at some point. When they told me that she had cancer then I suppose that I thought that she was going to die. Surely, that is what everyone thinks when they hear the word cancer. I had certainly thought it, but I had tried to push the thoughts from my mind as being too morbid. I suppose this was a denial of sorts. With the news that mum was going to die, sooner than expected, I became rather numb. I knew that we needed to pull together as a family, but it was hard. I just wanted to withdraw into my own little world where I could get away from it all and pretend that most of it was not happening, or maybe it was happening to someone else; not to me. I was learning that burying your head in the sand was not the best option to take though. I withdrew into my world and tried to pretend that it was not happening. I was so tired of it all. What I realise now is that I had started to grieve before she had died. You start the process earlier than anyone would think that you did.

Now

Daniel found that his work would not be neglected forever. Before Claire had died, he had submitted his last completed manuscript to his publisher. *Charlie's Song* had gone through the editing stage and the publisher had declared that it was ready for publication. He was obliged by his contract to take part in a few book signings and talks in order to promote the book.

This was the side of publishing that he hated the most. Yes, it got him out of the house and he got to meet his reading public and it was always good to meet the 'fans' who loved his work so much. They felt that they knew him even though they had never met him before. In reality they knew nothing about him, but they felt that they did and he was happy to let them go on thinking that they knew him. It was like acting. What they knew was the Daniel that he projected. Daniel the writer, rather than Daniel the man.

He found that he had to put his grief to one side for the moment and get on with the work that he had to do.

'It will do you some good to get out of the house,' said Jordan when he came around for coffee.

'I don't feel that I need to get out of the house. I've developed a sense of agoraphobia.'

'Well, that isn't good for you. I don't think you have been out of the house since the funeral, have you?'

'No. Thank God for online groceries. In the modern era there is no need to leave the house any longer.'

'That may be the case, but it isn't good for you. You need to get out and about and show yourself.'

'I don't think that I need to do that at all.'

'Well, whether you need to do it or not, it's something that you should do. You want to be a famous recluse writer?'

'A lot of them have done it in the past and done very well out of it. Hell, it's even expected of some of us.'

'Well, I hate to see you like that.'

'You'll get over it in time. Besides I am not a recluse I've agreed to do this book tour thing.'

'What's going to happen to Toby?'

'He's going to be fine. I'm only doing a local tour so I won't be away for all that long and he is more than capable of looking after himself.'

'How's he handling Claire's death?'

'Better than I am. He seems to be capable of a great many things. At least that's the show that he puts on for me. What goes on behind the scenes in the privacy of his own room I couldn't tell you.'

'He keeps himself to himself?'

'He keeps his grief very private. Everyone seems to expect me to write about mine and make it very public. I'm sure that Toby would hate that.'

'It might be good for you though.'

'So you've said. I'm not entirely inclined to it myself.'

'It's something that you should think about, that's all I say.'

'I think of little else but Claire.'

'So, what would be the harm in writing some of that down? Make some good out of it.'

'You know, that's exactly what she said to me.'

'Well, she was right. I see no reason why good can't come

of what is a terrible situation and you might be helping others.'

'Others?'

'Yes, other people that have lost someone and are struggling to come to terms with their grief and loss. You could do a lot of good out of it. Make people realise that they're not alone, make you realise that you're not alone.'

'I realise that I'm not alone. Not everyone feels the need to write about their grief though.'

'Not everyone is a writer.'

'Well, that's true, and thank God for it or the world would be a terrible place.'

'There'd be more bookshops though.'

'You think?'

'Supply and demand.'

'Also be a lot of crap books on the market.'

'There's a lot of crap books on the market anyway.'

'I know, I've written some of them.'

'Your bank account would seem to disagree.'

'Just because a book is a bestseller doesn't mean that it is any good. Plenty of bestselling authors that I could mention that couldn't write serious fiction for toffee.'

'You can name names if you like.'

'I wouldn't want to get sued.'

'I still think you should turn it to your advantage.'

'I don't know. It makes it sound like it's a business transaction. That her death is just another excuse for me to churn out another book. It somehow cheapens it for me. Makes it all seem like… I don't know what.'

'You could be turning some good out of it all.'

'So you say, but I'm not convinced.'

'Well, perhaps you should work on a novel that has nothing

to do with Claire.'

'I've thought about it.'

'Good, you should do it.'

'I'm not sure that I've got the energy for it at the moment. Writing a novel requires a great amount of staying power and I just don't have all that much at present. I feel sapped of all my energy.'

'It's inevitable, but the moment will pass and you will be able to work again. Perhaps this book tour is what you need to kick you into shape. Get out there and sign a few books and shake a few hands.'

Daniel was famous enough now that he could expect queues for his book signings to be out of the shop and around the corner. He remembered the first one that he had done when only six people had shown up to have their books signed. He had a number of signed books himself, not his own ones, other people's. He had Neil Gaiman and Terry Pratchett that he was particularly proud of.

Some authors found it curious as to why people would queue up to get a signature on a bit of paper. It seemed a strange thing to do when you thought about it. There wasn't any other profession outside of the arts where this happened. You didn't get a new kitchen fitted and then ask the workmen to sign the worktop for you. It was a bizarre thing to do, but it seemed to make people happy so who was he to argue?

'What's with the beard, anyway?' asked Jordan. 'Are you trying to appear more author-ish?'

'No, I just couldn't be bothered to shave.'

'I hate to say it, but it suits you. Gives you an air of knowledge.'

Daniel snorted. 'I'm not sure about that.'

'Maybe every author should be made to wear one.'

'Not a bad idea, that way people would be able to single them out in the street and avoid them.'

'Do you think people should avoid writers?'

'Probably a sensible thing to do.'

'Do you find that everyone you speak to wants to be a writer?'

'Not everyone, I mean you don't want to be one.'

'There must be a lot of people that want your advice though and want to know how they can be a writer.'

'Yeah, I get a lot of that, particularly at signings. I particularly hate those that turn up at book signings with a manuscript in their hands that they would just like me to read and give them my opinion on.'

'What do you tell them?'

'I politely tell them that I have not got the time and if they really want an expert opinion then they should send it to my publishers.'

'So, you pass the buck?'

'Pretty much.'

'And what do you do with those that say they want to be a writer, but don't have any manuscripts to show you?'

'Oh, they are easier to deal with. I just tell them that if they want to be a writer then they first have to learn how to read. I tell them to go and read as many books as they can in the genre that they are interested in. Get a taste for what it's all about. Find out what is happening in their chosen field and what people are writing about.'

'Sound advice.'

'Well, it's the advice that I was given when I started out. Seems to be the sensible thing to do. You have to learn how to read if you want to write.'

'What about creative writing courses?'

Daniel waved his hand in dismissal. 'They are all right if you believe in that kind of thing.'

'But you don't?'

'I don't really believe that writing is something that can be taught, although it is something that can be learnt.'

'You might have to explain that one.'

'Well, if you haven't got it in you then no amount of creative writing courses are going to help you to write. But, you can from scratch learn how to write.'

'By reading?'

'Exactly. We will make a writer out of you yet.'

'I don't think it's something that I would be any good at. They say that everyone has a novel in them, but I'm pretty sure that I don't.'

'Best to know your limitations. If you want to do creative writing courses then all well and good, but I would be inclined to keep your money and buy books with it instead.'

'Why?'

'Because it's like when you send a book to a publisher or an agent and they turn you down – it doesn't mean that your book is rubbish, although it can be the case, it might just mean that it is not right for them in their opinion. Your acceptance or rejection is based on the opinion of only a few people, initially only one if you are rejected.'

'I see.'

'It's the same with a creative writing course. You have the advice of your tutor and that is it. Who's to say if their advice is right for you. They may think you have no talent whereas someone else might think that you are full of potential.'

'I understand where you are coming from, but aren't they meant to be objective?'

'Meant to be, but writing is something that is very personal, so it's difficult to segregate your personal opinions from what you are reading. You know what it's like, sometimes you read a book and you just can't get on with it. That doesn't mean it's a bad book. Someone obviously thought that it had worth or they wouldn't have published it.'

'I suppose so.'

'Definitely. But you can't get on with every book that is published. That's just too much to ask.'

'You seem to do all right for readers.'

'I've been lucky. I've a good fan base now, but that doesn't mean that they will always like my books. I don't write to a formula. I write what I want to write, which means that the next book I write they may hate and reject in droves.'

'It's likely to still sell though because they are buying it for the name rather than the book.'

'Absolutely they are, but if they hate the next one, then they are less likely to buy the one that comes after that, even if it's really good.'

'Fame is fickle.'

'You know, I don't really see myself as famous.'

'Well, no one is queuing up to get my signature.'

'Yeah, but it's not as if I am Brad Pitt or anything.'

'Fame comes in different shapes and sizes.'

'I guess so. I still don't see myself as famous though. I'm just a writer that got lucky.'

'I think this new book and the associated promotional side of things will be good for you.'

'Because it will get me out of the house?'

'Partly because of that and partly because it might help in taking your mind off of Claire for a while.'

'I don't think there's anything that will enable me to take my mind off of Claire.'

Daniel had not stopped thinking about Claire. He figured that it was something that was going to occupy his thoughts for a long time to come. He thought about her first thing in the morning when he woke up and he thought about her last thing at night when he went to bed. He couldn't imagine that there would ever be a time when he wouldn't think about her.

He knew the maxim that time was a great healer, but he didn't really believe that. He didn't believe that it would get any easier as time went by. He still thought that he would think about her every day, but maybe he would get to a stage when she wouldn't be the first thing on his mind when he got up and wouldn't be the last thing on his mind when he went to bed. Perhaps normal life would intrude and a level of normality would return.

He thought that this was the way that things went. He thought that you continued to remember the pain all the time, but eventually the pain would go from acute to a dull ache that was almost in the background. Still there, still reminding you that you had lost something, but not as painful as it had been before.

That's what he hoped at any rate. He couldn't bear for the pain to remain so acute all of the time. That would be too much to cope with. No one would be able to live like that with it going on forever. He could just about get through the day now without feeling the need to lie on the floor, curled up in a ball and crying his eyes out.

He didn't feel that he was all that far away from being like that. Just one memory away from curling up on the floor was how he largely felt. It didn't sound all that much, but he felt it was an improvement on how he had been before. It had been some months since she had died now and he knew that he should really be getting on with his life. He had promised her that he would continue to work. He had managed to avoid promising her that he would date again because he had absolutely no intention of doing so. Maybe that would change in the future when years rather than months had passed, but he just couldn't imagine getting into all that again.

How did you meet anyone anyway? He couldn't imagine going onto some internet dating site, which seemed to be what a lot of other people did these days who were too busy to have much of a social life. He didn't really want to meet a woman in a pub or a club. He wasn't really one for nightclubs anyway and doubted that, even if he was, he would be able to find a long-term relationship in one. He just couldn't imagine that he would ever be in a situation that enabled him to meet women who weren't after him because of what, Jordan referred to, as his fame or his money.

How did you decide who was genuine and who wasn't? It just seemed to be too much of an effort as far as he was concerned and he couldn't see the point of it. Best to leave these things alone. He had married the love of his life and now she had died. There was nothing else to be said about it. He had lived, he had loved and perhaps Wordsworth had been right when he said that it was better to have loved and lost than to have never loved at all.

Who knows? He didn't consider himself an expert, but maybe with the death of Claire he was an expert. He had known what it was like to have loved and lost. He had lost her love, but he still was in love with her. He was in love with her memory if he could not physically be in love with her any longer. Love didn't die just because someone was dead. He was only discovering this for himself. He hadn't really thought about it before, but it was true. Love continued beyond the physical existence.

He liked to think that Claire still carried on somewhere, in some form or another, and he was sure that if she did then she was still in love with him and was watching over him. Like he promised her, he still talked to her on a daily basis. Usually when Toby was at school so that he wouldn't think that his dad had gone mad. He didn't think about it as a madness, but perhaps some other people would think of it as being slightly crazy. Talking to someone who was no longer there. Who couldn't hear you, as some people would have you believe, but Daniel was convinced that Claire could hear him, so he spoke to her all the time.

He didn't tell anyone about this. It was a form of therapy for him. He didn't really fancy the idea of going to therapy and seeing a grief counsellor. He didn't think that was something that would help him at all (although he understood how it could help some people). He had always been someone that had wanted to sort things out for himself though and not rely on others when it came to sorting out his problems. He was a very private man, despite his writing and didn't like sharing his inner most thoughts with a stranger. It was different when you were writing things down on paper, you didn't get to see the other person's reaction to what you were writing, well not usually, unless you were at one of those horrid talks where they expected you to read out a couple of chapters of your book.

Writing was a therapy as well, but it was a little too close to the knuckle to consider writing about Claire. He didn't feel like doing that at all. It was all too close and personal for him. The wound was still open and raw to be thinking of prizing it open and digging about inside. He couldn't imagine that it was a project that he was ever likely to work on, but you never knew what the future might hold. He never liked to say never. He might feel that there was a need for something like a book on grief. He might be able to make it impersonal... but then if he did that, what was the point of writing it?

Maybe he could distance himself slightly by turning it into a novel. He was a novelist after all. That would allow him to write about grief but keep it at an arm's length. It seemed like it might be an option, but he didn't want his next book to be about grief. He didn't know what his next book was going to be about, but it wasn't going to be about grief and loss. If he was ever to write that book then it was too soon to write it yet. That would potentially be a bridge that he crossed at some point in the future. It wasn't something to worry about at the moment.

Something that he did need to worry about more immediately was Toby. Toby had always been something of an introvert (he took after Daniel in that regard) but since Claire had died, he had withdrawn into himself even more. Daniel had allowed him to have his peace and spend time on his own, doing his own thing, but this had gone on for several months and it seemed that it might be getting a little too much now. He needed to come out of his shell a little and interact with people a bit more.

Daniel felt like a bit of a fraud in thinking that Toby needed to be more interactive when he had been more interactive than he had. At least he had been going to school and seeing his mates. Daniel hadn't left the house. The only time that he saw Toby was at meal times. The rest of the time he preferred to stick to his room. Daniel realised that this was not necessarily a grief thing, but rather a teenage thing. Daniel remembered spending most of his time in his room when he had been a teenager, it was the kind of thing that teenagers did, wasn't it? They preferred their own space rather than spending their time with their uncool parents. That's the way that he thought about it at any rate, and he was sure that, to a degree, he was right. He decided to speak to him at dinner that night.

'Are you okay?' he asked as they ate their lasagne.

'Yeah, fine.'

'How is school?'

'Yeah, good.'

'Any problems?'

Toby narrowed his eyes at him. 'What sort of problems?'

'Well grades suffering because you are distracted or any bullying or stuff like that really.'

'Why would I be being bullied?'

'Well, some kids are cruel and they know that your mum has just died and they might decide to bully you over it.'

'Dad, I'm almost sixteen not in kindergarten,'

'Even so, kids can be cruel at any age.'

'I'm not being bullied.'

'I'm pleased to hear it. You would tell me if you were being bullied though, wouldn't you?'

'Yes, I would. I would make a special point of telling you.'

'And your grades?'

'My grades are doing just fine. Nothing to worry about there. I'm sure that I will be able to pass all my exams.'

'That's good. Do you want to talk about it?'

'Talk about what?'

'Mum.'

'What's there to talk about?'

'Well, I know that her death has hit you hard, it's hit us both hard. We haven't really talked about it. Maybe we should.'

'She died. It's not fair that she died. She shouldn't have died. She shouldn't have got bloody lung cancer when she didn't smoke.'

'It's all unfair, isn't it?'

'Yes, but talking about it won't bring her back.'

'It might make you feel better, Toby.'

'I doubt it. I feel that it will probably just make it more painful to keep opening the wound.'

'You sound exactly like me.'

'Mum always said that I took after you more than her.'

'You developed her taste in classical music. Always preferred a bit of prog rock myself.'

'That's because you are so retro.'

'Yes, I suppose so. You know I'm here if you want to talk about mum, don't you?'

'I know. Do you want to talk about her? Is that what this is about?'

'Me?'

'Yes, you, Dad.'

'We are talking about you.'

'But it seems to me that you might want to talk about mum more than I do. Is that the case?'

'Well, I don't know. I was thinking more about you.'

'It's okay if you want to talk about her. I miss her.'

'I miss her too. I always thought that she would be there and to have her gone so early seems so damn unfair.'

'It is unfair.'

'Yes, yes, it is. It's bloody unfair, but there isn't really anything that we can do about it is there?'

261

'No there isn't anything we can do other than what Churchill used to say.'

'What did Churchill used to say, Toby?'

'He used to say "keep buggering on."'

'Yes, he did, didn't he?' Daniel said, laughing. It was the first time that he had laughed for what seemed to be an age. He was slightly surprised by this as a few sentences ago he had felt like crying.

'Death is the one thing that we can be sure of.'

'That's true. It will come to us all at some point. Just seems a shame that it came to your mum so early.'

'None of us can say when our time will come. I could be hit by a bus tomorrow.'

'I'd rather you weren't.'

'Just saying.'

'You are okay though?'

'As okay as you can be. How are you?'

'I'm okay.'

'You need to get out of the house more.'

'I've got a book tour coming up, you know that. I will get out of the house to do that.'

'You need to socialise though. Go see some friends.'

'They rather come and see me.'

'Not the point. You need to get out and see them in a different environment to these four walls. It's not good for you.'

'I'm doing all right.'

'I don't think you are. I think you need to get out a bit more and what's with the beard?'

'Just an author thing going on.'

'Oh right, because I thought it was because you couldn't be bothered to shave.'

'That may be an element in it.'

'Not sure it suits you.'

'Thanks.'

'Well, what do you expect? I've spent all my life seeing you clean shaven and now you are suddenly some hairy monster.'

'I don't think that it's that bad.'

'Maybe if you trimmed it a bit it would be better. Less of a caveman thing going on then.'

'You think I look like a caveman?'

'Just an opinion.'

'Thanks.'

'You're welcome. I would have thought that as an author you were used to constructive criticism.'

'I'm not sure making comments about my facial hair is constructive criticism. More of a personal attack.'

'Not much of an attack saying that you just need to have a bit of a trim. I'm sure that it will be fine if you trim it up a bit. Look a little more normal and a little less wild.'

'Well, you might be right. I suppose I don't want to scare people on the book tour.'

'No. They might not buy your book if they are scared of you.'

'I don't know, maybe it will scare them into buying the book because they fear the consequences if they don't.'

'Well, that's one way of looking at it.'

'I know I have been a bit absent, but then I haven't seen all that much of you. You spend all your time in your room.'

'I like spending time in my room. It's my personal space.'

'Yeah, I get that.'

'Well, there you go then. Nothing to worry about at all.'

'I'm your dad, I will always be worried about you.'

'I'm more worried about you.'

'Me?'

'Yeah, of course. I mean, I may have lost my mum, but you lost your wife. Seems much more serious to me than losing a parent. You expect to lose a parent really, maybe not as early as mum went, but you expect to lose them at some point. It's not always the same with a partner.'

'This is true.'

'And then, of course, you have been hiding in the house all the time and growing beards and stuff. It's not good for you.'

'So they tell me.'

'Maybe this book tour will help you a bit. Get you out to meet people, shake a few hands, take a few photos, sign a few books.'

'That's what I do.'

'You haven't done it for a while though.'

'Well, it's going to be difficult now. I am only doing a local tour so I don't have to leave you alone too long. If I do a big tour, I won't be able to leave you alone.'

'Dad, I'm almost sixteen.'

'Yeah, almost, but not quite and there are laws against these kinds of things and you wouldn't want me to leave you with your grandmother, would you?'

'God no.'

'Exactly. I don't think you have done anything to deserve that level of punishment.'

'If I didn't have exams then I would come with you.'

'Maybe you will one day.'

'You used to tour the world.'

'Well, bits of it. I'm still not that big in America, but I can't criticise the number of sales that I do have there. Enough to make a lot of authors happy, just not in the Stephen King league.'

'Not yet at least.'

'Your faith in me is admirable.'

'I suppose it's because you were an author before I was born, so it's all I have ever known you do. If it was something that you had turned to later in life then I might have been a little unsure of your potential success, but you were having success long before I came along.'

'Well, I don't know if I will go that far. Moderate success maybe.'

'You were published, that's more than some people.'

'True.'

'You know, it's okay to talk about mum to me if you want to, Dad.'

'I know.'

'I don't mind talking to you about her. I just don't really have anything to say about her that's all. Maybe with time I will.'

'I don't want you to forget about her.'

'Of course I won't forget about her. I'm almost sixteen—.'

'Yes, you said. Several times in fact.'

'—not four. I will have my memories of her just as you will have your memories of her as well.'

'That's good.'

'So, you can talk to me any time you want and you can talk to me about anything you want to, okay, Dad?'

'Okay, Toby.'

Daniel felt that at some point during the conversation he had lost his way and wasn't entirely sure that he had been able to find it again. It all seemed rather surreal. Perhaps Toby was handling things better than he thought. Or, maybe he was just really good at putting a brave face on things. Daniel wasn't really sure which it was and whether he should continue to be worried about things. He could take Toby on face value, in which case everything appeared to be all right, but what if he was harbouring deep filled grief and would ruin the remainder of his childhood and result in him having to see psychiatrists in the future?

Maybe he over thought things too much. That was always a possibility. It was the kind of thing that he did as a writer though. He couldn't help but think, hell, most of the time he was paid to think. It was what he did for a living, near enough. Not that he had been doing all that much of it lately.

I sometimes felt that I was the parent and it was dad who was the child. He didn't seem to be handling things as well as I thought he was. I suppose that is only to be expected. It was hard for me, but it must have been ten times worse for him. I can't imagine what it must have been like. There was probably a degree of survivor's guilt going on. He was probably asking himself why he had survived and mum had died. I'm sure that he would have changed places with her if he could have. I doubt that she would have wanted him to though. I have no idea if I will ever find someone to share my life with the way that they did. I've never really had a steady girlfriend. Just casual flings. I know what you will say, that there is plenty of time for that sort of thing and maybe you are right. We will see what happens.

Then

'You want me to what?' Daniel asked with disbelief.

'When the time comes, I want you to help me to die. I don't want to carry on with the pain and suffering before falling into a coma where I'm not able to say goodbye in my own time and in my own way.'

'You have got to be kidding me.'

'I'm not kidding you.'

'You can't be serious.'

'I'm deadly serious. I want you to help me go. My way. Not giving into this disease, but going with some dignity and when the time is right.'

'I can't believe that you would ask me to do that.'

'Who else am I going to ask? You're my husband. The love of my life. There is no one else who can help me do this. When the time comes, I will probably be too weak to do it myself.'

'You've really thought this out.'

'Yes, I have. You can give me an overdose on the morphine. They have left us enough to do that and no suspicion will fall on you as they don't know how much I'm taking. It's just as and when required.'

'I'm not sure I'll be able to do something like that. It's one thing that you are dying, but to kill you is… unthinkable.'

'Don't look on it as killing me, look on it as saving me from further pain and misery. Look on it as a last act of love.'

'I don't know what to say.'

'Say you will think about it. I know I have launched it on you, but I have been thinking about this for some time and I would rather go out on my terms instead of being dictated to by this terrible thing.'

'Okay, I will think about it.'

'That's all I can ask of you. Now I need to rest. I'm so very tired. No matter how much I rest, I never seem to feel any better for it.'

Claire had told Daniel that he should think about what she had said, but the problem was that he didn't know what to think. How could he even find the words to articulate what she had said to him? There wasn't anyone that he could discuss the matter with, as by the very nature of what she had asked him it had to remain a secret. He would have to keep his own counsel on this. The only one that he could remotely discuss it with was Claire, and she seemed to have very strong opinions on what it was that she wanted.

He had thought about discussing it with Jordan, but that would put Jordan in a very difficult position as well and would raise suspicion when Claire eventually did die. He decided to examine the situation as best as he could from all sides.

He didn't want Claire to die. That much was a given fact, but it was something that was rather out of his hands. She was going to die, regardless of what it was that he decided to do, or not do. The only question was whether she would die at his hand or not. He didn't want her to die, but did he really want to draw out her pain and suffering for the purely selfish reasons of spending a little longer with her? Did he really want to see her in pain? Wouldn't it be best to allow that suffering to stop and for her to exit this world on her own terms?

Daniel found that there were so many questions going

around that he really didn't know the answers to them. He didn't want her to die, but nor did he want to see her in pain, but that didn't mean that he wanted to kill her either. What would happen to him if he did kill her? Would he be arrested? Stand trial for her murder? That's how the police would look at it, surely? It wasn't legal to commit euthanasia in this country. They would have to fly to Sweden, or Switzerland, or wherever it was that had the clinics that allowed you to die on your own terms. He didn't think that Claire was up to that sort of thing. She had a more immediate solution at hand.

He had to decide if he was prepared to help Claire achieve what it was that she was after. It was a big decision to make. He wasn't really all that concerned about what would happen to him afterwards and what the police might think about it all. He could imagine the headlines though *Bestselling Novelist Murders Wife*. It would probably improve his sales somewhat, but wouldn't be particularly good for him, or for Toby for that matter, who would probably end up living with his grandmother, which was not a scenario that any of them wanted.

So, if he was less concerned about his own well-being, he had to make the decision of whether he was prepared to commit the act that would enable Claire to die. He was caught between the two worlds of loving her so much that he didn't want her to die and loving her so much that he didn't want her to suffer. Of course he didn't want her to suffer, that was obvious. He just had to work out if his love for her was sufficiently strong that he was prepared to be the hand that killed her rather than allow her to suffer.

'Have you made up your mind?' Claire asked him when she awoke from her sleep.

'I've hardly had all that much time to think about it.'

269

'It's a simple enough decision to make I would have thought.'

'It's not that easy a decision.'

'Are you worried about being caught?'

'Not particularly.'

'Because we can take steps to ensure that you are not caught.'

'You can never cover all the bases when it comes to things like that, but that isn't what's worrying me.'

'What is worrying you.'

'The fact that I would be killing you.'

'Don't look at it as killing me, look at it as relieving me of a lot of unnecessary suffering. You would really be doing me a favour.'

'Yes, that is true and is certainly one way of looking at it, but I will forever have to live the rest of my life knowing that it was my hand that killed you.'

'Yes, you will have to live with it, but maybe you don't have to play such an active part. Maybe you can just give me the morphine and then let me take it on my own.'

'Is that how you want to do it, morphine?'

'It seems the logical way to do it. It is the only real thing that we have to hand that would make it easy to do. If you hit me over the head with a lead pipe then the police might get suspicious.'

'Yes, I suppose I would find that a difficult one to explain.'

'If they even notice that the morphine has gone you can just tell them that you flushed the surplus down the toilet. I am sure that they will not even pay it that much mind. They know that I'm dying. It won't be a suspicious, unexpected death. They probably won't even look twice at it.'

'I suppose not.'

'Does that mean you will help?'

Daniel sighed. 'How can I refuse you? We have always done everything together. There has never been anything that we have not consented upon as a couple. I can hardly abandon you now when you, arguably, need me the most.'

'I love you.'

'I love you too.'

'I know this is something big that I'm asking you to do and I know that it is a burden that I'm asking you to live with for the rest of your life.'

'I certainly won't be able to tell anyone about it.'

'No, you won't. It will be a secret that I'm asking you to keep until the day that you die, which will hopefully be many years in the future.'

'I think I can bear it.'

'I think you can as well. I wouldn't ask you if it wasn't for the fact that I thought you were strong enough to be able to cope with it.'

'So, when do you want to do this?'

'Not yet. I will let you know when the time is right. I will know when I don't feel that I can go on any longer.'

'In the meantime, we shall have to make you as comfortable as possible.'

'Have you told Jordan what is happening?'

'About the euthanasia?'

'No, about the diagnosis and prognosis?'

'No, I haven't.'

'You should tell him.'

'There just doesn't seem to have been the time.'

'He deserves to know.'

'Have you told your mother?'

'Yes, she is no doubt already choosing the best funeral outfit that she can so she looks her best. She didn't seem to show much other emotion.'

'That woman staggers belief,' said Daniel, shaking his head.

'She is what she is. There's no changing her now.'

'If only one could change your parents.'

'I would have changed my mother a long time ago. Must be someone out there that would have been a better mother.'

'I should think that there are any number of candidates that would be able to fulfil the office better than she has.'

'Have I been a good mother?'

Daniel took Claire's hand. 'Of course you have. You only have to look at what a fine boy Toby has grown up to be.'

'That could be because you are a good father.'

'It's because of a joint effort that we have put into raising him. He is a well-adjusted kid who knows what he wants in life.'

'I wish I could see him turn out to be a man. There are so many possibilities that he has.'

'He will be a fine man and caring and considerate. He will make a woman very happy one day to be her husband.'

'Well he might turn out to be gay.'

'Doesn't matter what he does. He has to go the path that he is most happy with and it wouldn't matter in the slightest what he turned out to be so long as he wasn't cruel and nasty.'

'Not like my mother, in other words?'

'I'm sure he is more likely to take after you than he is to take after your mother. He doesn't care all that much for his grandmother.'

'Probably because she has never been like a grandmother to him.'

'Can I get you anything? Some soup or a cup of tea?'

'I could try a cup of tea, but I'm not sure that I'll be able to take much else. Everything seems to be such an effort. Who knew that dying could be so difficult?'

Daniel went to make the tea. He found it difficult to get used to the gallows humour of Claire. She was taking dying as something far better than he was. He was pretty sure that were he in her shoes then he wouldn't be able to find the humour in everything. He would probably be living in fear for what was about to happen to him. It wasn't something that he particularly liked to think about. She was able to joke about it though and was clear headed enough to be able to plan her own exit with calculation and determination. It truly staggered him.

'I don't want to die; you know that, don't you?' Claire asked him when he returned with the tea for her and a coffee for him.

'I don't imagine that you do. Nobody really wants to die.'

'And yet it is something that all must do at some point. Whether we want to or not.'

'That's true.'

'I don't think it's the moment of death that people fear. That's a momentary thing that will either result in an oblivion that we will not be aware of or a continued existence that will presumably be better than this one.'

'You'd like to think that it'll be better. Would be a bit of a bummer if it turned out that this was heaven and the next life was worse than it is here.'

'I think it's the long-drawn-out death that people fear and the pain that comes with it. People fear pain.'

'Yes, they do.'

'If we could have a life without pain then maybe this would be a better life for all.'

'I don't know. Maybe we need to experience pain to know

what it is like when there is no pain and to appreciate it as such.'

'Yes, I suppose that's one way of looking at it. You should have done a degree in philosophy.'

'If I'd done a degree in philosophy then it is a real chance that we wouldn't have met.'

'I don't know. I think it was fated that we would meet and end up together. We would have found a way to meet despite studying different subjects.'

'Do you think it was fate?'

'I do. Don't you?'

'I suppose it was. I feel like I was always meant to be with you. I only wish that I had met you even sooner so that I could have loved you even longer.'

'We met pretty early on in life. If we had met too early then you might have grown bored with me.'

'I doubt that very much.'

'The point of all of this is that I don't want to die. I'm not choosing to end my life because I don't want to be with you. The choice of living or dying has been taken out of our hands. If medical science offered any hope of a recovery, then I would grasp it with both hands, you know that, don't you?'

'Yes, of course.'

'We have reached the end game though. There's nothing more that they can do for me and so we have to work with the cards that we have been dealt. I don't think taking my own life at such a late stage of things is going to cause any issues over hanging around for a sudden cure to be found.'

'That's what the politicians would have people believe. That there's always hope and so you must cling to life without the chance to choose your own end. That's why they won't make it legal in this country to euthanize.'

'They might do one day. One day they might come to their senses and realise that people have a right to determine when their own deaths should be.'

'I think it has to be judged on a case-by-case basis though. I mean, okay, you have been given a terminal diagnosis and there's no hope of a recovery. Then that is a clear case, but suppose you had a wasting illness that effected your quality of life and meant that you couldn't do anything for yourself. There's no immediate chance of a natural death, but your life is no longer what it used to be. Should you be allowed to end your life in those circumstances when there's a possibility that one day someone might make a breakthrough that would give you better quality of life?'

'I see your point.'

'I think it is those circumstances that frighten the politicians. The chances where you can argue that there's still hope, regardless of how much of a small glimmer of hope it might be.'

'It's easy for politicians to make decisions that affect the lives of others though when it has no come back on them.'

'Perhaps they're also aware that there might be mad doctors that will euthanize people left, right and centre when there's no real need to.'

'A bit like Harold Shipman then?'

'Exactly. Maybe that's what they're afraid of.'

'They could have special clinics that deal with it only so not just any old doctor would be able to issue a lethal injection to someone. Something where it's carefully regulated and only certain people are allowed to end their lives there.'

'It's worked in other countries.'

'Sometimes I feel that other countries are a little more forward thinking than we are. The government try to protect people so much that they don't realise that they're smothering them.'

'I think they realise. I just don't think that they care.'

'Yeah, that's probably true.'

'I think it's been a long time since the government actually cared about anyone other than themselves. If, of course, they ever did care about anyone else that is.'

'I suspect not.'

'No.'

'Are you writing?'

'Not really.'

'You should write. You shouldn't stop writing because of what is happening to me.'

'I think I've other priorities at the moment.'

'But you still need to write. It's important that you do.'

'I'll write when the mood takes me. It's not good to write every day anyway. Need time to allow the brain cells to recharge and the creative juices to flow again.'

'If you say so.'

'I do.'

'I will take your word for it then.'

They lapsed into silence for a while Claire tried to drink her tea, which Daniel had to help her with as she found her hands were shaking a little and she was unable to balance the mug without spilling some of it.

'I've always been grateful that we have been able to speak,' she said after her exertions with the mug had proven to be something that she didn't feel was worth the effort.

'How do you mean?'

'Well look at literature.'

'What about it?'

276

'Well look at all the stories where trouble has come calling because couples were not able to talk to each other and clear up misunderstandings and mistakes.'

'Like Othello and Desdemona, you mean?'

'Well, they're a prime example. Just look at them. If Othello had spoken to Desdemona instead of putting all his faith in Iago, then none of it would have happened and they probably would have both lived happily ever after.'

'That's true. Wouldn't have made for much of a play though, would it?'

'Perhaps not, but they would have been happier. It's the same with Thomas Hardy. Half the time the lovers in the books misunderstand each other and get themselves into all sorts of scrapes and situations purely because they don't actually talk to each other.'

'Isn't the best story about conflict and misunderstanding though?'

'Well, there are all sorts of stories. They don't have to all be about conflict and misunderstanding.'

'Most of the best ones are though.'

'Well, probably. That's not the point though.'

'What is the point?'

'The point is, Danny, that I'm glad that in this marriage we have always been able to talk about problems and have never allowed the situation to get the better of us and put us in the position where we have that conflict and misunderstanding that exists in so much literature.'

'So am I. What made you think about that all of a sudden?'

'I don't know. Partly because you have been reading Hardy to me and partly because I have been reflecting on my life rather a bit.'

'Have you?'

'Of course. There's little else to do but reflect upon your life when you discover that it's very nearly coming to an end. You think about all the decisions that you have made. Have I made the right choices? Regretting things done or not done. Thinking about all the times when you could have done something different. Reliving past humiliations. That kind of thing.'

'Do you have many regrets?'

'No. I don't think so, at any rate. I always wanted to live my life so that I had no regrets when the time came. My one big regret is that I'm leaving you too soon. Should have had at least another forty years with you before it was time for one of us to go.'

'Life can be very unfair at times.'

'It can, but it's death that's the most unfair of all things. I'm not ready for it and yet it's calling me. I know that I don't have as long as I would've liked.'

'You don't have as long as any of us would've liked.'

'But we do, at least, have this time. It's a chance to say goodbye. It's a chance to ease out with some dignity rather than being killed in a car crash or dying when there was no chance to speak to you.'

'That's true. I hadn't really thought about it like that.'

'It's important that we are able to spend this time together,' she said as she took him by the hand. 'You have to learn how to let me go though.'

'I know. It won't be easy.'

'It won't be easy, but you have to do it. I'm going to go whether you let me go or not. It would be better if you were able to let me go and be at peace with it.'

'How can I be at peace with it? It's such a stupid bloody

thing to happen.'

'I know it is, but it's what it is, and we have to live with it – well you do, I don't, as it turns out.'

'I do wish you wouldn't joke about these things.'

'Who's joking? I'm just stating a fact.'

'That's as maybe.'

'I'm glad I'm not losing my mind though,' said Claire after a moment or two of thought.

'What do you mean?'

'Well, supposing that Alzheimer's had been my end. I don't think I could face losing all that I had known before the end eventually came. Or think of all the other ways that you can lose your mind before your body eventually gives in. I don't think I could have faced that.'

'But when you lose your mind, you wouldn't be aware of the fact that you have lost it. You would exist in a state of oblivion.'

'True, but there would be the period when you would know that it was going to happen. When you would forget words, or people, memories and all of that. They would just slip away from you and you would have the frustration of knowing that they are there, but unobtainable. Something that you constantly reach for, but are unable to get a hold of.'

'Rather like a bar of soap in the bath.'

'It's as good an image as any, I suppose. Yes, there would be that scary period before you eventually forgot all when you didn't know what was going to happen, or rather you knew only too well what it was that was going to happen.'

'Not an easy thing to live with.'

'And not an easy way to die, I should think.'

'I doubt that there's any way that will be an easy way to die. They all have their disadvantages, namely that the result is always going to be the same. But, really, Claire, do we have to talk about death so much?'

'It's the elephant in the room and there's no sense in ignoring it. It's going to happen, Danny, and you have to be prepared for the fact that it's going to happen. I don't think I want people to wear black to my funeral.'

'Well, it's your funeral.'

'I want people to be happy.'

'I doubt that will be a possibility for many that will be going. Your mother might be happy, I suppose, particularly if she has a new dress that she is able to show off.'

'I know, I expect people will be sad, but I want it to be a celebration for my life, rather than a big scene of mourning.'

'I can't promise not to cry.'

'So long as you don't cry for too long and too loud. I want you to remember the happy times that we spent together, rather than being depressed by the fact that I'm no longer here.'

'A rather tall order, I feel.'

'I don't want it to be a religious ceremony either.'

'Well, we have never been particularly religious, so that makes sense.'

'My mother won't like it, but it's my funeral and I see that I should be allowed to do things the way that I want to do them, regardless.'

'Well, your mother can do one.'

'She might be a little difficult when I'm gone.'

'She's been a little difficult when you were here, I don't see why there should be any particular change.'

'I also don't want any hymns. I can't see the point of having hymns that nobody sings and people just feel awkward about.'

'That shouldn't be a problem.'

'I would like songs and a bit of classical music.'

'Do you have anything in particular in mind?'

'I'm not sure. I can't quite make up my mind. I might give you a list and let you choose.'

'Well, I will do my best.'

'I'm sure you will.'

'Is there anything else that you want?'

'No flowers. They're just a waste of people's money. Let them donate to a cancer charity if they want to, but it is pointless just buying flowers that are going to be left on a grave and nobody is going to see them. Complete waste of money.'

'You want to be buried then, rather than be cremated?'

'Yeah, I suppose we should have discussed that before. Yes, I want to be buried. I can't face the idea of being burnt to a pile of ash. Doesn't seem right to me. Rather let things go naturally.'

'That's fair enough.'

'When you go to book the funeral though I want you to choose the most inexpensive one that you can find.'

'Why?'

'Because I think funerals are a waste of money. I can't see the point of an elaborate funeral.'

'It's the last act of respect that someone can do for someone else. It's a way of saying goodbye.'

'And as such the funerals are more about the mourners than they are about the deceased.'

'I guess so.'

'Well, I don't think that's right. I want my funeral to be about me and I don't want an expensive one.'

'I really don't think your mother is going to like that.'

'Screw my mother.'

'People will think I'm just a cheapskate.'

'People can think what they like. It's the way that I want it to be. No expensive coffin, just your basic one will do. It's only going to be buried at any rate. You will be lucky if you see it for an hour at most.'

'Well, that's one way of looking at it, I suppose.'

'It's really the only way of looking at it.'

'Well, if that's what you want, then that is what I will do my best to ensure that you have.'

'Thank you.'

'Do you want some of that tea?'

'I would rather have a little morphine, if I'm honest.'

'You in pain?'

'All the time, near enough anyway. The morphine helps a little, but not enough. It turns it into a dull ache rather than an acute pain, so I suppose that is something.'

Daniel went to the bedside cabinet and poured out some of the morphine that they had been supplied with and gave it to Claire who took it eagerly.

'I feel like a drug addict,' she said as she swallowed the liquid.

'I wouldn't worry too much about that.'

She handed the cup back to him.

'I don't know how I'm going to be able to drink an overdose of that stuff. You're really going to have to help me out and virtually pour it down my throat, I think.'

'Well, let's not worry about that now.'

'I think I need to get some sleep again.'

'Okay, let's settle you down.'

Daniel helped to get her comfortable and then left to take the empty cups back to the kitchen and put them in the dishwasher. He tidied up a little and gave some thought as to what was to be had for dinner. Claire wasn't really eating all that much so it was just Toby and himself that he had to worry about. He would probably knock something together from out of the freezer tonight, or maybe he would order a Just Eat delivery. It wasn't their regular takeaway night, but what the hell, live a little.

Claire had said that the elephant in the room was the fact that she was going to die, but upon reflection Daniel thought that this wasn't the case. He thought that the elephant in the room was more the fact that she had asked him to assist her in dying. He wasn't entirely convinced that her plan of a morphine overdose would work. Firstly, he didn't know how much morphine it took to kill someone, so he didn't know if they had enough of the stuff. Secondly, he wasn't sure that she would be able to get enough of the stuff down before she passed out or gagged and vomited it all back up again. He wasn't convinced that it was the best plan, but then he wasn't sure what a better plan would be other than to let nature take its course, and Claire had made it clear that it wasn't the way that she wanted to go.

Daniel wasn't sure that he agreed with Claire. He could understand where she was coming from, but he didn't think it was something that she should really do. He had agreed to help her though, and help her he would. It probably was something that needed more discussion. It just wasn't a discussion that he particularly wanted to have.

I'm not sure that I believe in an afterlife. Of course I would like to believe that mum has gone on and continues to exist in some form or another; I'm just not sure if that is just wishful thinking. Sometimes I find it hard to know what I believe and not just about this topic, but about everything. I know that I'm young and I'm only just finding my way in the world, so maybe I am not expected to have all the answers at the moment. Maybe none of us are meant to. I know dad still talks to mum though. He doesn't realise that I know, but I've heard him. The walls are really not that thick and I can hear him talking to her. Maybe he believes that she can hear him, or maybe it is some kind of forlorn hope that she still exists on another plain. I don't know. Sometimes I wish I did have all the answers. It would make things easier.

Now

Daniel's book tours were never really something that he looked forward to. He enjoyed the writing side of things, not so much the business side of things. He considered that all the promotional work that he did took him away from times when he could be writing. Okay, so he wasn't writing all that much since Claire had died, well nothing at all really, but that was beside the point, it was the principle of the matter.

He knew the logic behind it though. If you wanted to sell books then you had to do a certain amount to promote them, otherwise they were not going to shift off the shelves on their own. Okay, maybe if you were as famous as Stephen King you didn't have to go around promoting your books because they would sell on your name alone, but Daniel wasn't that famous, despite being reasonably famous. He still had to promote his books if he wanted them to sell. Only a few of his dedicated readership would buy his books on his name alone without there being any need for additional promotional work.

It was also a time to get out and "press some flesh", as Claire referred to it. As a writer, you spent so much of your time in isolation, hardly seeing anyone else. Promotional work was time to get out and meet the reading public whose book-buying put food on your table. It was payback for them. They finally got to meet one of their favourite authors.

Daniel wasn't entirely sure why people got so excited about meeting authors. He could, sort of, understand it when it came to movie stars and rock stars, but couldn't really see the excitement that came with meeting authors. The book world was usually more restrained than that. More often than not he expected to meet people at signings that would be critical of his work. Tell him all the things that they thought were wrong with his last novel and where he could go right. Everyone had an opinion on writing a book just because they had read one.

He didn't begrudge people that. He just tried to smile politely and pretend that he was interested in what they were saying, when he knew damn well that he was just going to go off and write his own thing the way that he had always done. If they liked him as a writer, they must like him because of the fact that he wrote what he wanted to write and wasn't pigeonholed or stuck in a rut of writing the same thing all of the time.

His publishers would probably have liked it if he was able to constantly repeat bestselling success by writing to the same formula all of the time, but he preferred to do his own thing and go his own way. It had worked out for him most of the time. Occasionally he would be asked if he could write another book like... whatever it may have been. He just smiled and would go away and write whatever it was that was in his brain that was demanding to be written.

That was the thing though. He didn't really get any say over what should be written. It wrote itself in many regards. That isn't to say that he didn't have to put the work in, he did, but it dictated to him what he was going to write and when he was going to write it. He had no more say over it than anyone else did.

'I so love your books,' said the rather overweight woman who was next in the queue at the signing.

'Thank you very much,' replied Daniel with a fixed smile on

his face. He was always wary of the enthusiastic fan. He thought they were one step away from being a stalker.

'*Dystopia* was so like, oh my God, I don't know what, but it was like you were talking to me directly, like you knew my life and everything about me and were talking to me directly, it was amazing, I have never read anything so beautiful in all my life, it was *the* most amazing book that I have ever read and I hear they're teaching it in schools now, which is so like amazingly out there that it's fantastic and you must think it's great.'

Daniel was impressed that she had managed to not only talk as far as she had without an apparent full stop, but also didn't appear to need to stop for breath at any point. She must have a healthy set of lungs on her. He wondered if she was an opera singer.

'What's your name?' he asked, taking the copy of *Charlie's Song* that she wanted him to sign.

'It's Julie. You must remember me, I've been to every signing that you have ever done, I am convinced of it, I have signed copies of all your books, I wouldn't buy one if I couldn't get it signed, I mean it's just the done thing that I have to do, I have to get my books by you signed, you must remember me, I've been here before.'

'I'm sorry, I see a lot of people at these signings, I can't remember everyone. I don't have much of a memory for faces.'

Now that she mentioned it though, she did seem to be rather familiar. He suspected that she would be the kind of woman that would be difficult to forget, even if you were trying to. He started to sign her book.

'Can you write *To the great love of my life, Julie,* in it for me please? That would be, like, so cool, if you could do that, I mean who am I kidding, that would be an amazing thing if you could do that for me. Could you do that for me, Danny? You don't mind me calling you Danny do you? Only I feel that I know you so well having read all of your books and all that, I feel like we have a special bond.'

Yep, she was definitely a stalker. Daniel began to wonder if the bookstore had laid on any security. He didn't normally have a problem with that kind of thing, but you could never tell when someone was going to come out of the woodwork who was a little deranged.

'I'm sorry, I can't sign that. There's only one love of my life and it wouldn't be fair to her to write that to someone else.'

'But I heard your wife was dead.'

'That's as maybe, but she is still the love of my life.' He handed the book over to her.

'Oh,' she said in disappointment, reading the message that he had scrawled inside the book for her. 'Well, anyway, you're not a patch on Matt Haig.'

With that she took her book and stormed off in the direction of the exit. Daniel wondered if he would be seeing her at future signings, he was sure to remember her in future. Perhaps she would not attend any of his signings after that barbed comment on the way out.

Daniel didn't mind being compared to other authors. He didn't see them as competitors or rivals, but all part of a brotherhood and sisterhood of the written word. They were all in it together and they all faced the same problems and had the same issues. Very often a lot of them were friends. He couldn't see the point of rivalry between authors. They all had their different styles and their different agendas so what did it matter if one sold more books than you or was more famous? Granted you all wanted success, you wanted to be a full-time writer and in order to do that you had to have a degree of success. You couldn't be a full-time writer if you only sold thirty books a year – unless you had a second income that meant that you didn't have to work and could dedicate all your time to writing. Daniel had been lucky that success had meant that he could be a full-time writer and not have to work in anything else. He doubted he would know how to do anything else now anyway.

'What's your new book about?' Jordan had asked before he had gone off to get involved in the book launch.

This seemed an innocuous question. For Daniel though it ranked second after his number one irritating question *Where do you get your ideas from?* The reason for this was that Daniel rarely knew what his novels were about. Yes, he had written them, but he was so close to the coalface that he had no idea what they were actually about and he would always sigh inwardly when someone asked him what his novel was about. He had worked too long and too closely on the project to know what it was actually about.

Besides which he didn't think it was necessarily the role of the author to tell the reader what the book was about. That was up to them to make up their own mind about it. He might have meant one thing when he had written it, but the reader might take it a different way entirely. Who was to say who was right? Well, the truth of the matter is that both interpretations were right. The book would be about whatever you wanted it to be about.

'I don't know,' he had replied to Jordan. 'Why don't you read the book and then tell me what it's about.'

'That seems a bit trite.'

'It's the best that I can do. Honestly, my opinion means little once the book has gone to print, if it ever meant anything to begin with. It's in the public domain now and it's up to the public to determine what it's about.'

'Yeah, but you could say that it's a love story or a thriller or whatever.'

'Yeah, but even so, that's open to interpretation. Trust me, I struggle when the publisher asks me to write the blurb on the back of the book. I would much rather that they did it for me.'

'Really?'

'Yep. I get so confused about all of that stuff. Much better for someone else to read the novel and then tell me what it's all about.'

'How very strange.'

'Do you think so? I've never really thought about it before.'

'Are you going to keep the beard for the book tour?'

'Don't see why not. I'm told it lends a distinguished air to my appearance.'

'I'm not entirely convinced of that.'

'That's because you have beard envy.'

'I'm not sure that I do.'

'Yeah, you just don't want to admit to it.'

'I don't think so. I think your perception might be a bit off there to be honest with you, Mate.'

Daniel was surprised by the amount of time that was taken up in not writing when you were a writer. Constant emails back and forth with your publisher, interviews that had to be given, book launches, book signings and a whole host of publicity that went into publishing a book. He found that he could sign a thousand books in an hour if he had someone who opened them to the right page so all he had to do was sign his name. These were the books that he was required to sign that went out to the bookshops with just his signature on them. It took a lot longer when you were at actual book signings and had to sign the book along with a dedication and then also chat with the person that you were signing for. It all took up a lot of time.

He had published enough books now that he was getting used to the publicity machine. He had found it difficult to get his head around when he had first started out. It had just seemed to be something that was bigger than he was. And it was. It was huge. Publishers were out to make as much money from you as they could and you were naturally trying to make as much money as you could as well.

You had to go through the publicity machine if you wanted to sell books, and selling books was the thing that you were there to do. It was in everyone's interest to sell books. You wanted people to buy them and in return you had to give something back to the reading public that wanted to meet you. That was the deal and most of the time Daniel was fine with that.

Daniel was finding it hard to do this particular book tour though because it was something that he was doing without Claire. She didn't always come on the book tours with him, she had other things to do and her own career to pursue as well, but she was always on the end of the phone and he could talk to her whenever things were tough after a long engagement. She would sympathise with him and boost up his energy levels to keep him going on to the next event. He was doing it all without her. This was the first publicity tour after she had died and he was feeling her absence like a hole in his heart. He didn't know if he would be able to do all this without her.

He saw himself as becoming a writer recluse. Not doing any publicity and living off his name alone, hoping that would be enough to sell his books. Signed books would become collector's items as the rarity of them grew. It could, of course, mean that doing this would be a shot in the head for his career and he could see sales plummet. He could argue that he had made enough money to live frugally by, but it was going to run out if he didn't keep the money coming in.

He would have to have a deep think about what he was going to do with his life now that Claire had died. Was he going to carry on as he had done while she was alive, or was he going to take his career in a new direction? Trouble was that without Claire he was a little directionless. He was just beginning to realise how much he had depended on her and how she had helped him over the years.

Thy had been blessed with a good marriage. A marriage of equal partnership where they worked together. Daniel found that he was missing her in all sorts of ways. There was the big way of missing her in the fact that she wasn't there any longer. In the fact that she wouldn't be coming through the door from work. That she wasn't there for him to turn to with his problems, or to listen about her day and the office politics.

He was also missing her in the small ways. There being no longer a need for making her a cup of tea in the morning. The scent of her shampoo in the bathroom after she had had a shower. The smell of her on the pillow next to him. The thousand and one little tells that remarked on the fact that she was no longer there.

It wasn't necessarily the case that you missed someone until you realised all the ways that they were not there any longer. There was a degree of truth in the matter that you didn't miss something until it was gone. Daniel had known that he would always miss Claire, even when she had been there. Even before she had got cancer, he had appreciated the love that they had, and knew that he would miss her when she was gone. He had just never expected it to happen so soon.

'How's the book tour going?' asked Jordan when they were in a coffee shop one day. Jordan had been able to lure Daniel out of the house for something other than business. Something which Jordan considered to be a great success.

'Slowly. It's more difficult than others have been.'

'Because of Claire?'

'Yes, I suppose so. I don't have the incentive to work that I did before.'

'You've got to work.'

'Why?'

'It's good for you.'

'I'm not sure that it is, you know.'

'Well, okay, I can understand that it might not be good for everyone and most people would probably choose not to work if they had the choice, but you are doing a job that you have always enjoyed.'

'Well, I certainly used to.'

'Are you saying that you don't enjoy it any longer?'

'I haven't really done any writing since Claire died. I'm only doing the book tour because I'm under contract, which was signed before she died. Who knows? I might give the entire thing up and retire quietly to a Scottish mountain somewhere.'

'Sounds idyllic, if somewhat extreme.'

'Well, I don't know what I'm going to do at the moment. I'm just taking one day at a time. Putting one foot in front of the other and all the other clichés. It's just about all that I can do to get out of bed in the mornings. If I had my way then I would probably stay in bed all the time.'

'Wouldn't be very good for Toby.'

'No, no it wouldn't. Toby's the reason that I get up every day, if I'm honest with myself.'

'It's a good reason to get up.'

'Yes, it is.'

'You finding it hard without Claire?'

'Of course I am. What do you think?'

'Stupid question, I suppose. I just wanted to check in with you and see how you're doing.'

'I know, I'm sorry. I didn't mean to snap at you. Yes, it's hard, it's damn hard. Harder than I ever thought that it would be. There's simply nothing I can do about it though. I have to carry on with life, without her, and that hurts a great deal. The fact that she is no longer here to experience things with me.'

'It must he hard. I can't imagine what you are going through.'

'I hope you don't have to, although the odds are on that one day you will have to experience something similar.'

'I know it may sound selfish, or self-destructive, but I always hoped that I would die before Natalie, so that I didn't have to experience the pain of losing her.'

'No, I can understand that.'

'Not everyone can. They don't want to die; they want to outlive everyone.'

'But they're the kind of people that probably wouldn't feel the pain of losing anyone else. They are so wrapped up in their own lives that they would rather live on their own, after everyone has died, just so that they can have the extra time to themselves.'

'No sense in living like that. Love is the utmost important thing in life.'

'Yes, I believe you're right. Maybe I should write a book about it.'

'I thought all your books were about that anyway.'

'Did you?'

'Yeah. Aren't they?'

'I've never really thought about it like that, but it's as I said to you before, my books are anything you want them to be and about anything that you think they are about. I've often been confronted by people that have seen more in my books than I ever did when I was writing them.'

'Hardly seems possible.'

'Oh, it is, believe me. For me a lot of the writing takes place on the sub-conscious level so that I'm not entirely sure what it is all about. My brain takes over and writes the words, and others interpret them however they like.'

'I've never really thought about it in those terms before.'

'It's not the same with all writers. I'm sure that there are ones that agonise over every single word before they commit it to paper, but I've never been one of those kinds of writers.'

'You're more free-flowing.'

'That's one word for it, another might be careless.'

'I'm sure that's not the case.'

'Or lazy.'

'You seem to be selling enough books for someone who classes themselves as lazy.'

'Well, everyone thinks that they can write a book.'

'I couldn't.'

'You would be amazed the number of times that I'm told at signings by people that they could write a book, if they only had the time.'

'That must be annoying.'

'Well, it can be extremely annoying, but you're never allowed to let on about that, you just have to smile knowingly and sympathise with them as if we would all be writing books if we only had the time.'

'Writing a book is one thing, getting it published is another.'

'That's something that people don't seem to understand. They think that the writing is the hard bit. They don't realise that the difficult bit starts afterwards. Claire understood, being in publishing. She knew that she would always reject more manuscripts than she would accept.'

'Must be difficult to dash someone's dreams though.'

'I read some of the manuscripts that she would get and the thing is that so many of them were just dross. People think it's so easy and it isn't. Writing is difficult.'

'You wouldn't encourage people to go into writing then?'

'Oh, of course I would. Writing isn't easy, it's difficult and there are a lot of hurdles to jump over, but it's a worthwhile thing and we need new authors coming up. We always need the next generation to be coming in and taking over. It's essential for the writing trade.'

'Yes, I can see that.'

'I would just warn them not to expect it to be easy or to be given something on a plate. Nor would I caution them to expect their first book to be a huge success, sometimes it happens, but more often than not it doesn't work like that and most writers have to take a second job to supplement their income and enable them to write.'

'I suppose you have to enter into it with realistic expectations.'

'Absolutely. I was lucky. I was one of the success stories and I sold enough to help me to write full time, but when I started out and wasn't earning the money I was supported by Claire. I've a lot to be thankful to her for.'

'For sure. You were good together.'

'Yes, yes, we were.'

'She wouldn't want you to give up on the writing. She believed in you.'

'Yes, she did. She believed in me when no one else did. I couldn't have made it as a writer without her. It helps if you have someone, other than yourself, who believes in what you are doing and thinks you will make it.'

'Yes, I can imagine.'

'She was always my first reader. I always gave her the manuscript to read first before it went to anyone else. Always took her advice about it as well. She had sound advice about what needed to be changed or included, what needed to be taken out.'

'Being in publishing must have helped with that.'

'Absolutely. She made me a better writer because of it. By the time that it went to my agent and publisher it had already been through her so was a better manuscript than when it was that I had finished it.'

'I can see where that would have helped.'

'Now I don't have her, I will just submit slightly inferior novels. My publisher will think that I have dropped my ability to write well.'

'You're going to write more then?'

'I don't know. I'll tell you one thing though. I'm tired. So tired that my eyeballs ache. Have you ever been that tired?'

'Probably not. Are you not sleeping all that well then?'

'No, not really. I find it difficult to get off to sleep. I lie awake for hours and then when I do get to sleep, I wake up several times during the night and then I wake up early in the morning and can't get back to sleep again. This tour isn't helping. Every bone and muscle in my body is aching from it. I never seem to be able to find the time to regenerate my body.'

'Doesn't sound good.'

'No. It's not good. I don't know what the answer is.'

'Maybe you could get some sleeping tablets.'

'Never really found them to work with me. Always seemed to be a bit snake-oil-like.'

'Well, if it works, so what?'

'Yeah, but they don't work for me. I wish they did. If I take one I still can't get to sleep and when I do eventually wake up I have a pounding headache from taking it.'

'Sounds like you can't win.'

'Doesn't seem to be that way.'

'They say that you get used to it after a while. Grief, that is.'

'They say that, but I don't know if it's true. My last thought at night is about her and the first thing I think of in the morning is her and then I sink into a depression when I realise that it's true, that's she gone, it isn't a nightmare. Well, it is, just a living one.'

'I wish I knew what to say to you.'

'Mate, I use words for a living and I don't know what to say to me, so I wouldn't worry too much. It's just one of those things. It happens to thousands of people a day and yet when it happens to you, you feel like you are the only one in the world who has ever felt like it.'

'Does it help at all knowing that you are not alone though. There are presumably support groups that you could go to.'

'No, it doesn't help in the slightest. I know there are other people out there suffering from grief, but I have no particular desire to meet them. It would only compound the matter.'

'Perhaps you could see a grief counsellor.'

'To tell me what? I know what the problem is. I just can't help feeling like it.'

'Maybe they could help. Give you some advice, maybe little tricks of the trade to help you manage it all better.'

'I don't know about that. I don't really fancy that as an idea at all.'

'But if it helps then surely it is worth it?'

'Thing is, Jordan, I don't know if I want to feel better. Claire is gone and grief is all that I have left of her. All that I have left is the gaping hole of where she used to be. If I fill that hole up then I will lose her a second time. At least this way I get to remember her and still feel that she is there.'

'I think I understand what you mean.'

'It isn't easy, I know. But when I wake up and realise that she is no longer there then I carry that pain throughout my day. I carry it with me like a stone around my leg.'

'That can't be healthy for you.'

'Maybe not, but it's what I do. It's what I have been doing over the last six months and it hasn't gotten any easier. Maybe it will with time, or maybe it will be that I will be stuck like this for the rest of my life and if so, that's fine. I can live like that.'

'I'm not sure you can.'

'What other choice do I have? Claire forbade me from suicide.'

'You thought about suicide?' asked Jordan, alarmed.

'I thought about it. I thought about the pain of going on without her and the fact that all that pain could go away if I just took the right number of pills or cut my wrists with a knife.'

'Jesus.'

'Not sure he enters into it. I thought about it, but I promised her that I wouldn't do it. She knew me so well, you see, that she knew that it was something that I was likely to think about.'

'You have to stay around for Toby.'

'Yeah, I know and she knew that as well and maybe that's why she made me promise that I wouldn't end my life. Otherwise, who knows? Maybe I would have gone through with it, if Toby had not been around.'

'Jesus.'

'Yeah, you said that. I don't think religion has all that much to do with it though. We were never really religious so I don't have any fear that I would be punished for taking my own life.'

'Do you think you will see her again?'

'Maybe. If there's an afterlife then I'm sure that I'll see her again. If there's nothing but oblivion then at least I'll join her in the darkness, and from where I am sitting, darkness and oblivion is not all that bad a thing.'

'I'm not sure I want to believe in oblivion.'

'Why not? Free from pain, free from suffering, nothing to worry about any longer. Just endless sleep without any dreams.'

'I'd quite like to believe that there is more to it than this.'

'Well, none of us will know that until the moment comes. Claire knows the truth now and, in a sense, I envy her.'

'Envy her?'

'Yeah. Towards the end of her life, she was in a lot of pain. Wherever she is now, whatever state of consciousness or unconsciousness she is involved in, I would like to believe that she's no longer in pain. At least I have that comfort, if nothing else.'

Jordan thought about this for a while. He wasn't sure what to think about all of it. It distressed him a great deal to think that his best friend might have contemplated suicide, or might be thinking of suicide in the future. It was a hard thing to take in. He wasn't sure what he could say to make things easier for his friend. Nobody wanted to see a friend in pain.

'More coffee?' he eventually said.

I think dad compares himself to Stephen King too much. He is always using him as the benchmark for what is success in a writer, just because of the fact that he has sold a trillion books. Don't get me wrong he is a good writer and a very successful one, but there are a lot of others out there that are much better. King is never going to win the Nobel Prize, for instance. Dad is pretty convinced that he won't either and maybe he is right on that front. I don't think winning the Nobel would make him any happier. He has been extremely sad since mum died. He tries to hide it from me, but you can't really hide something like that. It shows through the cracks too easily. It's best to try and get on with things, but I know that he is finding that hard. Things that were once familiar and that he took a comfort in have become like a bad taste in his mouth. I don't suppose that he will ever think that things will get back to normal again. I know that he has thought about ending his life. I can see it in his eyes. Maybe it is me that is preventing him from doing that. Maybe it is fear. I don't know. I don't particularly want to become an orphan. Death is part of life. It's something that we all have to get used to. There is no escaping from it. There is nothing that we can do about it. It doesn't make it any easier though.

Then

Daniel had to tell Jordan that Claire was dying. He was sure that he would be able to handle this. The difficult part had been telling Toby. That was the hardest of all. He was pretty sure that he would be able to handle their best friend, if he had been able to tell his son. It wasn't the easiest thing in the world to tell your son that his mother was going to die. It wasn't easy at any age, but at fifteen it seemed all the harder. Daniel supposed that it would only have been harder if Toby had been even younger. At least he had experienced fifteen years of having his mother about. He would have memories of her and wouldn't forget her. It would have been harder for him if he had grown up with only vague memories of his mother; or no memories at all.

He hoped that those memories would be a comfort for Toby as he got older. He knew that it would be no substitute for having his mother around, but he hoped he would take some comfort from remembering her. He would have to sort out a photograph of her that he could give to Toby to put in a frame and keep in his room so that he didn't forget her, not that he imagined that he would, but grief could be a funny process.

Daniel had been a lot older than Toby when his mother had died, but it had still been a hard time. You think that your parents are going to be there forever. You take them for granted as such. One day you wake up and they are not there any longer. All you are left with is memories, and perhaps some regrets. Regret that you didn't spend enough time with them, that you were so busy following your own life that you didn't think about looking after them in their age, the way that they had looked after you in your youth.

It didn't matter how much attention you had paid them, there was always the regret that you could have done more. Daniel had been busy in his own life trying to establish himself as an author. She had never lived long enough to see him have the success that would come later. He liked to think that she was proud of him, but then if he really thought about it, he was sure that she had been proud of him before he had been successful. A lot of parents were proud of their children without them having been successful in some famous adventure.

Telling someone some bad news was never an easy thing to do. You never quite knew how the other person was going to react. Whether there would be disbelief and argument or whether they would collapse in upon themselves. It depends on the person and the kind of news that you were going to tell them. Toby had handled the news of his mother's approaching death better than Claire or Daniel could have imagined that he would. At least, he had handled it well in their presence. God alone knew how he felt about it when he was on his own and didn't have to put up a façade.

Daniel didn't expect that Jordan would handle the news badly. Yes, he was close to Claire, but if Daniel and Toby could take the news without falling to pieces then there was no reason why Jordan couldn't handle it well either. Daniel just didn't like telling people bad things. He wasn't used to it. Thankfully, it was not something that he had to do every day. Not for the first time he wondered how doctors, nurses and police officers got on with telling people the really bad news that they were dying or someone they loved had died. It wasn't something that he could

303

ever have imagined himself doing, and yet at some point he would have to tell people that Claire had died. It was something that he would have to tell them soon as well.

Daniel had decided that the best philosophy for telling people bad news was to be blunt with it and come straight out with the news in a way that couldn't be misconstrued. If you used euphemisms then there was a fair chance of misunderstanding the situation and creating great confusion. It was better to be on the nose and come straight out with it rather than drag out the inevitable. With that in mind he had arranged to have coffee with Jordan.

'There's something I need to tell you,' he told him as they sat down with their lattes.

'That sounds ominous.'

'Yes, well, I'm afraid that it is, really.'

'Is it about Claire?' Jordan was nothing if not on the ball with the situation.

'Yes, it is.'

'Okay, you'd better tell me then.'

'We went to the hospital and saw her consultant. The thing is that there is nothing more that they can do for her.'

'It's terminal?'

'Yes, as they put it, it's only a matter of time.'

'Jesus.'

'Yeah, I used slightly stronger words when I found out, to be honest.'

'How long do they think?'

'Not long. Not long at all. I think we are talking a matter of weeks, if that. Certainly not months.'

'I'm so sorry.'

'Not your fault, Old Boy.'

'I know, but even so… How are you both holding up?'

'As well as can be expected really. Claire seems to be taking these things better than I am. She has retained her sense of humour, which is nice to see. Even if I don't appreciate some of the things that she is joking about.'

'It must be hard.'

'It isn't easy, let's put it that way.'

'Should I see her?'

'She said she would rather you remembered her as she was. She isn't really taking any visitors, nothing against you. They tire her out and she gets tired so easy. Plus, she says that she is finding it difficult to cope with all the pity that people bring with them.'

'Yeah, I suppose I can understand that.'

'She just needs to rest. She is too tired to talk half the time. All the treatment has really drained her. She feels that she is not the woman that she used to be.'

'I suppose I can see that. Must be very difficult. I don't know how the two of you are coping with it all. I never have done. Can't imagine it myself. It goes without saying that if there is anything that I can do for you, or Claire for that matter, then all you have to do is ask.'

'I appreciate that, Dude. It's going to be a difficult few months ahead. It's all so damn pointless. I just can't understand it. Claire takes it all with a remarkable degree of philosophy, but I just can't get my head around what I think of as the injustice of it all. I asked, "why her?" and she replied, "why not me?" I just can't behave like that. It makes no sense to me at all.'

'I don't suppose it is going to make much sense.'

'I don't think it ever will make any sense though. Some people think that everything happens for a reason, but I can't for the life of me see what the reason is behind this.'

'There isn't any. You will drive yourself mad in trying to find any. It's best not to even try.'

'I mean she never smoked in her life. To get lung cancer when you have never so much as touched a cigarette is an insult. If she had been a smoker then you could argue that she had no one but herself to blame. It just doesn't make any sense to me.'

'I can't imagine what it is like for you both. I don't have the words to be able to help you.'

'There are no words, Jordan. Nothing makes sense any longer. There is nothing that can be done. Nothing that can be said. We just have to wait for the inevitable.'

'You seem to be coping with it all better than I would be able to cope with it.'

'I don't think I'm coping with it all that well at all. It's just about all I can do to get up in the morning. If I didn't have to see to Claire and make sure that she is all right then I don't think I would get out of bed at all.'

'I can understand that.'

'Each morning I get up I wonder if this is going to be the morning that I wake up to find that she has gone during the night.'

'It must be unbearable.'

'And yet, somehow, we bear it. I suppose because we have to. I bear it because I don't want Claire to see how despondent I am. I don't want her to see between the cracks where things are starting to fall apart.'

'I can understand that you feel you have to be able to keep it together, but someone has to be there for you as well. Someone has to help you through this.'

'I don't think there is anyone.'

'Well, now that you have told me about this, perhaps I can help. Perhaps I can be someone that you can unload to. Let all your negativity out with. Someone that you can speak your mind to.'

'Thanks, Mate, I appreciate that. A lot of this is something that I will just have to bear on my own though.'

'You don't have to. You are not alone in this. You have a lot of friends that would support you if you asked them to.'

'I find that it isn't always easy to ask for help, though.'

'Well you should, because the support is there for you. If not from me then I'm sure that there will be others who will equally be prepared to help.'

'Thanks. It feels like I'm rather on my own at the moment. It isn't easy, I will admit to that.'

'Of course it isn't easy. It isn't going to be easy. This is going to be the hardest thing that you have ever done.'

Jordan didn't know the half of it. If he thought living with Claire during her final illness and watching her die was going to be hard, then he had no idea how hard it was going to be given that he had agreed to help her to die. This was something that Daniel couldn't share with him though. It was something that Daniel couldn't share with anyone. Not if he wanted to avoid going to prison and being all over the news. It was something that he was going to have to bear on his own, despite Jordan's reassurances that he was there for him. There were some paths that you just had to walk down on your own.

'How did he take it?' Claire asked when Daniel returned home.

'Much as you would expect,' Daniel replied as he sat on a corner of the bed. 'Shock, horror, offers to help. Sends his best wishes to you and says that if there is anything that he can do then just to let him know.'

'Bless him.'

'Everyone wants to help.'

'Except my mother.'

'Well, yes that's true. That's your mother for you though. We know what she is like.'

'I've been sleeping for much of the day. It annoys me that I'm dying and it seems that I'll be spending the rest of my life in sleeping it away rather than enjoying it.'

'It does seem a bit harsh.'

'So much reading to do and no time to do it in now. I'm too tired to read. I wish I could read; it would make being in bed all the time something that was more bearable. Instead, I just lay here.'

'You have music to listen to though.'

'Yes, I have my music and that's a blessing. I love music so much, what would life be without a little music? I can't understand people that don't have music in their lives.'

'I can't understand people that don't have books in their lives.'

'Well, I believe there are such people out there. They should probably be avoided at all costs.'

'I think they would avoid us. A writer and a publisher. Hardly the kind of people that you would seek out if you hated books.'

'That's true. Could I have a sip of water?'

'Of course. Is there anything else I can get you?'

'No, the water will be fine.'

Daniel poured her some water and helped her to take a few sips from it.

'I hate feeling so damned useless,' she said as she settled back on her pillow.

'We both feel useless. I'm useless because there's nothing that I can do to make this situation any better for you.'

'There's nothing that anyone can do about that. I wouldn't let it worry you. It will just drive you mad.'

'That's pretty much what Jordan said.'

'Well, he's a pretty intelligent person, well, for someone who works in HR he is.'

'Never knew how he managed to end up doing that.'

'How do any of us end up doing the things that we do. It's just something that happens, I guess.'

'More often than not.'

'It occurs to me, Danny, that I may have been a little unfair on you.'

'How so?'

'Asking you to help me… You know?'

'Well, it's not as if there is anyone else that you can ask.'

'It's a huge burden on you though. Something difficult for you to have to live with.'

'I'm sure that I'll be able to cope.'

'You say that, but will you? I know you. I know what you are like and I know that you will most likely just beat yourself up about this.'

'Well, that's nothing for you to worry about.'

'But it *is* something that I worry about, don't you see? I may be gone, but you will have to live on with things. Maybe I'm being unfair on you.'

'I don't think you're being unfair. I think this entire situation is unfair, but I don't think that you're being unfair. It's just one of those things.'

'I wish it was just one of those things. I have asked you to do something that is very important. I wouldn't want anything to happen to you as a result of it.'

'Nothing is going to happen to me. I'll be fine.'

'I hope so. I was going to say that I wouldn't be able to live with myself if anything happened to you, but that really won't be a problem for me, will it?'

'I hate to lose you, Claire.'

'I hate to be going, but it seems that it's something that I don't have all that much choice in.'

'I love you.'

'I love you too.'

'I would do anything for you, you know that don't you?'

'I do.'

'That's why I agreed to help you. I don't want to see you suffer. I don't want to see you in pain. I want you to have as easy an exit as you possibly can.'

'I hope that there is an afterlife. If there is then I will be waiting for you.'

'I'm convinced that we will be together again. Love is something that lasts for eternity. I don't think that being separated by death is something that will kill it off.'

'Do you really think that?'

'Yes, I do.'

'You weren't always that way inclined, to believe in an afterlife.'

'Perhaps not. It takes someone that you love to be dying to really focus the mind though. I want to believe that you will continue. I don't want to believe that when you die, that's it. That the Claire I know and love is no more. I want to believe that you will continue in some form or another.'

'I hope that is the case.'

'You can come back and tell me about it all if you want.'

'You want to be haunted?' she chuckled.

'Certainly. Can't think of anything better than being haunted by you.'

'I'm not sure that it will be allowed. I'm sure that if we were allowed to come back and talk to our loved ones then someone would have reported it by now.'

'Maybe. I don't know. Maybe it's part of the deal that it has to remain secret.'

'It would be a big secret to be keeping. Would change the world if there was irrefutable proof that there was an afterlife.'

'Would be the biggest discovery in the history of humanity. I doubt you would be able to keep the lid on that.'

'Oh, I don't know. Perhaps those who have come forward have just been dismissed as insane or cranks.'

'I'd like to think that there was something more to this than what we see.'

'Well, if I can let you know then I'll be sure to come back and tell you about it.'

'I appreciate that. I know if there is a way then you will be the one to find out about it and make it happen.'

Claire had been reading a lot of books on the afterlife since her diagnosis with cancer. It was inevitable really. It was as if she had sensed that she wasn't going to get through this and had needed some reassurance that there was more out there than just this life. She had read a number of books on near-death experiences and was trying to work out if they were telling the truth and were evidence that there was an afterlife, or whether it was evidence of a mass delusion.

She had pretty much concluded that there was something in it. Maybe this was because she was being hopeful. Maybe she felt she had nothing to lose by believing in it. It gave a certain degree of hope. She could only hope now that there was little left. She was going to die. We are all going to die, but it focuses the mind when you are pretty much given a rough date on when this is likely to happen.

Claire had shared some of the books with Daniel, who had thought that it was a bit depressing to be reading that sort of stuff and had tried to encourage her to have hope. This was back in the day when there had been hope. He had wanted her to take a more optimistic view of the future. It turned out that she had been right to take the view that she had.

It's true that before all this started Daniel had been sceptical on the suggestion of an afterlife. He had always linked afterlife with religion and had never been particularly religious having felt that most, if not all, major religions failed on one thing or another. He had made the mistake in believing that you had to be part of a religion in order to believe in an afterlife or in having any chance of going to one. This was what they wanted you to believe.

It had never occurred to him that you could be spiritual and not be aligned with any particular religion to believe that there was more to life than just the life that we were living. Claire had become increasingly spiritual over the last year or so. She believed that there was something more than just the here and now. She didn't go weird and start doing strange practices – which some people seemed to think that being spiritual meant that you did. She just became more content in her inner self. She believed that we were all part of something much bigger and we would get all the answers and all the knowledge when we died.

Some might say that it was a dream. Something that was almost impossible and something we only believed to bring us comfort while we were on this planet going about our lives, but what was religion if not exactly the same thing? People flocked to religion because they wanted hope. They wanted to believe that there was more to this then just our everyday lives. They wanted to believe that there was a grand purpose to it all. That the universe was designed. That it had a plan and a maker. They didn't want to believe in random stuff that meant that there was no purpose to any of it.

This is what humans did. They sought out a pattern to it all. They wanted there to be a design to suggest that this wasn't just evolution. That things had been designed with a purpose. They wanted that comfort. Okay, so there were those who didn't believe any of that. There were those who believed that when you died you just blinked out of existence. They seemed to be happy with this as an option. They didn't want to believe that there was a supreme being and they sure as hell didn't want to meet one.

There was a philosophical school of study called Pascal's Wager, that said that you should believe in God. The reasoning was that as followers, if you didn't believe that there was a god and when you died there was a god, then you might logically be in trouble for not believing. If you did believe that there was a god and when you died it turned out that there wasn't one, then you hadn't lost out anything by believing in one. Therefore, logic dictated that it was better to believe than not to believe.

It was, perhaps, a cynical way of looking at things, but it didn't hurt to hedge your bets. The problem was that you couldn't fake belief. You couldn't believe in something because logic told you that it was the best thing to believe. You either believed it or you didn't. It didn't really work any other way. You couldn't logic yourself into believing in God if your heart and mind just weren't into the concept.

Claire had become spiritual, not through logic, but because she had really started to believe some of the things that she was reading on the subject of near-death experiences and the afterlife.

When you started to look at it there were a surprisingly large number of books that were out there. When you looked on the internet there were even more experiences to look into. There were a lot of people out there who were prepared to swear that they had experienced an afterlife during a near-death experience.

The critics would say that this was an experience that was fake. That it was the brain reacting to drugs and you were imaging it all. There were those who claimed that it was just a belief that you wanted to believe in so much that when the brain was in extremis it created what you expected to experience. It was all fake.

Others contradicted this position by stating cases where they discovered things that they couldn't possibly otherwise have known. Dead relatives that they had never met but afterwards identified from photographs that they had not previously seen. Times when they were clinically dead and there was no brain activity shown.

The two sides would argue it out for ages. They would not concede a thing to the other side. What it eventually boiled down to was the only way to find out for sure what was going to happen to you when you died, was to die. Few people were prepared to run forward to experiment with this idea.

Claire didn't believe that there was a heaven or a hell. There was just an afterlife. The concept of heaven and hell was something that had been developed by religion as a means of keeping people in their place. She just believed that we all went to the same place and a lot of the things that you had done on Earth didn't matter when you got there. It would all be sorted out. We were all going to the same place, no matter how we had acted on Earth.

Some people might think that was a little unfair if they had lived a virtuous life and they ended up in the same place as someone like Hitler. The books that Claire had read were very clear about this though. When people died, they had a period where they experienced their life through the eyes of those that they had enacted with. They felt the pain that they had inflicted on others in the same way that they felt the love that they had caused. You went through this period of experiencing the pain and suffering that you might have caused before you were allowed to continue to the afterlife for real. It was a period of what the Catholics might call purgatory.

It wasn't an excuse for you to be able to do whatever you wanted in life though as you would still have to experience that pain when you died. It was in your own interest to lead a good life so you didn't have to experience any of the suffering when you died. This is what Claire believed and she had tried to make Daniel believe it as well. Daniel had gone along with her for appearances sake, but he was not entirely sure what he believed. He just wanted to believe in something where Claire continued to be. Where he wouldn't be without her and where one day they would unite together. Was that really too much to ask for?

'I want to believe that there is something else waiting for us,' she told Daniel a few weeks later.

'I know you do and I'm sure that there is something out there. This can't be all that there is.'

'What if what is waiting for us is not all that nice?'

'I'm sure that isn't the case at all.'

'It might be. None of us actually know.'

'Well, none of those books on near-death experiences you lent me suggested that there was anything nasty waiting for you.'

'Some people have had near-death experiences that have been truly frightening for them though.'

'Well, perhaps they are not very nice people and they are just getting what's coming to them.'

'What if I'm not a very nice person and I've got what's coming to me?'

'Well, that's just ludicrous speech. You're a good person.'

'Am I though? We don't know by what standards they judge these things. Compared to Mother Theresa I might be as bad as Hitler.'

'Now that's just the morphine talking. You're not as bad as Hitler. There will be nothing unpleasant waiting for you.'

'You can't know that for sure though, can you?'

'As sure as I can be about these things. I don't think you have anything to worry about.'

'What if there is a god and I was supposed to follow one of the religions?'

'If there is a god and you were meant to follow one of the religions then I am sure he would be a forgiving God and would only be interested in whether or not you had led a good life, and you have, so don't worry.'

'Lying here in bed all the time I have precious little else to do, but to think and to worry. It seems that at times it's all I have left.'

'Well you have us. You're not alone in this. Toby and I are here with you and we both love you very much.'

'I know you do. It's what has kept me going these last couple of months or so. I've never felt so wasted away.'

'You have an aggressive disease that is eating away at you. It's relentless and you are doing very well to stand up against it.'

'It's a fight that I shall lose.'

'Yes, yes, it is, but it's how you go that matters now. You can't beat it but you can fight it all the way.'

'I have been, but I don't know how much fight I have left in me.'

'You've done remarkably well, Babe. I love you so much.'

'I love you as well. Our love will never die, even when I do. If there is somewhere else for me to go then I will still love you there.'

'And I won't stop loving you just because you're not around any longer.'

'You better not, Mister. Although it is all right if you found someone else. It's a long time to be on your own.'

'Well I have no interest in finding anyone else. You are the only girl for me.'

'You might feel differently to that in a few years to come. Don't make any promises to me that you won't be able to keep in the years ahead. You are facing potentially decades without me, don't forget. It's a long time to be alone.'

'I can't speak for how I will feel decades from now. I can only tell you how I feel at this moment and how I feel at this moment is that I found my soulmate and there is no sense in trying to engage in a pointless exercise in finding anyone else who won't be able to measure up to you.'

'You shouldn't judge other women by me.'

'But that's the thing. I will judge them by you. I won't be able to do anything about it. It's not their fault. It's just the way that I am. I can't thank you enough for the years that I have spent with you. Ever since I saw you in Dr Larson's literature class, I knew that I wanted to be with you, come what may. That's why I had to ask you out for a coffee.'

'I'm glad that you did.'

'So am I. I have no regrets. I hope you don't either.'

'No, I have no regrets. Danny?'

317

'Yes, Babe?'
'I think it's time.'

In all this thinking about how I felt about mum dying and how dad felt about mum dying, I had not really given all that much thought to how mum felt knowing that she was going to die. How do you deal when you know that you are going to die? Yes, we all know that we are going to die, some day; but that's something that is in the abstract. We know that we are going to die, but it is perhaps something that we don't give all that much thought about. We don't really know when we are going to die. It's just some date in the future, which we hope is distant from now. How do you cope knowing that you are going to die in a matter of weeks, or even days? I can't imagine it. I can't imagine what it is that she must have been going through. Was she scared; or was she resigned to it? Perhaps she was even looking forward to a relief from the pain and the suffering. I suppose you can only really relate to it if it is something that you are going through yourself.

Now

The book tour was really starting to drag now. It was only a short tour of local bookshops. His publisher had wanted him to do the big tour that he normally did, but he argued that there was childcare issues and he couldn't be that far away from home for so long. Toby would have been insulted as he was more than sensible enough and capable of looking after himself, and probably would have done a better job of it than Daniel did. Daniel just wasn't sure on the legality of leaving a fifteen-year-old on his own while you toured the country. There was probably some law against it.

Aside from the legality of it all he also didn't feel that it was right to leave Toby on his own for such a long period of time while he fulfilled contractual obligations. It was work and if Daniel had learnt anything, it was that work was less important than family. Family had to come first.

So, he had agreed to a short enough tour that meant that he could be at home each night. It was something that was designed to please everyone, but probably didn't please anyone. He had signed a thousand books which were being distributed to the bookshops that he would not be visiting. It would have to be enough, even if his publishers would have liked him to do more.

It was a real drag on him at the moment. He had never particularly enjoyed the publicity side of things when it came to writing. He found it even more difficult now that Claire was no longer there to support him. He was finding it difficult and was only going through the motions.

He thought that he might become one of those writers who was a recluse. Add an air of mystery about him. Perhaps it wouldn't hurt his sales, but actually create a mystique that would generate more sales as people were more interested in him. To be honest, he didn't really care about the sales any longer or what people thought about him.

He wondered if this would be his last book tour. He wondered if this would be his last book. True, he did have others that he had written and not yet published; he just wasn't sure that he had the energy for it any longer. It had been six months since Claire had died and he just didn't have the energy for anything any longer. He knew that he was suffering from depression, but he was reluctant to go to the doctor about it. He knew that he would be put on pills and he only had a certain amount of faith in what pills could do. All that would probably end up happening was that he would become addicted to taking them and they probably wouldn't do him any good anyway. He felt that we had moved into a society where everything was solved by medication and it didn't always work.

He was just going to have to sort it all out for himself. The book tour and the signings gave him something to do, so he had a sense of purpose for the first time since her death, but he really wasn't enjoying it, not like he used to. A lot of the joy of life had gone out of him. He knew that the medication might be able to help with that, but it was something that he was, nevertheless, reluctant to take on. He felt he would just have to get on with it and work through it.

'If you break your leg,' Jordan had said, 'you don't try and fix it yourself. You go to the hospital and you get it treated.'

'Your point being?'

'So, if you would go and treat a physical illness or injury, what makes you think that you can cure a mental one without getting the appropriate help?'

'I don't know. Maybe it's because of the stigma that's still attached to mental illness. Maybe I don't want to be in the headlines for taking medication for depression and receiving treatment for such.'

'Your wife has died. It's perfectly understandable that you should be depressed. Anyone in their right mind would understand that.'

'Well, I for one am not in my right mind, clearly.'

'You know what I mean.'

'I know there shouldn't be stigma about mental illness and I know that a lot of people suffer from depression so it's hardly something that I should be ashamed about, but I don't think that medicine is the way to go in this instance.'

'You can't necessarily cure these things on your own though. It's not just a case of pulling yourself together. That's poor advice from the ignorant. You need professional help to learn how to put your life back together again.'

'Maybe.'

'There's no maybe about it. It's the logical thing to do. The sensible thing to do. You put your faith in medicine to treat Claire's physical illness; so why not put your faith in medicine to cure a mental illness? You need to be able to move forward.'

'What if I don't want to move forward?'

'How do you mean?'

'Claire is in the past. Moving forward means moving away from her. What if I don't want to move away from her?'

'You have to. It's not healthy to cling to the past. That, if anything, is what is making you depressed. You need to be able to let her go and move forward with your life. It's what she would have wanted.'

'Maybe she would have, maybe she wouldn't have.'

'Oh, you know she would have wanted the best for you. She wouldn't have wanted you wallowing in a pit of misery. She would've wanted you to be happy.'

'How can I be happy when she is gone?'

'It's not going to be easy. I can't begin to imagine the pain that you're going through, but you have to be strong. You have to carry on.'

'That's what everyone tells me, but I can't see the attraction in it if I am honest.'

'You have to for the sake of Toby, if nothing else.'

'That's what everyone tells me as well.'

'Well, everyone is right. You should listen to everyone for a change. Do what they are telling you.'

'Have you finished the lecture?'

'Not entirely. Not until I know that it's seeping into your brain.'

'I hear you. I just want to do things my way. I don't want to go and see a doctor; I don't want to be admitted to a mental hospital.'

'You won't get admitted to a mental hospital. It's extremely difficult to get admitted to a mental hospital. They are not going to admit you because you have natural depression because your wife has died.'

'Maybe, but why take the risk?'

'You're being unreasonable.'

'So you say. It's not you that would be facing them.'

'Just go to the doctor and get some pills. You'll feel better for it.'

'I don't want to go on medication. I'll never get off of it. I'll end up stuck on it for life.'

'So what?'

'It's not something that I want to do.'

'I can understand that, but really what's the alternative?'

'Sorting it out on my own.'

Jordan threw his hands up in despair. 'There's no reasoning with you when you're in this mood.'

'Nope.'

There was no reasoning with Daniel. He had prejudices about mental health that he couldn't get his head around. He knew that he shouldn't be prejudiced against it. He was an intelligent man and he knew there was nothing to be prejudiced about, but he hated the stigma that was still attached to mental health, even in this day and age. It was getting better, but it still hadn't quite got there yet.

It was partly the fault of his parents. They hadn't really believed in depression. They thought there was nothing like that which couldn't be cured by having a good long walk in the country. Get some fresh air into your lungs and you will feel fine. He had been raised, therefore, on the principal of self-help. It was a philosophy that his parents lived by and which they had raised their children. They would only go and see a doctor if there was something that was seriously wrong that couldn't be cured by natural means. As such, they rarely went to the doctor for anything.

These days they would probably be reported to social services, but it had been a different world back then and it was difficult for Daniel to shake the things that he had been indoctrinated into. All of us are subject to received wisdom, whether it is right or it's wrong. Most of our politics and religion we get into purely because of the fact that it's what our parents believed or followed. We pass the same onto our children.

Occasionally it is possible to break from the mould and go into a different direction. That depends entirely on the kind of character you are and what you are like. It's possible. The cycle can be broken, but then not everyone wants to break the cycle. Many are perfectly happy to be that way.

Claire and Daniel had broken the cycle with regards to religion. Although their parents had been religious, they had not felt any particular need to follow a religion when they had been old enough to choose their own path and make up their mind about these things. They had raised Toby to have no particular religion enforced on him. They had allowed him to do what he wanted in the hope that he would follow his own path. It didn't matter to them which direction that he took. He could grow up to be an atheist or a priest. So long as he was a good man, that was all that mattered to them. They wanted him to be happy and he would always be their son no matter what path he went down.

Daniel had not been able to shake his mistrust of doctors though. Yes, it was okay to go and see them when you had something seriously wrong with you, like Claire had done. You had to put your faith in them at that point. No amount of herbal tea and strong walks were going to cure cancer, but as it had turned out the doctors had not been able to cure cancer either. There were some fights that you clearly just couldn't win, no matter what you threw at it.

Family values were important to Claire and Daniel, but they didn't think that this had to revolve around religion or any particular philosophy, other than to be good to each other and treat others the way that you would want to be treated in return. They knew that was a Christian doctrine, but one that was hardly kept to if the Church was anything to go by. They had their own set of family values. For instance, no matter what they had been doing during the day, they always came together for meal times. Claire insisted that they all eat dinner at the dining table, rather than having trays and sitting in front of the television.

It was something that had stuck and since her death, Daniel and Toby still sat at the dining table for their dinner. It was on one of these occasions that Toby decided that he wanted to talk.

'Why did mum have to die?' he asked with an innocence that made him seem to Daniel to be a little boy again. It had been a question that Daniel had been dreading, even though he had not known it was coming.

'Oh boy, that's a good one,' he said. 'I worry about that question myself and I wish that I had an answer for you, I really do. I don't know why she had to die. Sometimes things happen that we can't explain.'

'I just don't know why she had to die. She was a good person and there are evil people in the world that are still alive. One of them should have died instead of her.'

'Unfortunately, the world doesn't work like that. I wish it did.'

'It should work like that.'

What was he supposed to tell him? That life wasn't fair? Surely he knew that already. Claire's death would have taught him that if he hadn't been aware of it before.

'I wish I had answers for you, Toby, I really do, but sometimes things happen for reasons that we can't explain or understand. We just have to hope that it all works out in the end.'

'I don't see how it can possibly work out in the end. Mum is dead. How can anything work out?'

'I don't know. You just have to believe that it does.'

'Does that mean you believe in an afterlife?'

'I would like to think so,' Daniel said cautiously. 'The truth is none of us can know the answer to that. I just have to hope that I will see your mum again one of these days.'

'I hope that I'll see her again as well. I don't believe in a god though.'

'No?'

'No. I don't believe that if there was a god that they would have allowed mum to get ill and die. Not when she hadn't done anything wrong.'

'People do die that haven't done anything wrong though. Just look at babies who die. They've done no harm to anyone and yet they die. I suppose it's just a matter of the way that life works. Some of us are here for a long time and others of us are taken away too soon.'

'It's so unfair.'

'Yes, it is unfair. The way that I look at it though is that we shouldn't focus on the fact that mum left us too early, but really, we should focus on the fact that she was here at all. We should be grateful for the years that we were able to spend together. That's better than not knowing her at all.'

'I suppose so. I hadn't really thought about it like that at all. I suppose it makes sense.'

'It's something that I like to hang on to.'

'How do you deal with it? The loss?'

Daniel sighed. 'Damned if I know. I just live day to day and try and get through it all in the hope that it will all make sense at some point.'

'It must be hard for you. I mean she was my mum, and that is bad, but she was your wife.'

'Yes, but it's still hard to lose your mum. Mustn't forget that and it's okay to be sad about it.'

'I am sad. I can't help but be sad. Sometimes I think the sadness will overwhelm me.'

'That's only to be expected. I feel exactly the same way.'

'Are you going to stop writing?'

'Why do you ask that?'

'I've noticed that you haven't been doing that much writing since mum got really sick. I wondered if you were going to give it up.'

'I haven't really thought about it. It's true with her illness I was distracted and didn't feel much like writing and since she died, I have probably been too sad to really be able to get any work done.'

'Are we going to lose our house if you stop working?'

'No, we are not going to lose the house. This is bought and paid for. You don't have to worry about that. It will always be your home.'

'What about paying the bills?'

'You don't have to worry about that either. We have enough money in the bank to cope with everything, even if I don't work for a little while.'

'Are you rich?'

'Well, not compared to Richard Branson or the Queen. Comfortable is what I would say. We are comfortably well off. The books sell enough to keep us going.'

'Are you very famous?'

'Well, I suppose that would depend on your definition of fame. If you mean, am I as famous as Tom Cruise, then the answer is no. Do I get recognised in the supermarket? The answer would, again, be no. Can you walk into Waterstones and see my name on books on the shelves? Well then yes, you can. Fame is relative I suppose.'

'Would you like to be recognised as you walk down the street? Would you like that kind of fame?'

'Good God no. Fame is the add-on to the writing career. I don't want to be so famous that my privacy is sacrificed.'

'Why do you write then? If not for fame?'

'I write because there are stories that need to be told. There are things that compel me to write. There is nothing that I can do about it. I would still be writing even if I wasn't published. Even if there was no money in it for me. I would still be writing.'

'Sounds like a passion.'

'It is a passion. It's a vocation. It's also the only thing that I've ever done. The only thing that I'm good at and know how to do. I doubt that I could do anything else.'

'I'm sure you could if you put your mind to it.'

'Maybe. Hopefully I won't have to.'

'I'm not sure what I'm going to do with my life. I'm not sure where my passion lies.'

'You have time enough to work it out.'

'Not really. GCSE's are upon me and then it will be A Levels and university after that. I'll have to choose subjects to specialise in. A path to follow.'

'If you take my advice, you will study subjects that interest you and you are happy studying. You have to be pleased with yourself. When I was doing my A Levels there was a guy studying mathematics and politics, philosophy and economics and it was all because his parents wanted him to be an accountant, but he didn't want to be an accountant. He hated every minute of it. Studying subjects that he hated, but felt that he had been forced into. Don't fall into that trap. Go where your heart leads you.'

'I'd like to study literature and music.'

'Then go for it. Your mum would have been very proud of you for studying those subjects. Two subjects that she absolutely adored.'

'Then I'll either be a musician or a writer, like you.'

'Sounds like you've got a plan, after all.'

'Maybe I have. I didn't think I had, but when you put it like following your favourite subjects it all makes sense.'

'There's no reason, of course, why you can't be a writer and a musician. Why not do both?'

'Feels a bit greedy.'

'Go for it. Why not?'

'I suppose so.'

They resumed their meal and spent the rest of it in silence. Each to their own thoughts. Daniel was pleased that he had been able to get Toby to talk about his mother, but also to move off from her. He was pleased that Toby was able to think and plan for the future. He just wished that it was something that he could do as well. Perhaps he would one day, perhaps he would be able to move forward. He wasn't really sure. He would carry on the way that he had been in the hope that he would eventually see the light at the end of the tunnel.

There were a couple of messages on the answerphone from Claire's mother. Daniel chose to ignore them. She was like a stopped clock, repeating the same thing over and over again. All she would go on about was how she felt that Toby would be better with her than he would be with Daniel.

Daniel was bemused as to why she was showing such an apparent interest in her grandson when she had paid little attention to her daughter. He suspected that it was because of the fact that if she looked after him then she could plead to her cronies how she was forced to look after her grandson because his father wasn't up to the task. It was a terrible burden that she had taken on, but wasn't she doing so well at it? She would no doubt get the sympathy of her cronies and be the centre of attention, which was ultimately what Daniel suspected she wanted. She wanted to be the centre of attention. Always had to be it. She had tried to get the attention drawn to her at Claire's funeral. Daniel concluded that she just wasn't a particularly nice person. It was a conclusion that Claire had reached a number of years ago.

Daniel didn't want to deal with her at the moment. Truth be told he never wanted to deal with her. With any luck if he ignored her, she might just go away and forget all about him and Toby. He didn't believe her threats about involving solicitors. What solicitor in their right mind would take her case against the father of a boy that had just lost his mother. It was another reason why he didn't want to go on medication. If she found out that he was on medication for depression he was sure that she would use it against him to try and win some form of custody suit to get hold of Toby. To try and claim that he was in some way an unfit father and not able to deal with bringing up a child.

He didn't have the energy for that kind of battle. He would just leave things and hope that she got bored and went away. He didn't think that she would be prepared to take him on in a lengthy battle of wills. He didn't think she had the mindset for it. She must realise that there was no hope of her getting hold of Toby, but that was the problem, she wasn't thinking rationally. She just had some strange scheme that she was up to. Daniel couldn't see the full picture, but what he did see was enough to convince him that Toby would be far better off with him rather than her. He was convinced that there wasn't a court in the land that would disagree with him on that front.

You didn't really need this kind of crap when your wife had just died, but that was her mum all over, not thinking about anyone else, but herself. She hadn't even come to see Claire in her final illness. She had expected Claire to come and see her. It was what she had always expected. Despite the fact that Claire was bedridden at the end, she had nevertheless expected to have everything come to her and so she hadn't seen her own daughter in her final illness. That was something that Daniel could never forgive her for.

'I just don't understand what she wants,' Jordan had said when Daniel had explained all of this to him.

'Who knows what she wants? The woman is deranged. She's seriously unhinged.'

'I think she must be. You say she never visits you?'

'Nope, that's a blessing, I suppose.'

'Perhaps you should change your phone number then.'

'That's a thought. Maybe then she will leave us alone. She won't come and see us. I'm surprised she actually even came to Claire's funeral if I'm honest.'

'That may be your answer then. Change your number and you won't have to deal with her any longer. She will get fed up and eventually go away forever.'

'It would be nice to believe that, but I'm not sure that I can.'

'She can't pester you forever.'

'It feels like she can. The woman seems to know no limit. She is relentless. She is just what I don't need at the moment.'

'I don't think you need her at any point judging by what you are saying about her.'

'Sometimes I think I'm doing her an injustice, but then I remember that Claire felt the same way about her, and she should know what she was like after all.'

'Well, she should know.'

'I always try and see the best in people, but I just can't do it with her. No matter how hard I try.'

'Sometimes you can't see the good in people because there is no good there to see. It's just one of those things.'

'Yes, I suppose so.'

'So, have you made up your mind?'

'About what?'

'What you are going to do.'

'About what?'

'The future. Are you going to move on with your life? Are you going to go back to writing now that your book tour is over?'

'I don't know. I know I don't want to do any publicity for a while. I've had enough of all of that. If I go back to work then I just want to write and leave it at that. I can't be doing with all the baggage that comes with it.'

'Will your publishers allow you to do that?'

'They will if they want to publish my future books. If they don't then I will move to a publisher that is prepared to accept the manuscripts without having me on as a publicity machine. I'm sure there will be several out there.'

'Well, that's good then.'

'It's going to be on my terms from now on, or not at all. I don't care what the results may be. I have built up a sufficient name for myself that I'm sure to get published regardless of anything else, and they will still sell books without me prostituting myself to get them sold.'

'Do you really see yourself as a prostitute?'

'Of course. We are all prostituting our talent for money. It's what we do. We are no better than those in the sex industry in that regard. We are all selling what we've got to people that we hope might be interested.'

'I've never really thought about it like that before. I think I understand where you're coming from though.'

Daniel wasn't the first artist to consider himself a prostitute when it came to plying his trade. The chances were that he would not be the last one either. For countless hundreds of years, artists, musicians, writers, and actors (to name but a few) had all considered themselves as prostitutes to their art. It wasn't a new idea by any stretch of the imagination. You had to jump through a number of hoops if you wanted to be involved in the artistic community.

There were two real types of artists, no matter what your particular art form was. There were those that stayed true to their calling; that did what they wanted to do and usually made no money from it. They were poor and they were usually starving and for some reason history usually had them staying in Paris or some such cosmopolitan city where the lights were bright and the wine flowed freely. These people remained true to their calling but they never made it as a commercial success in their lifetime. They might make it as a success when they had died, but during their lifetime they would be stuck with poverty, hunger and frustration, but they would be true to their art. Think Van Gogh and you are in the right sort of area on this front.

The second group of artists were those that had made a success of things. This might be because of the fact that they had sold out and were prostituting themselves to make a commercial success rather than following where their heart led them. Many people had felt that Daniel had fallen into this category because he had become successful.

They assumed that because he was successful, he was

writing for popular demand rather than writing what he wanted to write. They assumed that he had made a pact with the devil and would not be satisfied because he was no longer following his true calling. Daniel knew this to be a fact because he had been pretty much accused of it. Some of his early novels (before his success had kicked in) had reached an almost cult status among certain members of the reading public. When he had become successful these people reacted with much the same way that people reacted when Bob Dylan had gone from acoustic to electric. Granted nobody had actually called him Judas, but they might as well have done for the reaction that he got in some of the press and the way that some of the readers spoke to him at book signings.

The truth of it was slightly different though. Daniel hadn't felt that he had sold out because he was successful. That was just a fortunate by-product of his writing. He was still writing the kind of novels that he had always written and felt that he always would. He couldn't really write novels to order and he would have hated to write novels that were part of a series. He just couldn't sustain that level of commitment. Occasionally his publisher would ask him, very politely, if he wouldn't mind writing a novel that was a sequel to the one that he had just published, or they would ask him to write something that was similar to it if not actually a sequel.

Daniel had always declined. He declined because he wasn't that sort of writer. He couldn't write to order, he had to write what was demanding to be written next. That was the way this worked. He had less say over it than anyone else did. So, his publishers would be upset when he produced something that they didn't really want, but then it would go on to sell well anyway and they would be happy again, so naturally they would ask him if he could write something similar to that again. So, it went around like a Ferris wheel.

If nothing else, Daniel had learnt that you can't please everyone and it was pointless to even really try. Just do your thing and hope for the best.

I think it was pretty cool that dad was a writer. None of my friends had parents with such interesting jobs. I think they were a bit envious of me as it felt to them, perhaps, that dad was doing something that was a little exotic. It was something that I had grown up with and so I didn't really see anything unusual in it at all. Dad came into my English class one day and gave a talk on what it was like to be a writer and to answer any questions that the class might have. My teacher was something of a fan of his and she had been trying to get him to come in and share his knowledge for some time. I think he hated every minute of it, but he did it for me so I might look like the cool kid. Dad didn't consider himself a writer, he considered himself a novelist. He wrote novels and not much else. He had tried his hand at opinion pieces in the newspapers, but that was when he was starting out and he had given them up when his books started to take off. He didn't need the money from them. He thought that you could only be classed a writer if you wrote in more than one genre; otherwise, you were whatever it was that you wrote in. I can see that.

Then

Daniel didn't have to ask what Claire meant when she said it was time. He had, in a sense, hoped that the time would never come. He didn't know if he would have the courage to do what was right. Some would argue that it wasn't the right thing to do, of course. He just couldn't, with all conscience, sit back and allow Claire to suffer any more than she already had. It had been bad enough seeing her suffer this far. If she thought that she had reached her limit then that was good enough for him. Who was he to try and get her to stay against all the pain? Everyone should have the right to choose when they die under circumstances such as these. Those were his thoughts.

She had had enormous strength to get this far. She had put up with a lot that had been thrown at her. Had it really only been a year? It seemed like this was something that had been around them for a long time. Daniel found it hard to remember a time when cancer had not been in their lives. It had seemed to be there forever. It worked its way into your life until it consumed everything, not just the body, but the soul as well and the souls of those around you. It was a truly terrible disease.

Claire had always been a fighter and there were those that would suggest that her determination on her present course of action was a defeatist attitude. That really wasn't the case. She had been fighting this disease as best as she could. She had taken it as far as it was going to go and it wasn't defeatist to admit that you were beaten. No matter how much of a fighter she was, she wasn't going to be able to win this one. She could sit it out and wait for the end while enduring pain or she could take matters into her own hands and defeat the disease by robbing it of its final victory. That was the way that she viewed it. She was taking some control over her end.

'Are you sure you want to do this?' Daniel asked her as he sat on the end of the bed.

'It's the right thing to do.'

'How do you want to do it?'

'Morphine overdose. We have enough here and I haven't been taking the full amount prescribed to me so that there is a little stock pile. I've read on the internet that it should be reasonably easy to overdose from taking it.'

'You sound so clinical.'

'It *is* clinical. It's just another form of treatment.'

'I'm going to hate losing you, Claire.'

'I know, but that's going to happen regardless of what we do. If I don't die by my own hand then I will die soon enough from the cancer anyway. It's just a matter of time, as the doctors say.'

'I know, but this is a big step.'

'You agreed to help.'

'I know I did, but you can't blame me for having reservations.'

'No, I expect that you would have reservations. You're probably wondering if there will be any suspicion attached to my death, if there will be any blame that falls on you as a result of it.'

'I'm not really thinking about myself. I'm thinking about you.'

'Then this is the best thing that could happen for me. I can't go on with this any longer. I want to go out on my own terms, in my own way.'

'I can understand that.'

'Then you'll help me to do this?'

'Yes.'

'Good.'

Daniel was helping of his own free will, but he also felt that he didn't really have that much say in the matter. If he loved Claire then what else could he do? He had to help her with her final wish. It was the best thing that he could do in the circumstances. If you loved someone, would you really want to see them continue to suffer beyond their time? He had many questions that were going through his brain. He did wonder if any of it would come back and bite him. *Famous Novelist Kills Wife* would be the headline if this ever got out into the public domain.

He couldn't really worry about that though. He did worry about what would happen to Toby if he went to prison. He really didn't want him to end up with his grandmother and there were very little other options. He was pretty sure that Claire's mother would have a field day if it ever got out what they were planning. She would be the centre of attention for ages as the grieving mother whose daughter was killed by her ruthless and unloving husband. That would be how she would spin it at any rate. She would love every second of the attention that it would bring her. He wasn't prepared to give her the satisfaction.

Nobody could ever know what had happened though. It would have to be a secret that he would take with him to his grave. They were unlikely to discover the true cause of death. Claire was expected to die and it was only a matter of weeks before it happened naturally, so there was very little chance of a post-mortem being carried out. He was pretty sure that they only carried out a post-mortem when the cause of death could not be easily ascertained. He didn't think that there would be a problem with the doctor signing a death certificate in the circumstances of Claire's death.

He had spent a fair amount of time thinking about it since Claire had made her request so was more than prepared for what was to come. He was pretty sure that things would remain a secret and there would be no issues surrounding her death. If it was ever queried where the missing morphine had gone, he would just say that he had disposed of it down the toilet. A trifle irresponsible perhaps, but hardly something that they could haul him into the dock for.

He would dearly have liked to have taken Jordan into his confidence, but he couldn't take the risk. He hated keeping such a secret from his best friend, but he really didn't see that he had much choice in the matter. He was pretty sure that Jordan would be supportive and would understand the reasoning behind what they were planning (hell, he might even agree to help out if they asked him) but there was also the risk that he might think it is a step too far in friendship. Daniel didn't think that he would go running to the police, but it might damage their friendship completely. He just wasn't prepared to take the risk.

'You have to be prepared to let me go,' Claire told him.

'It will be the hardest thing that I've ever done.'

'The pain is really quite difficult to bear. The morphine isn't touching it any longer.'

'I can't imagine what it's like.'

'The pain will continue until I slip into a coma and then I won't know anything about it, but I won't get the chance to say goodbye or go the way that I would want to go. I don't want to be a burden.'

'You're never a burden, Babe.'

'I just don't want to lie here in a long-drawn-out coma and you never knowing if I'm going to go at any minute or whether it is going to be drawn out. I want you to be here with me when I go. I don't want you to have nipped to the toilet or to be asleep. I want you to hold my hand and tell me that you love me. The last thing that I want to hear is your voice.'

'Okay, Babe, we can arrange it exactly how you want it to be.'

'I want you to put Elgar on the stereo. I want to go listening to the things that I love.'

'I will make it as perfect for you as I possibly can.'

'That would be nice. I can't control this illness, but at least I can control my own end. Not many people get to do that.'

'No, I suppose not.'

'I love you, Danny. You are the world to me. I can't imagine my life without you. You've made me so happy all of these years and given me a wonderful son.'

'I couldn't have done any of it without you. I'm only the person that I am today because of you.'

'We have a lot to be thankful for.'

'You're my life, Claire. I don't know how I will survive without you. You have been the reason for why I get up every morning. Without you I just won't be able to see the point any more.'

'You must try your best. I know that it isn't going to be easy for you. I know, because if our situations were reversed then I wouldn't find it easy at all, but you have to try and do the best that you can. You have to promise me that you will go on. Don't mourn too long. I mean, you can mourn a little bit, but don't drag it out. Get on with your life.'

'I can try my best, but it won't be easy.'

'I know, Babe.'

'When do you want to do this?'

'I'm ready when you are.'

'So soon?'

'No sense in hanging around.'

'I was hoping that we might have some more time together.'

'We have had all the time in the world and time is the one thing that I don't have that much of any longer.'

'I understand.'

Daniel held her hand, reluctant to let her go. She squeezed his hand in return. 'Please, Danny.'

'Okay, Babe.'

He got up and walked to the stereo that they had deliberately moved into the room so that Claire could listen to some music while she was in bed. He selected a CD of the *Enigma Variations* and placed it in the machine. He adjusted the volume as the familiar strains began to sound in the room. He stood listening for a moment, allowing the music to flow over him. He knew that he was trying to delay the actual moment for as long as he could. He wanted the world that contained Claire to continue for as long as it was possible to do so, before he would have to adjust to the world where she was no longer in it. It was going to be a cold, bleak world and he feared that it was one that was going to go on a long time.

He turned back from the stereo and took a long look at Claire. The illness had devastated her. She had lost her hair because of the chemotherapy. She had lost so much weight that she was barely the shadow of the woman that she had once been, but it wasn't just that. The illness was etched into her face. There were dark rims under her eyes and lines that had not been there a year ago. Yet, through it all Daniel could easily see the woman

341

that he had loved and married. To him, she was no different from the day that they had met. She was the love of his life and always would be. He couldn't imagine going with anyone else. He never wanted to get married again. He believed that you had one soulmate in this world and when they were gone, that was that. There was no finding a second.

He moved over to the bed and took her hand. 'Are you ready?'

'Yes.'

He took the bottle of morphine from the night stand. He looked at it for some time. He also took a tablet from his pocket and gave it to Claire.

'What's this?'

'Anti-sickness tablet. In case your body tries to reject the morphine and you end up vomiting it up.'

'You've thought this through more than I thought you had.'

'I did some research on the internet.'

'I hope you wiped your browser history.'

'Yeah, but if they ever found it, I can just claim that I'm a writer. We research all sort of things that would make other people look like psychopaths.'

'I always thought there was a very fine line when it came to writers.'

'Well, you would know. You've dealt with more writers than I have over the years.'

He gave her a glass of water to take the tablet and helped her take a sip from it.

'Give that a few minutes to kick in before we issue you with the big stuff.'

'You're better planned than I thought you'd be.'

'Well, it's the last thing that I can do for you. I think it's important to get it right. Don't want anything to go wrong.'

'This is the best path to follow. With it being so close to Christmas I don't want to die on Christmas Day and ruin the day for you for the rest of your life.'

'Don't you worry about that.'

'I do worry about these things. It's going to be bad enough dying this close to Christmas as it is, but it would be worse to die on Christmas Day.'

'Charlie Chaplin died on Christmas Day.'

'I didn't know that.'

'And then they stole his corpse a couple of months later and held it to ransom.'

'Well, hopefully you won't have that problem. I don't think anyone would want to steal me.'

'You never know.'

'Well, don't pay any ransom demands to get me back. When I'm gone this will just be an empty husk. Whatever is left of me will be long gone.'

'You will remain in my heart forever,' he said as he placed her hand over his heart.

'I know I will. There will always be a part of me alive while you are. I know that and I take comfort from that. I'm also certain that I'll see you again.'

'I hope so.'

'I'm certain of it. I've read a lot on the subject and it's what I believe to be true. I don't think that this is all that there is.'

'I hope not. It would be a big disappointment if it turned out that this was all that there was. I would so like to believe that there is more to it than this. That there's some plan, or something in place that will explain it all at some point.'

'I wish I could let you know.'

'I know you would if you could.'

'I shall be trying my best. There will be a link between us, you know that, don't you? We will not be separated, even by death. I will still be a part of you and you will be a part of me. Death can't separate us, not really.'

'I'd like to believe that is the case.'

'Trust me, it's true. Soulmates can't be separated by a little thing like death. We found each other out of all the people in this whole world. Death won't stop us from being part of each other forever.'

'You have a perfect, dream-like view on what will happen.'

'Don't you believe it?'

'Yes, I do, to a certain extent. I'd like to have the level of faith that you have, but I'm the one who is being left behind. I don't know what will happen.'

'You'll just have to trust me on this one and go along with what I say.'

'Okay then.'

It had started to rain and they sat listening to it beating against the window for a few minutes. It was clearly not going to be a white Christmas again, but when was it ever? Daniel couldn't remember the last time that there had been a white Christmas. Sometime in the seventies, maybe? He wasn't sure. Certainly not something that he could remember. They just didn't seem to happen.

'Is it time?' she asked him when they had watched the patterns on the window for a while. It was dark out now. The nights came quickly in the middle of winter. They had been sitting there for some time, what with one thing and another. Toby had already gone to bed. Claire had said her goodbyes to him without making it obvious to him that he was actually saying goodbye. She didn't want him to think that this was going to be the last time that they saw each other. She preferred him to have no suspicions that would make things difficult for Daniel. He was a sensible boy, but he might not fully understand the reasons behind what they were doing.

'Yeah, I suppose it's time.'

Daniel had been holding the bottle of morphine in one hand and Claire's hand in the other.

'You sure about this?'

'Yes.'

'I love you.'

'I love you too.'

'I'll see you soon.'

'Not too soon, I hope.'

Daniel smiled and unscrewed the child lock on the cap.

'Ready?'

'Yes.'

He handed her the bottle and she took a long swig from it.

'Drink it all. I don't know how much it will take to work, but there should be more than enough there.'

She took another swing of it. She had probably swallowed about half the bottle, which had been near enough full when they had started.

'I might need your help.'

Daniel came up to her and took the bottle in his hands and started to pour some of it into her mouth while she took little gulps of it. A little bit at a time. She coughed a couple of times as the body tried to reject the overdose that was coming, but the anti-sickness tablet appeared to be doing its stuff. Eventually the bottle was empty.

'Now let's just see what happens.'

'I feel so tired,' she said as she settled down. 'Stay with me.'
'Of course I will.'

They stayed like that for a while until Claire fell into a deep sleep. Daniel holding her hand and reading to her from the other as it held *The Mayor of Casterbridge* so that she might fall asleep listening to his voice. When he knew that she was asleep he put the book to one side and held her hand with both of his as he watched her. Eventually the breathing became shallow and then before he knew it, it stopped altogether and he realised that she was gone.

All in all, it had been something that was quick and easy. Easier than he had been expecting that it would be. He thought that there would be difficulties and that it wouldn't be enough, but it turned out that it was easier to kill someone than he had imagined it would be. He didn't like to think of it as killing her though. He liked to think of it as releasing her from the pain and suffering that she had endured over the last year. She had borne it well. She hardly ever complained, but he knew that there were times when it had been too much for her.

He checked for a pulse and placed his ear near her mouth to check to see if she was breathing. There was no sign of either. She was definitely gone. It was all over. All her pain and suffering had come to an end. Daniel reflected on how things could change. One minute he had been married and the next he was widowed. One minute Claire had been in the world and then she was gone. It could all happen in the blink of an eye. It would take some getting used to.

He left the music on and turned out the light and made his way to the kitchen where he placed the mugs in the dishwasher. He was amazed that he could still act in such an ordinary way now that his wife had died. There were still things that needed to

346

be done though and he was numbly going through the motions. He knew that he would have to sort out funeral arrangements and all of that soon. The business of dealing with death would start in the morning and would no doubt take up a lot of the time.

He didn't want to cry in the kitchen. He didn't want to risk Toby coming in and catching him and finding out that his mother had died. The plan was that he would 'discover' Claire in the morning and then would break the news to Toby. Let him have one more night of restful sleep before the pain of loss and grief came upon him. With that in mind, Daniel knew that he would have to keep up appearances. He would make Claire a cup of tea in the morning, as he always did. He didn't want anything to appear to be out of place or suspicious. Everything had to be normal.

He felt like he had taken part in a great crime and in a sense, he had. He had, in every textbook definition of the word, murdered his wife. Maybe the morphine that she was able to take would have been enough to kill her on its own, but he had been the one, with his own hand, that had pushed her over the edge into the abyss.

Perhaps it was true that the legal system needed more flexibility when it came to cases like this. There was no public interest in prosecuting him for the crime of a mercy killing. The law needed to understand that there were cases like theirs that needed to be considered separate from legislation. Daniel could understand why you would want to prevent doctors from going mad and killing all their patients as an act of 'mercy', but there were cases when it was genuinely something that needed to be done.

Daniel left the kitchen, turning off the lights as he went. He turned the lights of the Christmas decorations off and made his way into the bedroom that he had until recently shared with Claire. He had missed her when she moved into the spare room and now, he knew he would miss her permanently in all cases. He got undressed down to his boxers and slipped into the cool sheets. There was a definitely chill in the air now that they were in December. He noticed all the things in graphic detail. How the sheets clung to his body. The ticking of the clock on the bedside table and the noise that the rain made as it pelted the window. If it kept raining then there was a chance that there wouldn't be a frost tonight.

He was amazed that he could still think about things like that. He thought that the world would have ended, that there would be a huge thunderstorm and cracks in the Earth at the fact that Claire had died. None of that had happened. It had surprised Daniel that it hadn't happened. He expected the heavens to be angry at her death, or the manner of her death. He expected there to be something to pay for what he had done. Maybe that would come later. He would have the rest of his life to ruminate on it after all.

That would be his punishment for what he had done. He had no real regrets over what had happened. It had been the right thing to do, but he knew that not everyone would see it that way. The police for starters were bound to take a different view of the matter. He would have to try and keep them out of the picture as much as possible although he saw no reason why they should get involved. Problem was that the unexpected had a way of happening. You never knew what might happen.

It was a bit late to be thinking about it now though. Now it was all over and done with and he was pretty confident that his 'crime' would remain undetected. If it didn't then he would just have to fight it out. There wasn't really much choice in it really.

What he couldn't do would be to give himself away by acting guilty. He had to act as normally as possible.

Fortunately, the fact that his wife had just died was sufficient reason for him to act in a bizarrely uptight way if anyone were to question him about it. They could put it all down to the fact that he had just lost his wife and was suffering from grief. That was what he reasoned with himself as he lay there in the dark thinking that it was likely to be hours before he actually managed to get to sleep.

He had heard once a rumour in the police that you could always tell the innocent because they were able to fall asleep in their cells overnight whereas the guilty tended to stay awake. He wasn't sure if he believed this. He was pretty sure that some hardened criminals would have no problem in sleeping at all. He was also sure that if he had been arrested for a crime that he had not committed that he would probably be awake all night worrying that the criminal justice system was going to fail him and he was going to be sent to prison for something that he did not do.

Yet, as he lay there now, unable to sleep, he wondered if there had been a certain amount of truth in it. He was pretty sure that his guilt was what was keeping him awake, as well as thoughts of Claire. He was pretty sure that those thoughts were not going to go away, and then he was also sure that he didn't want them to go away. He didn't want to stop thinking about her.

He thought about the time that he had first seen her in the literature class and how he had been captivated to hear what she had to say about the book that they were reading. She had seemed so intelligent and sexy. Truth was that she was both of those things. She would go on to prove that in the years that they were to spend together.

He thought about the first coffee that they had had together. The first of what would turn out to be thousands of cups of coffee, if not tens of thousands. He had listened to her with rapt attention and been fascinated by every part of her. He knew then that this was the woman that he was going to spend the rest of his life with. Only it would turn out that it wasn't for the rest of his life, just for the rest of her life.

He remembered the time that they had lived together in a student flat. How the place had been a hovel, but how they had not cared for the place at all. They had been so caught up in their love for each other that it had not mattered where they lived. They would have lived in a cave if it had meant that they could be together.

He thought about how she had helped him with his aspirations to be a writer. How she had encouraged him and made him see the good in what he was doing. He had only been able to become the writer that he had because of her. If he had not had her at his side then he would probably still not have published a single thing. She had made him the man that he was, but she had also been instrumental in making him the writer that he was. He had no doubt that his success was entirely down to her.

He thought about the time that they had taken refuge in a dingy café in Bournemouth to escape the rain when they had been on holiday. He thought about how they had laughed and not cared about the fact that they were soaked to their skins.

He remembered sitting with her on Brighton beach and complaining that there was no sand to be seen, that it was all stones. She had laughed and made him start a barbeque that hadn't really taken and she had laughed even more.

He thought about how radiant she had looked when she was pregnant with Toby and how he had been there for the birth of his son. Holding her hand throughout the entire procedure.

So many memories crammed into his head that he didn't think that he would have room for them all. He was sad that there were no more memories that would come and that his lasting memories would be of the pain that she had suffered and how she had ended her life. He would try to concentrate on the earlier memories and not focus on the bad things. To be honest they had been together for most of their lives and the only bad times that they had had was over the last year when she got sick. Even then they had not stopped loving each other. They never argued. They were always there for each other. They had a marriage of equality.

And now he would have to face it all on his own. That was what made him sad. Her not being there for him to share things with. A joke that he had found funny. A memory that he had. She wouldn't be the first person to read his new manuscripts. She was gone. But she was right – love went on. He would never stop loving her. He knew that he had to get up in a few hours and start the ball rolling on her death, but for the moment he thought of her as he drifted into a restless troubled sleep.

I found this manuscript among my dad's papers after he had died. I had a family of my own then. Two daughters, and a wife that I loved as much as dad loved mum. I shouldn't have been shocked that he did what he did. I can understand the reasoning behind it all. Who knows? Given the same circumstances I might do the same for my wife. I do think we have a right to choose when we are terminally ill on how long we prolong our suffering when we are no longer really living. I don't know if there is an afterlife – I hope there is; and I hope that I see them both again.